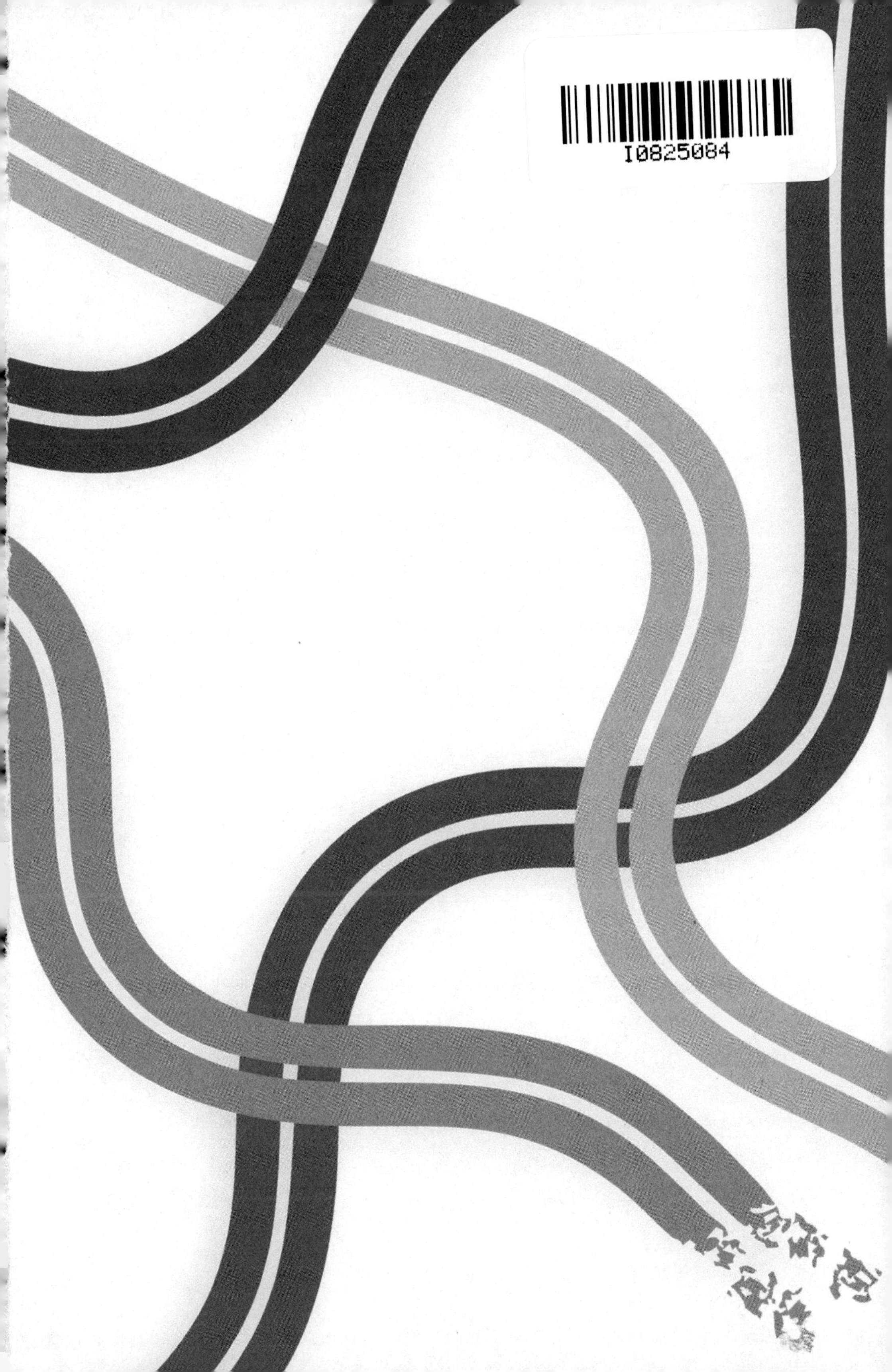
I0825084

"*I'm the Undertow* is a stunning debut, an intimate, emotionally charged portrait of loss and the unlikely relationships that help us endure it. Eric Scot Tryon writes with sensitivity and grace about the fragile, necessary connections that carry us through periods of grief and guide us toward forgiveness. Compelling and beautifully observed, this novel announces a powerful new voice in fiction."

— ANDREW PORTER
author of *The Imagined Life*

"A powerful and vividly rendered debut that deftly portrays the delicate and difficult work of rebuilding one's life in the wake of tragedy. Even as it fearlessly plumbs the depths of grief and guilt, *I'm the Undertow* brims with warmth and life."

— GINA CHUNG
author of *Sea Change* and *Green Frog*

"Propulsive, evocative, and atmospheric, Eric Scot Tryon's *I'm the Undertow* launches readers into Conner Robbins' world of upheaval following an accident that upends his life. So compelling you'll want to read it in a day but swimming with beautifully written scenic and emotional sentences that will make you want to linger. A fantastic debut novel!"

— AMY STUBER
author of *Sad Grownups,* winner of the 2025 PEN/Robert W. Bingham Prize

"Tryon's moving debut is a paean to grief, a navigation of the labyrinths we wander when confronted with our greatest shame. A powerful examination of humanity in tragedy's aftermath, this book explores how far we must sometimes go in order to forgive ourselves."

— DAVID JAMES POISSANT
author of *Lake Life* and *The Heaven of Animals*

I'M THE UNDERTOW

a novel

ERIC SCOT TRYON

central avenue

2026

Published by Central Avenue Publishing, an imprint of Central Avenue Marketing Ltd.
centralavenuepublishing.com

Printed in the United States of America

1. FICTION/Grief 2. FICTION/Family

I'M THE UNDERTOW: A Novel

Trade Paper: 978-1-77168-448-4
Ebook: 978-1-77168-449-1

1 3 5 7 9 10 8 6 4 2

For my girls, Aleja and Silvana:
this book, like everything I do, is for you.

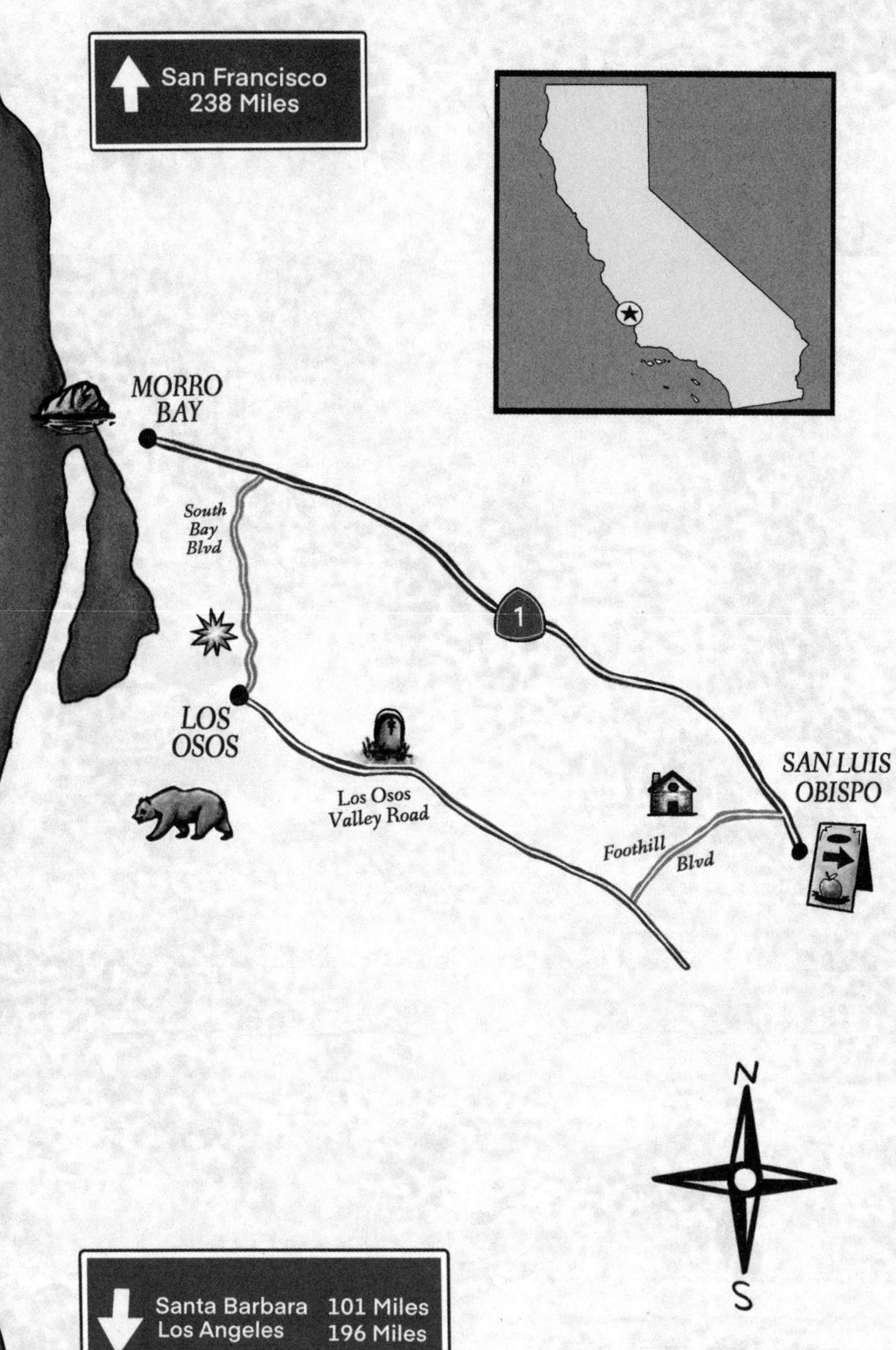
San Francisco
238 Miles
MORRO
BAY
South
Bay
Blvd
1
LOS
OSOS
Los Osos
Valley Road
SAN LUIS
OBISPO
Foothill
Blvd
N
S
Santa Barbara
101 Miles
Los Angeles
196 Miles

I'M THE UNDERTOW

CHAPTER 1

OUR PADDLES DIPPED INTO THE BAY WITH ONLY the slightest whisper. And as with every Wednesday morning, the first several moments of our meeting were silent. We slipped around the bay, Travis in his orange kayak, me in my yellow one, like a pair of cat burglars. Travis said it was out of respect for the ocean, our morning kiss on the cheek to Mother Nature. But for me it was the extra few moments I needed to shake the sleepy syrup from my head.

The bay was still beneath the fog, and just a light brushing of the water propelled our kayaks forward, each stroke creating mini whirlpools behind the paddles, a vortex sucking millions of amoebae and plankton to another universe. And today, I would be creating a vortex of my own.

"It's freezing out here," I said. "What do you think about holding these meetings *after* you close?"

"That would defeat the purpose," Travis said. "Listen." He extended his neck and held out his hand. There was only the gentle clanging of carabiners against masts and the occasional cry of a seagull. "So fucking peaceful," he said. "And c'mon, how many Bakersfieldians do you hear?"

"Okay, okay. I get your point."

Side by side we paddled. Left, wait, wait, right, wait, wait, left. We passed one white hull after another. The masts, sails, and cabins all hidden somewhere in the thick wet cotton that sat on the water. And as if seeing familiar friends, I read the same names I read every week—*Oh My Darling, The Crew's Ship, Kilgore Trout, Otter This World . . .*

"I got a text from Kayla last night," Travis said.

"Seriously? That girl is nuts."

"You'd be proud though. I didn't write back."

"Good," I said, paddling a little harder than I wanted just to keep up.

Travis made a new girl fall in love with him every day. He'd been doing it since high school, and the only reason we didn't all hate him was that he did it without meaning to. He said it was more of a curse than a blessing. But we had trouble feeling sorry for him.

"And what about that other girl?" I asked. "Adrienne, right?"

"Adriana."

Tomato, tomahto. I knew it would get him talking. And maybe if he got sidetracked enough, we wouldn't have time to get to business today. Maybe I could wait one more week to drop the bomb. As we paddled, parting the fog like a thin white curtain, Travis started in on his half-feelings for Adriana while I half listened. I was more focused on the knot in my stomach. And then the one in my throat. If they were to somehow meet in the middle, my chest might simply petrify.

Whap-whap-whap! He slapped the water with his paddle. "I now call this meeting to order," he boomed in a deep voice, chin tucked to his chest.

"Oh, Jesus."

"First order of business . . ." He sounded like a drunk Englishman, and with the paddle across his lap, he took a pretend pipe out of his mouth and puffed invisible smoke rings. " . . . is to establish attendance. Conner T. Robbins?"

"You're really going to do this every time?"

Whap-whap-whap! "Conner T. Robbins?"

"Present," I sighed. "What happened to honoring the quietness of the bay?"

"Travis R. Ellington the third?"

"The third? Please."

He slouched his posture and returned his voice to normal. "Present and ready."

We steadied our pace and headed toward Fairbank Point. We couldn't see it, but we'd kayaked the bay enough to know exactly where it was, and we also knew that there would be a hundred white herons there waiting for us. Half of them sleeping on chopstick legs, the others pecking breakfast off the water's surface.

"I have big news," Travis said.

You have no idea, I thought.

"Big," he repeated.

"Okay, so . . ."

"I talked to Pauline last night." He picked at a webby piece of green moss wrapped around his paddle. "She said the place on Higuera is ours!" And with the end of the sentence he flung the moss like a Frisbee. "They chose our application!"

"You didn't call me?"

"I wanted to tell you in person. Thought you might leap right into the ocean."

I looked down at the water as a traffic of bubbles moved past me, some popping soundlessly against the kayak.

"So?" he said. "We're taking it, right? I know it's smaller than we wanted, and it'll need new stoves. But it's ours. And it's on Higuera!"

"But are we really ready? I mean financially."

"C'mon, you know Horizons has been trying to buy my place for a year. I just have to say the word." Travis lifted his paddle out of the water and rested it across his lap. Water streamed off the ends back into the ocean, and we slowed to nearly a standstill. The water like glass beneath us. "And Pauline has the business loan all lined up. We're ready. I thought you'd be more excited."

"No, no, I am. Just a little surprised. It happened fast."

"And besides," he said, "what's your stupid saying?"

"*I take care of the grub and booze. You take care of the ones and twos,*" I said in a tone mocking myself.

"Exactly!" He picked up his paddle and sliced at the water, sending a rainbow of cold spray into my kayak and across my legs. "It's happening, you dick!

It's really happening!"

I paddled faster, skimming out in front of Travis. The fog poked at my face with tiny wet needles, and my arms gave rise to a field of goose bumps. As if I could actually outrun him, I paddled hard, chin down, the whirlpools behind me growing larger with each deep stroke.

Last night, running the words over and over in my head, I'd envisioned this conversation taking place while we were moving. My limbs needed the distraction. But the news from Pauline was unexpected, and I tried to convince myself that maybe it changed everything, maybe it was a sign that I should keep my big mouth shut.

"Out with it," Travis said, arriving at my side. He knew me too well.

"Huh?"

"Something's up. Out with it."

"Nothing's up." Sucking in the cold air, my chest tightened and ached. Travis kept up with me effortlessly. "I don't know, I just thought I'd throw something on the table."

"Okay, great. Let's hear it."

"I'm not even throwing it on the table, exactly, but you know . . . throwing it . . ." I could hear myself the way he was hearing me. It was embarrassing. "Throwing it out there."

"Jesus, what's wrong with you? Just say it."

"What do you think . . ." I pushed hard through the water. Left, right, left, right. "What do you think of opening the restaurant in San Francisco instead?" And with that, I was in a full sprint, throwing water behind me like I was bailing out a sinking ship.

"Easy there, Speed Racer." Travis again pulled even with me, no signs of strain on his face.

I picked up my paddle, and the kayak glided another several yards before slowing to a crawl.

Up ahead there was a pocket of fogless ocean, and we spotted a pelican no more than forty yards out, next to a black and red sailboat called *The Masked*

Marauder. The bird's enormous gray and pink beak tucked tightly in a fold of white feathers.

"Because of Rian?" he asked.

"No, no. She doesn't even know I'm thinking about this." Though I couldn't fully deny the Rian factor. "I mean, it would be nice to be closer to her."

"Well." This time Travis began to move, slowly, and I was forced to follow. "If it's not about her, then I assume this is a business proposition. In which case, I'd like to hear your pitch. You can't tell me that was it."

My pitch? I thought maybe he'd tell me I was crazy. At least give me a "fuck off." Travis and I used to catch blue-bellied lizards in the ice plant on our walk home from middle school. We used to rent low-budget erotic thrillers and hit pause every time we thought we spotted a nipple. And now he was asking me for a sales pitch as if we were sitting at opposite ends of a conference table.

"Yeah. That was it. You love San Francisco too. What do you think?"

"What do I think? I think we're a phone call away from renting a place in San Luis. I think uprooting to San Francisco negates everything we've done the past four months. I think trying to open a place in San Francisco costs twenty times as much."

He let those words hang in the air around us, amid the salt and the fog. The air too still and heavy to let them dissipate. We didn't look at each other, but instead stared at the pelican, which still hadn't moved, now only twenty yards in front of us.

"And I think it'd be hard to run a restaurant in San Francisco when I live in Morro Bay and you live in Los Osos." Then he looked over at me. "Which is where we live."

It was the first of many lectures I expected. Others would involve my timing, my reliability, my follow-throughedness, or lack thereof. Self-sabotage. Why hadn't I brought this up four months ago? With my track record, how could I be trusted to stay in one place long enough for water to boil? And on and on he would go, and on and on he'd be right. But I hadn't realized how depressing it would be to be back on the Central Coast. I had no idea how pathetic it would feel to run into Paul Cross at Mother's Tavern and find out that he was *still* dating Yvette and *still* working at Lemos Ranch and *still* playing pool every Friday night at Sweet Springs. I had no idea how painful it would be to bump into Shawn Stribling's mom and Ms. Gatwick at Ralphs on the same trip. Memories of your hometown far surpassed their reality. It was like trying to fit into my favorite pair of basketball shoes from rec league when I was ten. Small towns didn't grow at the same rate as people. And I couldn't imagine spending the rest of my life folded and crammed into my high school self.

As we approached the pelican, we didn't speak. We took another couple strokes, just enough to give us momentum to pass by the bird silently. We held our paddles on our laps and remained still. The pelican shook itself awake, lifted its head, and out came its large beak—orange and pink and gray. Travis and I were about ten feet apart, slipping slowly and quietly across the skin of the water, the pelican directly between us. It blinked its large eyes and looked at Travis, then me, then Travis again. Tiny red bumps dotted the skin that outlined its eyes. It was prehistoric. The pouch that hung loose from its bone-hard beak looked as though it were made from the skin of dinosaur elbows. The bird stared hard at us until we passed, and as we put our paddles back into the water, off it flew. Two loud flaps, and it vanished into the fog.

"There's no way," Travis said, shaking his head. "And how many times have you . . . ?" But he didn't need to finish his sentence. "It would change everything. The capital we'd need to raise. Even with selling to Horizons, this would add another year to us being ready. Or we'd need to find investors. Who knows how long that takes."

"A year? Whatever, I fart and a year passes."

"But you're not only making a business proposal. You're asking me to move my entire life. It's a big fucking something to throw on the table."

"I can't live here, man."

"But you do," he said. He sounded like a parent. Not like my parents, of course. My parents never sounded like parents, but he sounded like I imagined parents were supposed to sound. Then, like a mother stomping out of the kitchen, Travis turned his kayak hard to the left and paddled away. It was best to leave him be for now, so I turned right and headed toward the sand spit. I couldn't see it through the fog, but I trusted it was there, guarding me from the vast expanse of the Pacific Ocean.

In eighteen years, Travis and I had never fought. We came close a few times, and it always made me feel out of sorts, like the universe was tilting to the left and everything was sliding down to one end.

But going off in separate directions wasn't a dramatic action. It was a normal part of our Wednesday meetings. My favorite part. Sure, we usually spent most of the time talking about the restaurant—the menu, the décor, the vendors Travis was meeting. And there was always a little time to discuss Travis's latest girl, whether the Dodgers' rotation was good enough this year, and inevitably Travis had some gossip about someone we knew from high school. Someone who never moved away. It was usually a divorce. Or another baby. Or both.

And yet we always found a few moments to explore the bay on our own. We'd drift apart, then come back together, paddling silently, unconcerned with space or time. The quiet stillness of the morning, the soft, undulating water beneath me, and even the salty, fishy air I breathed in, had a way of making everything seem manageable. It was the only time mornings and I saw eye to eye: *Maybe you're not so bad*, I'd say, patting seven a.m. on the back. *Gee, thanks, you're not so bad yourself*, she'd respond, and then she'd show me the goods—sometimes just a single strand of sunlight poking through a crack in the fog, illuminating a patch of ocean that was a million shades of blue and green, some of which had never existed before. Or sometimes a whole bed of kelp wandered over: a swarm of flies, a small crab, a piece of driftwood—a whole world within its sheets. Or sometimes, a lone pelican.

Travis was probably doing some managing of his own. A spreadsheet up and running in his head. A list of pros and cons between San Luis Obispo and San Francisco. I felt as though I had no control except to wait and see what the bottom line read. But maybe even that was too optimistic. Maybe he was over there trying to figure out a way to do this without me.

I caught movement up ahead. It looked like another kayak, but Travis was clearly the other direction. I moved toward it, curious to see who or what else might be out here at this hour. My strokes were slow but deep, and the stingy fog disappeared before me an inch at a time. It wasn't a kayak but a canoe, painted at one time, but now the wood was cracked and sun-bleached. In it was a kid, maybe seventeen. He had rust-colored hair, and his long arms and slouched shoulders filled the space between his knobby knees. He held a fishing pole in his hands with the same slack he used to hold the cigarette between his lips.

"Morning," I said and offered a hand up.

The kid gave me a quick nod.

"Catch anything?"

"Not yet," he said, and for all his scrawniness, his voice was unusually deep. He took the cigarette out of his mouth for a moment before putting it back in. "But I will."

"What are you fishing for?"

"Easier than surfing, ain't it?"

"Heh, yeah. I meant what type of fish are you trying to catch?"

He looked at me with eyes thin as slits. "The kind that bite the hook."

I laughed. I caught it quickly, but not soon enough. He hadn't meant it to be funny. He gave a kind of snort, the sound a bully makes right before he throws the first punch.

"Yes, well, good luck with that," I said, and began to turn my kayak around.

But right before the fog moved in to close off the space between us, the kid said, "Thanks. And good luck with the sarcasm."

I didn't respond as I paddled quickly back to where I had left Travis. I certainly didn't need an altercation. The two of us standing in our vessels swinging paddles at one another like aquatic gladiators. Ridiculous.

"Hey." It was Travis. "Look what I found." He was holding up something with both hands, but I couldn't make it out.

"What is it?"

"Trash." He let it drop into his lap. Two aluminum cans and a plastic grocery bag. "Can you fucking believe it? These tourists are morons."

"Speaking of," I said as we pulled our kayaks alongside one another. "I ran into some weird kid out by the spit. In a canoe. Fishing."

I went on to tell him about my interaction with the gangly redhead. And he proceeded to tell me that he knew the kid. Of course he did. Between living in Morro Bay all his life and running Yakety Kayaks the last four years, if someone sneezed on the Embarcadero, Travis could tell you what color his snot was and how many *God bless you*s he received.

The kid's name was Jimmy. He had just moved out from Utah and could often be found piddling around the bay in that canoe, out on the driving range crushing golf balls, or roaming up and down the Embarcadero. And always by himself.

"He's not much for conversation though," Travis said.

"Yeah, I got that."

"Always wears camo too."

"You think he's still in high school?"

"Gonna be a senior this year."

"Strange cat."

"Anyway, so some quick head math, at about seven hundred fifty square feet of serviceable floor . . ." Travis gazed upwards and danced his index finger around as if typing on an invisible calculator, but we both knew he already knew the numbers. "You want to calculate about twelve to fifteen feet per head . . . carry the one . . . let's say conservatively that gives us eighty heads. Given that rough menu we came up with, you need to figure out food costs and check averages. Then we'll have a good idea of how many covers we need a night to make this work."

"I know, I know, and twenty-five percent, right?"

"Yeah, if you—if *we* can figure out a way to keep our food costs at or below twenty-five percent, we'll be in good shape."

"Alright, but—"

"Yeah, okay, so tell me this much, Magellan. What if you get that coaching job you so desperately wanted? How does that fit into your plans to return to Frisco?"

"Magellan?"

"Didn't he discover San Francisco?"

"I'm pretty sure that was Drake."

"Whatever. You're going to get that job. And then what?"

"Nah, I told you that interview was a disaster. Coach Rich hated me. Think he always has, really. And don't call it Frisco."

"Nah, he's just an asshole. I'm sure you'll get it."

"I dunno," I said. The interview had been so brief and awkward that I had completely written it off. "I guess I'd—*we'd* cross that bridge when, *if*, I come to it."

"He runs a pretty tight ship. Don't think he'd be too keen on you running up to San Francisco every other weekend. Which we'd pretty much have to do right away if we tried to open up there. Which we're not, so I guess it doesn't matter."

"Speaking of a tight ship, don't you run a pretty tight kayak? Shouldn't we head back?"

"Nice save. Yeah, we should. But you're not getting off that easily. You got to figure your shit out, man. You're not in your twenties anymore."

"I know, I know," I said, and now it was my turn. I sounded like a rebellious teenager tired of the same lecture from Dad. Again, it was a tone I never used with my actual dad, but I imagined it would have sounded something like that.

The fog was starting to lift. It wasn't any thinner, but raising up like a curtain. The seagulls were more noticeable now too, their squawking arguments picking up right where they left off the previous day.

"Did you hear about that kayaker last week?" Travis asked. "Rescued by some fishing boat like hundreds of yards offshore."

"Oh shit, no." I was grateful he'd changed the subject. "One of yours?"

"No. Thank God. A local. Wanted a better photo of the rock or something. Paddled way too far out around the spit. That's a weird little area, you know. Some undertow, some like underwater current, just took him. By the time he realized, he was too damn far out there. Exhausted himself trying to get back. A fishing boat found him and picked him up."

"Jesus."

"Yeah, you don't mess with the ocean. The ocean is no joke."

We paddled the rest of the way in silence, and I thought about the power of the ocean and the power of friendships. For the first time in my life, I could really feel the shift in ours. We no longer just needed the other for standard best friend bullshit, asking favors, getting drunk, complaining about parents or jobs or girls. If we were going to follow through with this restaurant idea, our lives would be tied up together. Decisions I made, needs I had, now affected Travis's life. And vice versa. It sounded an awful lot like a marriage. Which made me think of Rian. Which made me miss her, but also made me realize how many unknowns were still in front of me. A feeling I thought I was trying to leave behind when I turned thirty. I didn't regret bringing it up, though. I didn't know what came next, but it had to be said.

When we reached the dock, there was much more movement along the water than when we had left. The businesses along the Embarcadero were beginning to yawn and stretch. A second wave of fishing boats was heading out to sea to catch tomorrow's dinners. Above them were swarms of seagulls, screaming and circling like giant, angry bees. And of course, we could now hear the crying of the sea lions from the aquarium. A half dozen or so, sitting in tiny cement cells on top of one another. But man, how the faces of tourists lit up at the barking sea lions, which could be heard along the full length of the Embarcadero. People reacted as if they were hearing the call of a mythical creature they'd only heard rumors about. And now, here, they would be able to see them up close, even feed them. But there was nothing mythical about the sea lions in the Morro Bay Aquarium. Just sad creatures living in sad puddles, while the beautiful, endless ocean lay but yards away on the other side of their dirty walls. Depressing.

"Do you think it's *Bakersfieldians?*" Travis asked as he climbed out of the kayak and onto the wooden slats of the dock.

"Huh?"

"Earlier. I called them Bakersfieldians. Is that right? Or maybe Bakersfield . . . ites? Bakersfielders."

"Those all sound pretty dumb." I pulled my kayak out of the water with both hands and placed it on top of Travis's.

"I guess *Valley of the Dirt People* will have to do." Travis was still laughing as he untied the thick knot that held a stack of kayaks in place. He then moved up a short ramp and unlocked his shop: a white shack with a large yellow sign on top. The sign was in the shape of a kayak, and the words *Yakety Kayaks* were written in orange, blue, and green letters arranged in an orchestrated wobble, as if being bounced around in a popcorn machine.

"Hey," I said, following him into the shop. "It's the Valley of the Dirt People that keeps you in business."

"Indeed." He pushed open the shutters, and we looked out to the long aluminum ramp that led to the sidewalk. There were a half dozen people waiting, their hands either tucked into their armpits or clutching white Styrofoam cups leaking steam.

"You going to stick around and help a buddy out?" Travis asked as he added more bright orange vests to the stack in the back corner.

"Do you need help?"

"Of course not."

"Then no." I sat on the lone stool in the shop. "And besides, I think I have the lunch shift today."

"Sweet. Say hi to Donnie the Dick for me."

"Luckily, I think he's gone all week. That dude is always disappearing."

"Hey, I gotta . . ." Travis jingled his keys and nodded toward the people atop the ramp.

"Yeah, okay. I'm outta here." I hopped off the stool and followed Travis out of the shack.

Our steps made thin, metallic *clunks* as we ascended the ramp.

"Hey," I said. "Fried baba ghanoush balls."

"What?"

"Thought of it last night! Doesn't that sound amazing?"

Travis laughed and unlocked the gate, and as I headed left toward my truck, he yelled to my back, "We're not moving, you know!" And then with the flip of a switch, I could hear him start in on the tourists. "Fog, schmog! It's a beautiful day for kayaking, folks! Come on down and . . ."

I climbed into my silver pickup and headed toward South Bay Boulevard, the winding two-lane road that served as the sole connector between Morro Bay and Los Osos. I had driven it probably half a million times and could take the turns with my eyes closed.

Los Osos and Morro Bay were sibling towns (with San Luis Obispo acting as both mother and father). Morro Bay offered caged sea lions, surf spots, saltwater taffy, and of course the postcards, T-shirts, and photo ops of a giant rock. Morro Rock. It was a local celebrity. Los Osos, then, became the nondescript celebrity sibling no one even knew existed: the Michael McCartney of the Central Coast.

But Morro Bay didn't have a middle school, so during seventh and eighth grade, all the kids from Morro Bay were bussed over to Los Osos Middle School. And Los Osos didn't have a high school, so come ninth grade, all the kids from Los Osos were bussed over to Morro Bay High. If it were Los Angeles, this setup would be ripe for rival gangs, but in our sleepy coastal town, calling each other *Lost* Osos and *Moron* Bay was about as territorial as it got. Pathetic. Needless to say, after four years of living in Los Osos and going to high school in Morro Bay, I knew South Bay Boulevard like the proverbial back of my hand.

I drove the curves at forty, worrying about all the things I didn't have control over. We hadn't started an actual restaurant yet, and already I felt things were out of my hands. I didn't fool myself. Travis ultimately called the shots. If he didn't want to move to San Francisco, I'd probably stay. And he knew it. And I'd be miserable, but I'd stay. I'd stay until I absolutely couldn't take it anymore and then I'd bail, abandoning Travis and the restaurant. But he'd expect it. And he'd forgive me. Again, this was all the shit I promised myself I would leave behind in my twenties. And for the most part, I had. Finishing culinary school, turning thirty, moving back and committing to this crazy venture with Travis. Conner 2.0, I called it. And the last four months I had been a machine—the tastings, learning the numbers, vetting the farms. When I had presented Travis with my series of detailed sketches last week, showing him the smooth rhythm of how the kitchen should flow—like a finely tuned orchestra, like the ebb and flow of ocean tides—I saw the side-eye smirk he gave me. He was surprised. He was impressed.

"Conner 2.0," I had said, chest puffed a little.

"Don't get me wrong. I'm loving the new you, but shouldn't it be Conner 3.0?" Travis had said. "You know, since you turned over this new leaf when you turned thirty?"

But things were starting to shift within me. I could feel them start to flow the opposite direction. And then there was Rian. It had been two days since we talked, and it was beginning to make my shoulders tense. And I initiated the last three calls. People say absence makes the heart grow fonder. But people also say out of sight, out of mind.

The Sea & Sky Cafe was a second-tier—at best—seafood and chicken restaurant in Morro Bay that fed the overweight out-of-towners that had come from Fresno or Bakersfield to see the rock, feed the sad sea lions, and breathe in the fishy air for the weekend. We also had our handful of locals, all of whom were over seventy and preferred routine and familiarity over taste and cleanliness. The Sea & Sky was something I was beyond overqualified for, but it was a job. A job where I still got to make people happy with food. A job where I cringed every time I had to drop halfway decent ingredients into the deep fryer. A job that had only one rule: don't serve yellow tartar sauce.

The place was run by a brute named Donnie, a large man with perpetually red cheeks and a bulbous nose who could have been the mascot for Eastern Europe. The only thing Donnie had going for him, as far as I was concerned, was that he was out of town a lot. Where he went, I had no idea, but the less I saw of him the better. When he was there, he did nothing but complain about the slow waitresses, the lazy busboys, and the vendors that were stiffing him.

But for the most part, he left the cooks alone. For one, he couldn't afford to lose us. And two, the other head cook—I'd never use the word *chef* in a place that served rubbery Shrimp Louies in plastic dishes—was Nikki. Nikki couldn't cook her way out of a bag of microwave popcorn. But she was sleeping with Donnie. And she was half his age.

Like many midweek lunch shifts, this one was slow and uneventful, which normally I would welcome, but today it gave me too much time to think. The one upside, however, was that in the downtime, I experimented with new dishes for our restaurant. Yesterday, I had come up with an idea for guava chicken pops with a garlic-soy dipping sauce. As I sliced the wings that had marinated overnight and pushed the meat down the skewer, I thought about how Travis had to call Pauline back tomorrow, Friday at the latest. Would we talk more before he did? We had to. When the handful of chicken pops sizzled as they hit the hot grill, I realized that I hadn't thought this through nearly enough. Any of it.

Nikki and her cleavage came to relieve me at five, we exchanged sarcastic jabs, and off I went. Still no call from Rian, I drove a little faster down South Bay, my fourth trip on it today. The sun was still a ways from setting, but it was already casting an orange glow over the estuary that hugged the road to my right. The tide was out, which meant the soggy grassland was a mix of mucky browns and grays and greens. One stream of water twisted and snaked through the estuary much like South Bay Boulevard did, and in my periphery, I spotted two herons walking with stilt-like legs along the stream, hunting for dinner.

I was in serious need of dinner myself. And after a day that was spent entirely too much in my head, I wanted something greasy and salty. Something to get me back into my body again. I craved a stomachache. I stopped in at Sylvester's, the quintessential family-owned burger joint. On the side of the wooden shack were the words *Big, Hot, 'n Juicy,* along with a large hand-drawn cartoon hamburger with googly eyes. Everything was big and dripping with grease and secret sauce. On the wall inside was a corkboard, home to a couple dozen or so Polaroid pictures of large men, pimply teenage boys, and exactly three women who had conquered the *BIG ONE*: a five-pound burger with all the fixings consumed in thirty minutes or less. No thank you. Food was to be loved, not attacked.

I picked up a half-pound *Old Fashion*, large fries, extra seasoned salt, and a Coke. It would pair well with the Dodger game that started at seven. If a food-induced coma and three hours of a droning announcer weren't going to knock me out, then nothing would.

When I entered my apartment, I was taken aback at how dark it was already. Although the sun was still an hour or so from setting, my apartment was surrounded by tall pine trees and my blinds were closed. Before I had a chance to flip on the light switch, I saw the blinking red light of my answering machine. It blinked twice, then stopped. Blinked twice, stopped.

Travis had always given me shit for still owning the antiquated technology. "You have a cell phone. Why do you need two phones, let alone that goddamn answering machine?" I could never offer an answer that would satisfy him.

But, like anyone born before the '90s, you had a phone in your house. And the phone had an answering machine. Even after cell phones came along, I could never shake the conviction that a house needed a phone. And there was a certain anticipation to a blinking answering machine that cell phones couldn't convey. A blink for every message. It was always the first thing I did as a boy when we came back from vacation. Count the blinks. One time, after a week at the Grand Canyon, my parents and I had come home to a machine that blinked forty-seven times. My head nearly exploded with excitement. I had had no idea what that could mean, but it must mean something, and something big. Unfortunately, it turned out my mom had called a psychic hotline before we left to make sure nothing bad was in the cards for us as we donkeyed our way down the deep canyon. So our machine was filled to capacity with automated messages from Madam Zora, Edwina the Enchanted, and every other hack with a deck of cards and a 1-900 number. Sure I was disappointed that day, but the blinking red light still carried a mysterious promise. Like anything was possible. Like hitting the play button might change my life.

I turned on the kitchen light and set down my dinner, the white bag already transparent with grease. One of the messages was sure to be Rian, though I wasn't sure why she didn't call my cell first. But the second one? It couldn't have been Travis. He boycotted that phone on principle.

I placed my elbows on the white tile counter and hit *play*.

The first message was not from Rian. It was a high-pitched voice I had heard only once since I moved back down from San Francisco.

"Conner, dear, how *are* you? This is your mother. I'm quite sad that I've missed you. Your father and I are doing great. New Mexico is heaven on Earth. We're hitting the road tomorrow, and who knows when we'll be by a phone next. You know how it is. We'll call when we can. Tell Rhonda we say hello. Are you two still together? Okay, be a good boy."

Jesus. Getting her name wrong? And still without a cell phone? Prancing around New Mexico in corsets and tights and feathers. How useless and embarrassing they had become. I clicked *erase* and waited for Rian's sweet sing-songy voice.

But as soon as the second message began, it became clear that it wasn't Rian at all. In fact, it was a man's voice. He spoke in a rushed, agitated manner.

"Conner Robbins. Coach Rich here. Morro Bay High School. I want you coaching my JV squad this year. Summer league starts next week. See you in the gym Monday at four. It's a big commitment, but you're the man."

Just like that.

And suddenly I became aware that I was a lot of things at the moment but wasn't sure "the man" was one of them.

I was a long-distance boyfriend who waited too anxiously by the phone. I was a long-distance son to parents lost in another century. I was a cook at a restaurant I hated. I was a best friend who was unsure about mixing business with friendship. I was a business partner throwing monkey wrenches in already-made plans. I was a guy ready to pack up and move for the sixth time in twelve years. And now, apparently, I was the head JV coach for the Morro Bay High School boys' basketball team.

CHAPTER 2

MANNY WAS AT THE COMPUTER WHEN I WALKED through Travis's front door. A scene not all too unfamiliar.

"Mi amigo! Qué pasó?" He flashed me a quick smile before returning to the computer. "Travis is walking Jack, but come take a look at this one."

At eighty-four, Manny had to be the oldest sex addict in the world. He wasn't always that way, he'd told us, but since retiring, it was the only hobby that held his interest for more than a week.

On the screen was a thick middle-aged Hispanic woman lying on her back atop a pool table. Bad lighting, a pile of laundry towering behind her. Far from professional. She was attempting to cover both breasts with one hand, but they spilled out in all directions.

"What do you think, amigo? Looks fun, no?"

I could only laugh. Billiard balls lay scattered around her on the green felt table, except for the eight ball. It sat in the soft, doughy middle of her stomach.

"Let's see what she has to say." Manny scrolled down, reading. "*Looking for a mature man who doesn't play games but knows how to play me.* Oooh, mamacita. Come to Papi!"

"Go get her, big guy," I said, squeezing Manny's large, round shoulders. Manny didn't seem to shrink with age, but rather expand. He said all the sex made him stronger. "I'm going to grab a beer and clean the grill. Need anything?" I asked on my way to the kitchen.

"No, no. Let me send this one a message and I'll join you."

"No rush. We're going to wait for Rian. And besides . . ." I poked my head around the corner. Manny was hunched over the keyboard, poking away with his two index fingers. "Take your time. Sounds like she could be the one."

"Maybe the one hundred and one." He let out a loud singular laugh. "Not that no one is counting."

The backyard was small but inviting. An old wood deck extended out the door, just big enough for a Weber and a handful of patio chairs. The grass beyond the deck was lush and in need of mowing, and there was an orange tree in the back right corner. The grassy area was about the size of the key on a basketball court, and when I returned four months ago, Travis and I installed a hoop extending up from the back fence. He refused to cement the backyard, so there was no dribbling, but we practiced free throws while we talked about menu items or girls we used to know. But today, seeing a hoop took on a slightly different meaning.

It had been two days since I received the message from Coach Rich, and one day since he called back, an awkward, stilted conversation in which he not so much asked but rather congratulated me on landing the position, while I fumbled over one-word sentences. But I hadn't told anyone. When Rian had called the next day, she said she was coming down for the weekend, and that became all that mattered. So I told myself I'd wait, tell her in person. And when Travis called me this morning to invite me for a BBQ, he also said he was calling Pauline on Monday morning. To tell her what, he didn't say.

On the deck, I scrubbed halfheartedly at the black-crusted grill and nursed a Firestone like it was my first-ever beer. With an empty stomach and a full head, I didn't need to push it. Potentially moving back to San Francisco, yet one phone call away from leasing a place here in San Luis. Mix in the coaching job I just accepted in Morro Bay, and fold in a long-distance girlfriend . . . all these things swam around my head like goldfish in a bowl. Each unsure if the other might attack, so they didn't so much swim around my head as they dipped and dived to avoid one another, only occasionally and accidentally bumping fins.

Before hearing the voices in the living room, I heard the scratching of nails on the hardwood. Jack tore through the house and exploded out the back door through a trucker's mud flap that hung over the doggie door.

"Hey buddy, what's up?" I bent down and ruffled the fur behind Jack's ears. An extremely large black lab, he was the type of dog that made parents clutch their children tight when he passed. But really, he didn't want anything more than to lick any ankle, palm, or face he could get his tongue on.

"What's up, asshole?" Travis joined me on the deck, Firestone in hand.

"Nice walk?"

"Met a cute girl."

"Of course you did."

"Shoot?" he asked, nodding to the hoop.

I put my beer on the railing and dug the ball out of the grass behind the orange tree. As was customary, we each took five shots while the other rebounded, and then switched. All the while talking about mundane stuff. What time were we expecting Rian? Half hour or so. What did you buy for the grill? Burgers and dogs. Did the Dodgers win last night? No, lost in extras. And with each change of subject came a shot or two in silence. Miss, rebound, pass, sip, swish, rebound, pass—the perfect chorus for a Friday afternoon.

The sky was white but not glaring. Smooth, but still heavy. And over the rounded top of the orange tree, much of Morro Rock was visible, as it most always was from anywhere in Morro Bay and even parts of Los Osos. To me, it was nothing more than a large hunk of rock. Sure, it was more than five hundred feet tall, but really it was no different than what might get stuck in your shoe. Yet it defined this town. Hell, the rock was our biggest industry. I thought it more fun to imagine it as a sleeping mythic creature. As if its lumpy brown-and-green shell might unfurl at any moment, releasing a prehistoric beast that would terrorize the coast, tossing tourists into its mouth like popcorn. Travis told the out-of-town kayakers it wasn't a rock at all, but rather a giant piece of petrified shit. Earth's dingleberry.

"So," Travis said, spinning the ball in his hands. "Have you told Rian about your crazy idea?"

"No."

"How come?" He was looking at me when he shot. The ball fell short, barely grazing the front of the rim before landing in my hands.

"It doesn't concern her right now." I threw the ball back. "It's between you and me."

"And since it's not happening, there's no use in getting her hopes up, right?"

"Will you at least think about it?"

"Because if it is about her . . ." He took another shot that went through the net cleanly with a *snap*.

"It's not."

"Because I thought she was moving down here."

"She is!" I passed the ball back. A two-handed chest pass with perfect form. "Well, she might. She was going to, but now . . ."

"I told you I have to call Pauline on Monday about the lease."

"I know. So we should talk about it before then. You know, really talk about it."

"Fuck, man." He shot and again it went in without hitting the rim. "It's a big curveball to throw at me all of a sudden. I mean, do you really want to go from competing against the likes of what, Tahoe Joe's and that crappy place on Marsh, what's it called? And instead you'd rather open up against . . . shit, Thomas Keller, Gary Danko, the Zuni Café!"

"Wow. Look at you," I said. "I thought I was supposed to be the scared one in this partnership." I threw the ball back with a little too much zip.

"Not scared. I'm just saying . . . for our first restaurant, you want to skip college ball and the minors, and you want to go straight to Dodger Stadium."

"You keep saying 'the first restaurant.' Like there'll be others. This is it, man. This will be the one. And in your little analogy, don't you think my training at Culinary and all your years running Yakety, that was our minor leagues?"

"It's not as easy as trading in life vests for salad plates." He shot the ball, and it clanged off the rim, jetting off into the grass. "And taking classes on the perfect crème brûlée is not the same as running a professional kitchen."

"Of course, but—"

"And no offense, but I thought you were done with all the wishy-washy bullshit. You have been a rock, a fucking beast these last few—"

"Baby!" Rian came tearing out the back door, similarly to how Jack had done earlier, though she opted not to use the doggie door. I tossed the ball aside, and Rian jumped on my back, her legs wrapping around my waist. She was petite, but the weight felt good. And for that one moment, it felt as if she were the only thing keeping me tethered to the Earth.

"Hey! How was your drive?"

"Boring, but who cares?"

"Refills?" Travis said, and disappeared into the house.

I reached over my shoulder, grabbed her under the ribs, and flipped her small frame up and over my shoulder, placing her feet on the deck. She landed with such grace, as if we'd done it a hundred times. She wrapped her arms around my neck and attacked my face with quick, sharp pecks.

"I missed you," I said.

"I missed you too."

Rian was an unassuming girl from a distance. Typical shoulder-length brown hair, brown eyes, not very curvy, yet clearly feminine. We had been dating almost a year now, but we were quickly approaching the point where more of our relationship was spent long-distance than not. And even though she was younger than me by five years, she was the older, wiser one.

She pushed me backwards until the back of my knees hit a chair, and I fell into it. She sat on my lap, and again, I found relief to feel her weight on my body.

"Cervezas!" Manny came through the back door, shoulder first, bottles in hand. He was followed by Travis, who also backed out, carrying two plates of food.

And here was my family.

"Who wants a burg, who wants a dog?" Travis asked. "Wait, don't answer that. Everyone gets one of each."

It took a bit of willpower, but I always let Travis man the grill, usually without comment or suggestion. Unlike in the kitchen, he knew what he was doing if it involved charcoal.

Despite the frenzied goldfish in my head, it was a pleasant evening. Rian seemed unfazed by the nearly five hours she'd spent in the car. Travis appeared equally unfazed by the San Francisco bomb I had dropped on Wednesday. And Manny was Manny: perpetually happy, perpetually shirtless, and, I assumed, perpetually with a hard-on.

As for me, I was happy to have Rian there. Even without me telling her about everything, she was able to bring a calm to it all. For an hour or two, I allowed myself to become more concerned with shooting her playful glances than with what I was going to do if Travis vetoed my idea. More caught up in sneaking ways to pinch her ass or kiss her neck than I was with figuring out how taking a new job here while trying to move north made any fucking sense at all.

Surrounded by people you love, it's easy to become lulled into a sense of comfort. We sat on the deck with paper plates in our laps and beers by our feet, talking a whole lot about nothing. One of those moments you wanted to snap a photo of and live forever in that still shot.

"Manny, tell Travis and Rian about your latest chica," I said, which was all he needed to launch into a story, which would trickle into another, which would bubble into another. Rio Manny, we called him: a complicated river system with endless tributaries of stories.

He came up from Hermosillo, Mexico, in the 1940s. He told us he rode up the whole way on the back of a burro, with nothing but a sombrero and a handful of pesos. He told us a lot of things. Somehow, the handful of pesos became a handful of dollars, became *several* handfuls of dollars. We never did get the full origin story. But in 1954, Manny opened a hotel in West Hollywood. Casa Lola. Within two years, it doubled in size and became the hot spot for celebrities to hide out or have affairs with B-listers and tabloid journalists. As we understood it, the place was run mostly by undocumented immigrants, including the famous Señora Garces, who ran the kitchen. "Best mole sauce north of the equator," Manny would say, and all our mouths would water. Rio Manny had stories upon stories—all with varying degrees of truth—about the Hollywooders of the time: Burt Lancaster, Marlon Brando, Natalie Wood. Peter O'Toole was the biggest tipper. Vincent Price scored the most ladies. And Ava Gardner always signed in under the name *Fantasia*. He sold the hotel in 1978 for enough money to buy all of Mexico. But instead, he settled down in Morro Bay to take up surfing and internet dating.

"You don't go to their house, do you?" Rian laughed. "God, they probably have husbands. And kids."

"Grandkids!" Travis chimed in.

"Hotels, mamacita. I've got hotels in my blood." Manny rubbed his smooth belly. "Hotels are sexy!"

"Yeah," I said. "But when you're boinking these women at the Best Western in Morro Bay, I don't think Spencer Tracy or Elizabeth Taylor christened the room before you."

"Yes, not all hotels can be Casa Lola." And as with every time he uttered the name, Manny sat back, closed his eyes, and let a smile spread across his face, as if his memories were playing out from an old movie projector against the backside of his eyelids.

"Enough," Manny said, shaking himself out of 1957. "Mamacita, you are the guest tonight. Tell us what is new up in the area by the bay."

"Well, let's see." Rian reached down to rub Jack's head. "Oh, I do have some news. Pretty silly, really. I could never compete with your stories, Manny."

"And I could never compete with your beauty."

"I don't even think I've told this to you," Rian said, looking at me. I prayed we weren't going to start the game of *things we haven't told each other yet*.

"So," she started, "I know you guys are all going to tease me. But I've been chosen as the president of the *Chee* Club."

"The Cheese Club?" Travis asked. "Nice."

"Haha, no. Chee. *Q-i*."

"You lost me, mamacita."

"It's essentially the Bay Area Scrabble Club. It's been renamed the Qi Club. Qi is the only acceptable two-letter word using Q."

"Hmm," Travis said, "I liked it better when it was the cheese club."

"Hey," Rian said, lifting her bottle as if giving a toast. "Words are the testicles, the *balls*, of life. If you don't jiggle them every now and then, what's the point?"

Manny erupted with a string of booming laughs.

Travis tilted his bottle back to Rian. "Cheers to that!"

"That's my girl!" I said. And she was. My little word nerd. She was never without the day's *New York Times* crossword puzzle. Joined book clubs, published the occasional poem, and she was always one letter-swap away from a cheesy pun. Even her fish was named F. Scott Fishgerald.

Eventually Manny disappeared into the house to clean up and do whatever it was that Manny did. Rian, Travis, and I continued outside with Jack asleep on the deck between us as we alternated sentences with sips of beer.

A long, smooth sip seemed to be everybody's way of setting their pace. Manny used it to stretch out a long story, and most likely to stretch the truth. Travis often took a sip to stall, giving the gears and cogs in his brain one more rotation to work something out. Rian, the wordsmith that she was, would take a swig at the end of her sentence, letting the pun, the wordplay, the linguistic cleverness hover in the air for another moment so the rest of us could catch up. And I'd been accused of literally hiding behind the bottle.

I sat back and listened as Travis told us about the redhead he met while walking Jack. Then somehow, the conversation drifted over to Travis's family. Rian was curious; after all, she and Travis had only really hung out a handful of times. Predictably, this led to a conversation about *my* parents.

So through a tone that was one part angry, one part amused, and two parts embarrassed, I offered details on their move to Madrid, New Mexico, to join one of the country's largest traveling Renaissance fairs. They would be touring all over the West Coast in the coming months, to which Rian and Travis made plans—through contained laughter—for all of us to visit them whenever they were within driving distance.

"What do they . . ." Travis took a sip of beer, the gear clicking into place. "What do they *do?*"

"Honestly, I have no idea. Walk around barefoot reciting poetry and handing out flowers?"

"Or maybe they put on those hokey versions of Shakespeare," Travis said.

"Yeah, yeah! Or a kissing booth!" Rian offered.

"I'm glad you two are enjoying yourselves."

"Hey," Travis said, holding his hands up in defense, "I haven't even mentioned corsets or your mom's cleavage once."

I took a long swig, finishing off another Firestone.

This led to a discussion of breasts (Rian's stepmom's were fake), which led to a discussion of the Sea & Sky Cafe (were Nikki's real?), which led to a discussion of shitty jobs (what was everyone's first?), which led to a discussion of other firsts (cars? kisses?), which led to my story about Gina Lee, which led to . . . which led to . . . and round and round we went, letting the beer and the cooling night air take us from one subject to the next, where making sense was starting to become optional. And it was only every once in a while that I would remember all the things we *should* be talking about but weren't.

Soon the conversation thinned until the three of us fell into silence. Our heads tilted back to look for stars in the small patches of clear sky. It was becoming increasingly cold, my arms awash in goose bumps, and even though I should have gone in for a blanket for Rian, I couldn't move. We were all content in the silent company of others, content to just be. A quick thought swam by: Maybe this could work.

It was a short-lived moment, however, as Manny swung open the back door, singing in Spanish.

"Oh geez, Manny," Rian said with a sigh. "Really?"

She was referring to his hands. In one was a large bottle of tequila. In the other, four shot glasses.

"C'mon, c'mon, mamacita. We have so many things to celebrate!"

"God, Manny. I don't know." I patted my belly. It was firm, the skin stretched tight, full of hamburgers, hot dogs, and beer. But Manny was carefully lining up four shot glasses along the railing of the deck. He leaned down, eye level with the glasses, pouring tequila with the care of a chemist.

Travis, Rian, and I shook ourselves awake and readjusted in our chairs. Tequila required some straightening up.

"Salud. Salud. Salud," Manny said as he handed each of us a full shot glass. When he picked up his own, he held it in the air and said, "To mamacita's new job as queen of words."

"Cheers," I said, lifting my glass, suddenly hit with the idea of mini orange-agave cakes.

"And to a wonderful dinner with great amigos," he continued. Orange-agave cakes topped with blueberries and pistachio dust.

"Cheers to that," Rian said.

"And to—"

"C'mon," Travis interrupted. "Bottoms up, huh?"

"*And to,*" Manny continued even louder, "the new possibility of mis amigos moving north. I will miss you like I miss Señora Garces's enchiladas. But it will be the best restaurant in San Francisco! Salud!"

And there it was.

Manny clinked his glass against each of ours, and we all instinctively slammed back the tequila. It burned its way down my throat.

"What?" Rian said, her face pinched from the shot.

"Manny doesn't know what he's talking about," I said. The burn reached my stomach, full and now glowing like a bed of embers.

"But why did he . . . ?"

Manny was oblivious, swaying side to side as he poured himself a second shot. And even in the dark, I could feel Travis looking at me.

"It was just an idea," I said. "We haven't decided anything. And I certainly didn't think we were *telling* anyone."

Travis began to say something but stopped as Rian spoke: "I'd like to think I'm not just anyone."

"Well," I started, but not sure where to go. The tequila, having bottomed out, was now starting its way back up my esophagus.

"Here's all it was," Travis said. "Conner was thinking out loud the other day. Naturally San Francisco came up, how much he missed you. But of course, we realized how unrealistic it was, the cost, and how much we love living here, yada yada, and that was the end of it. I guess I said something to Manny in passing. That's all."

Rian and I didn't have sex that night. It was only the second time since we started a long-distance relationship that we shared a bed and didn't. To all the downsides of being 250 miles apart, the one upside was the sex. When you only saw each other once or twice a month, you became rabbits. But not that night. I lay in bed thinking of all the things I needed to say to people. About what Conner 2.0 would do. And Rian, after a long drive and then some drinking, fell asleep almost instantly. At least I thought she did. She always slept with such grace, her breathing never belabored, that it was difficult to tell when she was actually asleep.

I was folding over her omelet in the pan when she blindsided me much like Manny had the previous night.

"Why don't we go see that place downtown you were telling me about."

"The restaurant?"

"Yeah. Have you heard anything?"

"Not yet." The lies stacking up like a wobbly Jenga tower.

Travis and I had checked out the place on Higuera maybe two weeks ago. Pauline had lined up several locations for us to see that week, but despite its smaller-than-desired size, the downtown location was too good to pass up. We put in an application right away. I had called Rian and told her all about it, but that all seemed like centuries ago now.

We ate sausage-and-cheese omelets with a side of berries, yogurt, and mint, with a warm cup of coffee and the *New York Times* crossword puzzle. But when "we" did the crossword, that meant Rian filled in the answers while I looked over her shoulder, amazed that she knew obscure Italian operas, Chinese dynasties from the tenth century, the creator of Archie comics. "If useless knowledge were hurricanes," she would say, "then I'd be the Florida coast." Or once it was *ex-boyfriends* and *Taylor Swift*. Each time she said it, she filled in the blanks with an analogy more clever than the previous.

"Sixty-seven down," she said.

I scanned the tiny font below the checkered puzzle, the paper littered with pink eraser droppings. "*What makes God good?*" I read. "Baby, it's been an awfully long time since I've been to church."

"C'mon, you can get this one."

"You already know it?"

"Yep," she said, kissing my cheek.

"Okay," I sighed. "How many letters?"

"Three."

"Three? How can a question like that be three letters?"

"Think," she said, then cleared our plates from the table.

There were no letters to help me out, and I didn't even know where to begin. It also crossed my mind that this might somehow be a test or lesson. Neither of which I was much up for today.

We eventually left the apartment without me figuring out what made God good. Any of the obvious words—life, forgiveness, mercy—were clearly too long.

"You're thinking about it too logically," she told me as we exited the staircase of the parking structure in San Luis. I smirked at the irony. Too logical? Not an accusation I would be hearing from Travis anytime soon.

"It's up there." I pointed up Higuera. "See the green canopy?"

"Nice," she said. "Perfect location."

I took her hand, and we walked the two blocks in silence. Even though we left Los Osos in fog, San Luis was clear and sunny. The sidewalks were busy but not crowded. Green sweatshirts in abundance even though Cal Poly recently finished up. Aside from college students, there were plenty of families, strollers, young couples. Even those who were clearly tourists had a different swagger to them than the tourists in Morro Bay. Yet I could only half enjoy the afternoon. I did, after all, have my first basketball practice on Monday. And I needed to tell Travis before he found out on his own.

"Nice, nice," Rian said, taking notice of the stores leading up to the green canopy. "A coffee shop at the corner. That's good for foot traffic, right?"

"Yeah."

"And an art store. Not the best, but not horrible."

I loved how she took interest in even the smallest details. "And not too far from the theater," I said.

"Dinner and a movie."

"Exactly."

She squeezed my hand.

We arrived at the restaurant, but the windows were covered in tinted cellophane, making it difficult to see in. Rian immediately walked up and put her face to the glass with her hands cupped tightly around her eyes.

"What's the size?" she asked.

"In total, like fifteen hundred."

"Looks like nice floors."

I joined her. Pressed my forehead and nose to the glass. It was cold against my skin. The inside was dark and empty, but we could get an idea of the size and layout. For the most part it was a long, narrow rectangle going back. The floors were hardwood. The long wall that ran down the left side of the space was old brick; the rest of the walls were plain and white.

"What did this place used to be?" she asked into the glass.

"It's turned over a couple times in the last several years. I think the last people ran a taco joint."

She continued to pepper me with questions about the kitchen (we needed new stoves), the delivery access (there was a back entry and an alley), and on and on she went, but neither of us moved, poised like a couple of Peeping Toms, conversing into the glass.

Rian and I had met my second-to-last semester at the San Francisco Culinary Training Academy. She was working at a little hipster cafe called the Back Porch, and I went there on a class assignment. It was a course on front-of-house management, and we were to go be the most annoying, high-maintenance customer we could, a real pain in the ass, then observe and report on how the staff handled it. Rian took every punch I threw at her, and I came back the next day to apologize and confess. She said I could make it up by buying her a drink.

"Besides needing new stoves," she said now, "I don't see a thing wrong with it."

"Not quite as big as we wanted, but it's pretty much exactly what we were looking for." And as I said this to Rian, I also realized I was saying it to myself. It was true. We maybe wanted something twice the size, but you couldn't argue with the location. Ironically, location was also the problem. Wrong city.

"*Further*, right?" she asked. "Still going with that name?"

"Yeah, what, you don't like it?"

"No, no, I do. It's just that . . ." Her voice trailed off into the glass.

"What?"

"It's just that . . . well, that was the name of that bus you told me about, right? Someone had written it up top? Like the destination of the trip?"

"Yeah, and?"

"Well, it's not right. Grammatically, I mean. If they were traveling, then we're talking about distance and so it should be *Farther*. Not *Further*."

"Wow, babe, really?"

"I know it's silly, but I can't help but think of that every time." And then she forced a laugh. "But whatever, it's just me being me. No one will ever know or think of that. Especially when the place becomes so successful."

"Ha, well, then you really don't want to know that when they first painted it on the bus, the guy spelled it wrong. He spelled it F-U-R-T-H-U-R."

"Oh God, are you serious?"

Then she made a weird popping noise with her lips that sounded like a loud drop of water. "Spelling, huh . . . something to think about."

I ended up barely passing that class on front of house. Which is like barely passing P.E. As much as I loved making people happy with my food, I didn't like dealing with them directly. But that was what Travis was for. Though he was a natural with people, he definitely didn't give two shits about the difference between a hollandaise and a béarnaise. Besides being best friends since middle school, we were a perfect match for this restaurant. And despite my shortcomings, he knew it.

Rian was the first to unstick her forehead from the glass. "I can't wait for opening night!"

I smiled and kissed her.

"N," she said, and kissed me back.

"Huh?"

"What makes God good. The second letter is *n*."

"Three damn letters?" I whispered. "Is it an acronym?"

"No, but I like that you're thinking differently."

We did have sex that night. We were already in bed, the lights off, and when we started kissing and hands started roaming, I worried that a certain tension would show itself in how we moved. I worried that our rhythms wouldn't sync. When two opposing currents meet in the ocean, they can create turbulent eddies and fronts, and what would this mean for our bodies? I worried that once naked, she would see all the things I hadn't yet told her.

"I think I got it," I told her while we sipped coffee the following morning, sitting in the white plastic chairs outside my apartment. "I know what makes God good."

She kissed me on the lips. "Let's hear it."

"Is it *end?*"

"Hmm. How so?"

"You know, because we all die. God's real gift to us is our mortality." The look on her face told me I was wrong, but I stood by my answer. As though if I gave a good enough explanation, maybe I could change the whole damn crossword puzzle. "C'mon, who wants to live forever? It's our expiration date that gives everything value, makes life worth living. So really, it's our *end* that is God's gift to us."

"You're overthinking it. It's not the right answer if it has to come with a dissertation."

"It's a good answer."

"It actually is. Kafka once said, 'The meaning of life is that it will end.'"

"See!" I said, feeling vindicated.

"But Kafka is not God."

"Well, maybe he should be."

The rest of the day felt like a blowout game. One of those where the score gets out of hand early, and players on both teams just go through the motions, checking the clock to see how much time is left. We ended it with one of our traditions, and things felt as though they were falling back into place: loud music, a nice bottle of wine, and Rian and I cooking a good meal together. That night it was Arcade Fire, a bottle of Prisoner red blend, and a half pizza, half calzone concoction called a Pizza Vesuvio.

Admittedly, a half pizza, half calzone, while fun, was a little childish. Reeked of an '80s hotel menu. But Vesuvio was also the name of the bar in San Francisco where I took Rian on our first date. To buy her my apology beer. We started meeting up there every Thursday to sit in rickety wooden chairs on the second floor and look out the window. Watching the people go by as we sipped Guinness. It was in that bar that I fell in love with a girl and a city all at once.

"I am still gonna move down," she said as she kneaded dough with floured ghost-hands.

"I know." Did I?

"Okay, I just don't want you to think that I'm not and then try running up to San Francisco for me and ruin the restaurant."

And then we let ourselves get distracted by fresh olive oil, salty soppressata, and Win Butler's voice crooning about lost love.

That night, while Rian slept with the grace of a dancer, I stared at the ceiling, thought about the absurdity of actually coaching a basketball practice tomorrow, and tasted the lingering briny earthiness of artichoke hearts. I had a professor at the Academy say that artichoke hearts were, very simply, the center of the universe. Chef Asato. The only midterm I ever failed. I didn't finish three of the four components in the allotted time. She wouldn't even try the dish.

"One thing at a time," she told me. I made a move to protest the ridiculousness of the comment, but she put her hand out. "One thing at a time," she repeated. And she said it in such a slow, confident way, there was no questioning it.

And she was right. Even though that seemed like the exact *opposite* of what I needed to do. Even though the dish failed because I couldn't juggle *multiple* things at the same time. She was right. I was in control of *one* thing every moment. The sauce could not be seasoned while I broke down the chicken. The vegetables could not be chopped while I was deveining the shrimp. It was literally and technically impossible. But if I did one thing at a time and did it well, then the next thing could be done and done well, and then the next and the next. And once I began telling myself that simple mantra—one thing at a time, one thing at a time—suddenly not one, but twenty things were done.

So that's all I had to do. I didn't have to solve Rian, Travis, San Francisco, Pauline, the basketball team, and God knows what else all at the same time. One thing at a time. And what needed to come first was abundantly clear. I needed to tell Travis about the basketball gig. And soon. And shit, half the fun of coaching was going to be doing it with Travis alongside me, reminiscing about our days as Pirates, passing along some of the same torture enacted on us. I'd tell him first thing.

Rian left early on Monday morning. So early that Los Osos was still asleep, plenty of cold, sticky fog crusted into the corners of its eyes. And as I leaned into the open window of Rian's Toyota and kissed her and told her I loved her, she stared at me, smiled, and said, "An *o*."

"What?"

"What makes God good. *God* . . . becomes *good* . . . when you add an *o*." She enunciated the words like a preschool teacher, then laughed and pulled out of the driveway.

I stood there and watched her car disappear into the fog of 11th Street, still only half awake myself. "That's so fucking stupid," I said, but no one and nothing was awake to hear me.

The answer made me feel tricked. That, plus not knowing when I would see Rian next, put me in a bad mood all morning. But it was more than that. Something wasn't sitting right, and I could tell it wasn't about Rian. But before I spiraled about all my unknowns and the opposing forces pulling my body in different directions, I remembered: One thing at a time. I had to call Travis.

"Good morning, this is Further, where good friends come for good food. How may I help you?" This was how he answered.

"Okay, screw San Francisco." I don't know why I said it. It just came out. Like I had surrendered my mind and now my body was responding, and it yearned for control.

"Whoa." I could feel him shaking off joke-Travis and tightening up. "What do you mean?"

"I don't mean screw San Francisco. I love San Francisco. But I mean the place on Higuera. It's ours. It's right. Call Pauline."

"Are you *sure* sure? What changed from Wednesday?"

"How many places have I lived since high school? Five. I've lived in five different—"

"And how many schools? Jobs?" As if he had been waiting to pile on.

"And in all those different cities, all those different starts and restarts, what's the one time it worked out?" I could feel myself gaining a certain momentum, but I wasn't sure where it was heading. "What's the one thing I finished? Where was I the happiest?"

"Uh, San Diego? With ol' what's-her-name? Anna, right? When you were going to be a what, a chiropractor was it?"

"You dick."

"I think I need an adjustment along my L4-L5." He was cracking himself up.

"Are you done?"

"Sorry."

"San Francisco. The culinary academy. For the first time in my life, I truly loved something, I was passionate about something, and I was good at it. But then I got down here and even though we were crushing it, it started looking and tasting and smelling like high school again, and I freaked out. So I thought I had to run back to the last place where something was good. But I wouldn't be going back to the Academy and that life and those years. They're done. It's not the place as much as it's what you're doing and who you're with. So it just hit me, like right now, that where I'm happiest isn't San Francisco. It's cooking good food and opening this restaurant with you, that's where it is."

"Well, well, well, if it isn't Robert fucking De Niro." I could hear him clapping.

"Huh?"

"That was about the best damn Oscar speech I ever heard. Conner 3.0, baby!"

"2.0," I corrected.

"I knew this shit about going back to Frisco wasn't really you. It was a knee-jerk reaction. Muscle memory. I'm telling ya, you been different these months. Dare I say like an adult. My little Conner's all grown up."

"Okay, okay, call Pauline. And don't call it Frisco."

"Call Pauline?"

"Call Pauline."

We hung up and my heart was racing. It was like Travis and I were both discovering that conversation together at the same time. None of it was planned, but it felt right. And it felt good to be intentional. It felt good to be in control of a decision, even if that decision was simply to stay the course. One thing at a time. Okay, so maybe I didn't tell him about the basketball gig, but that was okay. I accomplished something else. Something much bigger.

Names are important. And *Further* came from a good place. The impulsive, yet in hindsight, obvious, idea for opening a restaurant was hatched over several rounds of Guinness on the second floor of Vesuvio. The same bar in North Beach that Rian and I frequented, an area in San Francisco most noted for its Italian food and strip clubs. Travis was up visiting for a weekend as the three of us had tickets to see the Flaming Lips at Bimbo's. Travis and I had several hours to kill before Rian met us after work.

Vesuvio, like its partner in crime across the alley, City Lights Bookstore, reeked of history. Photos and bric-a-brac littered the walls. Of the days when Lawrence Ferlinghetti and Allen Ginsberg, Dylan Thomas and Bob Dylan, Neal Cassady and Jack Kerouac all gathered to have a drink and talk about things that mattered. We marveled like fanboys at these larger-than-life characters and what it must have been like to sit in the exact same spot in the late '50s, early '60s. At one point, Travis mentioned that Neal Cassady was actually the driver for Ken Kesey's bus that carried his Merry Band of Pranksters on its twelve-day, LSD-laden jaunt across the country.

"What a trip that must have been," Travis had said, staring into the coffee-colored foam atop his Guinness.

"Yeah, no joke."

"Further."

"What?"

"The bus was called *Further*. Someone painted it on the destination placard."

And without needing an awkward, sugary discussion on the importance of friendship, the importance of *our* friendship, we both agreed—quite easily—that would be the name of our restaurant: Further. And it wasn't minutes after that Travis pointed and nodded to a black-and-white photo on the wall.

The photo was of Jack Kerouac, Lawrence Ferlinghetti, and a young brunette with long, swooping locks at a table on the bottom floor of Vesuvio. Over time, black rust had nestled into the dark creases of their clothes and into the subtle lines of their smiling faces, while the light parts of the photo were beginning to vanish like ghosts. But their expressions still came through. Their smiles were not of the *Say cheese!* variety, but rather smiles that came at the tail end of a good, hearty laugh. Their eyes said that nothing else existed except for that moment. Kerouac and the girl were holding glasses of beer, while Ferlinghetti's sat half full in front of him. His arms were raised as if he had told the punch line to the joke they were all enjoying. At the bottom of the photo, in ink that was bronzing, a carefree loopy scrawl read *Where Good Friends Come for Good Ale*.

I looked at Travis and smiled, and he smiled back. "Further," I said. "Where Good Friends Come for Good Food."

Travis nodded then drank from his glass, and for a brief moment there was a glint in his eye that could have belonged in the picture on the wall.

By 3:15, I was climbing into my truck, full of adrenaline. There was an excitement from the call with Travis, the reality of the restaurant going from zero to sixty in the span of a couple phone calls. He was possibly on the phone with Pauline right now. There was also a new anxiety for this JV practice I was grossly unprepared for. Did I really know what I was getting myself into? And there was still Rian. Would she really move down?

But before backing out of the driveway, I reached down to grab the black

Case Logic stashed under my seat. Music was essential for this drive, and in the same way I stood by my old answering machine, I also still believed in the CD. I didn't want to scroll through a screen to see my collection. I wanted to gawk at the CD towers that dominated my living room. I wanted to open a plastic case and hold a disc in my hand, something physical.

Flipping through the options, I found myself annoyingly indecisive. Each disc seemed to carry so many memories. Music was the ultimate time-travel. Nine Inch Nails instantly brought me back to the melted days in the Lake Havasu heat, working pool construction with my uncle and a handful of drop-outs in the middle of the desert. It's a wonder I lasted as long as I did. Mos Def or Erykah Badu transported me to Anna's couch in San Diego. I could smell her grilled cheese sandwiches and the ever-present hint of cat litter. If I heard the bouncing horn section of Buck-O-Nine or Reel Big Fish, I was in college again, red cup in hand, waiting in line at the keg, staring awkwardly at all the girls I was too scared to talk to. Every chapter, unbeknownst to me at the time, was being defined by a song, an album, a band. Like handprints in wet concrete. Ten years from now, what song would transport me back to my apartment on 11th Street?

I finally landed on *Mirror Ball*. Neil Young with Pearl Jam. Pure 1995 guitar grunge. I slid in the disc, cranked up the volume to make sure I couldn't hear my own thoughts, and headed down the hill.

I don't know if it was the driving guitar riff or the freedom of accelerating on the gas pedal, but turning left onto South Bay Boulevard, I suddenly found myself more excited than I had been in a long time. Sure, it'd been exhilarating to see Rian and to envision the new future of the restaurant, but this was different. I was surprised to find myself this amped up to be coaching. And not only for the sport and competition of it, but for leading a group of kids, of young men, and at such a formative time. Maybe I was getting a little caught up in the anticipation, but I swear I felt like I was driving to go change lives.

This rush was also being compounded by my renewed excitement for Further. The talk I had earlier with Travis was mostly for myself. San Francisco was an incredible city, but Further was where I belonged. And Further was in San Luis. On Higuera. And it wasn't just an idea. It was real; you could touch it. I had just unstuck my forehead from its cold glass. I had finally found something I loved and I was going to do it right. I wasn't naive to the low success rate of restaurants, but I believed in Travis and in our idea. A focus on friendship wasn't only the catchy, albeit sappy, tagline of the restaurant. It was also reflected in our concept and menu. Shared dishes. Family style. I had pitched Travis the idea weeks after that night at Vesuvio. The concept of sharing, of coming together with your best friends and breaking bread. What promoted that idea more than sharing dishes? And when people went out, the best items, the mouthwatering, guilty pleasures, were almost always found in the appetizers. "But what if they weren't just appetizers," I had said to Travis. "What if our whole menu *was* appetizers? Like tapas in Spain. We make them the headliner, not the opening act."

"So just snacks and bar food?" Travis asked, more than skeptical.

"No, no, no. We're not serving a plate of sliders and jalapeño poppers. We're talking the good stuff and plenty of it. But instead of rationing your bites waiting for your entrée, we let them indulge and gorge themselves on what used to be just apps. And no TVs. Zero. Not one."

"What? Why? What says *hang out with friends* more than watching the game together?"

"For starters," I said, "we're not opening a sports bar. And secondly, I want to promote actual interaction. Remember that photo you showed me back in Vesuvio, with Jack and—"

"Yeah, yeah, I know the photo."

"Do you think they were sitting around watching a game? Do you think they were laughing at a fucking commercial? No. They were—"

"I see your point. No TVs, but that's going to lose us customers on big game nights."

"Hell, if you'd let me, I'd have a phone closet."

"A what?"

"Like a coat closet. You know, a place people check their coats. But instead of checking jackets, we're checking cell phones. Let people really hang out together. Face to face."

"Kind of a novelty, but actually not your worst idea."

Zooming down the hill, past the Nazarene church and the statue of the bear, I could see Morro Bay in the distance across the estuary. The pine trees that bordered the golf course, the three tips of the signature smokestacks, and of course, the large, rounded hump of Morro Rock. This all-too-familiar scene mixed with the drive and punch of the music wiped my mind clean. I let myself get swept away in the music and the anticipation. Fuck, it felt good to be excited again!

The second song began from the shitty speakers, and right as Neil was singing about how the fruit of love was just around the corner, I myself was coming around a corner. The timing of it was not lost on me, and I caught myself in a genuine smile.

As I veered left, rounding the first of many twists and turns along South Bay, I thought about which drills to run at practice. A good first impression was everything. I wanted to show the kids I wasn't messing around, but I also wasn't going to rule with fear like Coach Rich. He did nothing but run drills designed to put us in dire situations and push us beyond exhaustion. "Sink or swim!" he'd yell. "Sink or swim!" It was his mantra for everything, without ever throwing us a life raft. "Sink or swim, boys!"

I wound back to the right, the gray-green brush hugging the edge of the road while my thumb pounded the beat against the steering wheel. I was approaching the twin bridges. They were called "twin" because there were two of them not a stone's throw apart. At first glance, they were so unassuming you might miss them, but if you grew up in Los Osos or Morro Bay in the '90s, the bridges were a major player of your daily life. At least in the winter. Although they had since been rebuilt, back when I was still in school, they were old, made of rickety wood painted white. They were also so low-lying that any halfway decent rain would cause havoc. The timid Chorro Creek would rise and flood the bridges by three or four feet. And with South Bay Boulevard the only artery between the two cities, this would essentially cut them off from one another.

So as a teenager living in Los Osos and going to school in Morro Bay, this meant getting to school by driving the long way around, through San Luis Obispo. On a normal, sunny day, this might add an additional thirty minutes. Aside from the weather, an even bigger contributing factor to our increased travel time was the fact that we were teenagers, adept at milking any situation to its fullest. Once word spread that the bridges were flooded, Carlock's, the local bakery in Osos, had a line out the door. So while the poor saps from Morro Bay still had no problem getting to school at 7:50, oftentimes those of us from Los Osos wouldn't stroll into class until fourth period, chocolate and sugar crystals decorating our lips, and the teachers couldn't say a word. "Sorry, Mr. Kamegawa, the bridges were flooded."

But as I drove over the first bridge, long gone was the trademark *ba-thump-thump, ba-thump-thump* of the old wood. Instead, my tires hummed over the seam of the now larger, metal bridges built a decade or so ago.

When the third song crunched into the cab of the pickup with its fuzzy guitar riff, my stomach dropped, like when talking to Rian for the first time, and I turned up the volume until the plastic dial was pinned to the right. More than a decade ago I had listened to the opening six seconds of the song over and over and over again. Hitting the restart button more than two dozen times, letting that opening riff become part of my DNA before finally letting the rest of the seven-minute song kick in. I was lying on the back balcony of my apartment in Costa Mesa. Discman on my chest, earphones nestled in my ears. On still nights, or if the breeze was just right, I could hear the fireworks from Disneyland around nine. That night, however, it had been much later. The balcony, the size of a twin bed, barely fit my six-foot frame. I played the song on repeat for an hour and decided then and there that I was moving to San Diego the next day. Orange County was soulless, and it was draining me. I would apply for chiropractic school in San Diego, and I would be on the fast track to figuring my life out. At the time, nothing had seemed clearer.

The song had gone on to mean a lot of things at a lot of times, and that was part of what drew me to it now. It transcended any one specific chapter of my life. The drums were relentless and the guitar riff repeated itself throughout the whole seven minutes. Structurally it didn't do much, but that was part of the allure. Hypnotic. And as Neil began grooving into the second verse, I reached to turn up the volume only to find it already maxed out. I rounded the last corner to the right and accelerated out of the turn when a flash of white took over my windshield. There was a booming *crack* that swallowed the music whole for a moment, and in that same moment the weight against the front of the truck was immense, jostling the cab and my entire body. "Fuck!" I yelled, and slammed down on the brakes with both feet, trying to push through the floor of the truck. The back fishtailed before locking up to a complete stop. My body surged forward, and the seat belt tore at the flesh of my chest.

And then everything was still.

Except the music. The third song. The thumping drums rattled loose fragments of glass that hung from the caved-in windshield. The caustic smell of the brakes and tires filled the inside of the cab and then my head. I could taste it. The buzzing guitars didn't know any better, didn't know to stop. The music was incessant and only made the cab feel smaller. Through the dissipating smoke from my tires, I tried to eye the road in front of me, but the concaved, spider-webbed windshield blurred and distorted everything as though under water. It was then I became aware that my heart was pounding everywhere except for my chest. It pulsed in my eyes and in my ears and in my stomach and in each of my fingertips. With Neil Young's high, desperate voice still pleading from the crackling speakers, oblivious to the moment, I finally made a move toward the volume knob, and that's when I saw it.

Up ahead, on the opposite side of the narrow road, was the mangled form of a bicycle. The tires, the seat, the handlebars, all out of place, like a puzzle. None of it where it should be. And then my eyes caught the sight in the rearview mirror. There was, similarly, a mangled form of a body. The arms and legs also like a puzzle. Nothing where it should be.

CHAPTER 3

THE CONSTANT CLICKING OF THE PEN, THE FILLING in of my name and address in little box after little box, the mandatory field sobriety test, heel toe, heel toe, arms out, touch your nose please for me, sir, can you please explain in your own words what happened, sir, do you know this woman, sir. Justine Bardales's was just another of the blurred faces I saw amid the frenzy that afternoon, her name another foggy word in the chaos of questions. The police wanted to know if I had ever seen her before. This woman with tears flooding her face, shaking hands covering her mouth.

Justine lived alone in a bungalow overlooking the beach in Cambria. She was from Barcelona. Addicted to hiking. At thirty-two, she had hiked the Appalachian Trail, a 2,160-mile trek from Katahdin, Maine, to Springer Mountain, Georgia. And while the most experienced hiker can complete the trek in five to seven months, Justine did it in four months and eleven days.

It was this obsession with hiking that brought Justine into my life on that Monday. Her next goal was to hike the Pacific Crest Trail, and this meant getting in elite shape. This meant surfing every morning, and it meant hiking up and down Black Mountain every afternoon.

I knew all of this because of an email I received Wednesday night. Two days after. The subject line was empty, but the sender's name—Justine Bardales—was one of the few things I remembered from Monday. The email itself was brief and to the point:

We didn't get to meet, but I'm the hiker who witnessed the accident. I hope you are doing okay. I've included my phone number if you ever want to talk. I pray for you as I do the boy's family. —Justine

For reasons I can't explain, I wrote back immediately.

As my fingers worked independently from the rest of my body, I wrote to her that maybe we could meet for coffee. I'd like to talk, to learn about her, but I didn't want to talk about Monday. That was my one condition. I put it in bold, underlined, in italics.

"And where does that Pacific Coast Trail start?" I asked. It was Thursday. Three days after. We were sitting at a table outside Coffee 'n' Things down on 2nd Street. The tide was out, and the stench of muck made my nose twitch. There was a black coffee in front of me, but I hadn't touched it.

"Crest. Pacific *Crest* Trail." Despite the chilly morning, she wore an orange tank top. Her arms and shoulders were muscular, strung together by taut cords of thick rope. "The PCT starts down along the US–Mexico border and runs up into British Columbia."

"So that has to be longer than the Appalachian."

"Oh yes, about five hundred miles longer."

She had been answering my questions all morning, never once hinting at what had brought our paths together, and never once even asking me about my own life. As I continued to grill her as if I were writing her biography, I couldn't stop thinking about how when my truck made solid contact with the biker, she was on Black Mountain, watching. And when I sat frozen in the cab of the broken truck, Neil Young still rocking out of old speakers, she was on Black Mountain, watching. And when other cars came upon me and stopped and drivers rushed out of their vehicles, and when the swarm of police and ambulances arrived like a tsunami—sirens, lights, running, yelling—she was on Black Mountain, watching. Like some sort of sick Peeping Tom. She watched the entire thing.

"My goal is to start the journey on my fortieth birthday. So I still have several months of training." She smiled after every sentence, occasionally sipping at her green smoothie but mostly offering a cautious, measured smile. I could tell she didn't want to appear too happy. It wasn't an ear-to-ear tooth smile. But rather, she grinned, letting me know that she was someone who knew about empathy.

"That sounds like quite an adventure," I said. I didn't want her to go, but I was running out of questions. I looked out on the estuary and saw a group of seagulls fighting over something, a fish or maybe a discarded bagel. They squawked and beat their wings against one another. "I guess I should go," I said.

~

Travis had found out about everything two days prior, first thing Tuesday morning to be exact. It wasn't from any local news. And it wasn't from the *Tribune*, where the front page probably displayed a large black-and-white photograph shot from a distance, police cars, caution tape, and onlookers dominating a frame bordered by the thick brush that ran extra black in newspaper ink. And there, in the lower right corner, would be the mashed front end of my truck. If you knew what to look for, you might even see the outline of bicycle handlebars under my dented front grille. I never actually saw the paper, but I imagined it enough times to know it pixel for pixel.

But Travis didn't have the *Trib* delivered to the shop, which was where he was when he got an early visit from Officer Rugtive. Miller Rugtive had gone to high school with us. One of those nondescript students you might have four or five classes with and not even know it. He made regular stops into Travis's shop, checking on local business, asking about loiterers, any suspicious tourists, had he seen the missing dog? There never was any of those things; the real reason Miller stopped in was to be the town crier, which was exactly what Travis called him.

"Hey, Trav, my man," Officer Rugtive probably said Tuesday morning, poking his head into the open window of Yakety Kayaks. "Did you hear about Conner Robbins? You guys are still friends, right?"

~

"Yeah, we can go," Justine said with a smile. "But if you want to ask me about—"

"I don't."

"Okay. I'm sorry. I just thought . . ."

We both got up, and as we took the short walk to the cars lined up single file along the edge of asphalt and dirt, I assumed she was looking to see if I had the silver pickup. If it was drivable. If it already had a sparkling new windshield. If it had remnants from Monday still stuck to the bumper.

"I walked," I said, nodding to the right. "I'm this way."

"You need a ride?"

"No, I can walk, thank you."

Her hands landed on her hips like exclamation points. "Can I walk with you?"

"Sure." I didn't know why, but there was a strong pull inside me that didn't want her to leave. "It's a bit of a walk, though."

"Thanks for the warning," she said seriously, before letting her voice turn playful. "But I am planning to walk from Mexico to Canada. I think I can manage a trek across Los Osos."

"Oh. Right."

As we began walking up El Morro, I realized I was still holding my Styrofoam cup. It was still full and now cold, but it kept my hands occupied. We didn't talk for the first block, the only sound the occasional car passing or the crunch of needles below our feet. It was in these moments of near silence that I could still hear that song playing, the drums thumping out of faraway speakers.

We were approaching 4th Street when Justine spoke. "I'm going to do the Triple Crown too. Maybe for my fiftieth."

"The what?" I kicked a pinecone that dribbled in front of me.

"There are three long-distance hikes in the US. It's called the Triple Crown when you do them all."

I kicked the same pinecone, harder this time. "Appalachian, Pacific Crest.

What's the third?"

"Can I ask *you* a question?"

I should have known this was coming. Had she just been playing along all morning? Did she have an ulterior motive? I didn't answer; she was going to ask anyway. The third time, the pinecone bounced hard off a rut in the ground and shot off into the street.

"I'm pretty sure you didn't ask me to coffee because you wanted to learn about my childhood or about the intricacies of long-distance hiking. So, why did you want to meet me?"

~

Travis had arrived at my doorstep at 8:15 that Tuesday morning. I wasn't really awake but wasn't really asleep either. He brought food from Dorn's, but I didn't touch it.

"I don't want to talk" was the first thing I said when he walked through the front door. He hadn't even knocked.

"I don't want to talk either," he said, and put the bags of food on the counter.

We sat in the living room and watched a marathon on ESPN Classic of the 1986 World Cup. It went on for hours. I had no idea who won. The only thing I remembered was that it was hosted in Mexico. There was a green cartoon jalapeño pepper perpetually dancing around on-screen. He wore a mustache and a sombrero.

My two phones rang frequently. After I let the first call go to the machine, Travis answered all the others before the second ring. He took the calls to the kitchen, mumbled a few somethings, and was back on the couch in no time. He never told me who had called unless it was Rian.

"You should talk to her," he said after her third call.

"I will."

"When?"

The room slowly darkened that Tuesday night. We didn't turn on any lights, and eventually we were illuminated only by the flickering glow of the TV.

"You know, one of the calls was from an attorney."

"Okay."

"I didn't get the name, but he said you spoke with him yesterday."

"Yes, and?"

"He said he talked to the police and expects no charges, but it's still too early. 'Cuz you know, because of the witness. And then the parents said . . . Well, anyway, he's gonna call again next week."

Germany scored on the TV, and we watched in silence as they replayed the goal over and over. A crossing pass headed into the back corner of the net.

"Hey, I also talked to Donnie," Travis said in a measured tone.

"Yeah?"

"He said don't worry 'bout coming in these next few days."

"Okay."

"But he is expecting you back this weekend. Is that alright?"

"I dunno."

"Hey, look man, if you—"

"I said I don't want to talk about it."

Travis slept on the couch that Tuesday night.

Justine's question wasn't as bad as I was anticipating. It also wasn't, however, something I had the answer to. I had been wondering the same thing. I didn't rush to answer, and she seemed content to wait. I think partly I wanted to be around her simply because she wasn't Travis, and she wasn't Rian, and she certainly wasn't my parents. Or Donnie or Nikki or anyone from the Sea & Sky.

"I don't know," I finally said. "Because you were a stranger? You don't know a thing about me. I dunno, maybe it doesn't make any sense, but I think I need a stranger right now."

This time it was Justine's turn not to respond. She did her half-smile thing, and then we walked. Around 9th Street, we passed an older couple walking the other direction. They held hands. Later, we passed a teenage boy walking two dogs. Something wasn't sitting right with what I had told Justine, though. It *sounded* like the right answer, but it didn't *feel* like the right answer.

"I'm up here," I said, and we turned right on 11th, the street stretching out before us in a long, gradual incline. "You don't have to walk me all the way."

"I don't mind. Really. I could use the cardio. Missed my early surf this morning."

"Alright."

"And as long as you don't mind."

"Not at all."

"Do you . . ." She hesitated. I looked over at her. Her skin was an incredible shade of brown. Like raw honey. "Are you sure you don't want to—"

"No," I responded quickly.

She gave me a look like she was desperate to say something. It was a look not given between strangers. And in that look I saw the real reason I wanted to meet Justine, and why once I was with her, I didn't want her to leave.

On Wednesday, I had slept until noon, although the chunks of sleep arrived in jagged fits and starts. Coming over me like a spell, only to betray me with a jerk. Mainly I lay in a half-awake, half-asleep limbo that only left me more tired. And it wasn't even the images that haunted me. It wasn't the flash of white across my windshield. It wasn't the storm of activity—cops and EMTs and cameras and measuring tape and chalk marks and flashing lights. It wasn't the misshapen body that now lived in the rearview mirror of my mind. And it wasn't even the image of that same body being swallowed whole by the white sheet on a stretcher; it wasn't any of these things that held me back from sleep.

It was the weight.

The weight of the cyclist on the windshield of my truck. Such immense weight. The kind you can only measure in tons. Each time, right as I began to slip into unconsciousness, I felt the weight not on the truck, but on *me*, on my body. It would collapse my lungs and crush my bones, and I'd pull and push and struggle beneath the pressure that sat on my chest like a hundred elephants. And the weight was always followed by the song. As I took deep breaths to remove the pressure from my chest, there it was: the pounding of the drums, the driving guitars. Neil Young's haunting, scratchy voice, as if singing to me directly.

When I had finally staggered from the bed, Travis was still there. He was on the phone in one of the plastic chairs outside my front door. Seeing him on the phone, however, made me realize there were certain people in my world who still didn't know about Monday. Two of those being my parents. But I wasn't concerned with them. Another was Coach Rich. I didn't peg him as the type who read a newspaper or watched the news, but undoubtedly word would spread once he learned his new JV coach was a no-show on the first day of practice. I didn't know if Travis knew anything about the basketball job, but decided to see what was on ESPN Classic instead of worrying myself over what now seemed like such stupid, trivial bullshit.

When Travis came back in, he asked a series of questions. How was I? Did I know a Dale something from the *Tribune*? How did I sleep? Had I talked to Rian yet? Was I hungry?

"Dodgers, Yankees, '78 World Series," was all I said.

"I know what happened was fucked up," he said. "But you have to talk about it at some point. Right?"

"It's a rematch of the '77 series."

~

When I had watched the '78 World Series with Travis on Wednesday, I had already known the outcome. I wasn't alive yet when the series actually took place. But any good Dodger fan knows what happened in the late '70s versus the Yankees and Mr. October. So I already knew that Reggie Jackson was going to blast a homer in game six against Bob Welch to seal it.

But as we watched, there was this tiny, almost imperceptible part of me—I imagined it a pinhole-sized speck of white light that hid in the base of my skull—that wondered and hoped if maybe the outcome would be different. Maybe Jackson, somehow, would strike out this time. Or maybe he'd hit a soft line drive to Davey Lopes. This little white light was so far removed from all sense, all logic, all rational, intelligent thought. But of course Reggie Jackson hit the home run. It already happened. But that light, that hope, that moronic morbid curiosity still existed as Bob Welch threw the pitch. It was the closest I could come to understanding the feeling of insanity. If I tried hard enough, I was able to actually give it power, if only for a nanosecond, to find excitement and anxiety in that blink of a moment as the ball traveled to the plate. Wasn't it also this same part of me that checked the fridge four times in twenty minutes to see if maybe I did still have some milk, when every cell in my body knew that I didn't? This bizarre part of me existed solely to hold out hope even when everything had proven, beyond a shadow of a doubt, that there was none. It knew nothing of logic, of facts, of history, of any existence beyond that exact and particular moment and desire. In a way, it was the most primal of urges. I knew Reggie Jackson was going to hit that home run just like I knew that two plus two equaled four, but yet as Bob Welch released the pitch . . . wasn't there technically still a myriad of outcomes that could occur? He could ground out, strike out, hit a foul ball into the stands. Live or recorded, a pitch on its way to the batter, by definition, held different possibilities.

That was why I had to meet Justine.

As she and I walked up and down the low, rolling hills of 11th Street, we walked in silence. She wanted me to ask her questions. She looked burdened. *She* was the one that desperately wanted to talk about Monday.

And I was realizing that maybe if I kept her around long enough, maybe she would tell a different story. Maybe she knew a different outcome, knew something, anything, that I didn't know. Despite everything I heard and knew from the police . . . maybe, somehow, she had a different ending. It was fucking ridiculous, and it didn't make an ounce of sense. But it was there. That little pinhole speck of light that didn't want her to leave. If she was still there, then maybe the pitch was still on its way to the plate.

"The Continental Divide," she said out of nowhere.

"Huh?"

"That's the third hike. The Continental Divide. It's the longest one of the three. It also runs from Mexico to Canada, but you have to go through the Rocky Mountains and a lot of Montana."

"Oh wow."

"Fewer than thirty people try it a year."

We were only several houses away from my apartment building, and it quickly became clear that nothing was going to come of this. Reggie Jackson *did* hit the home run. The Dodgers *did* lose the series. And there *was* no milk in the fridge. I began to regret meeting Justine and now wanted nothing more than to be alone in my apartment.

"Okay, I'm here," I said, nodding to apartments two buildings down from my own.

"Okay, I guess this is where I head back."

I forced a closed-lip smile.

"Thank you for meeting with me, Conner."

"Thank you," I said.

"You have my number, right?" she asked, searching my face. "If you ever want to talk about anything."

"Yep, okay."

"Are you sure that . . . Maybe we can meet up again or something?"

"Yeah, maybe."

"I just—"

"Well, okay, yeah, good luck with your hike."

She leaned forward like maybe she wanted to hug me, but I turned and headed toward the beige stucco apartment building that wasn't mine.

I went through the black metal gate that opened into a courtyard. From there I stood and watched Justine disappear up and over the hill. When she reached the peak, right before vanishing from my sight, she broke into a run.

Leaving the gate of the foreign apartment complex, I only made it halfway to my own gate when I stopped. I could see up ahead that there was a car in my parking space. It wasn't one I recognized. A red Taurus.

"You want to switch it over to the Dodger game?" Travis had asked around four thirty on that drudge of a Wednesday afternoon.

"We *are* watching the Dodger game." Ron Cey was on deck.

"Very funny. No, today's game." He sipped a beer and kept one eye on the TV and one eye on me.

"We've come this far with the series. Let's finish it. You know, Reggie's home run? I think Lakers–Celtics are on next. '85 Finals."

"Speaking of basketball . . ."

I had almost forgotten.

"I know about the coaching job."

"I was going to tell you. How'd you find out?"

"Does it matter?"

"Guess not."

"Anyway, congratulations. You'll be a great coach. And don't worry, I didn't bring it up to bitch about you hiding shit from me or anything like that."

"Okay, so . . ."

"Just wanted to tell you that I called Coach Rich."

"Really?" Travis had been helpful, but even this took me aback.

"Yeah, right after I cleared your week with Donnie."

"What'd he say?"

"So is that where you were headed? The first practice?"

"Travis."

"Sorry," he said, and sipped from a beer that looked empty. "He was actually really nice."

"What'd he say?"

"He said he understands you might need a little time. He'll take the practices this week, and you can start fresh next Monday."

"Start fresh?"

"I think it'd be good for you to get out of the apartment. Working the Sea & Sky this weekend and then Monday . . . Yeah, you can start fresh with the basketball team. You know?"

"I dunno."

"You talk to Rian yet?"

"No."

"Why not? She's going crazy to talk to you. At least hear your voice."

"You've talked to her, right?"

"A couple times."

"She understands then. I'll talk to her soon. I just need . . . Fuck, I don't know what I need. But talking to people is not it."

"You know, I'm gonna have to go tonight. Gotta be at Yakety early tomorrow."

"That's fine. Like I said, I don't want to talk anyway."

"Okay, but you have to get out of the apartment. I know it's only been a couple days. But make sure you take care of yourself. It wasn't your fau—"

"Travis, please."

~

I eyed the red Taurus with suspicion, but the car offered no clues. There was nothing familiar about it, and I didn't see anyone lingering about.

"Oh, baby!"

"Holy shit. Rian."

She came running at me the moment I was through the door.

"What are you—?"

She jumped, arms and legs wrapping around me, and her weight hung on my body, suffocating my bones and tugging hard on my skin.

"Please," I said, and tried to move us to the couch. "I just . . ." And then, once we were both seated, I saw that she was crying.

"I'm sorry," she said, and cried into my shoulder. "I'm so sorry that I'm crying!" But then she cried harder, her tears wetting my shoulder, her hands grabbing fistfuls of my shirt.

I held her, and as her head rocked rhythmic sobs into my shoulder, it happened. I started crying too, big, heavy breaths. Unable to hold back. My face scrunched so tight the skin might have snapped. The harder she cried, the harder I cried, until our bodies jerked against one another, each of us grabbing at the flesh of the other's back like it was the only thing that would keep our heads above water.

I cried for the lack of sleep I'd had the past three nights. I cried for myself and why it had to be *me* and *my* truck at that exact moment at that exact spot. For this morning, for my meeting with Justine and all the things we both didn't say. For the boy on the bike and his carelessness or bad karma or the faulty asphalt or whatever the fuck it was that sent him in front of my truck. But mostly I cried for his family. His parents. Not for them at this moment or tomorrow or next Christmas, but for the knock on the door. For whomever it was that answered the door that afternoon, thinking maybe it was a neighbor wanting to borrow a mixer, a salesman wanting to talk about solar panels, only to find that their universe had been crushed from the inside out. I cried so hard for the knocking of that door.

And then, as quickly as Rian and I started crying, we stopped, our eyes raw and sore like skinned knees. We held each other more softly now, the salty smell of snot permeating my nose.

"Let's get something to eat," she said.

"I'm not hungry."

"You have to eat, baby."

"Whose car did you drive?"

"Mine was making a weird ticking sound since I got back from last weekend. My supervisor, Jaime, gave me his. Said he would have a look at mine in the meantime."

I peeled my wet cheek off of hers and pulled away so I could look at her. Her face was as red as I imagined mine was.

"You didn't have to come. I was going to call you tonight."

"Of course I had to come. Why don't we order something. You can eat it whenever."

She went into the kitchen and ordered chicken fried rice, beef and broccoli, and two large Cokes. When it arrived, we put something mindless on the television. I picked at the rice, and while she ate, she looked over at me every once in a while, checking on me as if I might do something, as if I were a stray dog she wasn't sure was friendly.

After she finished, she snapped leftovers into Tupperware and cleaned the kitchen, something neither Travis nor I had done all week. And when she returned to the living room, I clicked off the TV. I had a pounding headache.

"How are you?" she asked, cringing as if I might snap at the mere sound of her voice. No one had spoken for a while.

"Not good."

"Do you want to talk about what happened, baby?"

"No, that's the last thing I want to do."

"Okay, that's okay too. But I had to ask." Then she bit her lower lip. I could see her searching. She was several years younger and right then she looked it. "Travis said you were coaching a basketball team or something?"

"Yeah, I don't know."

"What do you mean?"

"I'm sorry, I don't want to—"

"I'm sorry, I'm sorry. I don't know what to do. Do you want to watch a movie?"

"I can't stare at that screen anymore."

"Just tell me what to do."

The thin thread holding me together finally gave. "I don't want to do *any-*

thing. I don't want to have to choose or decide or ask or answer, or . . . I just . . . If I hadn't come back to this fucking town. If I . . ." And then I got up, afraid I might say something I'd regret. I didn't want to hurt Rian, but I couldn't be around any more people. The way Rian looked at me was the same way Travis and Justine did. Like they were looking for answers written on my face.

"I'm sorry," I said, and went into the bedroom.

I lay in bed for hours in a state of underwater blurriness, not really awake, not really asleep. This had become the norm. What had also become the norm was that song, haunting me, so cruelly indifferent to it all, still buzzing through the speakers as if nothing had happened. It played and played in my head until I forced a sound of my own to disrupt it—a clearing of the throat, a rustling of the blankets.

It was after two when Rian quietly entered the bedroom. She slipped into the bed with the grace of a ballerina.

"Good night," she said, then kissed me on the cheek and turned away.

Time passed in that weird way it does in the middle of the night. Minutes might be hours. Hours might be minutes. Everything was quiet, save the occasional hum of a car going down 11th. As usual, Rian was as still as a corpse, which gave me no indication if she was awake or not, but something told me she was.

"Rian?"

"Yes?"

"Will you do me a favor?"

She rolled to her side, facing me, and wrapped one arm around my torso. "Anything."

"Will you read to me?"

"Read?"

"Yeah. Will you read out loud to me?"

"Of course. What do you want me to read?"

But I couldn't think of a single title. I wasn't even sure why I asked that of her. The silence during the last few days had been deafening, but the television or talking to Travis, Justine, that was even worse. I needed something to fill the space before I started replaying images for the hundredth time or heard that guitar riff creep and lurk in the muddy swamps of my brain. But now, as the silence between us sat like a third person in the dark room, my request felt silly and childish. I was about to tell her never mind, when she clicked on the bedside lamp and went over to the tall wood bookshelf on the far wall, filled mostly with books Rian had given me, so much so that books sat behind books and lay sideways on top of other books.

Rian returned with a large hardback. She had removed the cover. I didn't know what the book was. I lay flat on my back and closed my eyes.

She cleared her throat and then her voice began, soft, as if she were, in fact, reading to a child:

"She said noon, right?" Roger looked at his wrist, but there was no watch. There never was. But still, it was something he often did to emphasize Sara's tardiness.

"No, wait," I interrupted. "Are you reading from the beginning? Don't read from the beginning."

"You don't want me to read from the—?"

"No, I don't want to pay attention. I don't want to follow anything. I just want to hear words."

I heard the pages flip heavily in her hand, maybe hundreds at a time. Then she continued.

She regarded her new home while taking long, slow inhales, letting the smoke fill and expand each tiny capillary in her lungs. The apartment was small, but it was hers . . .

I still didn't know what she was reading, and I was glad. She read and read and read, her voice like mint. She read, and I let her words enter through my ears and occupy every space in my head.

She thought briefly of Roger, the nervous jittery way in which he spoke, the tightness with which he gripped her hand. She figured there were so many years of repressed and suppressed and depressed emotions that his ligaments and joints must be hardened and calcified by now.

Her watery *o*'s and *a*'s and *u*'s flowed down my face, filling the tiny crevices of my nose and the intricate labyrinth of my ears.

She read, and her slippery *c*'s and *s*'s slid under my tongue and between each of my teeth. Her tapping of *t*'s and clacking of *k*'s stacked themselves along the inside of my neck, tumbling into my shoulders.

She never paused or cleared her throat or stumbled over a word, and I let her *r*'s roll end over end down my chest, and her *b*'s and *p*'s bounced their way into my stomach, where they expanded and filled the space of my organs, some snuggling in between my ribs. She read until my entire core was packed tightly with her words.

I let her *-ings* and her *-lys* unravel themselves down the length of my arms like red carpets, soft and velvety to the touch, until they tingled the tips of my fingers. She read and read, and I couldn't even hear the turning of pages, only her words. I let her *h*'s and *w*'s blow their way down the long tunnels of my legs, where the *m*'s and *n*'s hummed their way to the ends of my toes.

And finally, once filled, I drifted off to sleep. Real sleep. Occasionally, I calmly wafted back into wakefulness, and her voice was still there, constant and melodic.

When Pearl got closer, she realized it was just a beheaded barbeque. Just the dome top. Its body nowhere to be seen. A ghost of a memory with Cynthia started to materialize . . .

She read and read and read.

CHAPTER 4

THERE WAS A FUNERAL ON SUNDAY. IT WAS TO start at eleven a.m. at Los Osos Valley Memorial Park. I knew the place well. Across from the Los Osos Oaks State Reserve, you couldn't help but see it every time you drove from Los Osos to San Luis Obispo. There was to be a reception immediately following at a family friend's house. Although if they lived in San Luis, why was the funeral here in Osos?

I didn't seek out this information. I didn't want to know this. But on Saturday, at some nebulous hour between Rian and me sitting and watching whatever was on ESPN Classic and going to bed early so she could read to me at random from some book I still didn't know the title of, I checked my email and found a message from Justine:

Conner, I hope you are well. I'm glad we got to meet a few days ago. I don't know if this is appropriate or not, but I am including the funeral information below. It's not my place to tell you if you should go or not. But you should have the option. I will be there.

I didn't tell Rian about the email. Nor did I respond. Nor did I attend. Nor did I go into the Sea & Sky for my Saturday dinner shift or my Sunday lunch shift. What I *did* do was spend every minute obsessing over what the funeral was like. How many people were there? Was there a picture of him? What did people say about him? Was he genuinely a good person that made people cry until every muscle ached, or did people spout clichés, crying dry, obligatory tears? What color flowers were there? Did I linger in the backs of people's minds as someone to blame and hate? Was it a religious ceremony?

Did they believe in God? Did *he* believe in God?

I also didn't show up at Monday practice or any practice that week, or at the Sea & Sky for whatever shifts I may have had. I didn't talk to Coach Rich or to Donnie, although both called several times. Some guy from the *Trib* kept leaving messages, and Travis called often, and sometimes he stopped by or even picked me up and took me out for dinner. I never let him talk about Further or Pauline or that Monday. And he was nearing the end of his rope with me. He had every right. Everyone did. I just didn't care. It was as though something bigger than me was in control now. Its weight immense.

But Rian called the most. I answered about half of her calls, and a couple of nights, she read to me aloud over the phone. But it wasn't the same. Something about her voice got lost in the airwaves traveling to and from the satellites.

It was Monday morning—it had been exactly three weeks—when the house phone rang. I had no intention of picking up, but for some reason, after the third ring, I did.

"Oh, Conner, my baby! I'm so glad I didn't get that horrid machine. How come you never pick up when I call?"

"Hi, Mom."

My mother was an art teacher most of her adult life. But she never did much in the way of traditional artwork: paintings, sculpture, jewelry-making, etc. Instead, she went through *inspired phases*. For a while, she worshipped everything Native American. She made feather headdresses and wore them everywhere. She even made a giant buffalo head that sat for a month on our living room floor. And when I rolled my eyes, she told me, "If you were a Choctaw, you'd not only understand, but you'd be proud of your mother."

There was also an alien phase, where she was convinced life on other planets was trying to contact us. She spent days and days making muumuu-like dresses with a long train that would get caught up in furniture and doorways she was in two rooms ago. Her peace gowns, she called them.

There was a Japanese phase, an ocean phase, and even a time when she wanted to go live with the Inuit in Alaska. But she kept a steady job as an art teacher at Baywood Elementary and paid her taxes on time, which made her eccentric, not insane. And she loved her family and cooked nutritious meals, so she was quirky, not crazy.

"How are you doing, my dear? It's so nice to hear your voice. Your father and I were talking the other day about you and we think—"

"Mom. Please don't."

"Are you sick? You don't sound well."

"I'm fine."

"Well, okay. Your father says hello. He can't talk right now but wants to know how your job situation is. Do you need money?"

My father, on the other hand, wanted nothing to do with art or whimsy. He was a history buff. So while my mother was out sprinkling the perimeter of our house with moon dust or painting a mural of Vikings on the side of our garage, he was sitting in his worn leather chair reading. He had taught American history at Cuesta College, but he didn't discriminate. The Roman Empire, the Spanish Inquisition, the Chinese dynasties, he loved it all.

"Dad never seems to be around to talk, does he?" It wasn't that I necessarily wanted to talk to him, but I felt it was my duty to make them feel guilty whenever I could.

"Well, dear, right now he's being fitted for a full suit of armor. Can you believe it? Your dad's going to be a knight!"

It was when my mom's inspired phase landed on Renaissance art that my parents created the perfect storm. Right about that time, my father was reading a book called *It Was Marlowe,* where the author sold the theory that Christopher Marlowe faked his death and then continued to write under the name William Shakespeare. It sent my dad through the roof. Soon every Shakespeare book in our house had a big black *X* through the author's name, with *Christopher Marlowe* scrawled underneath.

"A knight? Are you kidding? He's never ridden a horse in his life!"

"We're learning a lot of new things out here. You'd be so proud of your mom and dad if only you'd be a little more open to our journey."

It was around that same time that my mother had stopped wearing shoes altogether. She spent hours sitting on the back lawn, weaving head wreaths out of leaves and twigs. Luckily, I was already out of the house when their passions finally lined up and they quit their jobs, sold the house, and moved to Madrid, New Mexico, to join the nation's largest Renaissance fair. The company was hired all over the country to come for a week and transport a fairground back to the sixteenth century, putting on plays, reciting poetry, working with leather and steel, competing in joust competitions, and who the hell knew what else.

"That's great, Mom. I really do have to go, though."

"Wait, wait. Don't you want to know when we're coming to California?"

"Okay, when are you coming to California?"

"The tour is starting in the West. So we'll be there the last weekend of August. I'm not sure which venue yet, but—"

"Okay, great, end of August, got it. I really have to go to work."

"But you didn't even tell me anything about you, dear."

I could hear the sadness in her voice. "There's nothing to tell."

"Are you still with that girl—oh, I always have trouble with her name."

"Rian."

"Oh yes, the boy's name, that's right!"

"It's not only a boy's name, Mom. And she's been my girlfriend for almost a year now."

"How wonderful. I hope you are treating her like a real man should. I know how couples are these days—"

"Bye, Mom."

"Love you, dearie!"

"I love you too."

I loved them because they were my parents, but everything after that had always been difficult.

I wasn't totally lying. I did have to work. It would be my first day back at the cafe.

Travis had agreed to pick me up and give me a ride to Morro Bay. He hadn't said anything yet about my truck, and I hadn't asked. On the drive over, he filled the air with talk of this new girl he met. She was from San Diego, up here on vacation with her girlfriends. They had rented a kayak from him, yada yada. He knew I wasn't interested, but he was polite enough to stretch the conversation. He even spent a couple minutes detailing the annoying way she pronounced *sure*, as if two syllables. And I guess I appreciated the effort, but mostly I stared out the window, still wondering why Justine emailed me last week. If she wanted or expected me to go to the funeral. What would the boy's parents have done if I had?

"I'm doing this because it's your first day back, you know," Travis said. By *this* he meant continuing straight on Los Osos Valley Road instead of turning left onto the serpentine South Bay. "But don't get used to it." We were going the long way around to Morro Bay, through SLO, as if we were in eleventh grade again and a big storm had washed out the twin bridges.

"I know," I said. "Thank you."

But today the sky wasn't the least bit gray. And even though the sun had long ago begun its descent, it was still warm out. Travis also hadn't said a single word about Pauline or the restaurant on Higuera. If I had still been in San Francisco, if I had never moved back . . .

As we passed Los Osos Valley Memorial Park, I pretended to tie my shoes. Bending down, hiding in the cave under Travis's glove box, it was then I noticed that fuzzy guitar riff again haunting the back of my mind as if it had never really stopped. I saw an image of myself in my truck, on South Bay, reaching to turn up the volume. Had I been reaching . . . No, no, that was earlier. I was sure of it.

And for the brief moment I was down there, Travis clicked on the radio. Blind Melon was in the middle of "No Rain," a song not pivotal to my youth, but definitely there, playing somewhere in the background of my puberty.

"Hey," Travis said, "I talked to Coach Rich the other day."

"Yeah?" The music was blurring together now. The song on the radio and the song in my head. The way the beat of the drums bounced off the windshield was all too similar.

"Yeah, you're hanging on by a thread there too, man. You have to either quit or show up, you know?"

"I know." But I didn't care. "And I have to stop letting you do everything for me." Something that sounded like the right thing to say. The tinny guitars spitting out of shitty car speakers. Travis had new speakers, and the song was different, but it was also the same.

"That might be good for you."

"Can I turn this off?" I said, flipping the knob hard to the left.

When I walked in the back door at Sea & Sky, Nikki wasn't there, but Donnie was. Even worse, he was in the kitchen, sweat streaming down his face. In the three months I'd been there, this was only the second time I'd seen him manning the fryers. That meant he was covering for Nikki. And it meant he had most likely been doing a lot of covering during the last two weeks.

"What's the hell?" he bellowed at me while dropping in a new basket of fries.

"I'm sorry, Donnie. I should have called."

"I know the things have been crazy, but c'mon!"

Debbie, one of the veteran waitresses, came rushing into the kitchen, a plate in hand. A customer had sent back the lemon chicken, claiming it was undercooked.

"Bullshits," Donnie said, taking the plate from her. And it was in this word that you could hear Eastern Europe. It was all saliva.

He handed me the plate. "No time for chit-chat," he said, then nodded to the dozen or so tickets clipped above his head. "You have birds and fishes waiting." And he rumbled out the swinging doors.

I fired another lemon chicken, and Debbie flashed me a smile before returning to the floor. Her bleach-blond hair was strung up in a loose ponytail as usual and bounced as she left the kitchen in a hurry.

Apparently there was a summer wrestling tournament all week at Cal Poly. Debbie told me there were several tables packed with large, lumpy young men. They were taking full advantage of the chicken strips with endless fries, so I spent most of the night dropping basket after basket of frozen potatoes into a pool of scalding oil. I couldn't drop them in fast enough. I imagined tables of round, fleshy wrestlers with shaved heads and cauliflower ears, unhinging their jaws and dumping entire baskets of fries down their throats. I let myself get lost in the chaos of the kitchen, the pop of the oil, the high-pitched scream of the ticket machine. The louder the kitchen grew, the quieter my mind became.

Along with Debbie, Greta was also there. They were the two longest-standing waitresses at the Sea & Sky. They both offered me smiles when picking up their orders. At one point, Debbie asked me how I was. "I'm fine," I said.

"I'm glad," she said. And that was that. The other waitress, the hostess, and two busboys, however, looked scared shitless when they glanced in my direction. They stared at me like *I* was the one who crashed face-first into a windshield, as if *I* was the one that still had bits of glass and asphalt embedded in my chin and forehead. When they looked at me that way, I saw the flash of white take over my windshield. I felt the weight of the truck, which became the weight on my chest. I heard the song in my ears.

It was near the end of the night and I was finishing my last ticket, putting a plate of fried calamari on the pass, when I felt Donnie's presence behind me.

"Likes I was saying. I know things have been crazy. But Conner, Nikki and me covered lots of shifts."

"Yes, I'm sorry," I said.

"Don't fuck up anymore, yes?"

"Yes, I—"

"Good. No fuckups." He turned, and with one sausage fist through the flimsy double door, he was gone.

I took off my stained apron and threw it across the kitchen toward the wash bin. My hands were red and raw from splattered grease, hot plates, burning pans, and boiling water. The skin on a couple of my knuckles had split and now stung from the salt and lemon juice that filled the cuts. The muscles and joints in each finger and my wrists ached from disuse.

How petty. How goddamned fucking petty. How dare I recognize this pain. How dare I think of wrapping my hands in a cool, wet towel. I was still berating myself when Greta walked in.

"Debbie is on closing duties, so I'm outta here."

"Good night, Greta."

But she didn't leave. Not right away. She dropped her apron in the wash bin and grabbed her belongings out of her cubby, then walked up to face me. Her blue eyes, each one in its own bed of wrinkles, looked at me hard, and her skin was aglow with equal parts cheap makeup, grease, and sweat. She put both her hands on my shoulders and smiled. Red lipstick marked two of her top teeth.

"I pray for you and for that boy's family."

I looked down. She held on to my shoulders for a moment more before sighing. Then she left.

After cleaning most of the stations, I sat on an overturned crate by the doors and listened to the low murmur of the few remaining tables. Just then, two older ladies emerged from the women's bathroom at the end of the hall. The hallway was long and straight and replete with framed reviews and photographs from the early days, when everyone's hair was a bit longer, their faces a bit thinner, and no doubt the food a bit tastier. The old women were in mid-conversation as they approached.

"The busboy with the big eyes?" one of them asked.

"No, no, one of the cooks," the other said, her voice shaky. "The new one."

There was a good fifteen feet between the women's bathroom door and the double swing doors to the kitchen. Their feet shuffled slowly down the hallway.

"And the poor boy died!" the first voice said with a gasp.

As they moved closer, I could tell that one of them must have been using a walker. There was a metallic squeak and click to their walk.

"Yup," the second voice said. "Dead. Right there on the road."

"Oh my."

"Didn't even make it to the hospital."

Squeak, click, drag. They crept along.

"Oh, how dreadful."

"I know. Can you imagine?"

As the two tennis balls impaled onto the bottom of the walker's aluminum legs came into view of the propped-open kitchen door, I rose from the crate, clocked out with the machine on the wall, and walked out the back door and into the cold Morro Bay night. The Embarcadero was empty, save the occasional couple returning to their cars with Styrofoamed leftovers. The ocean breeze was cold, and I could feel the skin of my hands splitting at the seams. I didn't complete half my closing duties, but I didn't care. I survived my first day back, if barely. The problem with the old women's conversation was not the words they said or the shock and sadness in their voices. It was that that same conversation was happening all over the Central Coast. In grocery stores, at bus stops, in classrooms, across phone lines.

Travis arrived promptly at midnight.

"How did it go?"

"Got through it."

But then he didn't say any more. He drove with purpose. And it was about four turns in that I realized he wasn't taking me the long way home, through San Luis. But he also wasn't taking me home via South Bay.

"Where are we going?"

"Just want to have a beer with my friend is all."

Manny wasn't home when we arrived. *Out with a lady friend* was how Travis put it. "Let's go out back and have a beer," he said as he crouched down like a catcher to pet Jack's sleeping head.

"It's fucking freezing."

"I'll make a fire. You grab the beer."

When I walked outside, I received confirmation. It was fucking freezing. The night fog had rolled in like a new carpet. It rolled in and sat, saturating the sleepy fishing town, bringing a coldness that cut through several layers of clothing.

There were already orange flames in the fire pit that Travis had moved to the center of the deck. He pulled up two chairs, and I handed him a Lagunitas.

"So tonight went well?" He was zipping up a jacket and leaning back in a patio chair.

"Busy at first, then slowed. Typical."

"Donnie there?"

"Yeah, he gave me some shit, but whatever."

The fire grew as Travis fed it piece after piece of broken pallet wood. He peppered me with mundane questions about my night. I told him about the wrestlers in town for the Cal Poly tournament, and he told me about Manny's new lady friend. This was the third night in the last two weeks that he had seen her. Travis went in and brought us a second round of beers, and at some point, Jack joined us on the deck, lying belly down, chin down between Travis and the fire.

"Okay," Travis finally said, "I know you've been asked this a hundred times, but I don't know if there's any other way to ask it—"

"I'm fine."

"Are you?"

"Man, can we not . . ." I took a swig of beer. It laid a layer of ice down the back of my throat. "I mean, it's been a long night, Donnie is on my ass, and—"

"No, fuck you, we're going to talk about it." Travis took a long pull off his beer then set it down on the deck. "I've been compassionate and understanding, and I've helped your ass in every way I could for the past few weeks. But I'm not going to let you drown in this funk or this depression. Or whatever it is. So yes." He picked at his beer and crossed his legs. "We are going to talk about it. Until the fucking sun comes up if we have to."

"Fine." I didn't want to argue. I wanted to pacify him and go home, crawl into bed, and imagine Rian reading meaningless words from a random book. "What do you want to know?"

"Know? I don't want to *know* anything. I want to talk, like adults. I want to talk about the damn thing as if it happened. Because it did, you know. It's shitty and it's fucked up, but it happened."

"Okay. I had a horrible fucking accident. It wasn't my fault, but maybe somehow it was, I don't fucking know. And that's what happened. And we can sit here and talk until the sun comes up, but it's not going to change what happened. So there. What else is there to say?"

"I know. I know, man. And I'm sorry. But it was a freak accident. The investigation was thorough, that witness lady, all of it, you know, not your fault. He lost control. And yes, it was tragic, and there's nothing you can do to change that. But you have to move forward at some point. Be thankful that you weren't hurt and thankful for all that you have, and live your life."

"Ah, yes, be thankful. Doesn't that sound like a nice, neat little thing to do."

"Hey, I'm on your side here."

"I know. I'm sorry. But 'be thankful'? Jesus Christ."

Manny came stumbling through the doors. "Amigos, amigos!" He saw the two of us and the fire, and came to a staggering stop. "Shit, amigos. Lo siento, lo siento."

"Geez, Manny, tell me you didn't drive home," Travis said.

"No, no. Uber is my friend." Then he turned to me, and I could see the slow and strained brainpower working behind his glassy eyes. "Amigo," he said, and pulled up another patio chair next to mine. He wrapped his large arms around me, my face swallowed by his large soft shoulder. "I'm sorry, mi amigo." He reeked of whiskey, smoke, and sweat. Then, as quickly as he barreled into our night, he left.

The night returned to stillness. Travis added more wood to the fire and stepped into the kitchen for two more beers, though I hadn't come close to finishing the one in my hand. We sat quietly for several moments, our breath visible before our faces. The cold ate at my hands, the cracks and burns now stretching and tearing, my skin trying to pull itself away from the bone. The wood popped and cracked. One was loud enough to wake Jack. His head jerked up, and then, either cold or annoyed, he rose and ambled inside.

"Okay, man, so if you don't want to talk about what happened and how you're feeling about it, let's at least talk about the nuts and bolts of what's going on in your life."

"The nuts and bolts? What the hell are you talking about?"

"Let's start with your jobs. You need to go to all your shifts at the cafe. You need to show up to basketball practice and coach the team you agreed to coach. I'm done talking to Donnie and Rich for you."

"Tough love, I get it."

"Yeah? Good. Because it's all love, buddy, but—"

"Hey." It was my turn to bring something up. I didn't want to, but I needed to be in control of something.

"Yeah?"

"My uh, my truck?" The jostling of the cab. The back fishtailing before locking up to a complete stop. The sting-smell of burnt brakes. The music pouring out the shitty speakers.

Travis opened his mouth to answer, then paused, drank from his beer, and looked over at me as if to thank me for no longer fighting him. "It was towed. Tapia's Auto Body."

"And?"

"Should be good as new. They'll call me."

"How much?"

"Don't know yet. But don't worry about it."

I wasn't worried about it. Travis and I always squared up eventually. But now I was curious. How much did it cost to kill a cyclist? Was the price dependent on whose fault it was?

"I know you're exhausted," Travis said. "But you know we have one more thing to talk about. I've been really good about keeping my trap shut."

"It's late, Travis."

"Aren't you the least bit curious about what I've talked to Pauline about? I tried to buy us some time, but she, the owners, everyone is excited. They had plenty of qualified applicants. They liked our vision, though, they actually liked Further, that's why they chose us."

"Okay, and so?"

"So we sign the lease tomorrow."

"Tomorrow?"

"No, man. I can't believe I was able to string them along even this far. But you know what they say, it's time to shit or get off the pot."

"I don't know, man."

"You don't know what? What about that speech you gave me on the phone? Where your happiness lies? Conner 3.0."

"Whatever. That was before. I mean, can you imagine if I was still in San Francisco? If I *wasn't* living here? That would mean—"

"Stop. Listen. They're giving us the option of a five-year or three-year lease. What if we take the three-year, and see what's up after that?"

"What's the point? Put our blood, sweat, and tears into a place so we can bounce in three years and start all over?"

"Yes, but look at our situation. What the fuck am I, are *we*, supposed to do?"

I finished my second beer, deciding to leave the third one alone. It was too late to argue any more, and I was too tired. Staring into the orange embers, I let my eyes blur over. My breath more and more visible before me.

"I don't want to lose this place," Travis said. "We need to sign tomorrow."

"What time are we supposed to meet Pauline and the owners?"

"Two."

"Pauline's office?"

"No. At the restaurant. We have to do a full walk-through."

"What time are you picking me up?"

"You want to crash here tonight?"

"If you'll drive me, I'd prefer to go home."

It was after two a.m. when Travis drove me. There wasn't a discussion about it, but even at the witching hour that it was, he once again took the long way around.

When I exited Travis's car, he told me he would pick me up at one tomorrow afternoon. He also apologized for tonight, for being so harsh, but I told him I understood. What I didn't tell him was that *he* didn't understand. No one did.

My apartment was darker than the night. I couldn't even see my hand in front of my face. But as I fumbled for the light switch, I saw the blinking red light of the answering machine. It blinked only once, then stopped. Once, then stopped. I watched it several times before flipping on the kitchen lights. I was guessing a police officer, maybe that journalist, maybe my insurance, but the moment I heard the tone of the woman's voice, it clearly wasn't any of those people.

"Hello, Conner. My name is Lauren Thomas. I'm uh . . . I'm not sure if you know who I am."

She took such a deep breath the cheap answering machine speakers crackled.

"I'm Braden's mother." She took another breath. "Justine gave me your number. I hope that's okay. Anyway . . ." And then I thought maybe she'd hung up. There was a long silence.

"Anyway . . . I was hoping maybe we could meet."

CHAPTER 5

WHEN I CLOSED THE TAXI DOOR, LAGUNA LAKE SAT before me, drab and cold. The grass and bushes surrounding the small man-made lake were muted shades of green and brown. Even the water struggled to be blue. Travis had explained to me once that too many creek runoffs brought in silt and turned the lake to muck brown. The lake was a constant source of chatter in town, everyone with an opinion on how to bring back the brilliant blue it once had and along with it, the swimmers, sailors, and picnic-goers. But for now, Laguna Lake looked like nothing more than a lonely bird refuge. A family of beige ducks fed on the shoreline. Several geese roamed the grass slope.

I sat on one of the wooden picnic tables and waited. I had the taxi pick me up at eleven, even though our meeting wasn't until twelve thirty. I felt more in control if I was there first. But what exactly I was waiting for, I wasn't sure.

My phone call to Lauren the morning following her message had been oddly bereft of any emotion, like making a dentist appointment. She suggested the location and time. And that was that. She offered no indication of what she wanted or how she felt toward me. I didn't tell Rian or Travis about the phone call or the meeting. I didn't want to meet her—to put names and faces and voices to what had happened, to see who had answered the door that Monday—but it was something I needed to do.

I looked around to make sure that she hadn't arrived as early as I had, wasn't sitting on some other picnic table, waiting. But the only other person I saw was an older man walking his dog down by the water. The dog was no bigger than the ducks it was so feverishly trying to chase.

It was a few minutes after twelve thirty when a blue Subaru pulled into the dirt parking lot not fifty yards from where I sat.

A woman exited the driver's-side door, but then a man also exited the passenger door. Lauren had not mentioned bringing her husband. She hadn't mentioned anything at all. As they walked toward me, I watched them only in my peripheral vision. They looked excessively normal. Nothing like people of tragedy. They didn't look like grieving parents ripped apart by loss. They looked as though they might have just come from the grocery store or a soccer game.

He wore blue jeans and a green windbreaker, his hair the color of the Morro Bay sky—a wash of gray and white, darker in some patches, lighter in others. He could have been anyone's father, could have been my father. His hands were stuffed into his jacket pockets, and he walked with his head down.

Lauren looked younger than I had imagined. Not that I imagined a singular face. But oftentimes when I dreamt, there were mothers and fathers and brothers and sisters. All silently weeping. They floated by me endlessly on a loop, only visible from the shoulders up, not panicking or gasping for air, simply floating. And when Justine had told me about the funeral, I imagined everything: the mother's thin, graying hair pulled up in a tight bun; the wrinkles on her face and around her eyes acting like rain gutters. I pictured her in long, flowing, tragic dresses, a light sweater over her shoulders. A woman rocked by sorrow.

And Lauren most likely was that woman. But she didn't look it, at least not from this distance. Her brown hair lay around her shoulders in large, swooping curls. And she wore khaki pants with a blue-and-green plaid button-up shirt. Around her neck, she wore a red and gray scarf.

None of us looked at one another as they approached. I looked down at the table. The wood had been carved up a hundred times over, a bulletin board for the bored teenagers of San Luis. My fingertips traced a large heart that had been etched into the wood. Inside, it read *Matt + Sarah*. Below that, in black Sharpie, someone else had written *the only tru love is unrequited.*

I stood up as they neared the table.

"Hi, Conner, I'm Lauren Thomas," she said, extending her hand. And there it was. That's when I saw all the pain I was expecting. She carried it in her eyes. They were dry and strained and lost. "And this is my husband, Peter." I also felt it in the hollow timbre of her voice.

I shook both their hands without a word, and we all sat at the table.

"Thank you for meeting us," Lauren said.

I nodded, but I couldn't look at her. I watched my hands as I ran the fingernail of my index finger through the grooves of the large *M* and *S* from the lovers' names.

"I'm sorry if this was a strange location," she continued in her clear but distant voice. "But I was hesitant to meet at a restaurant or coffee shop. In case I started crying." She looked at Peter. "There has been a lot."

She came across as one of those people that always told the truth, no matter the consequences. That scared me. It wasn't how I was used to functioning, with everything such fair game. "It's okay," I said. "This place is fine."

"City council has argued for years over dredging," Peter said. "The lake, that is."

Again, I nodded.

"Would cost millions." He was looking out at the lake as he spoke. As if speaking to it.

"How have you been, Conner?" Lauren asked.

How had *I* been? I shouldn't have been allowed to answer that. I didn't deserve that question. Not from her. But she sat, looking at my face, awaiting an answer.

"Okay," I said. "Not good. You know?"

"I do know."

Two geese wandered close to our table. They looked at us with tilted, inquisitive faces atop question mark necks. The three of us watched as the birds played with the boundaries. They took one step toward us, then two steps back, then two steps forward, then one back. One of them chattering a low mumble as if whispering to us.

Lauren looked behind her at the dirt parking lot. All that was there was their Subaru. "How did you get here?" she asked.

"Taxi," was all I said.

Peter, who had remained fixed on the two geese, swung both arms up at them in a demonstrative motion. The geese fled, one running down to the water, the other bursting up into the air for a moment before landing in the lake with a splash.

"I'm glad to not see it today," Lauren said, meaning my truck. "To be honest, that worried me much more than meeting you."

"I don't want to see it either," I said. And at that, Lauren smiled. It didn't look forced or pained, but looked as though that was the natural state of her face, and maybe it was every other look that was labored.

As we sat in silence, I didn't try to think of something to say. It wasn't my place. This was their time. It seemed as though I should say *I'm sorry*. Like that was the most obvious thing in the world. But as I heard the voice in my head say it first, I realized that I couldn't say that to them. It was so fucking trivial, so mundane. You said you were sorry when you accidentally bumped into someone or when you showed up fifteen minutes late to a meeting. I couldn't do it.

"Conner?"

I looked up at Lauren. Her eyes were green and weren't afraid to look at me.

"This might sound a little odd. I don't know, maybe it won't. But . . . would you mind telling us a little about yourself?"

My mind went blank. "About me?"

"Yes. If you wouldn't mind."

"Well, okay. What do you want to know?"

"I don't know." Lauren looked to Peter. But he was staring out at the lake. "Anything you might feel like sharing. Everything from the police or the paper has been so . . . sterile. Anything that helps us know you as *you*."

"Okay, well . . ." I madly scanned the files of my life. But as I was searching for facts, anecdotes, idiosyncrasies, I didn't know if I should be rounding down—making things seem not so good. Maybe it would help her feel better to know that I was miserable, a failure, not a good person. I didn't want it to appear that I was taking joy in anything.

Or maybe I should be rounding up—maybe she would feel better knowing I was a worthwhile, productive, happy individual. That maybe my triumphs could somehow balance out her catastrophe, keeping the universe in balance.

In the nanosecond I contemplated this, I didn't arrive at a clear answer, nor did I have the mental capacity to pull off any sort of manipulation of the facts of my life anyway. "I'm a chef," I said. "Well, really just a cook right now. But I went to culinary school in San Francisco."

Lauren tilted her head and continued to look at me, waiting for more.

"I moved back to the Central Coast four months ago. I cook now at the Sea & Sky Cafe in Morro Bay. A chicken and fish place. It's a dumb name, really. You know, because chickens don't fly."

"We've been there, haven't we, Peter?"

He didn't say anything, just put his hands back in the pockets of his green windbreaker.

"Is that on Market?" she asked.

"No, it's on the Embarcadero, kind of across from the Shell Shop. You might be thinking of Dorn's."

"Oh, okay."

"I don't know. I guess that's all, really."

"You said 'back to the Central Coast.' Did you grow up here?"

"Yes. In Los Osos. Went to Morro Bay High. All that."

"And your parents? Siblings?"

And so I went on to tell them a little about my parents, but I made them out to be more like teachers and artists and less like freaks and eccentrics. I didn't tell them why they had moved to New Mexico, only that they did. When Lauren asked about marriage and children, I told her about Rian and how we met in San Francisco. For the most part, she nodded, occasionally smiled. Peter looked mostly at the ducks or down at the ground. He sometimes nodded, but it seemed less a reaction to anything I said and more to some dialogue running in his head.

For whatever reason, I didn't tell her about coaching the JV basketball team. Maybe because technically I hadn't done that yet. I didn't feel like a coach any more than I felt like an architect or a firefighter. I also didn't say anything about Travis, about Further, about signing the papers yesterday for the place on Higuera.

"Thank you," Lauren said finally, as though she had heard enough. Then she looked over at Peter.

"Yes, thank you," he said.

"Can I ask you one more question, Conner?"

"Of course."

"Have you met Justine?"

"I have," I said. I didn't know why she asked. And if it was better if I said yes or no. The truth just came out.

"We are so grateful for her. How fortunate for her to have been where she was, when she was. I mean, to be able to hear how everything happened. The not knowing would have been . . ."

And although I was the only one of us that was actually there that day, as Lauren spoke I felt as though she knew much more than I did. And really, she did. I think the knowing would have had the opposite effect on me. So I nodded and offered a closed-lipped smile.

"Well," Lauren said. "Maybe this is enough for today." She looked at her husband, who barely nodded. "We thank you again, Conner, for agreeing to meet with us."

I stood up, not knowing how the hell a goodbye like this was supposed to go. Peter shook my hand and then retreated to the passenger seat without waiting for his wife. Lauren stepped toward me, her eyes trying to meet mine. I looked at her too-white shoes, at the rusted table legs, and at the weeds sprouting from the dirt. She put both her hands on my shoulders, much like Greta had done a couple days ago.

"We don't blame you, Conner."

I shook my head, felt a large swell rising from my stomach up toward my throat and my eyes.

"We don't." Her voice like a ghost. Something sensed, but not really there. "It wasn't your fault."

My head couldn't lift. I stared at my own shoes, which kicked hard at a rock half buried in the hard dirt.

"I . . ." she started then stopped.

And right before it got to be too much, before I could collapse or run or scream, she simply turned around and walked back to her car, where Peter sat looking straight ahead, the seat belt already strapped across his torso.

I turned to face the lake and tried not to think about what Lauren had said or the pain in her eyes. I had just pulled my cell phone out to call the cab driver that had driven me here when I heard my name.

"Conner?" Lauren called again. I turned. She was halfway between me and her car. "Can we give you a ride somewhere? Do you need a ride?"

"No thank you," I called out instinctively.

"Are you sure?"

At this distance, I couldn't read her face. I couldn't tell if it was pleading or stoic or pained.

"Really, it's okay. Thank you," I repeated, then turned back to the lake. Moments later, I heard her car door close and the engine start up.

The cab driver had said he would grab lunch in the area and be ready to take me home whenever I finished. He was pulling into the dirt parking lot minutes after I called.

"Back to Los Osos? The apartment on 11th?"

"Yes please."

As we pulled out onto the paved road and I was in the safety of a car with a stranger, I was trying to make sense of why they had wanted to meet me.

Why did they want to know about my life? What could they possibly have taken away from that visit? It was so brief and inconsequential. In my head I was asking these questions with the pronoun "they," but really I was thinking only of Lauren. Peter was a statue, a piece of the scenery. The only conclusion I came up with was that she wanted to see that I wasn't this awful, horrible human being. Maybe she wanted to be sure it was okay to not hate me. And almost like waiting for a pill to enter my bloodstream and take effect, I sat there, still, in the back seat of the taxi, waiting for a reaction to hit me. I wanted the meeting with Lauren and Peter to *do* something. To *change* me. But nothing happened.

We were on Los Osos Valley Road, passing Laguna Lake Golf Course, when I realized I didn't want to be sitting alone in my apartment. Maybe it was good to be out. It didn't necessarily feel better, but it felt different.

"Excuse me," I said to the driver, an older, balding white man with a walrus mustache who listened to news radio.

"Yes?" He looked at me in the rearview mirror.

"I'm sorry, but I've changed my mind. I don't want to go back to Los Osos. Would you mind taking me to Morro Bay? To the high school." I didn't have my clipboard, my practice notes, and I wasn't dressed the part, but the time of day was nearly perfect, and I thought maybe I had better show up for once. Maybe I hadn't already been replaced.

"Makes no difference to me, son. As long as you pay the fare. I can turn on Foothill up ahead."

I arrived at MBHS a couple minutes after two. Practice started at three. I had the driver drop me off in the back parking lot by the gym, and even outside I could hear the varsity team practicing. Coach Rich's voice booming off the gym walls, the echo of the ball against the hardwood, and the unmistakable sound of basketball shoes squeaking and squealing with every stop, start, and change of direction.

I probably should have spent the hour watching the varsity practice, show Coach Rich my initiative or at least try to come up with some semblance of a plan for my first JV practice. But instead I roamed the campus. I hadn't been back since I graduated a dozen years ago. For the most part it looked the same, if a bit smaller, the colors a bit duller. The bushes hanging over the retaining walls begged to be trimmed, and there was a hand-painted sign on the wall. Something about an end-of-something in the quad, but the sign was ripped. In the 500 hall, the light-blue lockers were rusted and in need of fresh paint. My steps echoed. A high school campus in summer was a ghost town. A skeleton of its former self. As I roamed I saw faces from my past, but mostly I saw Lauren's, with her tired eyes.

Before heading into the gym, I called Travis to see if he could pick me up around six at the high school. He said he was supposed to meet a girl in downtown SLO around six thirty. He tried to play it straight, but I could tell he was excited that I was taking my first practice. He said he'd push his date back till seven or eight.

It was ten to three when I entered the gym. It smelled exactly as I remembered: sweat, rubber, and BO. The varsity kids were on their way out, sweatshirts and gym bags slung over their slick shoulders, their shiny red faces too tired to give me notice. Coach Rich was still on the court with one player. Coach was down in a defensive stance, feet wide, arms out. He slapped his thighs twice, got lower, and stretched his arms out again. It was then I noticed the group over on the far court that was presumably my team. They were sitting in a circle at mid-court being led in the butterfly stretch by one player sitting in the middle. Skinny elbows and knees stuck out like the wings of baby birds. A couple of them noticed me, whispering to others until most of them were stealing glances in my direction. I waited in the doorway while Coach Rich put the lone varsity student in a defensive stance. The scrawny boy was bent over as though he were trying to sit in a chair. Coach Rich straightened the boy's back, then pushed his shoulders down. The coach mirrored the boy, and they shuffled back and forth in the position several times until Coach Rich slapped the court with his palms and shuffled more vigorously. The boy struggled to keep up. And just when I thought he was going to trip over his own big feet, Coach Rich straightened up, slapped the boy on the ass, and they both headed my way. As they approached, Coach Rich's face gave no sign of how he felt to see me.

"Conner," he said and extended his hand.

"Coach Rich."

"I'd like you to meet Jimmy here."

It was then that I really looked at the boy. The red hair. I instantly recognized him: the kid I met out in the bay, fishing in a canoe and giving me nothing but smart-ass remarks. I quickly tried to recall everything Travis had said about him, but drew blanks.

"Jimmy," I said, shaking the kid's hand. "Nice to meet you."

"Jimmy, this here is our JV coach. Coach Robbins."

Jimmy nodded and let go of my hand.

"And Jimmy here is the best goddamned jump shooter Morro Bay has seen in a *long* time."

At this, Jimmy's face didn't change. He knew better than to smile. His cheeks were flushed and sweat ran down his temples.

"Now, if we can get him to play some goddamned defense!" With this, he slapped Jimmy on the ass once again, signaling the boy to leave.

"See ya tomorrow, Coach," he mumbled as he shuffled out of the gym.

"I'm telling you." Coach Rich turned to me. "Sweetest jumper you've ever seen."

"That's great."

"The kid's a goddamned basket case, though. So we'll see."

I was only halfway looking at Coach Rich. Mostly I was watching the younger kids over his shoulder as they changed stretches, still whispering and sneaking peeks.

"Anyway, let me introduce you to your team." He slapped my shoulder, and we started walking to the far court.

"Hey look, I'm—"

"You're here now, that's what matters. I'll let them tell you what I've been doing with them. See how much stuck. You have a couple decent players, lot of projects, though. We'll run through the roster after you've had a chance to learn who's who. First game of summer league is next week. Games are either Mondays or Wednesdays, over at Cuesta. I'll give you a schedule." With a hand out, he stopped me halfway. "It's only summer league, though, just JV. Get your feet wet. Run the kids to death. And fuck, maybe even have a little fun. Come fall we'll get you serious."

The players, there must have been fifteen of them, were standing now, doing arm stretches, when we came upon them.

"Alright, Pirates, gather 'round, listen up!" Coach Rich's raised voice echoed off the wooden walls of folded bleachers that lined each side of the gymnasium. The kids didn't hesitate to sprint over. "I want to introduce you to your new coach."

They all looked over at me with big moon eyes. They knew exactly why I had missed the first couple of weeks. They probably knew more about the incident than I did. They didn't want to stare, but they couldn't look away.

"This here is Coach Robbins. It wasn't too long ago that he was standing right where you are. A former Pirate himself. And a damn good one. Worked hard for me." His legs were spread wide, and when he paused he put his hands on his hips. "You are to respect him. You are to listen to every goddamned thing he says. And you all know well and good, he's the first person I'm going to talk to when it's time to call some guys up to varsity. I haven't told him a single thing we've been doing. I trust each of you knows every drill and can explain to him exactly how we ran it. Any questions?"

No one, of course, had anything to say.

"Alright, Coach Robbins, I'll leave you to it." He slapped me hard on the back, and I had to roll my weight onto my toes to stop from taking a step.

"Thanks, Coach," I said with a nod.

We all stood and waited while the coach squeaked his way out of the gym. And then I turned back to find more than a dozen young teenagers staring at me, waiting for me to say something, to do something, to tell them what to do. But I hadn't a clue in the world.

CHAPTER 6

"AGAIN!" I PACED BEHIND THE BASELINE AS THE kids staggered to the line, heads hanging as if too heavy for their necks. "Ready, go!"

They took off, sprinting as best they could, feet shuffling, backs hunched. It was the end of practice; they were running their ninth suicide. I couldn't stop.

"Five seconds! Four . . . three-two-one-time!" And as I yelled, there were still a handful that had not yet crossed the baseline. They let out a collective groan. "Didn't make it!" I shouted. "On the line!"

"C'mon, Coach!" one of the taller boys said. I hadn't yet learned their names.

"You have something to say?"

"This is . . . crazy," he panted. "We're doing . . . our best."

They all peered up at me from slouched positions.

"Is that what you're going to tell the refs when you're down in the fourth quarter? 'Hey ref, we're doing our best, can't you give us a few more points?'"

They all turned back to staring down at the court; they knew they weren't being pardoned. Except the one who spoke up. He rolled his eyes and continued to look at me.

"On the line!" I shouted. "Ready . . . go!"

They limped off the line and stumbled down the court on noodle legs. I was angry. Mostly at myself. How dare I for a moment act the victim. The only way to shake the image of Lauren's face, those eyes, was to suffocate my head with the noises and smells of the gym. The echo of the ball, the squeak of the shoes, the stink of sweat and rubber. And what really helped was yelling.

The louder I yelled, the emptier my head. So as the team crossed the baseline for the tenth time, dripping and red-faced, I yelled some more.

"I tell you what, damn it." I grabbed a ball off the rack and threw it to the kid with the big mouth. "If you're already in such great shape that you don't need to run . . . You make two free throws and we go home right now."

He dribbled the ball slowly but confidently to the free throw line, while the rest of the team, hands on knees or hips, halfheartedly cheered him on. "C'mon, Cody." "Let's go, Dee, you got this." Their voices were weak, but the desperation in their eyes was not.

It didn't start this way, but I had found myself becoming increasingly angry as practice went on. There hadn't been any real reason; they all did as I said as best they could. I skipped any pre-practice speech—didn't address where I had been, why I had missed—and I didn't get into any rah-rah shit either. We ran half a dozen drills, mostly the hard ones I remembered from my days as a player, and then we scrimmaged. With each drill, I found myself pushing them harder. Yelling more. But it didn't come from a competitive place; it didn't have anything to do with basketball. I couldn't shake Lauren's face.

Cody was taking his time at the free throw line. Dribbling the ball, spinning it, dribbling it some more, catching his breath.

"Let's go!" I yelled. "Refs aren't going to give you this much time in the game!" As he lined up his toes and prepared to shoot the ball, I found myself rooting for him to miss. I didn't want to go home.

The ball hit the left then right side of the rim softly and dropped through the net. The team cheered, now with renewed energy. One of the kids grabbed the ball and threw it to Cody. He dribbled, spun the ball, dribbled again, then lined the tips of his white and black basketball shoes to the edge of the blue free throw line. The second shot was well short, barely nicking the front of the rim. "Shit!" Cody yelled. The team groaned.

"On the line," I said, turning my back to the team. "Suicide. Thirty seconds. Ready, go!" I didn't watch as they ran, and I certainly didn't note the time. When they finally finished, they didn't even have the energy to look up at me. Hands on knees, they were all folded in two.

"Let's try those free throws again," I said.

"I'll shoot, Coach." It was Kyle. Throughout the practice he showed himself to clearly be the best player. *His* name I had taken note of.

"No, no," I said, throwing the ball once again to Cody. "Cody seems to be the one who likes to open his mouth. Let's let him shoot again."

Cody walked to the line without a word. He went through his routine and shot the ball. This time it didn't even hit the rim, but went straight through, snapping the net. The team gave a few claps, but no one cheered.

"Let's go, Cody," I said. "We're all ready to go home." This time I did want him to make it. I was tired. Tired of practice. Tired of being an asshole. It didn't feel right. But it also felt beyond my control.

The second shot banked off the backboard and shot straight through the net. It was ugly, but it went in. The group didn't cheer so much as they sighed, then all looked to me.

"Alright, let's meet at center court."

As I stood in the middle with all eyes on me, I noticed a stark difference from the way they'd looked at me two hours ago. Before it was with shock and a morbid curiosity, like seeing a dead bird. Now their eyes were tired, and they looked at me the way they looked at Coach Rich. The way *I* used to look at Coach Rich. Fearful.

"Alright, good practice. See you tomorrow, same time." No encouragement, no appreciation for how hard they worked. I heard my tone, and I hated myself for it. "We have our first game next week. Let's bring it in." I put my hand up in the middle, and they hesitated before following, as if they were expecting me to say more. About what, I'm not sure. About all the running, and how hard I was at the end of practice? About where I'd been the last two weeks? But with all hands up in the air against one another, I simply said, "Pirates on three. One, two, three!"

As the kids grabbed their gym bags and shuffled out of the wide double doors, no one said a word. Until Cody approached while I was putting the balls in the equipment room, his face still flushed.

"Hey, Coach, I want to apologize. I didn't mean to talk back, it's just . . ." He paused to adjust his bag. I closed the storage room door and gave him my full attention. "It's just that us sophomores are used to that kind of practice and all the running, but I felt bad for the freshmen. They're new to this, not even officially in high school yet."

"Thanks, Cody," I said, and made a move to leave the gym.

"I'm not normally the problem kid though."

"Okay, Cody, thank you for apologizing."

"Yeah, so, see you tomorrow then."

I wanted to tell him that I understood more than he realized. That I thought maybe a lot of us were not inside ourselves today. That he wasn't the only one playing an unfamiliar role. But I didn't say anything. I offered a closed-mouthed smile, and he turned to leave.

It didn't feel good to have my first practice under my belt. Not at all. If anything, the overriding feeling was guilt. Guilt for carrying on. Guilt for starting a new endeavor. And sports of all things. A luxury, not a necessity. Walking out to the back parking lot, I found myself trailing three players. One of them was slightly chubby, but the other two, like most of the boys, looked like clones of one another. They walked slowly, picking up their feet just enough to move forward. They didn't realize I was behind them.

"Wait, you *knew* him?" one of them asked the chunky kid in the middle.

"Yeah, I lived in San Luis when I was younger. My brother was in Boy Scouts with him."

At first I thought nothing of their conversation. I half expected them to be talking about me and what an asshole I was.

"What was his name?"

"Braden something, I don't remember. We weren't friends or nothing. But my brother kind of was. I definitely remember him coming to the house a couple of times."

"Fuckin' crazy," said the kid asking all the questions.

"Totally."

When they spotted their ride, a blue minivan, their conversation ended, and they got into the car. Once alone in the parking lot, I got a text that Travis was on his way. I sat on a brick planter box and thought about the different versions we have of ourselves that we hang in our closet like winter coats. Sometimes we choose which one to wear and sometimes the coat chooses us. But with each passing day, I found that fewer and fewer fit me anymore.

The house on Foothill was as nondescript as they come. The front yard, what little of it there was, sat on an incline. The driveway went up on the right, and the rest of the yard was ground cover that looked mostly like ivy. At the top of the slope was a little patio that led to the front door. There were a couple unremarkable bushes and a faded white railing. The house itself was wood, painted the drab color of stucco, somewhere between beige and gray. The two windows facing the street had thin white drapes that were drawn shut. It was a house you'd never look twice at. It could have been any house. Certainly not one you would guess held so much sadness.

The evening before, I was at home after practice watching ESPN Classic: Super Bowl XXX, the Cowboys and the Steelers. The game itself wasn't exciting. Sure, the score was fairly close, but the Cowboys were in the midst of their Aikman–Emmit–Irvin dynasty, and there was never really any doubt they would hold on. Somewhere in the second quarter, the song once again crept into my head, drums thumping like a haunting. I inched the TV volume louder and louder, trying to drown it out. By the fourth quarter, the TV was so loud it was a wonder I heard the house phone ring.

"Conner? It's Lauren. Lauren Thomas."

"Hi." Although not expecting it, when I had heard that first ring, I was half hoping it would be her.

"Conner, I don't know how you feel about this, or if this is inappropriate, but . . ."

"Yes?"

"I was wondering if you might be okay with meeting again?"

"Is there something—"

"No, no, it's nothing specific, I just, I don't know. I'd like to talk some more, if that's okay?"

I again thought of the look in her eyes. The emptiness in her voice. Why would she want to be back in that place again? Or maybe that place was actually better than where she was most days. I agreed. I didn't have the right to say no or to question anything she asked.

But as I made my way up the driveway to the plain house, the reality of what was about to happen crept up my spine. Meeting at the lake was one thing, but going into their house was something altogether different. There would be pictures of him. Pictures of them as a family. His clothes. His favorite drinking glass. His spot at the kitchen table. His room was in there, no doubt with a door permanently closed as if too dangerous to enter. But what if it wasn't? What if it was wide open?

As I neared the top of the driveway, a cool breeze brushed past my neck, and the wind chimes that swung from the overhang clanged together, leaving a resonant high-pitched hum that didn't dissipate. Where the driveway met the front porch was a small, wobbly table, as if a dinner plate was stuck onto a baseball bat. It was poorly mosaicked with broken pieces of colorful tile. Jagged edges, globs of grout. Nothing sat on the table, but on its surface was a *T* made from green and yellow tile. A lonely family art project.

Arriving at the door, I paused, took a breath, wanted to run. A thin metal mailbox hung next to the doorbell. It was black, and *The Thomases* was stenciled across the top in white paint, only the *o* and the *a* were faded now, almost invisible. A family without vowels.

I knocked twice, and Lauren answered immediately.

"Conner, thank you so much for coming. Welcome to our house." She opened the door and stepped aside.

She ushered me into the family room, and I felt my bones tighten. There were two couches forming an *L* in the corner of the room. Above the one to my immediate left was a large oil painting of a rocky shoreline. The waves were big and violent, crashing against boulders. The coffee table and the corner table were matching dark wood. There was a black upright piano along the wall that held the front window. On the coffee table lay several magazines. There was a lamp and a set of coasters on the corner table, but otherwise the room looked untouched.

"Would you like something to drink? Coffee, tea, water?"

"No thank you, I'm okay." I had taken three steps into the room. I didn't know if I was supposed to sit or continue walking. I didn't want to move, as if the entire house was made of glass and it could all break at any moment. The air was several degrees cooler than outside, and goose bumps rose on my arms.

"Please, Conner, have a seat." Lauren motioned to the two couches with an open palm. "I'll be right back. I'm going to grab some coffee for myself."

It was when I sat on the couch below the painting that I noticed the frame atop the piano. A large family portrait. Lauren and Peter, looking a bit younger than they did now, and two children, a boy and a girl. I turned away before my eyes focused on them long enough to see their faces. I looked to switch seats, but the other couch was directly facing the piano. I could hear the moving around of dishes in the kitchen and decided to focus on the magazines that lay fanned on the coffee table. The only one visible in its entirety was *Home Design*. On the cover was an elaborate stone fireplace; large flames burned in the hearth. The normalcy of the living room was overwhelming.

Lauren entered the room carrying a mug with both hands. She looked more casual than when I first met her at the lake. She wore blue jeans and a pink T-shirt from a cancer walk in 2009. Her brown hair was up in a loose bun, though I couldn't tell what was keeping it in place. Her face, without makeup, looked tired. And there was the slightest hint of old, faded freckles on her cheeks.

"Peter should be here any minute," she said as she sat on the other couch and crossed her legs.

"Oh, alright," I said. My voice sounded weird, as if I were hearing it on a recording. It didn't belong in this house.

"You know," she said, then took a slow sip of coffee, like maybe that was all she had to say. Like maybe that was a full sentence, a declaration: "You know." But she continued. "I'm really glad we met the other day, Conner. So we could learn things about you, get to know who you are."

Why? What the hell was the benefit of learning anything about me? How did that help? I wanted to ask these things, but my complete lack of understanding left me paralyzed. I smiled a closed-mouth smile.

"But I noticed something. And this is not a criticism at all."

My stomach dropped, bottomed out. I deserved everything that was coming, but I wasn't prepared. I looked down at the magazines as she paused again.

"I was thinking on the way home that you never asked anything about Braden. Not a single question. I wasn't even sure if you knew that was his name."

"Well, I . . ." I said to avoid silence, but that was all I could do.

"No, it's not a criticism, I promise." She placed the mug down on the coffee table. A little coffee spilled over one of the sides, but she didn't notice. "*I* was the one that wanted to meet, to ask the questions, to know you. I noticed is all."

My paralysis was momentarily postponed as the front door opened. I hadn't even heard a car pull up or a door close. Peter, wearing a gray suit and blue and yellow tie, entered the house and placed his keys on a hook by the door.

"Hello, honey. How was your day?" Lauren said. "Conner just arrived. Why don't you get settled and come join us."

Peter half smiled, nodded at me, then continued into the house, disappearing down a hallway to the right.

Lauren sighed and looked at me, shaking her head.

I waited.

Then her expression changed from sadness to anger. "Flowers, Conner."

"Flowers?"

"Do you know how many . . . how many flowers we receive? Hundreds. Mostly from people I don't know. What in the world . . . I mean, what are flowers going to . . . ?" She was getting herself worked up, but I couldn't step in. I sat there and took it. "I throw them all away. All of them. Right away. They make it worse. Screw the flowers, Conner. I hate them." But then she caught herself. She rubbed each fingernail on her left hand with the thumb of her right. Slowly. Moving from the pinky down to the thumb and then back again. "I'm sorry."

"No. Please." Singular words. That's all I had.

Lauren looked down the abyss of the dark hallway. "And I don't know what to do with him. Like what does he need? Do I just leave him be?"

I didn't know if she expected an answer. Moisture gathered along the base of her eyes, tears that stacked and balanced like a delicate house of cards on the thin edge of her lower eyelid.

"Twenty-one," she said, changing subjects again. "Braden . . ."

We both looked down. It had been easier at the lake, talking about myself. But talking about him, in his house—I wasn't sure if I could do it.

"You're still in your twenties, aren't you, Conner?"

"I'm thirty," I said, but instantly wished I had lied. I could have been twenty-nine for her.

Lauren nodded. "He's gonna be a lawyer."

It felt like an accusation. I couldn't respond. I let Lauren speak. And she did. She always seemed ready to talk, as if she was trying to get every thought, idea, and emotion from the inside to the outside.

And when she spoke, she used contractions, like most people, but she seemed to combine "he was" into "he's," which I was pretty sure was supposed to be reserved for "he is." Or maybe she was swallowing the "was," her tongue not yet knowing how to use past tense verbs for him.

"*He's* taking classes at Cuesta." "*He's* going to transfer to a UC and major in poli-sci." "*He's* even looking at fancy law schools back east." The effect was unnerving.

There was nothing I could say. I mostly looked down and nodded. There was a lot of nodding as Lauren fed me all the little bits and pieces of Braden's life. "He loved books," she said with a smile, and I felt a tinge of relief to clearly hear the "-ed" on the end of the verb. "He's working at Barnes & Noble downtown."

I had been to that Barnes & Noble a million times. How many times did Braden sell me a book or a magazine? How many times had our fingertips touched as he handed me my receipt? I suddenly became conscious of my hands. I was rubbing them together, my fingers still cracked and red from the kitchen, now numb from the cold.

"He's never popular, but he's a boy that everybody liked." She smiled again and tried to make eye contact. "A bit shy, but the kind of shy that's endearing."

Not being able to fully look at Lauren as she spoke, I kept one eye on her cheeks, looking for them to become slick with tears, and I kept one eye on the hallway, waiting for the large, silent man. But he never came.

"Conner, can I tell you a story? About Braden."

"Of course," I said, although that was the last thing I wanted. Up until now, it had been a list of facts. Singular statements that often didn't connect. I now knew Braden's favorite food was a meatball sandwich, about his love for fantasy novels and video games, his career aspirations in law, and how he collected coffee mugs from every city he'd been to. Lauren was drinking out of one that sported the arch from St. Louis. Braden had been there with his senior government class. It was like reading a bio sheet, a profile page. Bullet points. But a story would make me *hear* him and *see* him.

"I think it might help, Conner."

"Of course," I repeated. I could feel younger Braden watching me from the piano. His fixed fake smile and unblinking eyes.

"Well, when he's younger, Braden loved the Boy Scouts. Anything outdoorsy. Eventually he outgrew them, I guess like any little boy does." Lauren stopped, lost in an image or a memory, much like Manny did when talking about Casa Lola. Lauren was drawing little figure eights on her pants with her index finger.

"So one summer, I don't know, he must have been ten years old. His troop went away for a long weekend. Camping up near Yosemite. His first weekend away from home, but he didn't cry when we dropped him off at the bus. He just said, 'Don't forget to feed Bilbo.' That was his goldfish, one of those ones with the big bug eyes. He told us exactly how much to give him. 'Only a pinch,' he said. 'But your fingers are bigger. So use your pinky, like this.'" And Lauren lifted her hand and showed me her thumb and pinky pinching together like tiny lobster claws.

We both smiled forced smiles.

"Anyway, that's not the point. So he was away at camp and one evening around sunset, he went off to collect kindling for the night's fire. He was a good ways from camp with a box half full of twigs and broken branches when he heard something. He told me at first he couldn't tell if it was an animal or a child, but it sounded scared. Soon, however, he spotted a little boy, no older than five. He was crying, and he was alone. But Braden was trained for such an event and immediately took the boy's hand and started taking him back to camp, to the troop leader, to an adult. Be prepared. That's the Boy Scout motto, right?"

I nodded every now and again as Lauren spoke, making a point of showing her I was listening. As Lauren told the story, she mostly looked at my chest. She wasn't as dramatic as facing her head down to the floor, but she also had trouble making eye contact, and that was fine with me. That phrase rang in my head: "Be prepared." But weren't there some things, I wanted to say, you couldn't ever prepare for?

"But, you see, as soon as Braden started in the direction of his troop's camp, the little boy cried harder and refused to go. 'My family is the other way,' the little boy told him. 'We have to go the other way!' So instead of dragging the crying boy to his troop leaders, you know what Braden did?" Lauren waited. The question was not rhetorical.

"What did he do?" I asked.

"He got out his map, figured out where they were, made an educated guess on where the boy's family was camped, and then using his compass and visual landmarks, Braden—only ten years old, mind you—navigated this boy back to the campground he figured the boy came from." Again she waited. I could tell the story wasn't quite finished, but she wanted me to respond.

"Wow," I said, once again feeling Braden's eyes staring at me from the picture on the piano. But now I imagined ten-year-old Braden, head to toe in khaki and forest green, badges across his chest sewed on by hand, by Lauren's hands. "So resourceful," I said.

"Exactly!" Lauren's face lit up. "That's exactly the word. Resourceful! He used everything he had learned, each skill they practiced, and then applied it to a real-life situation. And not only that . . ." She looked me in the eye. "He even made the judgment call to go against one of the Boy Scout rules about finding the nearest adult. He's able to assess the situation and make a mature decision about what would be the best way to help this child." Lauren's eyes began to water, but they appeared now to be happy tears, as if it were her own five-year-old being rescued and brought back to her. "So anyway, they found the boy's parents, who were worried out of their minds. In fact, Braden said they were so overjoyed to see their son that they didn't so much as look in Braden's direction. Not a thank-you, not a pat on the back. And Braden didn't care. He did it for the boy, not for the attention. *That*, I told him, is what a true hero is."

"Thank you," I said. "For sharing that story." I said it because I felt it was what Lauren would have said to me if I told her a story.

"Were you ever in the Boy Scouts, Conner?"

"I was." A lie. "Only for a little."

Just then the front door opened. My first thought was that it couldn't be Peter; he was already in the house. Lauren and I both looked up. It was a young teenage girl with short brown hair, almost a boy's haircut. She closed the door behind her and looked at us with a suspicious glare.

"Abby, hi dear." Lauren's voice was different as she spoke now. Light. Airy. "I want you to come meet someone." Cautious.

The girl didn't move. "Who's this?"

"His name is Conner, dear. Why don't you—"

"What?" She took a step back. "He's the fucker that hit Braden!"

My forced smile disappeared. I wanted to run out the door, but Abby was still in front of it, backing up slowly as if I were pointing a gun at her.

"No, honey, please. I know this is hard, but please—"

"Why the hell is he here?"

"We were just talking. About Braden, actually. Maybe you want to share some of your stories?"

"Why the fuck would I want to do that?"

"Abby, honey, please . . ."

But Abby had already stormed off into the same hallway Peter had vanished into earlier. I saw a clear path to my escape. But as quickly as she left, she returned.

"Mom, this is so fucked up! I don't want him in our house. What's wrong with you?"

"But darling." Despite Abby's screaming, Lauren's voice remained calm, barely more than a whisper. "You know that it was an . . . No one was . . . Conner has been very gracious to talk with us, and I think—"

"You think? You think? *I* think you're crazy. I don't care if he's a nice guy. I don't care if it was an accident. He killed Braden. Don't you get it, Mom? Your son. Braden. This guy fucking killed him and he's dead, and now he's sitting on our couch!"

"I'm sor— I . . . I shouldn't be here. I'll go," I said.

"Conner, no." Lauren stood.

"Yeah, see ya!" Abby yelled, but she was just a voice now, already halfway down the hallway.

I looked to Lauren, and she was crying. She stood, half bent over, her head in her hands, shaking. She looked so alone.

How could I leave this woman alone, crying? But how could I possibly stay in this house for another second?

"I should go," I said again, and walked out the door so fast that Lauren didn't have time to catch her breath or say anything. When I hit the sidewalk, I turned right and kept walking. Abby's voice replayed in my head on repeat—*He killed Braden. Don't you get it, Mom?* The concrete soon gave way to dust and rocks. I contemplated calling Travis. The taxis were draining my already-thin bank account. And with all my missed days at the cafe, the next check would be pennies. But I didn't want Travis to know where I was. Hearing myself explain it to him in my head, it felt dirty. I was embarrassed. So I called the cab company I had grown quite familiar with, and the dispatch lady told me a cab would be on the corner of Foothill and Patricia in fifteen minutes.

I sat on a rock, in the one slice of sunlight that still shone on the street. It was warm on the surface of my skin, but the coldness in my bones was going to be there for a while. *This guy fucking killed him and he's dead, and now he's sitting on our couch!* I needed a distraction. I took my phone back out. There was a missed call and voicemail from an unknown number and several texts from Rian. Mostly *I love you* and *call me* and *thinking of you*. But I couldn't reply, not now, and I skipped past the voicemail the moment I didn't recognize the man's voice.

I put my phone back in my pocket and tried to stop the spinning in my head. Abby's words, playing over and over. The sheer hate in her voice. But I did remember hearing myself start to apologize. Although I was sure Lauren knew that was not *the* apology, but rather I was sorry for making her daughter so upset. I was apologizing for the fight that would undoubtedly occur that night, and for however long it might carry over, three broken people, all not speaking to one another. Now that I was removed from it, Abby's emotion was almost refreshing. It was anger, and it came from a place of hurt, and it was not filtered or edited. It was probably how all of us needed to be. But somehow, she was the only one who knew how.

The taxi pulled up, and I recognized the driver right away. It was the same balding man that drove me to Laguna Lake and then to practice. He didn't seem to recognize me, and I was glad. I had a feeling that when I told him I wanted to go to Los Osos, 11th Street, that would jog his memory. But even then, he didn't say anything. He clicked on the meter and pulled out onto Foothill, heading for Los Osos Valley Road, listening to his news radio. I sat back and closed my eyes. That stress of where to look whenever I was on the road was too much sometimes. Neil's song would start to play. Panic would settle on me like a weighted blanket. We were halfway there when the driver spoke.

"I know who you are."

I opened my eyes. We were stopped behind several cars, not at a light, but a series of three or four tractors were slowly crossing Los Osos Valley Road. We weren't as far as I had imagined, hadn't yet passed the cemetery.

"Yes. You've taken me home before. The apartment on 11th."

"Yes, 11th. But that's not what I meant." His eyes searched for mine in the rearview mirror. "I know you had that accident. On South Bay."

"Yeah," I said.

"I'm real sorry, man. I read about it. In the paper. Really fucked up." He shook his head. "Sometimes you get shit on for no good reason, right?"

"Yeah," was all I could force. I saw myself now as a story he told his friends.

"Some real shit," he muttered as he maneuvered the taxi onto the shoulder and around the line of cars and the last of the tractors. Speeding up the hill toward Los Osos, I could tell he was still thinking about it. He shook his head several times and checked on me often in the rearview mirror as if to see if I was still there.

CHAPTER 7

IT WAS THE FIRST GAME OF THE SUMMER, AND WE were losing to Atascadero by ten at the end of the first quarter. The players huddled around me, looking for an answer they knew I didn't have.

"Okay, let's forget man-to-man. Start the second quarter in a two-three zone. You all know what that is, right?"

They nodded. Some rolled their eyes. They may have been young, but they weren't dumb. They knew we were in for a good old-fashioned ass-kicking.

"Coach." It was Kyle. His mop of blond hair was sweat-stuck to his forehead and his cheeks were flushed. "What about offense? What are we doing?"

"Uh, pass and screen away?" It was the oldest play in the book and rarely effective.

Just then, Coach Rich and half of the varsity squad re-entered the gym. Their game was before ours, and now they were showered and changed, and most of them wanted to stick around. See what kind of talent the JV team had. Or more importantly, see what was up with this new coach. Half of the senior boys followed Coach Rich up to the top bleacher, where they sat back against the wall and extended their lanky legs onto the row below. Like spiders watching from ceiling corners.

"Okay! Starting five get out there!"

But nobody left the huddle. Cody put his hand up in the middle, and the rest of the team followed. The team looked at Cody, who looked at me.

"Pirates on three," I yelled. "One-two-three!"

I had talked to Lauren only once since the meeting at her house. Since the explosion I detonated. She had called me the following day. She wanted to apologize for Abby's outburst, the things Abby had said, and the way things ended.

There hadn't really been a moment since then that I wasn't thinking about Lauren. Or Peter to some extent. Or even Abby. I thought about what a mess they all were. But mostly I thought about how I felt when I was talking with Lauren and how I felt immediately after. It was awful. It was uncomfortable. Painful. All, of course, words that were trivial and not something I was worthy of feeling or acknowledging. But it also was the only thing that made sense. It was fucked up, yet it felt like the only thing I was supposed to be doing. I was clearly a disaster with the basketball team. I got through my shifts at the Sea & Sky Cafe only because they got me out of the apartment, and if I left the apartment, then maybe I would return to a message on my answering machine from Lauren. As if maybe if I didn't leave, she wouldn't call. And I found myself avoiding all calls from Rian and Travis. Keeping in touch just enough so they wouldn't show up at my door unannounced with a search warrant. They were such vivid parts of the former me. Conner whatever-point-oh. The me I no longer recognized.

We were losing by twenty-two at the half. I passed Coach Rich on the way to the locker room. He and the seniors had seen enough. Frankly, so had I.

"Hang in there," he said. "Only the first game." But his eyes said something altogether different. If that Monday hadn't happened, he would be singing a different tune. I wasn't sure how long that compassion, or whatever the hell it was—pity?—was going to last.

My halftime speech was nothing but a string of clichés I didn't mean and they didn't believe. And predictably, the second half was as disastrous as the first. At least as far as the game went. But it was somewhere near the end of the third quarter when Atascadero called a time-out to empty its bench, to put in the thirteenth, fourteenth, fifteenth kid on the squad. I let my team rest for those sixty seconds. They didn't want to hear anything I had to say, not that I had anything anyway. My eyes did a quick scan of the sparse bleachers to see how many spiders were still lurking. And there were still several handfuls, but from what I gathered, most were parents of the Atascadero players; some of our own parents, who cheered dutifully as if unaware of the score;

and a dozen or so kids who were set to play on the court after us. But then there was Lauren. I didn't know how long she had been there. It could have been the entire game. If that face hadn't been etched into my mind, appearing over and over through sleepless nights, I would have missed it. Anyone would have. She sat alone midway up the bleachers, at the far end against the railing. She wore the same plaid shirt she had worn when I met her at Laguna Lake.

When we had spoken on the phone, after she forcefully apologized for her daughter, I mentioned the game in passing, though I didn't recall offering the time or location. Merely that my first game was Monday. And here she was. And without Peter. Obviously without Abby. I was even more embarrassed about the score now.

"C'mon, boys," I yelled and clapped. "Heads up, boys! Hard fourth quarter. Let's finish strong!"

I coached that quarter as hard as if it were for a national championship. The kids looked at me as if I had lost my mind, but I used each one of our time-outs to design plays on the spot, trying to teach weeks of offensive philosophy in sixty-second intervals. And although I didn't once look up to catch Lauren's sad eye contact, I was always aware of the splash of plaid in my periphery.

But all my theatrics didn't make a lick of difference as far as the game was concerned. We lost 88–41.

In the brief post-game talk in the locker room, I could tell the kids were expecting me to ride them hard, as I had been doing in each of the practices. But I didn't. I was embarrassed. I apologized, told them they had nothing to be ashamed of and this was all on me.

"It's fine, Coach," Cody said. "Like, we get it."

When I left the locker room, the next game was about to begin. During the summer, they lined up the games like an assembly line until the stench of sweat and rubber began to radiate off the outside brick facade of the gym. A few of the parents gave me half nods and partial smiles as they put an arm around their sweaty sons and headed to the parking lot, to no doubt ask their child what he thought of the new coach. Thankfully, none of them approached me.

Lauren was gone, as if merely a ghost I had imagined sitting there this whole time. And when I hurried out the gym doors, aside from the slow, shuffling feet of deflated players heading toward the parking lot, the Cuesta campus was empty. With summer school not starting for another couple of weeks, there were no students standing around smoking and talking about their psych professor. There were no young couples lying on the grass with interlocked fingers. And there certainly wasn't a grief-stricken middle-aged woman waiting around to talk to me.

As I was becoming quite accustomed to, I parked my ass on a curb and dialed the number for a taxi. There were several drivers now that recognized me, but we still only exchanged pleasantries. The bald driver who listened to news radio was the only one to call me out for who I was. He only worked San Luis Obispo, and each time I was there, I prayed they'd send a different driver. I hadn't seen him since he eyed me curiously from the rearview mirror, muttering about how fucked my situation was. But sitting here at Cuesta, off Highway 1 in San Luis, I was definitely in his territory.

While I waited, I decided to text Rian. A brief *I miss you, hope you had a good day*. And I did miss her. I missed drinking wine and listening to music on full volume with her. I missed watching her do the Sunday crossword while I made her breakfast. I missed her stupid puns. But none of those things seemed possible anymore. And so with my head down, punching out the text with my index finger, I didn't notice the car pull up in front of me.

"Hey, you need a ride or something?"

I heard the voice, but I didn't look up. Assumed it wasn't for me. It wasn't a cab. It wasn't a voice I recognized.

"Hey, Coach Robbins?" It was Jimmy. The passenger window was all the way down, and the string-bean redhead was leaning over as best he could across the bench seat of a rusted old Buick.

"Hey, uh . . ." I hit *send* on the message to Rian and stuffed my phone back in my pocket. "Actually, yeah, I could use a ride. But only if you're heading to Osos."

"Get in."

The door creaked when I got in, and I immediately called to cancel my taxi. I was in no position to get blacklisted from the taxi world.

"Thanks, Jimmy."

"No problem. After that game, thought you could use some help." The words sounded like a joke, like friendly banter. But he didn't look over at me when he spoke, and he certainly didn't smile.

"I can't believe you stayed for the whole thing."

"Eh, what the hell else I gotta do?" He clicked off the radio, which was spewing static. It was one of the old knobs you turned to control a tiny orange dial. It popped and crackled as you moved it back and forth in a sea of white lines. "But fuck. That was awful, Coach."

"Yes, thank you, Jimmy."

"I mean, the guys looked clueless out there."

"Yeah, I'm aware."

We pulled up to the red light and he flipped his blinker to turn left out of Cuesta, which would lead us to South Bay Boulevard.

"No, Jimmy, man, you have to go the other way."

"What? Through Foothill and Los Osos Valley Road? Fuck that. This is way faster."

"Look, if you're taking me home, that's the way we're going."

"Coach, you're out of your—"

"Jimmy." Then the redheaded kid actually looked right at me. "Turn right. Please."

He didn't change his blinker, but when the light turned green, he spun the wheel to the right and off we went, taking the long way around once again. Heading southeast on Highway 1, the Buick accelerated with a loud collective rattle. It wasn't a loose piece; it was the whole car itself that shook and moaned. The sun was setting, and cold air rushed into my open window as we picked up speed. I grabbed the handle to roll it up, but as it turned with a squeak, nothing happened.

"Jimmy? The window?"

"Nope. Hasn't been one since I bought the thing."

As we clattered and clanked down the highway, my eyes burned and my skin turned to ice. And although the driver's-side window was present and rolled up, the entirety of the inside of the car was a whirlwind of freezing ocean air. Yet Jimmy drove without so much as a single shiver or teeth clatter. He had one hand on the wheel and one resting on the door.

"I got some plays you should use," he said as we slowed toward a red light, entering San Luis, the howl of the wind in the car now just a cold, quiet breeze.

"I know how to run an offense," I said. "I think."

"That pass-and-screen-away bullshit? You got to drop that, Coach."

"I know. We haven't had time to get into anything yet."

"I got some plays for Kyle. You got to use him. Kid can play."

"Yeah, he's pretty good. I think we'll be alright."

"Nah, man, even if you think you got plays. You're using him wrong. He's not a point guard. Use him at the two-spot. Take the ball out of his hands, run him off some double screens, some curl screens. He could drop thirty, no problem."

He was making sense, but I didn't want to hear it. Not now. Soon we would be on Foothill, which meant passing the Thomases' house.

"Know what I mean, Coa—?"

"Yes," I said quickly to appease him.

"I'll hook you up with some plays."

The increasing wind whipping into the car made my ears ring, and I welcomed the numbing white noise. And then we turned right onto Foothill, and I heard Abby's voice yelling in my head. *Mom, this is so fucked up! I don't want him in our house.*

"Can I ask you a question, Coach?"

Here it comes. "What is it, Jimmy?"

"Well . . ."

And as Jimmy searched for the right words, I was surprised he of all people was going to ask me about that Monday. He gave off the impression that he had enough shit going on in his life; he certainly didn't care to hear anybody else's. A real *don't dump your shit on me, I won't dump my shit on you* kinda guy.

"Spit it out," I said, motioning for him to continue straight through the next light.

"I wanted to ask you what you know about recruiting." His hands were gripping and rubbing hard at the steering wheel. "Like for colleges."

"Hmm, I don't know." I was a bit taken aback by the question. "What do you mean?"

"I need a D1 scholarship. Plain and simple."

The drive by the Thomases' house was anticlimactic. I looked down to my shoes and listened to Jimmy and the rusty jangling of his piece-of-shit car.

"I don't want one. I need one. And living in this tiny shit-hole fishing town, you know we don't get no love from the big colleges. Shit, no D1 coach outside of Poly and Santa Barbara has heard of Morro Bay."

I hadn't had any interaction with Jimmy aside from in passing, and that day in the kayak. But I could already tell his voice was different. There was a panic to it, a desperation that cut through the usual don't-give-a-fuck tone.

"Well, I wasn't nearly good enough to think about hoops after high school, so I don't have any firsthand experience. But maybe I could help out if you need."

"No, no, I don't need some type of fatherly advice. I got enough of that. What I need is . . ."

Then he fell silent until we made a right onto Los Osos Valley Road.

"I need someone to contact coaches. Get 'em at our games. Like an agent."

The wind in my open window picked up again as he sped too fast on Los Osos Valley Road, but my skin already felt numb and swollen.

"What about Coach Rich? Surely you guys have already talked about this."

"Honestly, man, fuck him. He ain't gonna do shit for me. Excuse my language, Coach. But no, he's not gonna do . . ." Again Jimmy searched for words, but I could see that there were few options. "Shit."

That last word hung in the cold Buick for the rest of the drive. There was something off-putting but oddly calming about Jimmy. The silence between us made me more comfortable than I'd felt in some time. Directions were made with pointing and head nods until Jimmy finally made the turn into my perennially empty parking spot with its oval-shaped oil stain, pulling up too far until his rusty bumper was buried in the thick generic bush that was in need of trimming.

"Jimmy, you want to come in and talk about this? If I sit in this damn car any longer, I'm going to lose my right ear to frostbite."

"Yeah, if that's cool."

As I pushed the key into the lock, my foot kicked at something soft on the doorstep. There was a large envelope, white with blue-and-red postal service lettering. Once inside, I saw it was from Rian, and I laid it on the counter and sat with Jimmy at my round breakfast table.

"Okay. So before you tell me what you need, talk to me about Coach Rich. What's the problem? Aren't you his golden boy? Best jump shot the Pirates have ever seen?"

"No, what he loves is the idea of my bringing him a second CIF banner."

"I doubt that's all he—"

"I've tried, Coach. Every time I even mention college coaches or scouts he flips out. He yells about getting ahead of myself, checking my ego at the door, playing some damn defense. Shit like that." Jimmy then pulled a quarter out of his pocket and began spinning it on the table with his thumb and forefinger. "And then he rides my ass so hard the next practice. Like he's trying to prove something. Only thing he says is if I play well, after the season he'll help me put together a highlight reel to send out. But that's too late, and that shit don't work. I need coaches in the bleachers."

"Alright. If you say you've tried."

"I've tried, Coach. All he cares about is winning league and then CIF. It's all about him."

"And Galey?"

Jimmy gave me a look. "C'mon, Coach."

Coach Galey was older and had always been Coach Rich's only assistant. He was good at keeping Coach Rich organized and mediating between Coach Rich and the players, but with Galey it didn't take long to realize that he had zero aspirations of ever being a head coach. In fact, in all aspects of his life, he would always be just an assistant.

"Okay, so then there's me?"

"Then there's you."

"Earlier, you said you didn't want a scholarship, but you needed one."

"Exactly."

"You really think you have a shot at going pro?"

Jimmy slammed his hand down on the quarter that had been humming on the table in a tight spin. "Fuck, Coach, c'mon. I know we don't know each other that good, but can't we just, like, talk for real?"

"Aren't we?"

"No, man." He rotated the quarter between his two thumbs faster and faster. "You're there acting like Coach Rich cares about my future. Asking me about Galey. We both know he's worthless. And now pretending that I need to get a scholarship because I have some NBA delusion?"

Hearing a word like *delusion* come out of Jimmy's thin, tight lips made me realize that maybe I didn't know him at all.

"I'm trying to listen to you, Jimmy. What do you want, man?"

He sat back in the chair. Put the quarter back in his pocket. The look in his eyes told me he was wondering if talking to me was a mistake. The look told me that maybe he was realizing I was no different than any other coach or teacher he'd ever had. And really, I didn't know that I wasn't.

"Can I smoke in here, Coach?"

"In here? No. Let's go sit outside."

Sitting on one of the white plastic chairs outside my front door, Jimmy rolled his own cigarette as the sun began to set behind the pine trees. He was clumsy at it, and I should have told him something about smoking and his age or health, but it wasn't the time. While I waited, I thought about Lauren and wondered why she didn't wait for me after the game. Why did she even come if she didn't want to talk to me? I wondered where she might pop up next, or if maybe it was my turn to show up somewhere. And as Jimmy was finally shaking, hitting, flicking and re-flicking his lighter, I realized exactly what I needed to ask him, and it had nothing to do with basketball.

"So you want to talk for real, Jimmy?"

"Always, Coach. The rest is bullshit."

"Okay. I'll help you. But why don't you tell me about your family."

He slowly exhaled smoke up into the darkening sky, full of movie drama.

"What about my family? Fucked up like everybody else's. What else is new?"

"You're right. But everybody's is fucked up in a different way."

"Is yours?"

"Oh yeah. In its own way. I'll tell you sometime if you ever need a laugh."

"My family is a cliché. It's embarrassing."

"Who cares. Let's hear it."

He leaned forward, rested his elbows on his knees, and sucked on his poorly rolled cigarette. "My dad is an ex-military asshole. Well, not an *ex*-asshole, he's definitely a current asshole. But he's ex-military. We moved around all the damn time. Now he's bored as fuck and angry. To be fair, he's always been angry, but now he's home more. I got an older brother who hates my dad more than the goddamned devil and hates the rest of us by association. He bounced years ago. I don't even know where he is. So fuck him. I got a little sister, but she's all messed up, man. She's only five and has had like a million surgeries on her eyes."

Jimmy sat up and stared into the sky, blowing smoke up to the silhouette of pine trees. He was thinking hard on something.

"And your mom?"

"What do you think? She hates my dad, as she should, and she spends every waking second taking care of my sister. My dad doesn't give two shits about my sister and somehow blames my mom."

"Does your dad drink?"

"Not a drop. Doesn't need to. He's an abusive drunk without the drunk. Shit, could you imagine."

"So college is your way out of here. And basketball is your way to college."

"Sherlock mother-fuckin' Holmes."

"I'll help you, Jimmy."

He looked at me with slits for eyes, shaking his head.

"I don't need a therapist, Coach. I don't need you calling protective services or some shit. I can take care of myself."

"I know."

"I gotta get coaches in bleachers."

"I'll help you." Though as I heard myself say the words yet again, I had no idea if I could help Jimmy at all. But it seemed like the right thing to say. I could figure the rest out later.

He looked around uneasily, probably partly to avoid eye contact and partly to take in the crappy apartments I called home. "So what's wrong with your family?"

Whatever I was or wasn't going to tell him was interrupted by headlights that swung off 11th and into the complex parking lot, illuminating Jimmy and me like a pair of crooks. The crunch of asphalt and dried pine needles under the tires was loud and dramatic as the vehicle settled in next to Jimmy's.

"Jimmy, we'll have to save that story for another time. I think you should go."

He looked back and forth between me and the headlights. "Sure, Coach. Whatever you say."

"Let's talk soon, though, set a game plan." More hollow words. What had Travis called that thing I sometimes did? Muscle memory.

"Yeah," he said, snuffing out his cigarette with his shoe.

There was no handshake or one-armed hug, not a thank-you or even a goodbye. Through all Jimmy's coarseness, I did appreciate his inability, or unwillingness, to bullshit.

Before he got in his beat-up Buick to drive home with cold wind frosting his ears to ice, Jimmy and Travis turned sideways to squeeze by one another.

Travis stopped and stood backlit by the headlights, silhouetted with his hands on his hips. "Well, it's finished."

Even though the lights were blinding, I had recognized my truck as soon as it pulled in.

"So it is."

"You wanna go grab a beer at Sweet Springs?" It was like his voice was tiptoeing on eggshells. That didn't come naturally to him, and it always felt strange to be around him like this.

"No thanks."

"Look, I'm not going to pretend you're happy to see your truck. I get it. But at least it should be helpful. Getting around and stuff."

Having conceded we weren't about to go for a joyride, Travis went to turn off the lights and retrieve the keys. All I could see now was a faint outline of the truck and a reflection of light off the silver hood. I had no idea what it had looked like when he took it into Tapia's, so to me it looked exactly the same as it always did. Yet also completely different.

"We need to talk." Travis took the seat vacated by Jimmy. It felt like back-to-back therapy sessions, though I had a feeling I was now on the other side of the desk. Travis started talking, but I wasn't listening. I was thinking about the truck. Sitting there. Looking at me. That blank stare.

". . . and how many times have you not answered my phone calls? Or texts? Hell, I even stopped by the other day, sat in this same exact chair like a chump for over an hour, waiting for you to show up."

"Sorry, man."

"I don't want you to be sorry, I want you to be present."

And like Jimmy before him, Travis had a way of being succinct. Of saying exactly what he needed to without any extra words. I thought about telling him about my two meetings with Lauren. I thought about how that would be anything but succinct. Or clear. A clusterfuck of words at best.

Like we often used to do floating in the bay, we sat in silence, listening to the world around us. And right now, the world didn't have much to offer.

There was the occasional car that hummed down 11th, an even less frequent bark of a dog. Then there was my truck, silently screaming at me. All of which played on top of the ever-present high-pitched chirping of the crickets.

"You have an appointment tomorrow," Travis said.

"Me?"

"Ten o'clock. At Central Coast Meats in San Luis. The guy's name is Carl. You need to price everything out. But dissect that menu beforehand, figure out exactly what we need, approximate quantities per day, week, month. See what kind of deals we can get depending on purchase size. But keep in mind our freezer space. Ask about delivery options. Check out the quality, you know, do the shit you know how to do." He didn't wait for me to answer, but took his phone out, and his right thumb began swiping and tapping. "I texted you the address. And you don't need a ride anymore, do you?" He nodded to the truck.

"I, uh—" I couldn't even look at it.

"And I know you been getting around on your own anyway."

"Ten o'clock?"

"I'll pick you up on Friday morning, though. We're meeting with a guy about the new stovetop. You're not working any morning shifts, right? You're free?"

"I'm free."

"And then when do you want to meet with *me*? We have a ton to talk about."

"Whenever you want. I can move practices around. And I only have a few dinner shifts a week now."

"Okay then. Friday morning. Out on the bay, before meeting with the stove guy?"

"On the bay?"

"The seagulls miss you."

"Okay, yeah, that works I guess."

"You alright?"

"Yeah, I am, I'm fine. Been busy. Scattered. I dunno. I'll be better."

CHAPTER 8

THE SUN WAS STILL A LITTLE WAYS FROM SETTING, but it was low enough to hide behind buildings, sending up a warm glow over Higuera and the throngs of people meandering up and down the four or five blocks of the closed-off street. I hadn't been to Thursday night Farmer's Market in downtown SLO in twelve years, but as soon as I exited the taxi, I smelled the smoky sweetness of Santa Maria–style BBQ in the air and knew that not a thing had changed.

I passed several local farmers selling large, robust vegetables. Zucchini like the forearms of bodybuilders, off-color tomatoes that smelled sweet as candy, and mushrooms so funky they seemed straight out of *Alice in Wonderland*. I also passed a booth featuring thirty-minute massages for $20, the ever-present Cowboy Cookie, and a table selling incense sticks and candles. The smell of tomatoes and cookies had been taken over by the pungent smell of patchouli. I was in high school again, meeting up with a pack of friends to eat tri-tip sandwiches and see what girls we'd run into.

I had missed my Tuesday morning meeting with Carl at Central Coast Meats. After Travis and Jimmy left on Monday night, I had found myself very alone in my apartment with a lot to digest: that disastrous basketball debut, seeing Lauren in the bleachers, the car ride home with Jimmy, the tone in which Travis spoke to me, my smooth truck preening in the driveway. I also opened the envelope from Rian and found an email from Justine in my inbox. Needless to say, Tuesday morning was sucked into the strong current of Monday.

I walked down the center of the street. The booths didn't interest me. Not as much as the people. Out of habit, I searched every face for recognition.

When I was sixteen, this was everything. At Farmer's Market, things were possible that weren't possible at school. Girls who wouldn't even look at you in an empty hallway would be excited to run into you here, and you'd talk in a circle for five minutes, each minute like gold, praying other guys would see who you were *hanging out* with. But I didn't know anyone here, not anymore. The teenagers now looked like little kids, and the adults all strangers.

Before opening Rian's envelope, I had read the email from Justine. She told me about a trip to Zion she was taking in a couple weeks with some friends. To get in some serious hiking, she said. She also mentioned these recurring dreams she was having but wasn't specific. But it was the last thing she said that hit me. She said she'd found a group. She said that word, *group*, several times and never with any other adjective. She said it was helpful, that she was able to talk to "similar people" with "similar situations." That I should contact her if I wanted to go. But what a privileged, self-indulgent thing. I could never.

At the end of the first block, there was a clearing in the intersection, and a band was setting up. Without any booths, the traffic of people thinned. The drummer was doing most of the heavy lifting. He had a dozen or so chrome-plated stands and pieces he was putting together with some sort of wrench. It looked complicated. A handyman's jigsaw. Another guy was unrolling some black cables while he joked with a third that held a guitar by the neck. There was a fourth member of the band, a girl, sitting on the curb. She had long stringy black hair and what must have been twenty or so bracelets on one wrist. She sat smoking a clove cigarette. I moved on as the drummer was setting the kick drum in place. The drum face was white with pink, blue, and yellow psychedelic lettering that read *13th Street Melting Pot*.

When Travis found out I had missed my meeting with the meat guy, he was disappointed but not pissed. His voice was defeated, but not angry. There wasn't a lecture, and in fact the phone call was quite short. That was much worse, like he was giving up. Tired of fighting for his friend to get his shit together and dealing with the reality that this was who his friend was now. I asked him how I could make it up, and he suggested Farmer's Market. He said Carl ran a booth most Thursday nights, large containers packed with crushed ice showcasing freshly caught Pacific red snapper and choice cuts of beef. He thought I should show up, apologize, buy something, start a conversation. And he suggested that since I'd already be there, it couldn't hurt to keep an eye out for other potential vendors as well.

"Alright," Travis had said. "Looking forward to a full report on Friday morning. I'll see ya at the shop at seven."

At the next intersection, after passing another handful of local growers, a psychic's table, and a married couple who sold handcrafted wood chimes, there was a man dressed like a circus ringleader performing a puppet show. A dozen or so kids sat on the asphalt in front of a puppet stage. He stood behind it controlling two puppets from above—making a giraffe dance with one hand, maneuvering a parrot hanging from strings with the other—and screeching bad animal voices into a microphone. The kids were fixated, but none of them were laughing.

When I had opened Rian's envelope I found a book, a homemade CD with my name written on it in blue Sharpie, and a note:

I miss you. I don't hear from you as much anymore, and we don't even talk about plans to visit. I'm hoping this book might help. And the CD too? I didn't know what else to do.

I love you. —R.

The book was a bright green and yellow paperback entitled *Why Me? An In-Depth Look at Overcoming Survivor's Guilt.* I tossed it into the corner of my room where a pile of unwashed clothes was collecting more unwashed clothes.

A couple blocks later, I reached the end of Farmer's Market. In front of the barricades sat two grungy guys on milk crates, each with a conga between their legs. One was white, one Black, both looked too young to be that dirty.

They synchronized their beat well, and they had rhythm, but it didn't take long to realize they were playing something fairly simple and repeating it ad nauseum. The hat in front of them held a handful of change, nothing paper.

As I made the turn to start heading back, I realized I hadn't seen the Central Coast Meats booth. Granted, I hadn't been looking very hard, but I needed to talk to Carl and make things right with him, and by proxy, with Travis. I promised myself I would do a better job looking on the walk back.

"Coach Robbiiiiins!"

I turned to see Jimmy emerge from behind a building with two other guys, both of whom looked much older than him. He staggered up to me, clearly drunk.

"What's up, Coach, how you doin'?"

"Jimmy, hey."

"Hey guys." Jimmy turned to his two friends. All three of them had eyes as red as roses. "This is Coach Robbins. He coaches JV at Morro Bay. The guy I was telling you about." He meant this last part to be quieter, but he had no control over the volume of his voice.

They both gave me a nod and lingered behind a few steps.

"Jimmy, what the hell are you doing?" I asked.

As he stood, I could see his body rocking itself as if waves crashed against the inside of his skin.

"It's Farmer's Market, man. Good times."

"You're wasted, Jimmy."

"It's cool, I'm fine, good times."

The stench of alcohol was sharp, and I felt a wave of something come over me. It was anger, but it was also something parental. It was a foreign feeling, and I didn't know what to do with it.

"Go home, Jimmy."

"Nahhh, fuck home, man."

"Hey, J-bones." It was one of the guys behind him. His voice was deep, and I realized not only did he not go to high school with Jimmy, but he probably hadn't seen a classroom in quite a few years. "Let's go, bro."

Jimmy turned to follow.

"Jimmy," I said.

"Gotta run, Coach, gotta run." And he jogged off with the two other guys, disappearing into the wash of heads. The crowd on Higuera had doubled since I arrived. Walking down the street was now shoulder to shoulder, elbow to elbow.

I joined the crowd too, wondering if I should have done more with Jimmy. Was it my job to stop him? To get him home somehow? As I squeezed my way down the street, I kept an eye on the booths. I snuck a handful of cashews from one that had buckets of all different types of nuts. I was handed two flyers, one for the Church of Scientology and one for a company that wanted to turn your house 100 percent solar powered. But still no Central Coast Meats.

It had been late when I finally crawled into bed that previous Monday night, and I was in no mood to listen to music—music had betrayed me, sat in my bones and rattled something awful. I was sure the CD was some indie band Rian wanted to introduce me to, something with wonky tuning and purposefully pitchy vocals, but something she promised I would fall in love with by the tenth listen. So simply out of respect for Rian, I decided to put it in. I could turn it off halfway through the first song and she would be none the wiser.

I placed the disc into the alarm clock radio—another antique, according to Travis—that sat on my nightstand and hit play. But there was no tinny drumbeat, and there wasn't a jaunty guitar rhythm. It was Rian. Her voice. At first I couldn't make out what she was saying. The recording was clear, but her words didn't make sense. Something about a church and clouds above that rolled like a herd of buffalo. I was lost. But then I realized. She was reading. I didn't know what from. It didn't matter. I skipped ahead ten minutes. There was her voice, smooth and melodic, reading dialogue between a child and teacher maybe. I jumped ahead again. There was the full disc—eighty minutes—of Rian reading to me. I thought it was sweet and thought maybe

I should try it. Maybe it was what I needed at the end of a day like Monday. I flipped off the lights, restarted the CD, and closed my eyes.

Just past the booth selling local organic honey—the sellers dressed as bees—was an old man with a sign that read *Repent Now! Or Burn for Eternity: Homos, Terrorists, Whores, Hippies, Gangsters & Sinners*. But apart from the frequent cringing side glance, people ignored him. His beard was long and wiry and gray, and he walked with a considerable limp. His lips were pursed together and off to the side, and had his eyes shown any hint of awareness, he might have looked like he was thinking real hard. He had his small clearing, and he walked it in a tight circle. He appeared lost and indifferent. Had I not been so consumed by searching faces for popular kids, I might have seen this same old man with this same sign walking this same tight circle twelve years ago. He might have been full of passion and stringent ideologies at one time. But now, he simply looked content with routine. This was all he knew. And for that, I bore him no animosity, despite what I thought of his sign.

By the time I got back to the clearing with the band, I had still not seen Carl or any meat booth. I couldn't honestly attest to double-checking every stall; after all, the crowd was dense and pulsed with energy, but I assumed it would have stood out—maybe the salty smell of fresh fish, or the unmistakable crinkling of white butcher paper around marbled slabs of beef.

The band, however, 13th Street Melting Pot, was in full groove. The girl with the bracelets, who now also wore a hat—a red beret of sorts—was belting out the chorus to "Layla." There were several people dancing. Mostly fifty-somethings, young enough to remember when this song came out, but old enough not to care about dancing in the street in front of hundreds of people. There was a fair number of young people too. All girls, eager to show off their midriffs as they twirled. The guitarist actually sounded halfway like he knew what he was doing. I bought a blackened corn on the cob, fresh off the grill and still in its husk, and sat on the curb, trying to hide and watch at the same time.

The CD from Rian, while sweet and thoughtful, had been a complete failure. I had lain in bed with my eyes closed, trying to concentrate not necessarily on the words, but on the sing-songy rhythm of her voice, the whoosh of her vowels and the clack of her consonants. But it was different now. Alone and listening to her voice coming out of the speakers made me hyper-aware of what I was doing. It was humiliating. I had fought this feeling at first, because the first time she did this, I had slept well, so well, in fact, that I hadn't reached any such state since that night. But the more I lay there listening to the slightly mechanized version of her voice, the more I was able to see myself. I felt exposed and pathetic. It was worse than going to some meeting with Justine or reading some poor-me book. I turned the CD player off, couldn't fall asleep, and not only missed my meeting with Carl, but I also didn't show up for the dinner shift at the Sea & Sky. When I had played Donnie's spit-laden message at six that evening, it was the first time I got out of bed.

The band sped through covers of CCR, the Rolling Stones, and even a lesser-known Doors song called "Peace Frog." Every baby boomer who wasn't dancing at least snapped her fingers or bobbed his head as they passed. Anyone younger than fifty had moved on from the dance floor. For them, something more promising always waited in the next block. As I sat and listened to the music, the girl's voice trying to let me hear old songs new again, I realized rock 'n' roll beats were still all too similar. And so even through the buzzing hum of the crowd, I heard that *bass-snare-bass-bass-snare-crash* as if it were the only sound. That same sound that had remained in the aftermath. And remained and remained and remained within me until it became a beat so clear I could see it and taste it. Neil's song, taunting me from inside the broken truck.

I shook the music out of my head as best I could and focused on the corn. The natural sweetness of it balanced with the salt, the smoothness of the butter balanced with the roasted crunch of the kernels. It was perfect. But the more I enjoyed it, the more I hid. There was a large blue trash can to my right, and the more people that stood above me, the better. There was such guilt attached to enjoying something as simple as a roasted piece of corn on a warm summer evening. I bit off one row at a time, devouring each kernel completely, neat and clean. I hated myself for indulging in it. For the most part, I had excelled at avoiding and depriving myself of such pleasures, but maybe if I ducked low enough below the crowd, then maybe it was like it never happened. Maybe God—if there was one—couldn't even see me down here, hunched on the cement curb, pecking at salty roasted corn, row by row, until the cob was as slick as bone.

As the band jumped into "Brown-Eyed Girl," a group of five teenage girls came running into the clearing. They quickly formed a circle and took turns dancing in the middle, jumping and laughing and screaming the chorus to each other. The older couples simply smiled, moved over a step or two, and continued to dance. For a moment, it was nice to see the two generations sharing the energy of the song, but the knee-jerk reaction I now had toward music quickly snuffed that out. My corn was about finished, and all I had to do was reach up and drop it in the trash can I was up against. I told myself I should make a real effort to find Carl. But as I picked a kernel of corn out from between my back molars, I saw Jimmy and his two friends stumble into the dancing circle of girls. The boys attempted to dance, their movements aggressive and unbalanced, but the girls didn't seem to mind. They widened their circle to make room for the lanky limbs of the boys, which flung about wildly like flags whipping in a fierce wind.

One of Jimmy's friends grabbed one of the girls around the waist and tried to dance with her. The girl didn't seem to mind as she continued hopping in time to the music and whipping her long blond hair back and forth, blurring her face. The boy, however, had no sense of timing and was far more interested in bringing the girl in closer.

Jimmy and the third boy took the cue and grabbed a girl of their own. I could tell the girls, for the most part, were just being polite, but their energy sapped by a small, barely perceptible amount. While Jimmy had one hand around the waist of a girl in a green tank top and long patchwork skirt, he noticed there were still two girls without a partner, and he wrangled in a second girl with his free hand. Her hair was cut short, but what she lacked in hair-whipping, she made up with her arms, which danced high above her head.

The situation didn't seem to be headed anywhere good, so I instinctively stood up. And almost as if my standing had prompted them, one of Jimmy's friends started whispering something in the blonde's ear—undoubtedly crude words uttered through rye-scented breath. He was smiling, and she was pulling away. The band had launched into the guitar solo. It was loud and fuzzy, and no one seemed to pay the group of girls any mind. I made a move toward them but then stepped back onto the curb. What was I going to do? But then the one free girl grabbed her blond friend's arm. For a moment the guy held tight to her other arm before he relinquished the girl to her friend. But his smile turned sour, and he said something that made the girls talk back.

I took a step forward then stopped.

Jimmy, with a girl on each hip, was doing his best to distract the two young girls, smiling and bouncing around more vigorously, but they were starting to overhear the argument. Soon, both of Jimmy's friends were jawing with three of the girls, only Jimmy's little threesome still pounding their fists in the air to the final chorus. A couple people stopped to watch, but nobody interfered, and without thinking, I made a move.

I marched with purpose across the street. With my adrenaline surging, my fingers flexed and unflexed. Had this been any other group, any other day, I would still be back with my butt on the curb, but I was counting on the fact that Jimmy knew me and seemed to like me well enough, and so I was hopeful I could defuse this situation quickly with minimal confrontation.

None of the group saw me coming except one of the girls with Jimmy, the girl with the bob. She eyed me from a pocket between Jimmy's shoulder and the other girl's messy brown hair.

"Jimmy!" I yelled.

He didn't hear me.

But before I could yell at him again, the girl with the short brown hair bolted from Jimmy's side in a demonstrative rage. "What the fuck are you doing here?"

Wait, what? This was directed at me.

It was Abby.

She came at me like a hit batter charging the mound. The other girl with Jimmy held her back. "Abby, what's wrong? Who the hell is this?"

"Coach?" Jimmy's foggy brain was having trouble catching up. "What you doing here?"

"What the hell do you want?" Abby screamed at me. "What? What?"

My hands went up in defense, but my voice was stuck.

But Abby's voice, like I heard in her house exactly one week earlier, was so guttural that even Jimmy's friends took notice.

"Why don't you leave my family alone, huh? What the fuck's wrong with you!"

The band hadn't stopped and now were strumming through a new song.

"Abby, who is this?" the blonde asked.

"Abbs, what's wrong, girl?" asked another. Three of them were at her side now, the one with blond hair holding her around the waist, while the final one was still pushing at one of Jimmy's friends.

"Hey, hey," I finally managed, my palms still facing the sky. "I'm trying to help here. Jimmy?"

"Fuck you!" Abby continued, and all the girls eyed me with a mix of confusion and contempt. Abby was trying to break free to get at me.

"Hey, buddy, why don't you leave the girl alone, huh?" It was one of Jimmy's guys.

"What the hell," the blonde yelled at him. "Now you're trying to *save* us? Asshole!"

Abby didn't let up; the excited energy I had witnessed only moments before was now redirected at me and gaining in velocity. It was contagious. Soon, the girl with the green tank top and another girl were pushing me and yelling for me to leave.

"Abby, I'm sorry, I'm sorry, I—"

But when I said her name it vaulted her to a new level of anger. And soon Jimmy's other friend was in my face.

"Why don't you leave, bro. You have a problem with these girls, you have a problem with me." The girls were at his hip like sidekicks. "Let's go, bro, let's go!"

His face was pockmarked with years of acne and scars of humiliation. Everything in my body told me to leave, to turn and walk away. But what had started as a rescue mission for Jimmy had now turned into something much more. I felt a dying need to prove myself to Abby, to prove what, I didn't know, but if I turned and left, there was no way I could help the hurt I saw in her eyes. I had to do something.

I took a step toward Abby, wanting to explain, to say something, *anything*, but before my foot even hit the asphalt, I had both of Jimmy's friends in my chest, dirty fingers bruising my sternum. And then I became acutely aware that the band had stopped. The white noise that hid our skirmish was gone, and all that was left was Abby: "Fuck you, fuck you, just go, just go . . ."

Then a hand came shooting in between the two assholes and me. I turned expecting to see Jimmy, but it wasn't him at all. It was a police officer.

"Okay, back up, sir. Back up, please."

I did as I was told, and he followed me. Behind him, another officer held his hands out, trying to wrangle in the eight of them.

Once I was several yards away, the police officer, who looked a good five years younger than me, asked me what was going on.

"Officer, I was only trying to protect those girls. The guys were getting a little too pushy. That's all."

"It sure looked like it was them trying to keep *you* from the girls."

"Well, yeah. They didn't want me breaking up their little party."

"Didn't look like the girls wanted you there either."

The band started playing again, easing into "Me and Bobby McGee." The ugly one who kept calling me *bro* and the blond girl were talking to the other officer. Abby was a few steps back, crying into her friend's shoulder, her back hunched and shaking.

"You been drinking, sir?"

"No. Not at all. I'd just like to go home. I'm not driving either, Officer."

"Wait right here."

The two officers met in the middle and talked while the band jumped into the chorus. Abby was still hugging her two friends. Jimmy and his buddies looked bored and lost now, the excitement of either getting in a fight or hooking up with the girls now vanished into the air like the smoke from the grill behind me. The other officer went back to the girls and Jimmy's crew and pointed down Higuera.

"Sir," the young cop said to me, his hands hitched onto his large utility belt. "Why don't you head on down that way, they'll go the other way, and everyone can go home safe and sound, huh?"

"Yeah," I said, trying to catch a glimpse of Abby's face in the crowd.

"Here we go." His hand was on my back, urging me forward. "No more trouble, tonight, huh?"

But I couldn't find her in the sea of people.

CHAPTER 9

"I HAVE ERRANDS TO RUN," SHE HAD SAID, HER voice as thin as tracing paper. "But you could come along."

Of course I accepted. I had to talk to her before Abby did. When I called Lauren late Thursday night after Farmer's Market, she sounded startled to hear my voice, and even more startled when I asked if she'd talked to Abby yet. Abby was staying over at a friend's, she said. But I didn't want to explain on the phone, so I accepted her invite even though I had a meeting on the bay with Travis at seven a.m. and we were to see the stovetop guy afterward. He would understand, right? Though it could be hard to understand what you didn't know.

Lauren said she would pick me up at 8:30, but it was only 8:04 as I stood on the edge of the road. Always anxious to leave wherever I was. And with my truck lurking behind me like a specter, I found myself inching farther into the street. So much so that with the last passing car I had to step back, felt its wind on my face, the driver honking at me after the fact.

At 8:16, she texted me that she was running a little late.

At 8:27, I decided to get into my truck. Not sure why, maybe leftover courage after jumping off the curb to confront Jimmy and his drunk friends? Or maybe it was my way of trying to end the silent standoff I'd been having with it the last twenty minutes. Hell, the standoff began on Monday. Every time I left or returned to my apartment, I passed by with my head down, afraid to make eye contact. Even when I was in my apartment, I felt its presence. Its weight. Whatever it was that propelled me to get inside, it was not the kind of thing I did.

The driver's-side door creaked open like it always had, the vinyl seat cold even through my clothes, and there were still vacuum marks striping the floor mats. I closed the door and looked up to find the windshield glazed by the night's fog, the world outside distorted as if I were looking through a marble. But as my hands instinctively found the wheel, my fingers gripped it like a vise, my heart leapt into a sprint, and my stomach bottomed out. I bolted out of the truck as if on fire, breathing heavy in the tiny parking lot, sweating in the bone-chill of early morning.

It was 8:41 when the blue Subaru crept up over the hill, pulled into the lot, and I got in almost as if nothing happened. Almost as if I hadn't just realized that what had been haunting my mind all this time was not only sitting in my parking spot but also inhabiting my body.

"Good morning, Conner." Her eyes were red, but not wet.

"Morning. And thank you again for coming all the way out here."

"It's no problem. You have no idea how much I've come to like driving."

As I sat in the passenger seat, I noticed right away that Lauren was dressed nicer than the past two times I had seen her. Her hair had been straightened. Not that it was excessively curly before, rather more natural, letting things fall where they may. But now it looked manufactured as it lay in thin, rigid sheets down past her shoulders. She had on a collared maroon shirt that buttoned up the front with round white buttons that looked like mints, and her pants looked freshly ironed. Besides the bloodshot eyes and lips that fell loose, indifferent, I saw for the first time that Lauren could be pretty. That she was probably very beautiful before. She took caution backing up into 11th Street, and I thought of a youthful Lauren, before there was grief and fear and loss. Back when she felt invincible. Her knuckles whitened around the steering wheel and guided us down the hill.

"The reason I called last night," I began. Even though I was with Lauren now and Abby wasn't, I still felt an urgency to get it out. "I wanted to tell you what happened. Last night. And I thought it important that you heard it from me."

"Before you begin, Conner, would you mind opening the glove box?"

I did as I was told, pinching the plastic knob and letting the door swing upwards.

"There's a paper in there. Should be on top. Yellow."

Inside there was nothing but papers, most of which looked like greasy mechanic receipts, yellow and pink carbon copies. There was also a pack of Kleenex and a mini flashlight tucked into one corner.

"It's got directions on it."

"Got it." As she said, it was on top. Cleaner than the rest. I shut the compartment and showed her the paper.

"Yes, thank you. You mind being my navigator?"

The paper was folded once in half, and when I opened it, there was a list of six to eight bulleted directions. I didn't recognize the street names, but what I did take notice of was her handwriting. It was immaculate, the thing of wedding invitations. Maybe she wrote it a long time ago, or maybe this was one small beauty that remained, that couldn't be tainted with bloodshot eyes. She only knew how to write one way.

She didn't need the directions right away. We were heading back out onto Los Osos Valley Road, back into San Luis, back where she had just come from, and this meant back by Los Osos Valley Memorial Park. Braden. Had she stopped on the way in? Did she plan on stopping now? Is that why she was dressed so nice?

"Okay, thank you," she said. "I'm sorry. You were trying to tell me something?"

"Yes. Last night." But I couldn't speak; the cemetery sat in waiting down the hill.

"You know, Conner, that . . ." She didn't slow down as we passed the cemetery, but she deliberately glanced toward it. "Peter's grandparents. They purchased a large plot there. For every . . . So that's . . ."

And then we were passing her son.

He was there, somewhere off to the left. Somewhere in that large green field. Where exactly, I wasn't sure. How often had she been? Were there flowers on the tombstone? I looked down to my shoes and waited for it to pass. I closed my eyes. I felt the inertia of my truck throw my body forward, the seat belt tearing at the flesh of my chest. I didn't know if she looked over, or if her eyes welled up with tears for the millionth time. When I felt we were safely past, I opened my eyes again, but kept them focused on my shoes, too afraid to see who now was driving.

When I looked up, the cemetery was a fleck in the side-view mirror.

"I'm sorry, Conner. Last night?"

I went on to tell Lauren about Farmer's Market, though I didn't tell her the reason for my trip. She didn't know anything about the restaurant. I told her about the roasted corn and the band who played classic rock covers, and as I did this, the guilt came back to me in one strong wave, like the flush that comes over you right before you faint. How could I admit to her that I was there, enjoying small things this way? Roasting corn, live music, warm summer evenings. Could I be more selfish? As I stumbled over needless details like the name of the band and the songs they played, I contemplated telling her why I was really there. How I was trying to make up for a past failure only to fail again. I realized as I was talking that I was currently committing yet further failures. Travis. We were supposed to meet at seven. He had left two voicemails already.

"And then I spotted Abby."

"Oh?"

"And at first I didn't know it was her. There was just a group of girls dancing, you know?"

"Yes, I knew she and her girlfriends were going to Farmer's. She's been out of the house almost every night this summer, actually."

I told her about the guys that came up to dance with them. I didn't mention I knew Jimmy. In the story they were simply *rowdy teenage boys*. And I explained how when I went to protect the girls, to shoo the boys away, Abby turned on me and was screaming and cursing and this got both the girls and the boys against me, though none of them knew why.

"And how did it end?" she asked.

So then I told her how the music stopped and two police officers came to break things up, and they thought *I* was the aggressor.

"And I wanted to tell you what happened, so that you didn't think . . ." I wasn't sure how to finish that sentence. What would the story look like if Abby had told her?

"Thank you, Conner. I wouldn't have thought anything other than what you told me."

Then neither of us knew what to say. Rows and rows of lettuce and strawberries blurred by our side windows. Los Osos Valley Road was particularly empty this morning. The dampness already behind us in Osos.

"I'm sorry for how she was with you," Lauren finally said. "We all have our different ways of grieving."

I wanted to ask her what *her* way was. If it was working. But I didn't. "I'm sorry it ended like that. I only meant to—"

"I know, Conner. And I am thankful you were there."

I glanced down at the yellow paper I had forgotten was in my hand. "Oh, up ahead, you want to make a left on Descanso."

As we sat at the red light, her left blinker the only sound in the car, I realized we were turning into a residential neighborhood. What kind of errand were we running? Before I could ask, the car was turning left into a labyrinth of residential streets, many of which ended in cul-de-sacs. I had to navigate: "Left again at . . . yes, here. Okay, then a right on Vista Del something, yes I think that's it, and now we're looking for 1492, evens are on the right, 52, 62 . . . Okay, yes, there it is, the blue one."

We were in front of a large two-story house the color of the sky. The sky in SLO, not the ghost-gray of Osos or Morro Bay. The white trim around the edges and bordering each window looked freshly painted. Like clouds. There were two stripes of rosebushes that followed the brick walkway to the large white door. A Lexus sat in the driveway, and a basketball hoop was cemented into the ground at the far left. I could even make out the handprints left in the concrete around the pole; there must have been four or five sets. The basketball net, however, was ripped and frayed, hanging from the fading orange rim by only two strings of rope. As far as I could tell, it was the only blemish in the otherwise flawless house. And really, I was guessing it was more a sign of time passing, of kids growing up, than it was of neglect.

"I have to drop some things off, Conner." Lauren pulled hard at the emergency brake and unbuckled her seat belt. "You can stay here. I won't be long." And then she cracked my window a few inches as if I were a dog and it was a hot summer day.

"Sure," I said.

She retrieved a brown grocery bag from the back seat and left the car. As she walked up the path to the front door, her tan pants a bit wrinkled in the back but otherwise nicely put together, it hit me that Braden used to sit in the same seat I was in now. Hundreds, maybe thousands of times, whenever he had successfully beat Abby to calling shotgun. He had grown up watching life through this side window. In all likelihood, he had spent more time in the back, however. I looked behind me. Aside from an empty water bottle, the back seats were spotless, and I wondered which side was his. In here, in the car, it was imagined memories of where Braden might have been. In his house, it was more of the same. Ghosts of the past. But we had just passed Braden, the *present* him, in the cemetery. He was physically, technically there. Wasn't he?

Lauren took longer than one might take to "drop something off." The door had been opened by a woman who looked the same age as Lauren, and they both quickly disappeared into the house. After what felt like thirty minutes but was probably only five, I decided to face the voicemails from Travis. They were looming overhead like gathering clouds. The sooner I listened, the sooner I could delete. The first one was from six thirty. He must have just arrived at the shop. I had left the message there instead of his cell to guarantee no pickup.

"What the fuck, man? What the fuck?" And then he hung up. The second message was a couple hours later. His anger was replaced by disappointment and defeat. "I don't know what's going on with you, but . . . And I'm concerned, but also . . . Jesus. Will you call me? Please. Seriously."

I did need to call him. I knew I did. And I would. But the guilt from his voice was a joke compared to real guilt. Oh, did I miss a meeting? Try driving by the cemetery with Lauren!

When the front door to the all-American blue house opened again, Lauren was not with the woman who answered, but now stood talking to a young man, maybe even a teenager. His hair was shaggy, and he wore dark shorts and a white T-shirt, no shoes, and both of them were nodding a lot as they spoke. Sometimes quick, short nods like they were agreeing on something simple like a meeting time or confirming an address. But sometimes they nodded slowly, deliberately, as if agreeing on something from the inside, confirming something they didn't want to be confirming.

And then they hugged. I turned away quickly. It didn't feel like something I should see. It was far too intimate. And as the boy's head reached over Lauren's shoulder, I also didn't want him to see me.

I didn't look up again until I heard the car door open. Lauren offered me a closed-mouth smile, which I was relieved to take.

"Sorry, Conner," she said, "if that took a little long." Her eyes, still mapped with red, now had a clear sheen over them. She wiped quickly at her nose.

"No, it's okay."

Lauren started the car and made a U-turn, backtracking the way we came in. Aside from a slight hesitation at one intersection, she didn't need my help. And she didn't appear to want to talk. She drove out of the neighborhood with a little more purpose. But when we reached Los Osos Valley Road, she made a right, heading back toward Los Osos. Was that really the extent of her errands? Did she get dressed up, drive all the way out to pick me up, drive back to SLO to drop off a brown bag, have another cry, and then take me back home?

"That was Toad," Lauren said. "I think his real name's Dominic or something, but everyone calls him Toad."

"Okay."

"I don't even know where the nickname came from. He's Braden's best friend."

I closed my eyes and prayed he hadn't seen me.

"I haven't even gone through Braden's room yet, Conner. I can't. But there was some stuff around the house and in the garage that belonged to Toad, and I thought he should have some of Braden's things too." She sniffed and rubbed at her nose again.

I didn't say anything as Lauren made a right onto Foothill. We weren't going back to Los Osos after all. For this I was relieved. And scared. This was also the way to her house.

"I have another stop to make. I hope that's okay."

"Of course."

"Peter wouldn't come with me. He won't do much of anything."

"Guess we all have our way," I said, mirroring her earlier comment. But it didn't feel like it was something I was allowed to say. I tried again. "I don't do much of anything either."

And this was true. I thought of Travis, of Rian, the Sea & Sky, Jimmy, the basketball team. Everything was getting worse. And then I wondered what in the world I was doing in this car, riding around with Lauren as she completed her grief errands.

"And Abby . . ." she said, but then finished the sentence in her head. Because of what the other words were or because of where we were—passing their house—I didn't know. But like the cemetery earlier, I simply looked down at my shoes again.

"Well, Abby does *too* much," she continued. "I didn't want to put any more on her plate. Not little things like this. Nothing is little for her."

I understood now what Lauren meant about driving. As she spoke, her eyes scanned the road, they checked the rearview mirror, side mirrors, crosswalks. They didn't have time to look at me or at passing cemeteries or empty houses, or even stare into nothingness. Meanwhile, her finger was busy flicking the turn signal, her hands passing one over the other on the wheel as she made a left turn, her feet controlling the car as if operating on their own. She was out of her head and into her body.

But it was impossible to watch her drive without thinking of my truck sitting heavy in front of my apartment. And how this morning I didn't last but ten seconds in my own driver's seat. We weren't even moving, but the truck felt alive.

As we zigzagged our way into downtown, crossing Higuera where I ate corn not ten hours ago, Lauren told me that she got a call from Barnes & Noble. They didn't know what to do with Braden's things. He had a cubby. Did they want them shipped to the house? Would someone come by for them? Should they throw them out? She told me she didn't ask what was in the cubby, if it was anything more than a Styrofoam box of leftover food. She didn't tell Peter or Abby about it either. Little things, she called them again, that neither of them would know how to deal with.

We pulled into the parking structure across from Barnes & Noble off Marsh Street. This time, she pulled the emergency brake, undid her seat belt, and turned to me.

"Will you come with me, Conner?"

"Of course." But as I undid my seat belt and took my jacket off to leave it in the car, I didn't know how far she meant. I could walk her to the entrance and then go grab a coffee from Starbucks. That seemed reasonable.

As we waited at the crosswalk, Lauren looked at me as if for the first time that day. Out of the car now and out of the gloom of early morning Los Osos, she could really see me. She smiled a closed-mouth smile again and told me she liked my shirt. It was a long-sleeve cotton shirt, gray, with orange threading along the seams. She said orange was a good color on me and that it wasn't a good color on most people. But Braden could pull off orange, she said. In fact, he had a shirt not too dissimilar to the one I was wearing. Her thumb and forefinger rubbed the fabric that hung loose off my shoulder.

At the front entrance to the large two-story bookstore, I hesitated, not knowing if she wanted me to follow her in, if *I* wanted to follow her in.

"Will you come with me?" She repeated the question like a mantra.

I nodded and opened the heavy wooden door.

Inside, the bookstore was nearly empty. I had to remind myself that it was still shy of ten o'clock on a Friday morning. By this evening, it would be a literary nightclub. But now, there was one old man reading the back of a hardback book at the New Fiction table and several people sitting at tables to the right at the store cafe. I followed Lauren, who also appeared reluctant to make a move.

To our left stood a long counter housing a half dozen or so registers. Only one employee was there. An older woman, with her hands clasped behind her back, pacing. And there was another one in front of the registers, a man restocking bookmarks, chocolate squares, and other impulse buys. Lauren eyed the two of them for a moment before approaching the woman—the softer-looking of the two with her thin gold-rimmed glasses, her graying blond hair pulled back in a bun. Librarian-like.

"Excu . . ." Lauren's voice wasn't ready. She cleared it and tried again. "Excuse me."

"Yes?" The older woman unclasped her hands and rested them on the counter. "May I help you?"

"Yes, hello. I'm Lauren Thomas. I'm uh . . ."

The woman's face was frozen in a smile as she waited for more explanation.

"I'm uh, I'm Braden's mother."

With that, the smile was gone. "Oh dear. Yes. I'm so sorry."

I begged and pleaded and prayed not to be introduced, not with the truth and not with some cheap lie either.

"Yes, well," Lauren said, ignoring me. "I was called to . . . They told me . . ." But then she lost her words. Standing a step or two behind her, I couldn't see her face, but I was able to watch the older lady as her sympathetic eyes urged

Lauren on. She was looking for enough syllables to garner the meaning of Lauren's visit.

"There's a cubby," I said. My voice strong, maybe a decibel louder than necessary.

"Oh yes, yes." The woman looked relieved to flee the situation and held her index finger up, motioning for us to stay as she went to talk to the man restocking the counters.

He looked middle-aged, his black hair greasy and in need of a haircut, his glasses thick and resting crooked on his face.

"Hi there. I'm Tucker." He shook Lauren's hand and then mine. "Follow me," he said, and tried to smile.

He took us past the New Arrivals and Bestsellers, and on past the business and computer section and past the messy, overstocked remainder shelf of books past their prime. Lauren looked back at me only once, but it reminded me of the way the taxi driver checked on me in the rearview mirror. To see if I was still there.

When we reached the back of the store, Tucker turned left, and Lauren and I followed, the three of us walking in a quiet single-file line. In the far back corner, there was a single door with a green sign that read *Employees only*. Tucker typed in a code, and soon we were in the back room of Barnes & Noble.

The room opened up in both directions. To the right, a cramped kitchen, a table and chairs, a water cooler, and a copy machine. And to the left was a series of cubicles, all of which were empty. We followed wordlessly past all of this down a short hallway to another room. Inside were two couches facing one another, olive green and navy blue with throw pillows that didn't match, and a coffee table littered with magazines. It made me think of the Thomases' table and their fan of home design magazines.

"Here you are," Tucker said. He extended his hand to the back wall, where there were rows and rows of open cubbies. "They're labeled by last name."

"Thank you," Lauren said, eyeing the columns and rows of cubbies like a climbing wall, plotting her route.

"I'll leave you two alone. Take your time." Tucker pushed his glasses up on his nose. "No one should bother you."

"Thank you," I said.

"Yes, thank you, Tucker."

I stood, waiting for Lauren. I didn't think I needed to follow her any farther.

Lauren watched Tucker leave and then walked immediately to the wall of cubbies. Even though their last name began with a *T*, she started on the far left. She looked meticulously over each name, some of which she ran her fingers over. Did she know any of these people? Was she close to Braden's friends? Did he have a lot of friends? Why didn't she know the way to Toad's house? She was silent, but her lips mouthed the names of his faceless co-workers.

She was past halfway when the door behind me opened and a teenage girl with long red hair pulled back into a ponytail entered.

"Hi. Tucker let us in. We'll only be a moment," I said to answer her quizzical look.

"Oh, totally. Noooo worries, man," she said, then popped her gum with a sharp inhale. I stood frozen in my spot, floating a bit aimlessly in the space between the lounge room and the hallway. I wasn't anchored to a wall or a piece of furniture, and my feet hadn't so much as shifted weight since Tucker left. The girl went to a cubby somewhere early in the alphabet, grabbed a lanyard, threw it around her neck, and was already hustling past me.

"I'm late! Ahh!" she said, her eyebrows almost lifting off her forehead. Her faux panic told me she was late to most shifts. "Don't tell, okay?"

When she was gone, I turned back to Lauren. She had found Braden's box. There was a green lanyard around her neck now, and she clutched a brown hooded sweatshirt to her chest. Braden's cubby, however, was on the top row. She rose to the tips of her toes and then fell back down. She lifted the sweatshirt to her face, and her whole body swelled with a large inhale. She did this two or three times and then stood on the tip of her right foot to try and see deeper into the square foot of space that was Braden's.

"Conner?" Her voice was barely audible. "Could you . . . ?"

I unplanted my feet only to realize my left calf had fallen asleep.

"I can't see to the back," she said. "I want to make sure . . ."

"Of course." When I arrived at Lauren's side, I could see the water that was drowning her eyeballs but somehow not running down her cheeks, and I could again see the whites of her knuckles as she gripped the sweatshirt.

The top and farthest right cubbyhole had a green and white label on it that read *Thomas, B.*. The typo of the extra period after the *B* made his name seem like a cliffhanger, like there was something about his name that wasn't quite finished.

I was a good six inches taller than Lauren and had to crane my neck a little to see to the back of the box. I didn't expect to see anything, but there was something there. Two things. I reached in and pulled out a book and a partially eaten bag of peanut M&M's. The yellow wrapper was twisted tightly at the open end. I handed them both to Lauren. She took the M&M's and laughed, which caused a few drops to finally spill from her eyes. Old tears that had been holding on for too long.

The book was a paperback. Shiny, it looked new. And upside-down, I read the title: *The Anubis Gates*. Lauren ran her hand over the cover, used her index fingers to trace the raised letters of the title and the author's name, Tim Powers. She turned it over in her hands. The price sticker was still attached.

"Do you think this is his?" she asked. "I mean, or the store's?"

"I don't know."

She flipped it back to the front side. "I don't care." With this, she made to leave, and so I followed. Between the book, the sweatshirt, and the candy, her hands were full, but I knew better than to ask if she needed help. It looked like it might be a while before she relaxed her grip on any of the items. And had I seen this scene in any other capacity or heard about or even thought about it, rich in fine detail, this mother clinging to the random, worthless things in her son's abandoned twelve-by-twelve work cubby, it would have crushed me, flattened me whole. But somehow, being tied to Lauren, if only by the two steps in which I trailed behind her, made it barely tolerable.

At the entrance to the hallway, Lauren turned back to look. She scanned the room. Left to right, top to bottom, as painstakingly as she'd read the last names moments before. Maybe she was memorizing every last detail: the poster on the wall stuffed with fine print about employee rights, the McDonald's cup and crumpled napkin that sat on the center table. Or maybe she was replaying imaginary memories—Braden's memories—in her mind. Envisioning her son in this space, maybe reaching on the tips of his toes to grab his M&M's, sitting on the couch during break reading one of his fantasy novels or recounting to his co-workers the struggle with a particularly disgruntled customer.

"Okay. Let's go," she said.

Back on the floor, there were a few more customers milling about, but the store still carried the slow malaise of a weekday morning. I didn't see the tardy redhead, but both Tucker and the older woman were behind the registers. The woman sucked her lips inside of her mouth as if to stop from frowning at us. Tucker smiled something genuine and raised his hand to us in a silent goodbye.

The walk back to the car was also silent, and when we arrived at the blue Subaru, Lauren still hadn't said anything. Nor did she put the things we picked up into the back seat, but rather, she piled them onto her lap, the sweatshirt, the book, the half bag of M&M's, the lanyard still around her neck. We pulled out of the parking structure, not there long enough to warrant a parking fee, and we were back on the road.

We were driving west on California Street when Lauren pulled the car over. It was done in such haste; this wasn't another errand. She put the car in park and hunched over in her seat, grabbing the sweatshirt with both hands and burrowing her face deep into it. I was waiting for the shaking to start, the up-and-down rhythm of her sobs. But she didn't jerk. She was rounded into herself, but she was still. And quiet. And then she uncurled herself and looked at me with wrecked eyes.

"They didn't do a fucking thing!"

I didn't understand.

"He loved that place. He worked his ass off for them and thought each one of his co-workers his close friend. He talked about that place, those people, nonstop." Lauren looked down at her fingers. She was rubbing the cuff of the sweatshirt between her thumbs and index fingers."And we walk in there like it's any other day. Like we were picking up a goddamn piece of mail." She threw the sleeve down into her lap."There was nothing there to honor him. To celebrate him. Nothing! Nothing, nothing. Nothing." She looked out the front window. Down at the gearshift. She looked back at the street."I thought maybe the manager would be there to greet me. What's her name . . . ?" Lauren looked to me as if maybe I had the answer, as if I knew her name."Anne. That's it, Anne something. Maybe she would hand me his things in a nice bag and offer me some kind words, maybe even some bullshit card that everybody signed. And all this stupid shit I'm talking about is just that. It's stupid, stupid little shit. But it's also not." Then, for a moment, the power in her voice subsided."It's important," she said, barely above a whisper."But no, we walk in and get the same treatment as an employee who had moved to . . . to Wisconsin or somewhere to be with a new girlfriend. Like he never even existed there, Conner."

And then she was done. She took steady, even, planned breaths, putting herself back together. She had no problem being honest with me, but I could feel she didn't want to break down. Sure, a couple tears made kamikaze missions down her face, that was beyond her control, but I felt her very conscious effort to stave off the *real* crying.

"I don't want to go home." She looked at me with beggar's eyes."Let's not go home. Not yet. Not right now."

But now I was supposed to speak. She wanted a response.

"Okay, but . . . but where . . . ?"

"It doesn't matter."

She put the car back in drive and re-entered California Street. Up ahead, a few blocks away, was the on-ramp for the 101. Without flipping on her blinker, Lauren eased onto the on-ramp and accelerated quickly. Soon we were on the 101 freeway heading south. But I had no idea where we were going.

CHAPTER 10

THE SUMMER AFTER I GRADUATED HIGH SCHOOL, I moved down to Santa Barbara. I didn't have my shit perfectly planned out like Travis. He knew he would stay local, major in business at Cal Poly, and open up his own something by the time he graduated. And the bastard followed it down to the last bullet point, opening Yakety Kayaks when he was just twenty-four.

My "plan," however, was to do two years at Santa Barbara City College, work, save up, apply for scholarships, and then transfer to a UC. I didn't have a major figured out yet, but there was time. Despite my parents' much more logical plea to stay at home and go to Cuesta, the idea of spending another two years at home with Dad, his legs crossed, nose deep in a textbook, and Mom conducting séances or rain chants, was enough to send me running the hundred miles to SB.

So I enrolled at SBCC for the fall and drove down with Travis on a couple scouting weekends in search of a job and a place to live. But Santa Barbara City College is a seventy-four-acre campus adjacent to a gorgeous beach, and up on the mesa. Up on the mesa means million-dollar views. And million-dollar views mean multi-million-dollar houses.

I had to drift down toward where the students were. This meant Isla Vista. IV was one of those places you wouldn't understand unless you'd been. And even then, still doubtful. With over twenty-three thousand residents in an area just under two square miles, it is the most densely populated community west of the Mississippi. And that only tells the half of it—ninety percent of the residents are students, and the other ten are either scared for their lives and locked indoors, or were one-time students turned burnouts who still went to the same parties and hit on the same freshman girls. But in a nutshell, it was Disneyland for teenagers. You could go a whole month in IV without ever seeing someone over the age of twenty-two. And in the summer, the telephone poles swelled with flyers for cheap work and rooms for rent. I found one of each fairly quickly.

So when Lauren suggested we go to Santa Barbara, a tiny smile creased my face. I could hear the muscles in my cheeks crack and splinter from disuse.

It was nearly ten thirty when we passed Avila and Pismo Beach. Places I had spent my childhood boogie-boarding and sunburning with Travis and Ollie, before Ollie's family moved to Alaska and we never heard from him again. Lauren didn't say much at first, and all the time I had been in the Subaru, she never turned on the radio. The hum of tires speeding along the asphalt would be our white noise.

When she did finally start to talk, it was a one-sided conversation about Braden and what he liked. She began in on his love for fantasy novels, commenting on the book found in his cubby. On the cover was an Egyptian god that looked like a regal Doberman pinscher. There was a lot of desert stone and what looked like a solar eclipse, with a stopwatch lying on one of the stones. Right in his wheelhouse, she said with a smile. How he loved reading. In fact, he used to read so much, Lauren said she had to regulate reading time like most parents regulated TV. As an eleven-year-old, he was allowed three hours a day of reading, and no more. He wouldn't get out of the house, she said, wouldn't interact with anyone. He only wanted to lie on his back, be it on the living room floor or his bed, and get lost in another world.

It made me sad at first. Someone running away from reality, escaping, pretending they existed in a different time and place. But then I realized that this was what *adults* did when they read, not kids. He wasn't running *from* something; he was running *to* something. And so naturally, working at Barnes & Noble, for him, was *it*.

I mostly listened, making sure to look over and nod every once in a while to show her I was still there. But inside, I was cataloguing an index of all the things I took away. And the smaller and more specific the details, the more they weighed stacked atop my chest.

"Did you like to read, Conner?" She startled me with the question. I had been lulled into the passive role of listener. "Like, as a kid."

"Not as much as he did," I said, and tried to start a joint laughter, however forced. But she didn't bite. She was genuinely interested in my response. "I read a little bit, though. Mostly biographies. Sports stars. Jackie Robinson, Magic Johnson, Joe Montana, stuff like that."

"So you were an athlete?"

"Kind of. I maybe read a couple of Stephen King books in high school."

"Oh, Braden loves Stephen King! When he wasn't reading swords-and-sorcery stuff, he ate up every King novel there was. Too creepy for me."

I never actually finished one of King's books. I think I started one about a car that went around killing people, but the way her face lit up when I mentioned the name, I had to play it up.

"Oh, what's the one with the dog?" she asked. "What was his name?"

"Uhm . . ."

"Cujo! Yes, that's it. Cujo. Oh, too much blood. And that poor dog."

After cringing at the thought of Cujo, there was an almost-smile on her face. As if there was a secret somewhere inside her, but she wanted to keep it there, hidden, and only the faintest shadow of it made it to her face.

After our book talk, she was quiet again for a while. We passed Arroyo Grande. I hadn't thought of AG for twelve years. Not since high school basketball. I always hated AG. They kicked our ass. But as with all the little coastal towns lined up like Pac-Man pellets between SLO and Santa Barbara, it was gone as quickly as it had appeared.

"He liked more than books, though. He had other interests."

She didn't say this defensively so much as she said it like there was an endless dialogue running in her head, and this happened to be the portion that made it to her lips. She started repeating things she'd already told me. He was taking classes at Cuesta, trying to figure things out. When she said that last phrase, it hit me again that we weren't talking about someone back at the house. There was no more figuring out to be done. But she went on about law school. That was the plan. That's what everything was building toward. She had stars in her eyes as we nipped past Nipomo. She fantasized about the trials he would win, the people he would save.

I sat and listened to all that I had taken away. Like penance. At some point, when she was talking about Braden wanting to move to a big city like New York or Chicago, I felt my phone buzz in my pocket. Rian? Travis? It was a fifty-fifty shot, though Travis had already called twice.

As we moved inland, we traded ocean views for perfect rows of lettuce. Lauren fell silent again. A small biplane made a low swoop over the fields to our right, and I waited for it to drop its spray of pesticide, but nothing fell from the belly of the plane.

"Can I ask you a question?" I asked, the mundaneness of Santa Maria pulling on me.

"Yes, Conner. Anything."

"What was in that bag? The one you gave to Toad."

She didn't answer right away. She stared out the front windshield. A red pickup truck and two semis were the only vehicles in view. So far, Lauren had been extremely forthcoming, almost too much so, but in those quiet moments between question and answer I would have given anything to take it back.

"Never mind, I'm . . . I shouldn't have asked."

"No, Conner, really, it's okay. Let's see," she said. "There were a lot of video games. They played together in the garage, and I don't know whose games were whose, but I figured Toad would want them. He had also left his hat at our house. Black baseball hat with an orange bird?"

"Orioles," I said.

"Yes, but the boys didn't care much for sports. Still, Toad never went anywhere without it." Lauren put on her blinker and passed the pickup truck on the left. As we passed the last Santa Maria exit, there weren't any cars in front of us, not as far as the eye could see. "And then . . . Well, and then I put in little things. Maybe it's silly. Maybe it's not something a twenty-year-old cares about, but he's Braden's best friend. I didn't know him well, actually. They met at Cuesta. But once they met, they were inseparable. I put in a picture of Braden. It was an old one, from high school. You know how pictures these days are all on computers. But it's different to hold a picture in your hand, isn't it? It's different to look at a photograph that's not a bunch of pixels on a screen. Maybe only a mother notices these things."

She looked at me for a response, but I felt underwater.

"I also gave him a T-shirt. It wasn't anything special. Something Braden got at a Barnes & Noble giveaway. It said 'Have You Hugged a Book Today?' or something like that. But clothes are important to me." She let go of the steering wheel with one hand to squeeze a handful of the brown sweatshirt in her lap. "Like a second skin. His smell, his feel, it's still here." She let go of the sweatshirt. "Almost."

That's when the tears started. Not real ones, just the runaways. She was good at containing. I shifted my body toward the window to be alone and to give Lauren her privacy, as much as either of those things were possible in the small blue Subaru.

In another half hour we were in Buellton, a gas-stop town in the Santa Ynez valley, made "famous" by Andersen's. A Dutch-themed restaurant that had been around since the '20s but was really a glorified Denny's. But it pushed its "world famous" split pea soup in larger-than-life billboards along the 101—two cartoon chefs chopping a pea in half with a mallet and chisel—and had thusly put itself on the map, if only as a smudge, another kitschy Americana roadside attraction.

Lauren pulled off the freeway and into a gas station. She asked if I needed anything, and even though she meant a bottle of water or a bag of pretzels, I thought it was a morose question for her to be asking me, but I said no thank you, and she exited the car to pump gas. I used the five minutes to check my phone. The missed call had not been from Travis or Rian, but rather the Sea

& Sky. There was a voicemail as well. Two, actually.

"This is Donnie." His accent spit into the receiver. "It's too much. You leave me too many times. How I cook food with no cook? You are no working here no more. I am sorry, my friend, but I have restaurant to run."

I skipped the second voicemail when I didn't recognize the guy's voice. Dale something? But my initial stomach drop from hearing Donnie's words didn't last long. Sure, the first reaction was one of panic, but as Lauren re-entered the car and accelerated back onto the freeway, the overriding feeling was one of relief. One fewer thing to bite at the back of my neck as I neglected it.

After filling up the car, it was as if Lauren had also recharged. She returned with a different energy. And she wanted to talk. But not about Braden. She started asking me questions. She had done this during our initial visit at Laguna Lake, but this time her questions were more specific, less edited. And as I was previously unsure if she was trying to confirm me as a good person worthy of forgiving or a bad person worthy of hating, I knew now that she was asking only to learn. Maybe I was a welcome distraction. Or maybe I had convinced myself of this because I wanted to open up to her. Or maybe it was the message I received from Donnie that left me feeling that I was on the fast track to having nothing else left to lose. Or the two stops we made this morning, penance I was paying that put me at my wit's end. But whatever the reason, I was finally and completely honest.

I told her the real story of my parents. That calling them teacher and artist was being generous. I told her about New Mexico, the Renaissance Faire, about my embarrassment of them. She didn't judge me or defend them in some sort of parental solidarity. She just listened. I told her about Travis and about Further. I told her about the menu ideas, the concept, how we were lifelong friends and now merging our two passions. She appeared genuinely happy for the idea. When I saw her smile, I decided not to tell her about how badly I was already fucking things up, the meetings I'd missed. But as I spoke, I didn't think about what Lauren might think of me or how any details of my life might make her feel. I talked and talked and talked.

By the time I was finishing my purge, we were back along the coast, passing through Gaviota. The first silence fell between us in quite some time, and it felt different than it had previously. It felt good to tell Lauren everything. Well, almost everything. And I could tell it changed her a little as well. She didn't grip the steering wheel so tightly, and she checked her mirrors less often. To our right, the ocean was a calming force. Maybe it was the enormity of it, or the way it rocked gently, alive, like a caring mother shushing and rocking us into a peaceful rest.

Neither of us spoke for another ten minutes or so, until Lauren broke the silence. "People don't look at me anymore, Conner, but they bring me all sorts of things."

I opened my mouth, but she kept going before I could choose the right word.

"It's amazing to see the lengths they go to in order to avoid eye contact. Like I'm Medusa." She said this with a forced laugh. "But socks, Conner. Handmade socks. And casseroles. Magazines. Lasagnas. Afghans. Why would I want a handful of magazines? Really? And cookies. Pies. I even got a check for two hundred and twelve dollars. One of Peter's co-workers came by. I guess they took a collection or something."

I gave her a look that let her know I was here, but I also didn't know what to say. She gave me a look that said it was okay to not always respond, and we continued down the 101 together. And even in the space where she wasn't talking, her voice still hung in the air. Particularly the way she said my name, enunciating the whole thing, where most people swallowed the end. And she said my name often. More than necessary. As if it were a period at the end of a sentence.

"El Capitan State Beach." She read the words of the sign slowly as if saying the name of an old friend. "Braden used to camp here. With the Boy Scouts, I mean." *Be prepared.* She slowed a little and searched both sides of the highway, though I wasn't sure what for. There wasn't much to see but wild brush and patches of sandy beach. "We dropped him off somewhere right around here."

She smiled so I smiled.

"Did you ever camp here, Conner? I mean, when you were in Boy Scouts?"

I opened my mouth to tell her I had never been in Boy Scouts, but even with my lips loosened up with the recent honesty, I caught myself on the inhale and remembered the lie I had told her back in her cold living room.

"No, not here," I said. "I just remember going to Big Bear." I didn't like lying to Lauren. Even if well-intentioned, it felt blasphemous. I promised myself I wouldn't do it again. But luckily, she wasn't listening as she slowed and pulled off the road at the next turnout. We came to a stop in a scrap of dirt that would fit no more than three or four cars. A sizeable tree canopied over us like an umbrella, and beyond it was a strip of ice plant, then an equally small strip of sand, and then the waves, no higher than my knees, which didn't so much crash as they fell onto the shore like a cat flopping into a patch of sunlight.

"Can we sit for a bit?" she asked, killing the engine. "It's nice out, yeah?"

"It is." But looking at the ocean made me think of that song. Neil Young's song. The only sound that remained. Taunting me from shitty speakers. Soundtracking tragedy with the same indifference it had been soundtracking my innocent, if eager, drive. Cruelly persistent. Cruelly indifferent.

Lauren turned the key in order to roll down our windows so we could listen to the rhythmic *whoosh* of the waves, but all I heard was the song, louder now as if someone off in the distance, up along the beach, was playing it out of a little boom box.

It was a nice enough scene, but aside from that fucking song, I also couldn't get the taste out of my mouth of the lie I had told Lauren about being in the Boy Scouts. I feared she might continue to ask questions about it now that we were at one of Braden's frequent campsites. I had to start a conversation of my own. And it had to be truthful.

"I never learned to surf," I said. She looked at me, confused. "I always wanted to. I've almost always lived near the beach. I even boogie-boarded a lot as a kid. But surfing never happened."

"Why do you think that is?"

"I dunno. One of those things."

"You could learn now," she said. "I mean, if you still wanted."

"Yeah, I guess." A couple runners bounced their way past us. "To be honest, I think it always scared me." Although it felt good to be honest, to try and cancel out my lie, it also felt like cheating. Being honest with something small, something that didn't matter.

"I get that," she said. "The ocean is so powerful. Did you hear about that kayaker that had to be rescued a couple weeks back?"

I nodded but didn't want to talk about people who escaped tragedy. Looking out at the ocean, I thought about how calm it looked on the surface. But there were currents lurking beneath, unseen. Giant undertows ready to sweep people away without notice.

"Braden's never really been athletic." She looked down and fingered the green lanyard that still hung around her neck. Below that lay the sweatshirt on her lap. Under that was the half-eaten bag of peanut M&M's and the Tim Powers novel. "I mean, he's good with the outdoors and even recently got into—"

Her sentence ran headfirst into a brick wall. We both finished it in our heads—*cycling*—and I think felt equally guilty for letting our filters soften. For not putting our words through a screening process before letting them out into this new, fragile world. We weren't allowed to be so frivolous. Even though Lauren was the one that ran into it, I felt as if it were me that said the word.

"Anyway," she said. "He liked this place. Even if it's pretty tame as far as wilderness goes, he was good at it."

And there it was. It was the first time I heard her say "was" in the same sentence as Braden. *He was good at it.* I don't think she noticed, but I certainly did. Her tongue had loosened, slipped, preoccupied with her previous near trip-up.

"Do you want to head back, Conner?"

We both looked at the clock on the mute radio. It was a little after noon.

There were so many days now when I wouldn't even be out of bed at this time. I wondered if that was the case for her too. Both of us buried under blankets while the rest of the world moved about, interacting and working and playing.

I didn't answer right away, but she started the car nonetheless. As soon as I thought about what I'd be returning to, the answer was easy.

"How about not yet? I mean, we're technically still twenty minutes or so away from Santa Barbara."

"Good," she said. "Let's keep going, Conner."

At first I had found the habit annoying, her always saying my name, like I was constantly being called out. But I was starting to like it, to like how it was something I could expect and depend on.

As for getting a job back in college, I had landed a random one in nearby Goleta at a place called Mail Movers. A large warehouse where businesses took their bulk mail to be sorted, stuffed, sealed, addressed, and shipped. There was a large Mexican contingency that worked the assembly line machines—tiny mechanical arms that shoved letters and pamphlets into envelopes sucked open by a tiny air hole. I, however, was stuck sitting on a metal stool stuffing envelopes by hand and then sealing them with a damp sponge. I got the smaller jobs that weren't deemed machine-worthy. Although smaller, by machine standards, could still mean a thousand envelopes, each with two to three sheets of folded paper. Paper cuts a daily occurrence. I shared the metal table with the only other gringo there, a scrawny kid named Tank that went to UCSB. He had a perpetually runny nose, always slurping up long strings of snot, and he rambled on each week about the perverted escapades he and his forty-something girlfriend were up to.

What this all amounted to—packed into a tiny, filthy apartment in a city of ten thousand drunk teenagers and trying to go to school a half hour away, a school where I was asked to focus on the teacher, where class was conducted on the beach surrounded by bikinied co-eds—was a recipe for disaster.

Classes became harder and harder to attend. I became adept at stuffing envelopes with a hangover the size of Morro Rock. And by the time I turned twenty-one, my parents had cut me off financially. If I didn't leave, I'd be on the quick-and-dirty track to being another IV burnout. So at twenty-one, I moved farther south to Orange County.

"I'm not really sure where I'm going," she said as we passed from Goleta to Santa Barbara.

"That's okay."

"It's not okay. If you don't say something, we'll end up in Mexico." But she didn't smile, and her tone showed no hint of sarcasm.

"I have an idea," I said. "Let's get off at Mission. It's either this exit or the one after."

She exited onto Mission Street, and I pointed to the left. We followed the road through several residential blocks, across State Street, and once we hit Laguna, I directed her to make a left, and we began a slow, steady ascent. Before long, without much forethought of why, we were pulling into the parking lot of the Santa Barbara Mission.

Lauren parked, and we both got out without a word. Fortunately, she didn't bring the contents of Braden's cubby that had been piled on her lap for the entire drive, except for the lanyard around her neck. At first, we wandered around the mission grounds with a handful of curious tourists. The chapel and its surroundings were beautiful beyond words. The building itself maintained the simple, elegant Spanish colonial style architecture, although the picturesque chapel entrance looked almost Greek with its triangle top and faux columns that adorned the front bricks. This entrance was flanked by two tall bell towers that briefly reminded me of a football goalpost. And in front of the chapel was a large grass field. The green was vibrant and bordered with full rosebushes, red and pink and orange. And to the south was a view of the rich blue Pacific Ocean, to the east the green and brown of the Santa Ynez

Mountains. Only two hours away from home, yet here at the mission felt like another continent.

"Founded in 1786," Lauren said, pointing to a plaque.

We quickly learned, however, that this was not the original building. An earthquake in 1812 destroyed it; the one we were looking at was constructed in 1820. The bell towers were again damaged in a 1925 earthquake but subsequently rebuilt.

"Damn earthquakes," I said, just to say something.

"But look here." Lauren pointed to a sentence that told us the inside of the mission was essentially unchanged since 1820. "That's beautiful," she said.

"But we haven't even seen the inside yet."

"No, that something sacred can remain the same for over two hundred years. That's beautiful."

We peeked our heads inside, but Lauren recoiled and told me there was a blanket in the trunk if we wanted to go sit on the grass for a bit. I wasn't sure what it was about the inside that made her withdraw, but I assumed it had something to do with funerals, or crosses, or maybe even God in general.

Lauren went to the car while I continued to roam around the exterior of the mission, reading plaques and running my fingers across the rough, chalky surface of the building. I thought about all it had seen. Battles, storms, sunshine, deaths, marriages, tragedies, miracles.

We picked a spot at random on the grass. She laid out a large quilt, checkered orange and yellow and brown.

"I had to build a mission in the fourth grade," I said as I sat.

"Really," Lauren said. "So did Braden. I remember we were up all night finishing it the night before it was due."

"I made mine out of sugar cubes. You know, to look like the white stone."

"We did ours out of Popsicle sticks," she said with a sad half smile. "Looked more like a log cabin than a mission."

"Well, the glue I used ate away at the sugar. Within a day, my mission looked like it had been pummeled by acid rain."

"I never did those projects with Abby. She always did everything on her own. But Braden . . ." She looked up toward the mountains behind the mission. "He needs me."

For the most part, today had been fairly awakening. I had shared small but important events with Lauren. I had opened up to her in ways I hadn't done even with Rian or Travis lately. But there were still many moments when I didn't know what to say. If I was even allowed to say something. *He needs me.* This was one of those moments.

"I read that the name Santa Barbara of course comes from Saint Barbara," I finally said, recalling one of the plaques. "But it said that she was beheaded. By her father. She was quite young and found Christianity and then refused her father's arranged marriage." It was a stupid thing to tell Lauren. "Wild, huh?"

Lauren gave me a forced half smile. And then we sat silently for several moments. While periodic silence seemed to work in the car, it was different here. Or maybe it was because it came on the heels of what I'd just said. Or the *He needs me* that still hung in the air like smoke. Our attention briefly turned to three college-aged guys throwing a Frisbee on the grass. They whipped it back and forth in straight, tight lines as if the disc were on a taut wire strung between them.

"Are you a Christian, Conner?" she asked. "I mean, are you religious at all, go to church and all that?"

"Not really, no. I mean, I told you about my mom. So you can imagine . . . When I was a kid, we tried all sorts. And I mean all sorts. Even some ancient dead religions."

"And now?"

"Well, when I was ten I started complaining. At that time she was dragging me to Buddhist meditations. So she said when I turned twelve she would let me make my own decisions on whether to go with her to whatever flavor-of-the-week church she was into. I haven't been to a church service of any kind since my twelfth birthday."

"I can see why. But that's religion. What about faith? God?" She looked at me in search of real answers, not quirky mom anecdotes. "Is it okay that I ask you these questions, Conner?"

"Of course." And then I paused to figure out my answer. My mind was blank. In the past couple of weeks, I had questioned everything, but I wasn't sure what verbiage I was using. Was I praying? Certainly not in the traditional sense. Was I blaming someone, something, some higher power for what happened? I didn't even know.

"You don't have to answer."

"No, it's just that I'm not quite sure what my answer is. I don't know what I believe. It's a hard question to answer, I guess."

"Maybe."

I could tell she was disappointed. I thought about asking her what made God good. Telling her the little crossword joke I had learned. But it wasn't the time.

"But don't you think it's an important answer to figure out?"

"I don't know." Despite my weak, terse answers, I felt she wanted to continue the conversation. She wanted me to ask her about her beliefs, but I wasn't sure I wanted to. Could I handle hearing about how I was responsible for crushing this woman's faith on top of everything else?

I didn't ask, not right away, and we took a break to watch the guys toss the Frisbee. A little dog was off its leash now and running after the Frisbee with each throw. An endless, hopeless game of keep-away.

"But what if you never figure it out?" I asked. "I mean, really, there's no way to know the right answer. Everyone thinks their god, their way, is the only way and that everyone else is wrong, meanwhile everyone else is thinking the same thing, and no one is ever gonna really know."

"But it's not about being right. You can't look in the back of the Bible for the answer key."

"If the Bible is even the right book to look in."

"Exactly."

"Then what?" I asked.

"I think that's different for everyone."

"What's it about for you?"

She looked away when I said this, her hair moved by a midday breeze that had just arrived. It had lost some of the straightness from this morning. I liked it better now. Natural. I couldn't tell if she was thinking of an answer or if I had gone too far and she was done with the conversation.

"Hey, I'm sorry if I—"

"Can I tell you a story?"

I nodded, though was cautious about hearing another Braden story. Each new detail made the Polaroid version of him come into clearer focus. It didn't take long, however, to realize the story wasn't about Braden at all.

"My parents," she said, "were Christian Scientists. Which has nothing to do with Scientology, by the way."

"Yeah, but aren't they the ones that let their kids die because they refuse to go to doctors? I think Mom did that one for a month until she needed stronger glasses and didn't want to feel guilty going to the optometrist."

Lauren looked defensive. "Yes and no. All we hear about in the news are the extreme cases. But aren't there extremists in every group? Anyway, but no, fundamentally they don't go to doctors. They believe our bodies are temporary. It's our spirit and our soul that make us who we are. And when we are feeling sick or hurt, it's not necessarily a physical problem that needs to be fixed."

I wanted to interrupt and play devil's advocate, but she needed this to be a one-sided story. The pace of her words was steady and her tone was even.

"They pray to correct the error in their thinking. They believe that God created us all in his perfect image and likeness, and that doesn't ever change. Everything is corrected through prayer and adjusting our way of thought. *Corrected* isn't even the right word, but I think you know what I mean."

I nodded. I was listening.

"Anyway, I'm no expert. And I'm not trying to convert you to a religion I don't even believe in myself. Let me start again."

She adjusted her position before she did. Her legs, which had been out in front of her, were now crisscrossed inwards. It was childlike and made her look younger.

"My parents. They were devout Christian Scientists since they were old enough to attend Sunday school. But they weren't the extremists I mentioned earlier. I went to the eye doctor. I went to the dentist. When my brother broke his arm, we went to the hospital. Rational people know their limitations. They were always learning and trying to grow, but they knew they couldn't walk on water.

"Anyway, so a couple years ago, my dad got sick. He was in his late eighties, and I didn't even know what exactly he was feeling because they were very vague and quiet about his condition. What it was, or how bad. And then a couple months later, he passed away. Just like that. A lot of people were upset that my mother didn't take him to a doctor. 'It was probably something so manageable,' they'd say. 'He could have lived for many more years with the help of doctors,' et cetera, et cetera.

"I wasn't there the night it happened. But I know for certain that my father was at peace when he passed. He believed so incredibly strongly in his belief system that for him, he knew this physical, earthly time was not the be-all and end-all of existence. I couldn't imagine him spending his last years in and out of hospitals and doctor's offices, going against everything his whole being had believed in for more than eighty years. *That's* what would be appalling to me, not missing out on a couple extra years."

And then she stopped. But she didn't seem to be finished. Her tone wasn't that of conclusion. I imagined she was seeing her father now in her mind. Maybe replaying a particular memory. She had the softest of smiles on her face.

"And my mom . . ." By now the smile was clearly there. "She had lost the man she was married to for sixty-two years. Sixty-two years. And she handled it better than anyone in the family. Sure, she missed him. More than anything. But because of how she believed, it didn't rock her to her core like you would expect. Like it did the rest of us. She was so at peace. They spent their entire lives together believing in a particular way that . . . No, it wasn't only what they *believed*. It was who they were."

"Wow." I felt I should say more, but it was another one of those times.

"So that's what I mean when I say you have to find out what it's all about for *you*. And you alone. And then be a hundred percent in. They sure did. I'm certainly not saying Christian Science is the one right religion. I don't even follow it. But for my parents, it worked for them like you wouldn't believe, and I wouldn't have had it any other way."

As I continued to digest her story, it dawned on me that it was prompted by my asking what it was about for her, and yet she told me a story about her parents. I didn't know if I should let the conversation be, or if I should push.

"Thank you for sharing that story," was all I said. She chose to answer the question that way for a reason. Who was I to say anything?

For a random weekday, the mission was now bustling with people. The fountain that sat in front and to the right of the chapel entrance was never without a photo in progress. And while the Frisbee-chasing dog was gone, the Frisbee was still whizzing about, and a handful of other dogs were accompanying their owners around the premises.

"Are you hungry, Conner?"

As soon as she asked, I realized I was. It was a jarring feeling. Something I hadn't felt in a while. I ate occasionally, usually not, but regardless, I hadn't felt that pang of hunger in weeks.

"I am," I said.

"Do you know a good place for lunch?"

As we folded up the quilt and headed back to the Subaru, I racked my brain trying to think of places I loved when I lived here. It didn't take long for Carlito's to jump to mind. An upscale yet casual Mexican restaurant on upper State Street with a beautiful patio and live music. It seemed especially fitting after our time at the mission. But as we got back into the car, I realized I didn't want to eat at all. Yes, I was hungry. And it felt good to be hungry again. I wanted to hold on to this feeling for as long as possible.

CHAPTER 11

LAUREN ORDERED SALMON WITH PAPAYA SALSA, and I had rock shrimp tacos. I ate all three, plus the cilantro rice and black beans. But even though the food was delicious and the weather was perfect, the conversation was clunky, like two people dancing together for the first time, constantly stepping on one another's toes. She asked me how rock shrimp differed from regular shrimp, and as I began rambling about how the texture was actually closer to lobster, the waiter came to refill our waters, and we fell silent. Somehow, once we left the quilt, the grass, the mission, we each left that conversation in a different place and had to find our way back.

I didn't know what was going on in Lauren's head, and for me that was half of it. Like dancers, if I couldn't read whether she wanted to go left or right, it left me frozen in place. The other part was that I didn't know what to make of our talk. We'd moved way past small talk and seemed to be moving too fast, but too fast to where?

The one thing we could silently agree on was that we weren't ready to go back home, so after lunch we took a walk down State Street.

Leaving Carlito's patio, I thanked Lauren again for paying, but she pointed across the street and said, "Let's go look." Across from Carlito's was the Arlington Theatre, Santa Barbara's largest movie theater and performing arts venue. Another gorgeous local landmark.

The large old marquee was white and beige, Spanish-style architecture with big red plastic letters that were placed there by hand. Today it advertised *The Deer Hunter* with several showtimes as part of its throwback series. Next week: *Animal House*.

On the exterior of the glass ticket booth was another plaque. Our history lesson continued. It said that the Arlington Theatre was built in 1931 on the same grounds that used to hold the Arlington Hotel—which made me think of Manny—which was destroyed in 1925.

"Another earthquake," I said, pointing to the words.

Lauren gave me a look that said everything was hopeless. That anything strong or beautiful could be toppled in an instant.

"I used to see a lot of shows here," I said. "Not movies. Concerts."

"Braden liked to go to concerts too." As we moved on, Lauren linked arms with me, looping hers through mine like a chain. My hands remained stuffed in my pockets. Our arms barely touched, and when they did it was only because of the unsteadiness of our combined gait. Nevertheless, it was distracting. I simply nodded to her comment.

"Rock. He mostly likes rock music. Not the loud, screaming kind. Stuff with a nice guitar."

The phrase *nice guitar* hit my ears like curse words, something raunchy and wicked. I fought against the riff. The opening fuzz that persisted throughout the song. Had Braden heard it too? When the stillness settled upon South Bay Boulevard that afternoon and the rest of the world fell silent, did he hear the unrelenting guitars? Was Neil's voice the last one he heard? Lately I had been getting better at keeping thoughts like this at bay, but sometimes they snuck up unannounced, pulling me under.

I fought to get out of my head and focus on the world around me. State Street was a grown-up version of Higuera. The stores were a little bigger, a bit nicer. Even the people—while still a mix of tourists and locals—were more cultured, certainly wealthier, and even a bit more attractive.

Walking by an Italian restaurant with blackened windows was when I got a clear look at us, arm in arm. For a flashing moment in opaque glass, I saw Lauren and myself as others saw us. Arms linked. Mother and son? Lifelong friends? A couple? We were none of these things. Not remotely.

We were passing by the Santa Barbara Museum of Art when Lauren broke our arm chain and reached into her purse for her phone. After glancing at the screen, she answered it and made an intentional move away from me, trotting up the stairs of the museum.

As I stood alone on the sidewalk, I was distracted by the gesture she had made to link arms the way she did. The more I thought about it, the stranger it became. But at the same time, moments prior, when we were talking or people-watching, it wasn't weird at all.

Lauren returned sooner, or rather more abruptly, than I expected, and we once again made our way down State Street in the direction that eventually ran down to the ocean. Black asphalt became slick concrete became warm sand giving way to endless water. She was walking quicker now, her arms folded across her chest.

"That was Abby."

"Oh?"

"She didn't sound good."

"What do you mean?"

"I dunno. Her voice. She was upset."

"What did she say?"

"She asked where I was, what I was doing, when I'd be home. I lied. Said I was still running errands and that I'd be home sometime later."

"Should we head back?"

"No, no, it's okay. Something about the roadside memorial. She also told me she wanted to talk to me. But not now. In person. She said she saw you last night."

"You sure you don't want to head back?"

"No. It's okay. She's going out again tonight with friends anyway."

I could tell it wasn't okay, though. Lauren's face said that she was working something over in her mind.

"What I told you last night. About Farmer's Market," I said. "It was the truth."

"I know it was, Conner." We stopped to wait at a crosswalk for the light to turn.

We walked the next couple of blocks in silence. But there was plenty to keep us distracted. The streets were busy, and the cafes, bars, and boutiques offered plenty in the way of window shopping.

"You know, Conner, I haven't been there."

"Haven't been where?"

"To that memorial thing. On the side of the road."

"I didn't know there was—"

"A cross, flowers, maybe a photo. That kinda stuff."

We passed a homeless man, though he didn't look up. He sat cross-legged, braiding colorful beads into the long, shaggy hair of his dog, who sat in front of him. Eyes sleepy, tongue lolling.

"Abby and her friends put it up a couple weeks ago. She was so mad I didn't go. Wouldn't speak to me for days. I know that kind of thing is common and comes from a good place . . . and maybe it's important?" We slowed, watching our own feet move one in front of the other. "But I don't want that image to be part of my memory. That's not how or where I see him and think of him. Maybe I'm wrong about this. And I don't know if it's symbolic or somehow meaningful, or if it's for show or . . . or I don't know."

"It's not about being right."

"It's like the cemetery. I know he's there, I do. But that's not where he is."

After that, Lauren kept her arms folded, my hands stayed in my pockets, and we only spoke—if at all—in short fragments about things we saw. A couple blocks farther down State Street, in front of a store called the Peace Store, she came to a sudden stop. Outside the store sat a young hippie dressed in dirty tie-dye playing the bongos, who mumbled something to us that we didn't hear.

"I gotta go," Lauren said. "I'm still a mother." Her face was tightening. She repeated the phrase as we reversed direction back up State Street. "I'm still a mother, Conner."

"Abby will be okay," I said, which we both knew was an empty line.

"Yes, but I still have to be there for her. I have to be the strong one, don't

I. I have to be a mother for a sixteen-year-old-girl."

We were walking more quickly now, as if the house was up the block. When in reality, the car was fifteen minutes away, and home was another two hours.

~

It wasn't until we were passing Santa Maria that I finally said something meaningful.

"Can I ask you a question?" We were constantly asking permission from one another to do the simplest things.

"Yes, of course."

"Why did you tell me that story about your parents?" When it came out, though, it didn't sound like the question I wanted to ask. I tried again. "I mean . . . why were you curious about my religious beliefs?"

With one hand, she was still holding the brown sweatshirt in her lap. The book and the M&M's sat in the center console between our seats. Up until that point, during the hour that we were in the car, there wasn't much said. We had not shaken the funk that had settled on us like a Morro Bay fog since we left the mission.

My gaze remained at its familiar spot down at my feet while Lauren answered my question.

"I didn't ask the question to judge you, Conner." As she spoke, her eyes darted between the road, her rearview mirror, and the side mirror. "I asked to get to know you. What you think and what you feel. Something a little beyond the interview questions I asked you at the lake."

I wanted to push further. To ask her why the hell she wanted to know me in the first place. What good could this possibly be doing her? But I kept my mouth shut.

"And I told you about my parents because . . . I dunno. Because I think it's an important story. My mother was not pretending or putting on a strong face. She was truly at peace with everything. I really feel that everyone needs to figure out what they believe. Religion and otherwise. Whatever it may be. What's right for them is not necessarily right for me. And what's right for me might not be what's right for you. But once you fully believe it, *if* you fully believe it, at your core, then nothing can shake you from it. It's not a belief that's separate from you. It *is* you."

She was talking to both of us. Making her pitch. Desperate for at least one of us to get it.

"It sounds nice when you say it like that," I said. And that was true. She made it sound so simple, so comforting. Like if I could find my personal answer, like finding your car keys, then everything would be better. But I couldn't have felt further from knowing what I believed. "You said that your parents raised you in their religion, in . . ."

"Christian Science. Yes."

"But then you said you didn't follow that anymore. When did you stop?"

She continued checking her mirrors though the freeway was fairly empty, chewing on her bottom lip as if it were a piece of gum she was trying to peel off her chin.

"We were young. Peter and I." After she said this, she switched to the left lane for no apparent reason. "We hadn't even been married a year. But in that time, we moved to San Luis, bought the house, and then I got pregnant. We were invincible. Everything was playing itself out like in a movie. Fairy tales, American dreams, whatever."

She stopped talking, as if deciding to continue the story in her head only. And the longer she was silent, the surer I was of how the story ended. But she took a deep breath and continued. "I lost the baby, Conner. Like many first-time mothers do. But we were devastated. When I finally arrived from the hospital and walked into our son's empty room . . . We had painted it sky blue, even the ceiling. Peter got on a ladder and painted puffy white clouds. He said it would make our son feel limitless, lying in the crib and staring up at the sky we created for him. He would be a dreamer. Peter used to be a dreamer too. But walking back into that room. There was a crib, a bin full of stuffed animals. His name on the wall in big wooden cartoon letters . . ."

She drifted off again to finish more details in her mind. I felt like shit for drumming up the memory. I was getting too comfortable. I reminded myself of my place in this relationship.

"I can't even say his name anymore."

"I'm sorry, I didn't mean to . . ." But I was too pathetic to even continue my own apology.

"It's okay. You didn't know. So anyway, as cliché as it may sound, I stopped going to church after that. I resented Christian Science. Hated it. Blamed it. Even though I did all my prenatal appointments and checkups, I couldn't help but wonder, if my parents hadn't grounded us in these beliefs, if maybe I would have gone to the doctors more. Maybe they would have found something? Maybe something could have been done. I even thought it was science's way of getting back at my family. I know all that might seem ridiculous now, but still, I was done."

So two sons had been taken from her. Decades apart, but still, more than any mother should ever have to endure. My guilt compounded. I instantly felt responsible for both losses.

"Don't you think it's odd," she said, "that I say Braden's name all the time, but I can't say his?"

It wasn't a question I was supposed to answer.

"I think there's something strange about that. I wonder if eventually I won't be able to say Braden's name either." She flipped her blinker on and changed back into the right lane. "I have actually been able to say Braden's name much more since I met you, Conner."

This time she finished as if she were expecting a response. A smile was all I could stomach. But she returned the smile, and before I knew it, we were exiting Los Osos Valley Road.

It was after four when we pulled into my apartment complex, and there sat the fucking truck. She must have known it was mine. She had to. Newspaper photos. Police reports. Or simply motherly instincts. The guilt was overwhelming. With the day we'd had I almost, for a brief moment, let myself forget why we knew each other. Or rather, I hoped for a moment that *she* had forgotten. But seeing the truck sitting there, silent and smug, a screaming, in-your-face reminder of why Lauren and I were together today, was like a flashing neon sign, and there was nothing I could do to hide it.

But when the Subaru's tires came to a stop atop the bed of dry pine needles, she put the car in park and looked over at me with an expression of gratitude. And suddenly I was shocked at the intensity with which I didn't want to leave her.

"Thank you, Conner. For coming with me today." She patted the sweatshirt on her lap to remind me of where the day had started. "You have no idea how much . . ."

Again, I could only smile. How ridiculous of me to think that road trips and rock shrimp tacos and old missions could distract her into flashes of forgetting. This wasn't something she remembered or forgot, this was simply something she now was.

"And thank you for telling me about last night."

Farmer's Market. The altercation last night seemed like years ago.

Before I could respond, she made a move to hug me. But we both still had our seat belts on, not to mention the center console and emergency brake, and I felt like we were stretching across the Grand Canyon to reach each other. My arms extended enough for my fingertips to reach her back as the seat belt tightened and pulled at my chest and shoulder. The green lanyard knocked against my chest as it swung like a pendulum between us. The hug was awkward and the opposite of intimate, or even friendly.

When I opened the door to leave, she stopped me. "Conner?"

"Yeah?"

"I would have driven to Mexico today."

"Yeah," I said. "Me too."

And that was our way. Our way of saying that today mattered. And that we would see each other again soon.

I opened the door to my apartment, the somber glow of twilight through half-opened blinds was enough to illuminate my world: Travis on my couch, elbows on knees, shaking his head. Rian at the dining room table, head in her hands, crying. My entire basketball team sitting in a circle on the living room floor, Coach Rich leading them in the butterfly stretch. Twelve sets of knees sticking up like leftover chicken bones. Even Donnie in the kitchen, frying something that spat and crackled on the stovetop. Jimmy next to him, leaning on the counter in a bony slouch, smoking a sloppy hand-rolled cigarette. And even through the hum of the crowded apartment and the roar of my truck's engine outside, I could hear my mother's shrill voice on the answering machine, pleading for me to call her. Her voice on a loop, never getting cut off by the beep.

I bypassed it all, and without so much as turning on a light, headed for my bedroom. I collapsed, back-first, onto my mattress. I hadn't been gone that long. Roughly eight hours by the clock, but it felt like weeks to my body. It was then I remembered that Donnie had fired me. Money was going to be a problem. It was already a problem, but it was about to get a lot worse. Mostly I thought of my day with Lauren. I replayed each event, trying to remember the things she said, the looks she gave, how the shrimp tacos tasted and how her car smelled. I was helping her. We were helping each other.

With what little natural light remained, I caught a glimpse of the book on my pile of laundry. The book from Rian. It was strange; part of me missed her terribly. But when I tried to think of why or what I missed about her, I had trouble coming up with answers.

I turned my phone over and over in my hand like a magician with a deck of cards. There were three voicemails and five text messages I had not yet opened or listened to. But that was not what I was mulling over. I assumed they were from Travis and Rian, and I would get to them eventually. But I wanted to call Lauren. I wanted to know what Abby had said about Farmer's

Market. I wanted to know if Lauren had thought about each event of the day like I had. I didn't even know what I wanted, but I wanted her to call me. Or me to call her. But I didn't. Even after our all-day trip to Santa Barbara. I wasn't allowed to call her. That's not how it worked.

Fully dressed, lying perpendicular across the bed, atop the covers, I fell asleep and fell asleep hard. I was awoken by a loud racket. At first, in my half-conscious state, I couldn't tell if it was down the street or in my apartment or even in my bedroom. Initially it was a bang, but as I began to come to, it changed into a scream. But not from a person. More mechanical. And it was getting louder. It was definitely in my apartment. When I was finally able to shake the sleep from my head, I realized it was my front door. Whoever was there was interspersing knocking and ringing the doorbell. It was rushed but not frantic. Purposeful but not panicked.

I stumbled through the apartment, running purely on instinct, not even able to guess at who it might be. I opened the door without turning on the porch light, so the only light came from the fragment of a moon. But I didn't need more than that to recognize the contours of Lauren's face. She stood at my doorstep, shivering and crying.

CHAPTER 12

THE NOTE LAY ON MY COFFEE TABLE LIKE EVIDENCE. Of what, I wasn't sure, but it didn't belong there. Yet I couldn't stop staring at it, at the handwriting. The whole mess felt like a crime scene I wasn't supposed to see. The way the letters ran one into the next, not quite printing, not quite cursive. And the *i*'s were topped not with dots, but with full, sloppy circles.

Lauren had pulled it out of her pocket when she first arrived, gripping it tight as she fell onto the couch. Maybe it was sitting down, or maybe it was my presence, but something dried her tears right away. She dropped the note, still folded in quarters, onto her lap and began talking.

"Abby," Lauren said. "I don't know where she is. She left. She didn't come home. And Peter was . . . and . . ." She started to get herself worked up again. She took a slow, deep breath and looked at me with puffy red eyes.

"Just tell me," I said. "What happened when you got home?"

And as if my voice alone had straightened her spine and wiped her eyes, she began again. "I got home and the house was empty. Dark. Peter's car was in the driveway, but I couldn't find him anywhere."

I wanted to reach out and cradle her hands in mine. She looked so lonely on the other side of the couch in a room foreign to her. But my hands remained in my lap, picking at nails already too short.

"After calling and calling for Peter and checking every room and trying his cell phone and then Abby's, I finally had no other option." She looked at me, her eyes asking for forgiveness. Pleading for me not to judge her.

"What?"

"It was my last option, Conner. I had to. I opened his door."

I instantly understood. She'd opened the crypt she had promised herself she wouldn't.

"And Peter was in there, Conner. In Braden's room. Lying on the bed as if nothing was wrong. He was still in his work clothes. Jacket, tie, even his shoes. I think he was sleeping. Maybe all my yelling woke him, because he was groggy and disoriented. I asked him what in the world he was doing, why he was in there, where was Abby."

"What did he say?"

Then Lauren laughed a sad laugh. "Nothing at first. I asked him again, and all he said was 'She went out.' That's it. I asked him where she went and with who and when she was coming back—I always ask—but he just kind of nodded, and I told him to get off the bed. To get out of the room. We had talked about not going in there, messing things up, changing things, changing the smell. He's going to ruin the smell!"

She stopped, and I knew well enough to stay quiet too. She had spat so much out that she needed to catch her breath. The clock behind her read 2:51. Outside was still, not so much as a car passing. Even the crickets had turned in for the night. And in the same way Lauren would have driven to Mexico earlier today, I was prepared to sit in silence until sunrise.

And then she continued, her voice a little quieter, softer. "So he came out. And he followed me into the family room, where you and I sat."

My mind flashed to the piano. The family portrait. The coffee table with the magazines. The cold of the room. So fucking cold. And then Abby's anger echoing off the walls.

"He told me a guy came to pick her up. A guy he had never seen before. And she left with him. That's all he knew. She's only sixteen, Conner, and he let her go. And he said he didn't even know how he ended up on the bed—he only remembered being tired and wanting to lie down."

I looked down at the note. She picked it up and rubbed the crease back and forth between her thumb and forefinger. "Oh yes, this," she said and handed me the paper, still folded several times over. "After Peter went to bed, to *our* bed, I stayed up. Paced around the house with my phone. I sent her a text, asking her to call me. But nothing. At some point, I wandered into her room and found this on her pillow. I don't know how I missed it earlier."

She nodded for me to open it. As I did, my stomach knotted and my throat tightened. It was like seeing a girl naked for the first time, wanting so badly to look, but also scared out of my mind. In black pen, in loopy handwriting, the note read:

I went out. Maybe I'll be back tonight. Maybe I won't. I told this to Dad, but we both know what good that does. I would tell you not to wait up, but I know you wouldn't anyway. I needed you today and you weren't there. You're a bad mother.

It was this last line that got me. And I knew that's what got Lauren. Most of it read like the angry rant of a moody teenager. But the last line—*You're a bad mother*—was so simple, so definitive. It would have been better had it read *I hate you*, because that you could write off as emotion, as lashing out with the intention to hurt. But this line seemed so calm, so matter-of-fact. *You're a bad mother*. I dropped the letter onto the coffee table and it landed writing-side open, but with its edges curled as if it were trying to fold itself back up.

"She's only sixteen, Conner. A baby."

"Have you heard anything from her?"

"No. I sat up and I waited and waited with my phone in my lap, staring at the time ticking away. I sat until I couldn't take it anymore, and then I came here. Didn't know what else to do."

"Have you called any of her friends?"

"No. I don't really know any of her friends. Maybe I am a . . . Well, I dunno, she doesn't even have that many."

I hadn't a clue what to say. How to find Abby. How to make Lauren feel better, if only for tonight. Or how to fix the family I had single-handedly destroyed. For the most part, we sat. I watched the dull green numbers on the clock behind her change every minute, but each one felt like five. Lauren mostly stared across the room. Technically she was looking at the TV and the cabinet with the DVD player and stereo. The messy piles of CDs, the dusty blinds, the stack of *Sports Illustrated* that slumped against the wall, leaning to the right, ready to topple. But she wasn't looking at any of those things. Not really.

Occasionally, we looked at each other. Brief glances, slow and purposeful, as if seeking validation. Checking that the other person was still there, and that it was okay for us to be there, sitting in the darkness of the early morning in complete silence.

It was after about ten minutes that it dawned on me that I couldn't speak first. It wasn't my place. This was what she needed, so I was going to give it to her for as long as necessary. When I came to this understanding, I felt a twinge of relief. I didn't have to think of the right thing to say. All I had to do was sit. To be here at the other end of the lumpy brown couch.

At 3:26 I thought about Lauren's mother. Had she wept in private for her husband, only appearing strong in front of others? Or was there really an inner peace that others couldn't comprehend?

At 3:51 I forced myself to stop staring at the note on the table and thought about the book in Braden's cubby. *The Anubis Gates*. Had he started it? Finished? Or maybe left off somewhere hopelessly, forever in the middle?

At 4:14 I thought about Neil Young and the song that was playing when I rounded that curve on South Bay. Bits and pieces of the lyrics coming at me in spurts, haunting me like a soothsayer. The damn song that kept playing and playing and playing. Unapologetic.

The next time our eyes met, Lauren's held mine. She wanted to say something. If she asked me if she was a good mother, I had the *yes* waiting on the doorstep of my tongue. But she didn't ask that. Not even close.

"Conner," she began as she usually did. "Do you think Braden ever had sex?"

Blindsided by the question, my throat seized up like an old motor.

"I mean, I know there's no way for you to actually know that. But I'm curious, and you're a guy, and I dunno, I wanted to ask it out loud. Part of me hopes he did, because I want him to have experienced everything. But I don't know, the mother in me, the part of me that wants to protect him from messiness and disappointment, kind of hopes he didn't."

Again I wanted to reach for her hand but sat paralyzed.

"Maybe it sounds silly and cliché, but sometimes I still think of him as seven years old. Shaggy hair, nose in a book."

Suddenly aware that my right leg was asleep, I shook it loose as I continued to listen.

"He didn't really have girlfriends. Sure, he's well liked and always with plenty of friend-friends. But not girlfriends. At least not that he told me about. So that makes me think that if he *did* have sex, it would have been the one-night type. And that's not the same thing. That's not the experience I hope for him."

Outside, a car sped by. It was alone and going much too fast. At this hour, at that speed, I worried for the driver.

"Conner, is that a weird question? Should I not have asked that?"

"I don't think there are weird or wrong questions."

Then we fell into a deep pause before she spoke again.

"Conner. It's late. Do you think I could lie down? I don't want to go home tonight."

"I think the night has come and gone. But yeah. Let me make up my bed for you." Walking to my room, I had no recollection of what state it might be in. I turned on the bedside lamp, and aside from the mountain of laundry and the cluttered desk, it wasn't too bad. The bed was still made, but it looked as though someone had been sleeping on top of the bedspread. Which I had, for several nights in a row now. I wanted to hide the laundry and remake the bed a little, but before I could take another step, I felt Lauren's presence behind me.

"Thank you, Conner. I just need to lie down for a bit."

"Yes, of course, I'm sorry it's not nicer, but—"

"It's perfect," she said, and moved past me into the room. She slipped out of her shoes and pulled the bedspread and sheet back enough to crawl inside.

I reached under the lampshade and switched off the light, then turned to head back to the couch.

"Conner?"

I froze mid-step.

"Will you lie with me?" Her voice was as thin and soft as an eyelash.

"Of course," I said out of habit, yet my body still hadn't moved.

"I just don't want to be alone."

The room was pitch black. I knew where the bed and nightstand were from muscle memory, but I didn't know exactly where Lauren was. I felt around gingerly and found the edge of the covers. I pulled them back and got into bed. I felt the weight of her on the mattress, the heat of another body under the sheets, but we weren't touching, not even accidentally. Not like how she linked arms with me a century ago on State Street. I wondered if maybe I should have stayed on top of the covers. But then I realized details like that were trivial now. A tiny island in this universe I had created.

"You know"—Her voice was soft, but I could hear it clearly. We were sharing the same space—"this bedroom reminds me a lot of Braden's."

I opened my mouth to say something meaningless like "oh," but nothing came out.

"Yeah, I mean like the layout. The way the desk is over to the left from the bed, and how there are two windows. One across from the bed and one to the, well, Braden's was on the left, but yours is on the right. But still, I feel like I'm in his room right now."

Even though we were in early morning Los Osos, in those frigid moments between the middle of the night and when the sun wakes up, the heat under the blankets was immense. I imagined if I looked under the covers, Lauren would be pulsing orange and red like the lazy coals at the end of a good fire.

"Do you have anything on the wall?" she asked. "I didn't notice."

"Not really, no. Even though I've been here four or so months, I guess I haven't fully settled in, you know?"

"I can almost see Braden's posters." She adjusted her legs, her left ankle crossing over my right shin. I didn't think she meant to do it, but she also didn't undo it. For the second time today, our limbs intertwined like vines of ivy.

"I used to have a lot of posters when I was in high school," I said.

"Braden had a huge *Lord of the Rings* one. And then he had one over his bed that was *Star Wars*. Or *Star Trek*, maybe. I always get those two mixed up. It drives him crazy. There was a third one, though, by the closet . . . What was it?"

She stopped, and I could feel her digging at her memory, walking back into his room, trying to visualize every detail. She wasn't allowing herself to go into the room physically, but she was in there now. And she wanted to bring me with her.

"It's blue with like . . . Or green, maybe. Damn it, why can't I remember?"

I heard the frustration in her voice. As if the poster represented how well she knew him. Or maybe how fast she was already forgetting those small, irrelevant details that meant everything.

"I mostly had sports posters." She was listening, but only partly. "You know, Michael Jordan, those types. But I would have loved a *Star Wars* one too."

We were creating a thin layer of sweat in the crease between her ankle and my shin. It was a small contact point, really, but it was now warm and slick.

She was quiet for a while, and I didn't know if she was asleep or still trying to remember the third poster, or if there was something else she was drowning in. I continued to lie still, so still that the muscles in my legs and arms and back were teetering on the edge of cramping, my bones petrifying. Dying to move, to stretch, to bend, but I couldn't risk it.

"Do you think Abby is okay?" When she broke the audible silence, Lauren also broke the stillness in the bed. Her ankle slid off my shin, and she rotated her whole body toward me until she was on her side, bent like a zigzag.

She put her hands flat on my shoulder, then her head on her hands as if on a pillow.

"I'm sure she is. She seems like a smart, strong girl." I felt Lauren's breath on my chest with her every exhale. It was warm and frightening. "I'm sure she just needs to be distracted right now. With friends."

"Oh, Conner, I had a horrible image. What if she comes home at this ungodly hour and I'm not there?"

"It's so late. You stayed until after two. If she were coming home it would have happened by then. You'll see her in the morning." I didn't even know what I was saying. My mouth functioning separately from my brain.

"You're right. Oh, but could you imagine?" Her hands created a light layer of sweat against my shoulder, and her breath continued to dig a path from my shoulder down to my stomach. A diagonal stripe of warmth across my chest.

"I dunno. Maybe I should go. Just in case."

"Yes, of course." My voice was no longer my own.

"I want to stay here."

And then we lay in that position in silence for lifetimes. Generations of stars made their way across the sky above us. I imagined the constellations circling us, Orion and the Big Dipper and the Little Dipper and all the others I didn't know, in orbit around our stillness.

If the sun was already coming up, only the living room and kitchen knew about it. The blinds in my room could keep out the radiance of heaven. They were dark and thick and worked like a force field against the day.

Even though Lauren didn't move, I didn't think she was asleep. Her breath told me as much. It was conscious breathing. And if her finger moved even a twitch, it sent screaming alarms through my entire nervous system. Once, when her index finger went from straight to a ninety-degree angle back to straight again, I worried about getting an erection. These things were beyond my control. I had to fight off the idea of a hard-on again when she adjusted her head and the softness of her hair fell around my shoulder and tickled the base of my neck. I wasn't turned on sexually, but the intimacy and the intensity were overwhelming.

"Braden had this alarm clock shaped like the Batmobile." The sound of her voice was a relief. A sense other than touch to focus on. "At night, you'd push this button and it showed the bat symbol on the ceiling. Then it woke him up each morning with that annoying theme music."

I tried humming the song, but it caught and stuttered in my throat. A dumb idea.

"He loved comic books, especially when he was younger. And fantasy novels. I told you that, right, that I used to have to give him a reading curfew? That didn't stop him. He kept a flashlight under his bed, but I never let on that I knew."

I could hear a faint smile in her voice. When she finished, she began running her finger up and down the length of my collarbone, the thin fabric of my old T-shirt turning to dust. I shut my eyes to concentrate. Not on any one thing, but on nothing at all. Not on her hand gripping my shoulder. Not on the weight of her head on me. Not on the feathery brushing of her hair against my neck or her breath swirling and moving like trade winds across my chest. And certainly not on the pad at the tip of her index finger that swam laps up and down my clavicle.

"The Beatles!" Lauren blurted out, and shot up in bed. She sat up straight, resting on her hands like stilts. She looked down on me, but the darkness of the room prohibited us from seeing each other's faces. For this I was grateful. "The third poster was the Beatles. Of course! The famous shot of them walking in a line across the crosswalk. *Abbey Road*."

"A classic."

"Geez. How could I forget?"

"It's been a long day. It's okay. You remembered."

"*Abbey Road*," she said again, this time as if saying the name of an ex-boyfriend she was remembering fondly.

"So he was a big Beatles fan?" Drums began in my head. That familiar, relentless, haunting beat of the song, trancelike.

"He wasn't big into music, but he loves the Beatles. When he was little, he always wanted me to sing them to him or put our old records on. You like the Beatles, Conner?"

"They're the best for a reason, right?"

"Braden used to say something like that."

In truth I had always been more of a Stones fan. The Beatles may have been innovators, but their stuff didn't hold up as well as the Stones. But none of that mattered now.

With that, Lauren lowered herself back onto the bed. She lay like I did, on her back, our arms and legs not so much touching as grazing one another as we breathed.

"That's where we got Abby's name from."

"*Abbey Road?*"

"Yeah. Silly, I know. But Peter and I used to be crazy for them. Had all their albums on vinyl. Do you have a favorite Beatles song, Conner?"

"Wow, I don't know. That's tough." I scrambled to think of something from *Abbey Road*. "Maybe 'Come Together'?"

"Really?" I felt her head turn toward me. "That was Braden's favorite too." Her body followed, and she hitched herself onto her side again. "Well, maybe, I dunno, at least one of his favorites."

Then her head returned to staring at the black of the ceiling as if we were stargazing.

"When he was a baby I used to sing him this Beatles lullaby every night as I put him to bed. And then as he got older, if he was sick or couldn't sleep, he always asked me to come hold him and sing our song."

"What song was it?"

"Well, technically it's not the Beatles, but John Lennon. 'Beautiful Boy.' He wrote it for his son Sean."

"Hmm, I don't think I know it."

And then we were silent again. In the dark of the early morning, I could feel she was on her side, facing me, her head held up by her hand, but I didn't know anything else. Where she was looking, *how* she was looking, what she was thinking.

"Conner?" When she said my name, she put her hand on my chest. Her full palm and spread fingers rose and fell with me as I breathed. "Can I . . . Can I sing that song for you?"

I lay still, staring into the black, feeling the warmth of her hand on my chest. But she knew the answer was yes.

"But can you do me a favor first?" she asked. "Can you turn the other way? Away from me."

I did as she asked and rolled to my side, my back now to Lauren. My body reveled in the movement. Muscles and bones yawning with relief.

"It's not that I'm shy, it's that . . . this was always how I sang it to him when he was little." And then her body came up behind me. Her bent legs fit like puzzle pieces behind mine. Her hips pressed flush against my butt, her stomach flush against my back. I felt her breasts pushed against my upper back, and finally her right hand wrapped around my body. It wrapped all the way around me until her fingers tucked between my ribs and the mattress, caging me within her.

"Braden didn't like to watch me as I sang. He just liked to listen as I held him."

As she said this, I closed my eyes and exhaled so heavily my entire body sank deeper into the mattress, deeper into Lauren's one-armed embrace.

"Thank you, Conner."

Her breath on me made the hairs on my arm stand at attention.

"The song actually begins with the crashing of waves. He always liked me to do that part too." And then she made a couple *whooshing* sounds, her breath warm as it blanketed the back of my neck. She inhaled ever so slightly and began to sing.

Her voice was soft and beautiful. As she sang, her lips brushed against the back of my neck, only occasionally, only on certain words. The lyrics were that of a sweet goodnight lullaby, a dad to his son, scaring away the monsters, though she changed "daddy" to "mommy," and her arm squeezed around my torso as she sang the chorus. Such a simple chorus. A father telling his son how beautiful he was. There was so much love in the words, so much love in Lauren's voice.

And with each repeated "*b*" sound, her lips brushed against the back of my neck, almost like a kiss. My body was pure electricity.

She continued to squeeze me closer, and I responded by leaning back into her, our bodies working together to create an incredible heat. The song a perfect, soft lullaby, a goodnight prayer, something that would fill a child with safety and assurance. Her voice in my ear was as smooth as her lips on my neck. I was sinking deeper.

The song called for the boy to take her hand, and I did. I grabbed the hand that held me tightly. My fingers interlocking with hers. Yet it was her voice that held us together. She tried to pull me in even closer, but we were already pressed hard against one another. I squeezed her hand in response and then she kissed the back of my neck softly, so softly that had my every skin cell not been on heightened awareness, I might have missed it.

As she continued to repeat the chorus, her voice wavered but didn't weaken. Even though she was singing the words, I could feel her need to say them, to repeat them, as if the words had been trapped inside her, frantic buzzing bees she was finally setting free. Proclaiming her love to her beautiful boy, and then with the last line she went off course, replacing the final word, her beautiful *Braden*.

And with that, I broke.

The tears fell individually at first, but with each successive one, they gained in speed and number. They gained their own momentum, and I lost control. Soon I was in a full sob, my wet face contorted and my whole body seized. It was the whole day upon me. It was the way Lauren looked at me, the way her body felt against mine. It was the Batmobile alarm clock. It was her voice as she sang. It was the posters on the wall. Her breath on my neck. The brown sweatshirt on her lap. It was his name in the song. It was every fucking thing. I cried and cried and cried, and I couldn't stop it. I was a runaway truck, no brakes, barreling downhill into oblivion.

Lauren continued to hold me as I shook and convulsed inside her embrace. She whispered the chorus once more, though it was barely audible, and I didn't know who she was whispering to.

Eventually, as my body wore down, my sobs became less chaotic and more rhythmic. It was then that I felt the wetness on the back of my neck. While my face was a salty, snotty mess, the wetness on the back of my neck was not my own. This made me stop crying altogether. While I was a bawling mess, she had been behind me, crying soft, quiet tears. Individual droplets ran down the curve of my neck until they could no longer hug my skin, and dropped to the sheet below.

Neither of us said a word or made another sound or even so much as shifted an arm or a leg. And I didn't know if it was five minutes or two hours, but we stayed like that until we both fell asleep at some unknown early hour of the morning.

Chapter 13

LAUREN WOKE UP IN A PANIC AND LEAPT OUT OF bed, thumbing her phone for missed calls, voicemails, text messages, anything. But there were none. None from her daughter and none from her husband.

"I have to go, Conner."

"Of course."

"I know I'm a bad mother."

"You're not a—"

"Please don't," she said, and put her hand up.

We made our way to the kitchen, which was bright with the morning sun. I offered her coffee or something to eat, but she declined and said she had to get home before Abby did.

As I walked her to the front door, she ran her hands through her hair several times and rubbed the salt from her eyes. My own face felt like a mess. My eyes were raw and dry; they burned.

"I know everything is okay with Abby," I said as I followed her to her car, my truck looming, a five-thousand-pound reminder in our peripherals. "But will you text me when you hear from her?"

"Of course, Conner."

She was still trying to get her keys into the lock when Travis's car came over the hill of 11th. He pulled into the parking space on the other side of Lauren's car. Our three cars lined up like one happy fucking family.

Lauren didn't bat an eye as she didn't know Travis. But Travis certainly saw Lauren, saw me standing beside some woman at seven thirty in the morning. He turned the engine off but remained in the car. I couldn't see clear enough through the glare of the windshield, but there appeared to be someone sitting beside him in the passenger seat.

"Goodbye, Conner," Lauren said.

I didn't even get out a goodbye before her car door shut. Lost in the sound of her door closing was the opening of Travis's door. And the passenger door. I felt his eyes on me as I watched Lauren back out and disappear down 11th. She gave one quick wave, and then she was gone.

It was Manny who emerged from the passenger side of Travis's car. He was the first to speak.

"Amigo," he said with caution. But neither of them approached. They stood next to the car and watched me.

"Hi, guys," I said as I made my way back toward the apartment. They still didn't move. "You, uh, want to come in?"

"No," Travis said. "Put some shoes on and come with us."

"What?"

"Put some shoes on," he repeated, slow and deliberate as if talking to a child, "and come with us."

"What? Why? Where are we going? It's not even eight."

But Manny was already stuffing his large body into the back seat, while Travis brushed pine needles off the hood of my truck.

What choice did I have? He clearly was not messing around. I went back into my apartment, which instantly chilled me to the bone. I didn't know if it was because I had been standing in the direct sunlight or if it was the ghost of Lauren still lingering in the apartment, but I was freezing. I put on my shoes and grabbed a thin blue sweatshirt off the pile of laundry in the corner.

"Okay, this is ridiculous," I said from the passenger seat. We were driving up 11th toward Los Osos Valley Road. "Tell me where we're going."

"It's kind of funny," Travis said, "that you're the one asking questions."

He was pissed. I got that. I'd missed at least three meetings within the last week. Not to mention the unreturned phone calls.

"Look, amigo," Manny said from the back seat. "We only want to help you, man."

"Yes," Travis said. "This is for your own good."

"What, kidnapping me?"

"Oh, stop being so dramatic. We're not kidnapping you. But you do need an intervention. Especially after what we saw back there."

We were on Los Osos Valley Road heading toward San Luis. But this didn't tell me much.

"You don't know what you saw back there."

"Exactly," Travis said.

Most of the drive was quiet. Whatever ambush they had planned for me, they were waiting until we arrived at our location. Manny briefly told Travis about a woman he had been chatting with online.

"Colombia makes the most beautiful women in the world, my friends," Manny said with a laugh. "Most people think coffee or maybe drugs is their biggest export, but they're wrong. It's women. They send to the world the most beautiful women."

"Did you just call women an export?" Travis laughed a controlled laugh into the rearview mirror.

"Por favooor. You know what I mean."

"Yeah," Travis laughed. "I know exactly what you mean."

"Talking of women, you hear about Travis, amigo? He's done. No more girls."

"I didn't say no more girls. Just that I'm taking a break." Travis paused to look at me purposefully. "You know, to focus on the restaurant a hundred percent."

"Sí, sí, we'll see how long that lasts, my friend."

"I mean it, no more bullshittin'."

Manny said something in Spanish quick like a dart, and they both laughed.

The banter continued back and forth as if I weren't even there. And in some ways, I wasn't. My hand rested outside my shorts pocket, anxious to feel a vibration from my phone, a text from Lauren letting me know about

Abby. My body was still in my bed, feeling the warmth of Lauren next to me, the weight of her body close to mine. But my mind was concocting a story that would explain a woman's presence in my driveway at seven this morning. Maybe she was a neighbor, and we were chatting this morning when I went out to get yesterday's mail? Or maybe she was a stranger who pulled over when her car broke down. I helped her call AAA. Each lie was worse than the previous. Whatever, when it came time, I'd pick one and be adamant enough about it that Travis had no choice but to believe me. But my mind was also swirling underwater from lack of sleep. Nothing was clear and thoughts were like fish, never staying still long enough for me to grab one.

When we turned onto Higuera, I knew exactly where we were going: the restaurant. I felt like an idiot for not figuring it out sooner. Travis noticed the realization on my face and smiled and nodded. After finding a spot directly in front of the empty restaurant, he popped the trunk, and he and Manny unloaded two large boxes.

Travis handed me his box when we got to the door so he could unlock it.

"What's in here?" I asked. The box was heavier than expected.

He swung the door open and motioned me in. The room was empty and smelled of dust and stale air. Our footsteps echoed off the hardwood floor. Manny and Travis set the boxes down and looked over at me, Travis with his hands on his hips and Manny scratching at his head.

"Well," Travis said, clapping his hands together. The echo reverberated dramatically throughout the space. "Should we give Manny a tour first?" He was smiling. This all seemed to be part of some premeditated plan.

We circled around the main rectangular dining area with its hardwood flooring, white walls, and long accent wall of old brick.

"I think," Travis said, rotating in place, "we could fit ten to fifteen tables in here. Then that alcove there . . ." He pointed toward the front door. To the right of it was a space that could maybe fit an L-shaped couch. "That's our waiting area. With the hostess stand to the left of the entrance."

"I love it, mis amigos," Manny said, looking the place over and rubbing his round, firm belly. "I love it!"

"And there . . ." Travis pointed to the white wall on the right, which only went two-thirds of the way up. "In that gap between the wall and the ceiling . . . I was thinking we fill that space with wine bottles . . . you know, with a nice antique wood rack."

Manny nodded.

"Let me show you the kitchen," Travis said, and motioned us both to the back right of the room. "Where Conner works his magic."

The kitchen was galley style: long and rectangular. A stainless steel island ran the length of the room. To the right, along the three-quarter wall, was endless counter space with metal cupboards hung above and shelves below. To the left was more counters, but also a series of black-crusted stovetops, and ovens where black and brown grease stains spread outward from every crack and crevice like a virus.

"Those," Travis said, looking at me and pointing to the stovetops, "are being replaced today."

"Today?" I said.

"They'll be here between nine and twelve."

None of this seemed important. I couldn't believe I still hadn't heard from Lauren. Whether she was with Abby or not, why hadn't she let me know? And what exactly happened last night?

Back in the main dining room, Travis went over to the boxes and bent to open them. "We're here for two reasons. Conner? Shit, man, are you even listening?"

"Yeah, yeah, I'm here. What's up?"

As Travis spoke, he began emptying the contents of the boxes: rags, paintbrushes, rollers, drop cloths. "For one, we're painting this side wall and the back wall."

And while painting was the last thing I wanted to do, I played along.

"Okay, whatever," I said. "And the second thing?"

Manny shot a look over to Travis.

"Like I said in the car," Travis said. "You need a damn intervention. I'm not joking. I don't know what's going on with you these days. I'll even ignore the fact that you've blown me off entirely, but I don't know where you've been or what you've been doing or what you're even thinking or feeling. Something is not right."

"What? Jesus. I'm fine. Fuck."

"And who the hell was that woman this morning? You're not fine, by the way."

The three of us remained still and looked at one another. The echo of our voices in the empty restaurant made each word more dramatic, shooting around the room like racquetballs. It was profoundly irritating.

"I don't want to talk about her," I said, shaking my head.

"Well, you're going to," Travis said.

By this point, Manny had broken into the other box and was taking out paint cans. Travis threw me a roll of blue tape.

"Here. Start taping off all the edges. Along the floor, around the door to the kitchen, the two windows in the back."

I obeyed and was soon on my hands and knees along the side wall, while Manny was doing the same along the back wall.

"Okay, so let's start with her. Who is she and what the hell were you doing?" Travis said as he tore new brushes and rollers out of their packaging.

"No one. I told you I don't want to talk about it." The tape I was placing along the floor was a drunken line. "Besides, it sure sounds like you have quite an agenda today. What other items are on your list?"

"Alright, fine, you don't want to talk about her right now. We'll start with something else. But we will get back to her."

"Whatever."

"Your job. The Sea & Sky? What happened?"

Shit. It hadn't even been twenty-four hours.

"So you know?" I said.

"What happened?"

"Obviously you know, so why you gotta make me say it?"

"Don't fight us here, amigo," Manny chimed in. "We here to help. Let's just talk, my friend."

"I got fired," I said. "As you already know."

"Because you never showed up?" Travis asked. He was now taping down large square drop cloths to the edges I had already cleared with tape.

"Yeah, but whatever, Donnie was a dick and that job sucked."

"I don't care if the job sucked or not. It's irresponsible. You're not a kid anymore."

"And you're not my dad."

Travis and I had never spoken to one another like that. But it surprised me how it didn't feel that weird. Everything was different now, so why should that exclude Travis?

"No, I'm not. But how are you going to pay rent? Buy food? Where's your money coming from?"

"Wait, what? Didn't you want me to quit that place anyway once we started Further? I'm here, right? We're starting."

"Yeah, we'll get to that later."

I didn't know what that meant, and when I looked at him, he saw that I was finished with the edge along the floor and pointed to the waiting alcove.

"There too," he said, and followed me with more drop cloths. "Okay, and so how's Rian?"

"What do you mean? She's fine."

"Is she?"

"When's the last time you called her, amigo?" Manny added.

"I dunno. Why are you guys ambushing me?"

Travis froze, dropped his hands to his sides, and looked at me. "Look, I'm sorry, man, I really am. And I don't mean to come off this way. But there's a theme here, don't you see? Rian. The Sea & Sky. Your meetings with the meat guy. Your meetings with me. God only knows how the basketball team is doing. We don't mean to ambush you, but we do want to help you."

"What if I don't need help?"

"Am I wrong about any of those things?"

I stretched the tape and ripped off foot-long chunks, then ran them in the crevice between the hardwood floor and the white baseboards. Travis continued to follow me, taping drop cloths, and Manny was somewhere near the back of the room. Our voices and steps continued to echo.

"She called me, you know," Travis said.

"Who? Rian?"

"She's worried about you. You don't call, you don't text. She's a million miles away and has no clue how you're doing. And it's safe to assume she doesn't know anything about that woman you were walking to the car this morning."

"And what did you tell her?"

"The truth. That I didn't know either. But I promised her I would find out."

I was finishing the last corner of the alcove, running tape along and around the front door. "I can't believe she called you," I said, more to myself. "I mean, she barely knows you."

"She's concerned. That's a good thing. She cares."

"There's a good girl there, amigo," Manny called from the back of the room, his low voice vibrating the floors.

"What do you want me to say? Promise to call her? I will."

Travis gave me a look.

"I will. Jesus."

With all our edges taped and the floors sufficiently covered, the three of us met in the middle of the room where the paint and brushes were. Travis shook one of the cans while Manny prepped paint trays.

"Let's all take a small brush and work the borders," Travis said. "Once we outline everything, it will be a piece of cake to knock out the walls with the rollers."

"You got a ladder?" Manny asked.

"Out back." Travis then popped open the top of a can, using his keys around the edges of the lid. He poured out a pumpkin orange into one of the trays.

"Wait, what's that?" I asked. "I thought we agreed on a natural palette, browns and greens?"

"We're going with this for the back wall. And rich blue for the side wall and the waiting area. We thought it would work better with the brick. You know, give the room more pop."

"Since when? And *we* decided? Who is *we*?"

"You haven't been around. Remember that meeting you were supposed to have with me on Friday? Manny has been helping a lot. Trust us, these colors will work better in here."

Wordlessly, Manny took the tray and a brush and retreated to start on the edges of the back wall. Meanwhile, Travis shook another can of paint and pried at the lip of the lid with his keys.

"Rian's not the only person who called me."

"Who else?"

"Dale Ruthemeyer."

"Who the hell is that?"

"Really, you don't know? He's from the *Tribune*. He's been trying to talk to you since the accident. He wants to do a full story about you and the boy's family. A person piece. Really sit down and talk to you."

It sounded weird to hear Travis refer to Lauren as *the boy's family*. He wasn't allowed to talk about them. "I've never heard of this guy," I said.

"Well, I talked to him a couple times right at the beginning. When I was answering the phone at your house."

"What did you tell him?"

"I said I'd talk to you. See where you're at. I'm supposed to call him back on Monday."

"What? I don't want to talk to him. Fuck that guy."

Travis didn't push, but he gave me a look. With my brush, I knelt on the floor and began painting the bottom edge with short, quick strokes. Sometimes there was too much paint on the brush and thick, heavy drips rolled down onto the blue painter's tape, sometimes all the way down to the drop cloth.

Travis was near the back, covering the edges around the door to the kitchen. "Amigo," Manny said, "he's going to write the story no matter. I'm not saying you should or should not talk to him, but just know he's going to write it."

"I think he's already talked to the family," Travis said.

"He what?" I let my hand fall to the ground, and a streak of blue striped across my leg above the knee.

"Yeah, he told me he's been talking to the boy's father."

Peter. I imagined what those painful conversations were like. The guy should consider himself lucky to get three sentences from Peter. I wasn't worried what he might have said, it couldn't have been much, but I worried about Lauren. Did she know Peter was talking to the paper?

By the time Travis and I finished the edges of our wall and the lounge, Manny had already begun rolling the back wall. At least the half he could reach; the ceilings must have been fifteen to twenty feet high. I didn't say anything to Travis, but already the colors were looking good with the wood flooring and the expansive brick wall. As I was returning to the center of the room to trade in my brush for a roller, I felt a vibration against my left hip. I put the brush down and looked at my hands. They looked like my legs and shorts, spattered in dots, splotches, and streaks of blue.

"I'll be right back," I said. "Bathroom should be unlocked, yeah?"

"Should be," Travis said.

There was one single toilet in the far back corner of the building near the kitchen.

Once inside the tight, stark bathroom with its single overhead bulb, I saw there was one new text message sitting atop the handful I hadn't checked yesterday. I sat down on the closed toilet lid and decided to clean them out and then see what Lauren had to say.

Scrolling to the bottom, I saw Travis's name once and Rian's name three times. I deleted their messages without reading a word, feeling bad only for a moment. The last message from yesterday was from an unknown number. It read:

Hi Conner, this is Justine. I'm back from Zion and would love to talk some more. Call me. I hope you're doing well.

Justine? A knot formed in my stomach and a lump in my throat at the sight of her name on my screen. I hadn't expected to hear from her.

I deleted that message without saving her number. That left the message from a couple minutes ago. From Lauren. I clicked it open and held my breath.

Abby's home, but she's not talking to me. Think she has a new boyfriend. Also had a message from Justine. Not sure. Please let me know how you are.

I wanted to call her. I wanted to have her come pick me up, rescue me from my intervention. But I couldn't. I had to text her and quickly, before Travis and Manny busted down the bathroom door. Although in the cramped, dirty bathroom, I didn't know what to say. I was glad Abby was okay. I was glad Lauren had the same aversion to Justine as I did. I was glad she was thinking about me. All of it. But only some of these were things I could say. I told her I was glad Abby was okay and that maybe a boyfriend was a good thing. That I also heard from Justine. I didn't know how to sign off, so I wrote *Call me if you need anything. Or just want to drive to Mexico.* It sounded stupid, but I could hear Travis getting anxious and needed to send it.

I flushed the toilet and jiggled and pulled several times at the doorknob before it finally clicked and gave way.

"Jesus," I announced as I re-entered the room, "we need to get that knob fixed."

Manny was already high up on the ladder, which I wasn't sure could support his weight. "You already stinking up the place, amigo?"

"Seriously," Travis said, roller in hand, "you trying to christen the place?"

Whatever. I'd take a silly joke over the third degree.

"We all know only Manny has the power to properly break in a bathroom," I said, feeling less agitated having heard from Lauren.

They both smiled but didn't laugh.

"Here," Travis said, "you start rolling on that end, and we'll make our way toward each other in the middle."

I grabbed a roller and a fresh tray.

"And don't put so much damn paint on the brush. I saw all those drips on the edging. It's gotta be smooth as Manny's game. No teardrops."

And so I started painting. With long, slow strokes, I made *w*'s across the wall, then doubled back. Then forward again. The paint went on wet and glossy. The drips were minimal and quickly smoothed over.

"Okay, fuck, out with it already," Travis said without stopping his own line of *w*'s.

"Out with what?"

"What do you mean, *what*?" Manny called from atop the ladder, his voice echoing even more from up on high. "The señorita from this morning."

"Yeah, man, what the hell?"

None of the half-assed lies I came up with would work. And after reading Lauren's text, I somehow felt empowered. I almost *wanted* to tell them. Maybe I didn't need to be ashamed.

"That was Lauren Thomas," I said, trying my damnedest to stay monotone.

"Who is Lauren Tomás?" Manny asked.

"Wait." Travis took his roller off the wall and turned to face me. "Thomas?"

I tried to read his face. To catch the moment of recognition and then read that initial gut response. And really, what was the right response here? I was hoping to find out.

"No way. Thomas as in . . . *Thomas*, Thomas?"

"Yes. Lauren Thomas."

"Someone better tell Manny who the hell is this Lauren Tomás."

"That was his mother," I said to Manny. "*Is* his mother."

And then I told them everything. Almost everything. With Manny still perched on the ladder and Travis standing frozen with the roller dripping a slow but steady drip onto the white cloth, I told them about everything from Lauren's first voicemail to the meeting at Laguna Lake. I even told them about the altercation with Jimmy and Abby at Farmer's Market. It was the longest time I had ever been in a room with the both of them where one or the other was not babbling on about something or making some snide remark. I went on to tell them about yesterday, our full day in Santa Barbara, brown sweatshirts, peanut M&M's, and rock shrimp tacos at Carlitos. And then I told them how I let Lauren sleep *on the couch* last night. Alone. I told them that I threw a blanket over her, went to my room, and then walked her to her car in the morning.

I did not tell them about her linking arms with me as we strolled down State Street. Or about the two of us lying in bed in the darkness. And I definitely didn't tell them how I wanted to drop this damned roller and walk to the beige house on Foothill with the wind chimes and missing mailbox letters.

Manny was speechless and looked hard at Travis, as did I. Waiting for the official reaction.

"I don't know, man," was all he said.

"Don't know what?"

"Doesn't seem right." He shook his head. "I mean, doesn't it seem a little weird?"

Weird? *Everything* since that Monday had been fucking weird. Maybe, finally, I was doing something that *didn't* feel weird.

"I mean, don't get me wrong, I think it's good that you met her and made peace and all that. But spending the day with her. Spending the *night* with her? Seems like there might be a line you're crossing."

"What line? How is any of this whole fucking situation normal? Where are the lines, and who's drawing them? It's helping her, man. And maybe it's helping me too. Isn't helping her the very fucking least I can do? Isn't that what I owe?"

"What you *owe*? So what, this is your community service? And then when you feel you've done enough time, you're going to snap back into your old self?"

"There is no more old self. This is me. How can anything be the same after that?"

We shared a look, hesitated, then reluctantly went back to painting. We zigged and zagged and rolled our way across the wall. Manny, however, stood still on the ladder, watching us.

"So you're going to see her again?" Travis asked as the space between us was closing in. Our rollers like magnets.

"Yeah, I'm sure I will. I don't know when or where, but I'm going to."

"Just be careful, amigo," Manny finally said, his booming voice a little softer.

"Careful of what?"

"About her daughter. Her family."

"Yeah," Travis agreed. "Look at the daughter, what's her na—"

"Abby."

"Yeah, Abby. Look at what's already happened the couple times you've seen her. Be careful."

They didn't understand. Travis and Rian, they wanted me to be sad for a week, get over it, and go back to how things were. As if nothing ever happened. That way it wouldn't inconvenience their lives, and they could keep doing what they wanted without me fucking it all up. I was working myself up to say all this to Travis when he got a phone call. It was brief, and when he hung up, he put his roller down and wiped his hands on his dirty jeans.

"The guys with the stoves are here. I'm gonna meet them out back."

We didn't see Travis for at least another hour. When Manny finished his wall, he brought the ladder over to help me. I worked on the lower half while he started painting the top. We still had the alcove to finish, but all in all we'd be done quicker than I expected.

As we painted, Manny and I didn't say much. And when we did, it wasn't anything serious. Talking just enough to keep the silence from getting too loud.

There was a lot of banging and voices coming from the kitchen; it sounded like there were at least three or four men in there with Travis.

When Manny and I turned the corner to tackle the waiting recess, he spoke up with a slightly more serious tone.

"You need to be careful about this place too, amigo."

"What do you mean?"

"You can't treat it like you did the Sky and the Sea place. Or like your basketball team, you know?"

"Yeah, yeah, I know." I felt another buzz against my left thigh. Lauren.

"Yes, but Travis has been asking me a lot of questions, amigo, like help with the place."

"That's great, Manny. I know he appreciates your help." I couldn't run to the bathroom to check the text message with Travis and the workers in there. Maybe I could check it here. "And I do too."

"No, amigo. Questions about food too. And the menu. Even asked me to meet with Carl next week."

Who the hell was Carl? Maybe I could step outside for a sec, tell him I needed to make a phone call.

"You know we love you, Manny. Hey, I gotta step—"

"Hey, I'm only trying to warn you, man. I don't want you to wake up in a week or a month or whatever and think I went behind—"

Travis emerged from the kitchen clapping his hands. "New stoves, guys, come check it out! Damn, these walls look fantastic. C'mon, put the brushes down and take a look."

The entire kitchen looked new, or at least cleaner, with the addition of the new stovetops. There were eight burners, two of which were twice the size of the others, and then a sizeable grill-top. Travis turned the burners on, all eight of them, and they glowed with blue circles. His smile covered his entire face, and his eyes lit up like the flames he left dancing on the stove. He patted my back and then Manny's. "Let's cook something, boys!"

One of the guys from the appliance company returned to the back doorstep with a clipboard and some paperwork. Travis and Manny went to deal with him.

I realized I had a smile of my own. A genuine one. I was happy to have finally told Travis about Lauren. Even if he didn't approve, having said it out loud, it legitimized our . . . our what? Our relationship, whatever it was. I wanted to call her right then and tell her that I'd told Travis. It sounded silly, but I knew she would understand.

And then with a quarter turn of each dial, the burners went *click, click, click,* and poof, the flames disappeared.

CHAPTER 14

RIAN'S LETTER ARRIVED ON A TUESDAY. IT CAME at the tail end of a long string of unanswered calls. I told myself to answer. I told myself to listen to her messages. I told myself to call her back. But I couldn't physically bring myself to do any of those things.

So after at least a week of seeing her name light up my phone, the calls came to a screeching halt. Cold turkey. Three days later, the letter arrived in the mail. Written words were her currency. Much like her calls, the letter sat unopened on the coffee table, alongside a half-empty canister of Pringles, two empty bottles of wine, and Braden's brown sweatshirt.

It was on that same Tuesday that I first accepted money from Lauren. At the time it felt dirty, illegal. She was driving me to the gym for basketball practice as she had been doing for several days. She had also driven me to the grocery store after the inside of my fridge began to echo. All in all, I didn't need to be many places. But when I did, Lauren drove me. Yes, my truck was in good health and sitting in my parking spot. But every time I caught a glimpse of it, I felt such a pang of betrayal. And anger. Like a cancerous organ or a cheating girlfriend. Something taken for granted, something trusted. Something you didn't think twice about that suddenly ripped the rug out from underneath you, upending your world. It didn't make sense; it was four wheels and a bunch of steel. But it betrayed me just the same.

She had pulled into the near-empty lot at MBHS and put the car in park when I began my feeble attempt to offer gas money I didn't have.

"Conner, stop."

"It's just—"

"I don't want your money."

The way she ended that sentence—with such finality—left us both suspended in silence, as if waiting for what it was she *did* want. But it seemed neither of us had the guts to entertain answers to that question, not even in the privacy of our own minds.

"In fact," she finally continued, "how are you doing with money for other stuff? Rent, groceries?"

I watched out the window as Cody and Kyle jogged toward the gym, unaware of their coach sitting in the passenger seat next to this strange woman.

"I know it's tough without the cooking job. Let me help you, Conner."

"I'll be fine."

From the front pocket of her jeans, she pulled out three bills—hundreds—and put them in my lap. It had all been premeditated, the bills already neatly folded and in her pocket.

"No way, I—"

"I know it's not a lot, but it will help, and if you need more, please let me know."

I hastily stuffed the bills into the pocket of my windbreaker. "I gotta get to practice."

"Promise me you'll let me know, Conner."

"I will," I said, mostly to get her to stop talking about it.

"Okay, so I'll see you back here at seven?"

"Seven's good."

As her Subaru raced through the parking lot, bouncing over speed bumps, I knew she wasn't hurrying to get home. She would go park by the rock as she often did and watch the tide creep in or roll out until it was time to pick me up. Seeing as how we were in the thick of summer, the sun would be taking the long way home tonight, so there might even still be a few surfers. But I imagined she mostly went to stare blankly at the sleeping sand dunes, listening to the rhythmic white noise of crashing waves. A far better option than the cold house on Foothill.

Before entering the gym, I put my hands in my pockets once more to feel the money she had given me. Peter's money. Peter's money from long hours spent at the power plant, doing whatever it was Peter did there to prolong going back to that same cold house on Foothill.

As for the basketball team, we were 0–3 and getting worse. I struggled to keep Coach Rich's schedule of practice five days a week. Games on Mondays or Wednesdays. I didn't run the kids anymore, and we didn't do difficult drills. In fact, we were doing fewer and fewer drills with each practice. We scrimmaged, mostly. They played loose and wild, their hormone-rich bodies running for two hours with ease. After each practice as they left the gym, I saw it in their red faces and sideways glances. Disappointment. Even at their young age, they knew they deserved better.

On this particular Tuesday, the one where I received Rian's letter and Lauren gave me three hundred dollars, I was watching them scrimmage, doing all I could to remain upright and interested instead of sitting against the wall, counting the minutes. Today they had to play four-on-four with one player rotating in for both sides. Only nine showed. We had started with fifteen. Three had already quit and on this Tuesday, we had three no-shows, which was typical.

Midway through the practice, Jimmy walked through the doors. He was in street clothes, not his practice uniform, his orange-red hair looking a bit more disheveled than usual. He remained fixated on the sloppy game on the court as he walked toward me.

"Hey, Jimmy, didn't you guys practice already?"

"Yeah, I'm not here for that. Can we talk?"

"Sure." I glanced at the court as one kid hoisted up a half-court shot that missed the rim by ten feet. I was embarrassed for Jimmy to see this mess I had created.

"So yeah, Coach, you know varsity got this Bakersfield tournament coming up?"

I didn't. "Sure, yeah, what about it?"

"You know there's gonna be some legit talent there. Some big high schools, right?" Jimmy reeked of cigarettes.

"Yeah, sure."

"That's my shot, Coach, you gotta get some coaches there." A yelling match broke out in the game. Jimmy turned to look, shook his head, then returned to me. "In our shithouse league, we ain't gonna play anyone worth a shit. I gotta showcase against these D1 teams. You gotta help me get some schools out there to look at me."

"Yes, Jimmy, you're right." I had completely forgotten. "And I'm sure scouts will be there."

"Nah. Universities don't scout summer tournaments. They think the games aren't serious enough or something. They wait till fall. But I can't wait till fall, Coach. No one's gonna come watch me play against shitburger teams like Templeton or Coast Union."

"Sure, sure, I understand."

"I'd make the calls myself, but no one's gonna listen to a little fucker like me. Besides, it might be like against NCAA rules or some shit."

"Yeah, you're right, no, no, you don't call anyone."

"So you gonna help me, Coach? You said you'd help me."

"Yeah, I'll make some calls." I couldn't even call my girlfriend back and I was supposed to cold-call D1 colleges? I cursed my past self for agreeing to this. But now I was in it.

"Yeah? Who you gonna call, you think?"

"Well, I dunno off the top of my head, but I'll get on it soon."

"Damn, Coach, c'mon, don't you think you should maybe ask me about my top schools? Where I think I could go, where I think I got a chance, who I think might give me a scholarship? Where I *want* to go?"

Before I could answer, he pulled a folded piece of paper from his back pocket and handed it to me. "Here," he said.

I unfolded the paper and found a dozen or so schools—Gonzaga, Baylor, UNLV . . . scrolled in messy, angular writing like a young kid's Christmas list.

"Jimmy, none of these schools are in California."

"Exactly." He turned and looked at the game being played behind him, then back at me. "Shit, it's like you ain't even listenin'," he said, and then he left.

It wasn't until several days later that I finally read Rian's letter. My initial reaction was that it was shorter than I was expecting. Though I also had no idea what I was expecting. Her handwriting was slightly slanted, sharp and uniform. Decisive. She told me that for her own self-preservation, she was choosing to end the relationship. And that really there wasn't much of a relationship left anyway, so hopefully this wouldn't come as a surprise. She said she wasn't giving up on me as a person but on the relationship as an entity. The letter was sweet, it was logical, it was well written. And just like that, Rian was gone. I was supposed to be sad, and I was. But not in the way I should've been. I didn't miss her like I used to. The letter felt like the snapping of one of the last cords tethering me to my former self, the person I used to be. Before. And now any remaining cords, if there were any, were weathered and worn and frayed.

I returned the letter to the envelope and stuffed it in the organizer next to the house phone, which was already bursting with bills, junk mail, and take-out menus.

Later that morning, Lauren picked me up and we headed for Morro Bay. Rian and the letter drifted into the background along with all the other debris of my life. And of course, without asking, Lauren took the long way around through San Luis as she had the dozen or so times she took me to and from practice. An extra twenty minutes each way. It wasn't until that trip, however, that it dawned on me that she wasn't avoiding South Bay Boulevard for *my* sake.

The worst part about taking the long way was that we had to pass by the Thomases' house. The innocuous beige house with its overgrown lawn and darkened windows. Neither of us ever looked at it as we drove by, and if there happened to be a lull in the conversation as we approached the house, one of us usually found something to say.

"Thank you for returning the sweatshirt, Conner." Lauren gripped a handful of the brown sweatshirt in her lap, rubbing the cotton between her thumb and forefinger. She had left it at my place several nights before, a night when I had made her short ribs and risotto, and we'd eaten with the windows and door open, listening to it almost rain outside.

"I really didn't mean to have you do all this driving just for me to make this stupid pickup."

"I wanted to, Conner, you know that. Besides, there's something I want to show you."

The impetus for our trip was making me more nervous than it should have. Donnie had left a voicemail a few days ago saying I could pick up my last paycheck when I returned the keys and picked up my things. What things I might have left at the restaurant I wasn't sure. What made it so idiotic, however, was that my paycheck couldn't have been for more than $100, and the keys I had weren't even to the entrance, but to the knife cupboard and the freezer.

As we pulled into the parking lot outside the Sea & Sky Cafe, I prayed Lauren wasn't making the same connection I was: returning to a former place of work to pick up petty items. It wasn't right.

"Hey, I know this is stupid," I said. "I'll be one quick second."

"Take your time, Conner. I'll be right here."

It wasn't yet eleven, and so I shouldn't have been surprised when I tried the heavy maroon double doors only to find them locked. But the Sea & Sky opened at noon for lunch, so the staff would already be there. I knocked three times, hard. No one came. I didn't want to draw out this task a moment longer than needed. I knocked again, harder.

When I had no other choice but to wait, I turned back to the car, but Lauren was sitting on one of the wooden planter boxes that divided the parking lot from the walkway, her once-white tennis shoes not quite reaching the cement. The brown sweatshirt folded neatly over her lap.

"Hey," she said, and even smiled. "No luck?"

"Locked. They're probably all in the back, prepping. We can come back later. Sorry."

She didn't make a move to get up. In fact, she slouched a little more. "It's okay," she said. "We can wait."

I took a seat on the planter next to her, the narrow wood edge uncomfortable on my ass. The breeze coming off the water gave the air a salty ocean chill.

"Peter talked to me last night."

"Talked to you?"

"Yes, like actually talked to me. Well, kind of. He doesn't talk to anyone anymore."

"I'm sor—"

"Which is fine I guess, right? I mean, everyone has their way, right?"

"But last night was different?"

"He wants to move, Conner."

"He what?"

"To move. Leave San Luis."

I immediately thought of Rian. Not because this bomb made me think of distance or geography, but because my stomach turned inside out as Lauren spoke. A feeling I should have had this morning when I read Rian's letter. But I didn't have that feeling then. I had it *now*. My heart began to play paradiddles against my ribs.

"What'd he say?"

"Well, not much. But I want to tell you what happened."

I shifted my weight from one side of my ass to the other, the wooden lip digging into my flesh.

"When I came home from dropping you off, he was at the dinner table. Eating. Abby wasn't home, and no lights were on in the house except for the one above the kitchen table. It was so dark. He had warmed up spaghetti from the fridge. That's all I ever cook. Pasta. I make the entire box like I'm feeding a Boy Scout troop. Then no one eats it and it sits in the fridge until it either goes bad or I make another batch, and the Tupperware multiplies. I warmed some up too, and sat with him. I asked him about his day. It was fine. I asked him where Abby was. He didn't know. This is how all our conversations go. And right when I'm ready to give up and leave him alone, he says, 'I think we should move.' Just like that. Of course, I was shocked. We had never discussed moving. Not even before . . . But, actually, I was more shocked that he said something real. So I asked him why, and at first he didn't answer. He sat there staring at his dry mound of pasta."

Lauren paused her story to look at a man heading down the walkway. It was Donnie; I could tell by the sound of his heavy gait before I even looked up. We both watched as he approached. Donnie stared at us as if we were strangers, and it wasn't until he was upon us that he finally recognized me.

"Conner, what you do here?"

"You called me. About the paycheck. Your keys. My stuff?"

"Ah yes, yes. Come inside. Why you wait? Girls no let you in?"

The smell inside was immediately familiar. A mix of lemon disinfectant and fish. Marcus sat at a table filling salt and pepper shakers, while Greta was hastily braiding her hair. They both gave me a smile. Marcus added a nod, while Greta gave me a "Miss you, honey" as she hustled by without slowing. All in all, no one was interested in me. But the feeling was mutual. In the doorway of his office, I handed Donnie two silver keys, and he handed me a check for $84.31.

"Sorry, Conner. Not the hard feelings, no?" Donnie's nose seemed to have grown in size and redness since the last time I had seen him. Cratered like the moon.

"I bet Nikki's happy, huh?" My hatred for the place was growing by the second, and I wanted to say something that showed it. He didn't have to be an expert in English to know what I meant. "She can have the kitchen all to herself. Might even learn to cook something."

"Fuck that Nikki." Donnie pounded his meatball fist against the wall as he said this. "She gone too. She turn out as real bitch."

"Sorry to hear that."

"And this." He held out a brown paper bag. I didn't recognize it as mine, but really it was nothing more than a standard lunch bag. Without a word, I grabbed it by the scrunched-up top and exited the Sea & Sky for the last time.

Lauren was still sitting on the planter when I returned. In the few minutes I was inside, the clouds had got together in dark little huddles in the sky, casting shadows across the Embarcadero. Goose bumps rose on my arms.

"How did it go?"

"It was fine, whatever, we didn't really need to come here."

"What's in the bag?"

I held it up. It barely weighed anything. "You know, I'm not even sure."

Lauren gave me a confused look and jumped off the planter, folding the sweatshirt over one arm like a waiter might do a napkin.

"But let's open it somewhere else."

"Do you mind if we walk?" She gestured to the street, away from her parked Subaru.

"Of course," I said, stuffing the check into my back pocket.

Once we hit Embarcadero and made a left, I opened the bag and peered inside.

"What is it?" she asked.

There were only a few items. The first thing I pulled out was a generic silver-chain necklace.

"This isn't even mine." I placed it back in the bag and pulled out an empty money clip with a *K* engraved into the metal. "Jesus. That's not mine either."

"Are you sure you took the right bag?"

"It's the one he gave me."

The last item in the bag didn't look like anything at all. From the paper-thin edge I saw it looked like maybe a 3x5 index card. I reached in and pulled it out, expecting it to also belong to someone else. But this was mine, and it wasn't an index card. It was a postcard. On the front was a picture of Vesuvio. A close-up shot of the front of the bar, with the word *Vesuvio* above the door in stained glass—green and blue and red and yellow. The building curved, like many corner buildings in San Francisco, as if molded on a potter's wheel. I already knew what was written on the back, but I turned it over. In a slightly drunken scrawl, surrounded by spattered brown circles that at one time were drops of Guinness, were the words *Further: Where Good Friends Come for Good Food.* I had taped the card to the kitchen wall my first day at the Sea & Sky. Motivation. There were better things waiting for me than dropping baskets of battered fish sticks.

Lauren was waiting for me to finish examining the postcard. She didn't say anything but looked at me expectantly.

"Not mine either," I said. "Idiot doesn't know anything." I put the postcard back in the bag with the other two items and dropped it into a nearby trash can. "So did Peter ever answer you? About why he wants to move?"

"Not at first. He just kept staring at his spaghetti. We were both born here in the Central Coast. Lifers."

The idea of living in one place for your entire life sounded depressing. Suffocating.

"So I asked him again. I was frustrated, but I was gentle. Like handling a bird with a broken wing. I mean, he had finally said something. So I waited. But then just when I thought he was going to start crying, he put his fork down and got upset. 'What do you mean, why?' he said. But he still wouldn't look at me. Just at the pasta. 'To survive,' he said, and then got up and left."

Lauren looked to me, and I looked away.

In Rian's letter, she had also said she was breaking up with me for *survival,* for mine just as much as hers. Though I wasn't sure what she meant.

Lauren and I walked past shell shacks and souvenir shops, the Embarcadero not yet teeming with tourists as it would be later. It was in our prolonged silence that I began to notice the sea lions. The ones crying from their dirty cement beds. As Lauren and I walked side by side in silence, their desperate songs hung in the air above the street, as sad and constant as the Morro Bay fog.

"What does Abby think about moving?" I said, which was my way of asking Lauren what *she* thought.

"I don't think she knows Peter's been thinking about it. She's not home a lot. She's got that boyfriend I told you about, which normally, Conner, would freak me out. But I think maybe it's good for her right now. Don't you think?"

"If he's a good guy, then yeah, someone she can talk to."

We approached an older man walking a dog the size of a cat, its little feet a blur of tiny steps as it kept up with the old man.

"Like you, Conner. She should have someone to talk to like I have you."

The old man smiled and nodded as he passed.

"Rian broke up with me." I wasn't sure why I was telling her at that moment. It just came out.

"I'm sorry. What did she say? Do you want to talk about it?"

"No." Which was true. I didn't. There was nothing to say. "It's okay, really. She wrote me a letter." In saying that out loud, I found a dime-sized bit of comfort in the fact that Rian's last interaction with me was with what she did best—perfectly crafted words.

We continued down the Embarcadero, the moaning of the sea lions growing distant as we moved farther away. The souvenir stores and the fish 'n' chip joints were endless, but we didn't bother peering into the windows. I was assuming we were both thinking about what Peter had said, but really, there were so many options on the menu; her mind could have been reeling about anything. I also half expected to run into someone I knew. Travis. Although Yakety Kayaks was at the other end of the Embarcadero. Jimmy, maybe. But he should be in school. Same went for any kid on my winless basketball team. Coach Rich? Someone I went to high school with? Or maybe we'd run into someone *she* knew. She had been here all her life, she must know every local to some degree. A tilted head and a hand on the elbow, they'd ask how she was holding up. How would she introduce me, if at all? Suddenly, I felt exposed walking around in public with her. Someone would see us. Someone would know who we were. Who we *both* were.

"Have you talked to Justine recently?" I asked to disrupt my own thoughts.

"No," she answered quickly. "But she keeps trying to get a hold of me."

"Yeah, me too."

"Voicemails, texts, emails."

"Same," I said.

"What do you think she wants?"

"I dunno."

"She keeps saying she just wants to talk."

"Yeah."

"About what? What does she want to talk about?"

"Are you going to call her back?

"I don't want to."

"Neither do I."

And there we made a silent pact not to call Justine. We passed surf shops and a cinnamon roll bakery that smelled like boiling sugar. I wasn't sure why Justine was so off-putting to me, but the fact that Lauren felt the same way validated that feeling. I moved on, thinking about other possible nightmare run-ins. What if we bumped into the police officers from that day? Would they recognize us? What if we ran into Abby? I thought again of the scene in the Thomases' living room. And Farmer's Market.

"Why are we so against her, Conner?"

"Who?"

"Justine." Lauren hadn't moved past it. "I mean, why don't we want to talk to her?"

"I'm not sure," I said, and I really wasn't. "She was nice enough the one time I met her."

We were nearing the home stretch of the Embarcadero. Morro Rock looming larger as we got closer. With its size, it always looked closer than it really was. Did she want to walk that far? Even though it was cold and seemed to be getting more so, we could do it. Could be there in twenty minutes if she wanted.

"You know . . . they investigated Braden too."

"Investigated?" I asked, genuinely confused. "What do you mean?"

"They called it a *twenty-four-hour profile.*" She used air quotes and a mocking voice with the last bit. "We had to help them account for his last twenty-four hours. Had he been drinking, using drugs, gotten in a big fight or something. Maybe to see if it was a . . ." She paused and wiped at her nose and looked away from me. "To rule out that anything was done on purpose."

"What," I said, but not really as a question. I was taken aback.

"Well, yeah, their little *investigation*"—again with the air quotes—"was over as quickly as it started. But how sad."

"Man." I shook my head and looked down at my feet.

"Your life being boiled down to the last twenty-four hours." She took a big, exaggerated breath, her chest rising and falling. Then she pointed. "Can we go in there, Conner?"

I looked up and saw the old Crills Saltwater Taffy sign. It was a blue and white wood building in dire need of a paint job. Although the place had been a staple of the Embarcadero and had been around long before I was born, I couldn't remember ever going in. There was a walk-up window that was vacant, but I followed Lauren in the front door. An electronic bell announced our arrival.

The place looked like a saltwater taffy place should look—bright, colorful, and cluttered. Every inch of wall was covered: shelves of knickknacks, vintage Coke signs, surf memorabilia, old black-and-white photos of Morro Bay. Back when Crills first opened and sea lions still swam in the sea. There were narrow walkways lined with large wooden barrels of saltwater taffy of every color and flavor imaginable. The place reeked of waxy sugar.

"Braden's favorite," Lauren said with a hesitant smile, tempered, as if smiling too big meant she was a bad mother.

"I've actually made it before."

"You have?" Her face lit up this time without holding back. "Oh, you have? Will you tell me about it?"

There was one other woman browsing the barrels, filling a long skinny plastic bag. And an old man sat on a stool behind a cash register along the far wall.

"It was at the culinary academy. I took a confections class, God knows why. I was horrible at anything involving dessert. Dessert is more chemistry than cooking. Science, not art."

Lauren readjusted the brown sweatshirt in the crook of her elbow and pulled a bag off a roll hanging from the wall. She began rummaging through barrels as if looking for one specific piece, and I followed her like a puppy.

"Anyway, for our final we had to learn, make, and present a type of sweet we had not yet covered in class. I chose saltwater taffy."

"Because of this place? Because you remembered spending your childhood here? Like Braden."

"Yes, exactly," I lied. "So, I had to learn how to make the taffy, which actually isn't that hard."

"What's in it? Do you remember?" She picked up an orange one—Tangerine Dream—sniffed it, then put it back.

"Sugar, cornstarch, corn syrup, um . . . glycerin, water, uh . . . I know there's a couple more. Oh, salt of course. And butter. Then whatever flavor and coloring."

Although she had picked up many pieces, only three sat at the bottom of her bag. She stopped her searching and looked at me as I spoke.

"With taffy, you have to pull it. To aerate it. That's how it gets soft. Places like this will have a pulling machine with large, rotating metal hooks. But I pulled it by hand. It was a disaster."

"I love it, Conner." She threw some green ones into her bag—Lime Sublime. "Wait, so there's not actually salt water in them? Sorry, was that a dumb question?"

"I mean, there's water and there's salt. But no, there's no salt water. Not in the traditional sense. Not like seawater."

"So why's it called saltwater taffy?"

"I'm not sure, actua—"

"Legend has it . . ." The old man on the stool spoke up then waited for our attention. We stopped and looked at him. "Hi, folks," he said, and waved. "You see, saltwater taffy originated in Atlantic City. In the late 1800s. On the boardwalk." He said the word *boardwalk* as if it were a mythical place only few had seen.

"Yes, but taffy itself has been around for about a thousand years," I said. It was childish, but I didn't like that he had encroached on our conversation. "Started in the Middle East. Iraq, I think."

"I don't know about no Middle East. But in the late 1800s along the boardwalk in Atlantic City, there was this great storm." He used both his hands to make big, circular motions. "Most of the stores were downright flooded." He paused for a reaction, but we gave him none. "And when the storm and flood dried up, the taffy in the candy store was covered in salt, on account of all the salt water from the great ocean storm."

Lauren nodded; she looked genuinely interested. I was genuinely irritated. We weren't brainless tourists looking for small-town wives' tales to make the place seem more magical. It was condescending.

"Well, wouldn't ya know it, the darned people went mad for this taffy that had been soaked in salt water. After that, them boys at the candy store started adding a pinch of the Atlantic to the recipe, and saltwater taffy was born." When he finished, he spread his hands outward slowly as if concluding a magic trick.

Lauren offered him a smile, but I turned and continued down the aisle.

"That's a nice story," she said.

"Sometimes it takes a storm to bring out the true goodness in things," he said.

When Lauren caught up to me, I whispered, "It's just regular taffy with a fancy name." But I could tell she didn't like hearing that, and I regretted saying it.

Lauren paid for her taffy, talking with the old man much longer than they should have. I assumed he gave her every wink and one-liner he fed the folks from the Central Valley, who ate it up like the waxed candy they were buying for $8.99 a pound.

When she exited the store, Lauren made a right to return back from where we had come. The rock was not in our plans.

She offered me a piece of pink taffy. "Peppermint Paradise," she said.

I didn't want it but took it. "Earlier, you said there was something you wanted to show me?"

She unwrapped one herself but didn't yet put it in her mouth. "It's up ahead."

Soon we were both smacking at the taffy, our jaws working like a sculptor trying to manipulate her clay. Mine was disgusting and tasted like candy cane and toothpaste.

The Embarcadero had picked up a little, though the sun still hadn't shown up, and I tried not to look passersby in the face for fear of seeing recognition in someone's eyes. After a block or so, there was a break in the storefronts, just a few strips of grass and some benches, and it was here that Lauren led me. A sign read *Anchor Memorial Park*. I had never noticed the sign before, and really, calling it a park was a bit of a stretch. It was simply a place to sit and look at the bay, the rock, the smokestacks. But now that Lauren was taking me here specifically, I became more aware of the details. The benches were actually in the design of boat cleats. There were several oval picnic tables covered in seagull shit but otherwise unoccupied. In the center of the patch of grass was an anchor statue. Sitting on a large cement block, the whole thing was about ten feet tall.

"This is what I wanted to show you, Conner." She led me to the anchor.

Besides its impressive size, the anchor was otherwise nondescript. Goose bumps rose on my arms for the second time that day, and I let Lauren guide me. She walked around the anchor a couple times, slowly, looking it up and down.

"You know, when I was little," I said, "I used to think this was an actual old anchor, something salvaged maybe from a giant pirate ship." I tried to laugh, but not much came out. "But I guess it's just a statue made to be a statue."

"It's a memorial." She looked it up and down again. "For all the local fishermen lost at sea." She stopped her circling and knelt down beside the cement base. On the side where she knelt was a plaque. It was black and shiny and home to a hundred or so engraved names. I knelt beside Lauren and noticed there was room for a lot more names on the marble plate. It wasn't complete. It was merely waiting for the next big storm.

We quietly read the names. They were listed as first initial and full last name, but not in alphabetical order. I quickly scanned for a Thomas and luckily found none. As usual, I waited for Lauren to speak first. As I waited, aimlessly scanning names of dead fishermen I didn't know—J. Burch, R. Hattersley, V. Woodward—I realized one horrifying characteristic. Nearly a third of the last names had multiple listings. Two Pierces, a pair of Congers. Fathers and sons, brothers. D. Lockard and A. Lockard. Entire families wiped out at once. Four Fannings. *Four*! I thought of the wives and mothers, daughters and sisters waiting onshore. How did they know which one to cry for first?

"People think being lost at sea is only something that happened centuries ago," she said. "Pirates, explorers, that sorta thing. But . . ."

I thought of the rescued kayaker. Wondered where he might be if the fishing boat hadn't seen him. Was there a place the ocean took all the people it swept away?

"There," Lauren said softly. She put her finger to the name *B. Pierce* and then fell back onto her butt, sitting cross-legged in the grass. Below it was *J. Pierce*.

"Braeden Pierce. My uncle."

I sat down next to her, my weight on the grass pushing moisture up into the butt of my jeans.

"We named Braden after him."

"Do you remember him?"

"I was real young. Maybe five. They were my mom's brothers." I assumed she was now referring to J. Pierce as well. "Their dad was a fisherman too. Tuna mostly. My uncles were hard workers. I never really saw them except maybe at Christmas. But the family always talked about them with such reverence. Their wives, my aunts, were quiet women. I used to think they were mean, but now I know they were lonely."

A cool ocean breeze swept across us, and my ears went numb.

"And then one day, my uncles didn't come home. At the time, nothing was told to us kids. But I remember the phone calls, the whispers, the worried faces. This went on for a long time. You see, they never found the boat. Or the bodies." Those hidden currents under the surface, taking boats and bodies worlds away from where they first went under. "So the waiting went on forever. But they never told us kids anything. Just that Uncle Braeden and Uncle . . . Well, they were both out working, and so we thought nothing of it. They always worked. But then one of my aunts moved in with us, the one without any children, and that's when I knew something was wrong. She stayed in the guest room all the time. Or she was on the phone. I remember the red of her eyes used to scare me, and I avoided her when I could. And then one day there was a funeral. All of a sudden. A double funeral. Even then, I wasn't told much except to be quiet and respectful and to be sad for my aunts and my cousins."

"Did they ever find out what happened?" A voice in the back of my mind wondered if they had headstones in the family plot at Los Osos Valley Memorial. If the family plot was bigger than I had realized.

"Never. I was a teenager when I finally asked my parents. They shook their heads and said there was a real bad storm and that the boat . . . the people on it . . . were never found."

"Jesus."

"My mother said that was the worst part for my aunts. The not knowing. Even though they knew in their hearts and their minds that their husbands weren't coming back, they couldn't handle not knowing where they physically were. Even though I was only fourteen at the time of that conversation, when she finally told me the story, I decided then that if I had boys, I wanted to name them after my uncles. So that maybe, in some small way, they would be found again."

I didn't even feel the tears approaching, but with that last sentence, drops began falling down the edge of my nose. I looked away so Lauren wouldn't see.

"I'm sorry to bring you here, Conner. Even if it's sad, I thought you might like to hear the story."

I didn't say anything for fear of the floodgates really opening up. I bit the inside of my cheek and nodded. But the more I cried, the more I felt guilty for crying, which then made me cry more. I couldn't tell if Lauren was crying too; I couldn't look at her. The few people that passed held curious stares.

I stood up and walked around the anchor, trying to shake the tears away from behind my eyes. I had cried in front of Lauren before, but that didn't make it okay. On the opposite side from the plaque of names, there was another plaque, smaller and oval in shape, cut into the cement base. I knelt before it. Engraved into the oval was a quote:

This Wonderful Memorial
Gives Comfort to the Living
And Honor to the Dead

The words were attributed to "A. Z." Why weren't they given a full name? I didn't notice Lauren get up, but soon she was behind me, her hands on my shoulders as she leaned down. Her fingers were bony, and even through my shirt I could feel their coldness.

"This wonderful memorial," she read slowly, as if waiting to digest every word before moving to the next. "Gives comfort to the living." She squeezed my shoulders, but I could tell it was involuntary. "And honor to the dead." She swallowed the last "*d*" as she let go of me.

There was a cross engraved above the quote, and I thought of our conversation at the mission in Santa Barbara. I thought of her mother. And realized now that her family had a longer and more complex relationship with God than I could ever understand.

When I stood, I felt something enwrap me from behind, but it was not Lauren. Well, it was Lauren, but not her hands.

"Here, Conner," she said. "Put your arms through."

It was the brown sweatshirt; she had draped it over my shoulders.

"No, really, I'm okay."

"You're not. You're freezing. Put it on."

I made to protest again, but she stopped me.

"Please. Conner."

So I slipped my hands through the arms of the sweatshirt. It was about a size too small, and my wrists stuck out of the ends of the sleeves. I began talking purely to distract.

"Pierce is Irish, isn't it?"

"That's right. So is the name Braden. My father's side all came from Ireland. How did you know?"

"For a while growing up I thought I was Irish. So I read up on a lot of Irish ancestry stuff. I think names can be important."

"They are, Conner."

"But I'm not Irish, not at all. Only my name is." If ever it was possible to be wearing something while simultaneously trying not to touch it, that was me in the brown sweatshirt that wasn't mine.

"My name has French origins, I believe," she said. "My mother's side."

"You won't believe where my wacky parents got my name."

Lauren looked a little disappointed, waiting for the rest of my story.

"Ale-conners. Apparently in England way back when, these ale-conners were put in charge of checking the goodness and quality of all the bread and the beer. I guess my parents thought that was a pretty good job. But naming your kid after beer testers? Pretty dumb."

I could feel myself in the sweatshirt, trying to shrink away from it, away from my own skin. But I was noticeably warmer.

"That anchor? That's a real memorial, Conner, not like that one on the road. You haven't seen it, have you?"

"No, I—"

"Abby talks about it all the time. How big it's getting. What people are adding to it. People? What people?" She paused as a loud sea lion interrupted her. Three loud barks and then quiet. "And why would you put something *there* of all places! I hate it."

The sea lions grew louder, and Lauren changed the subject. She told me about taking Braden and Abby to the aquarium when they were little, and it made her cry. She said she had hidden her tears from her children, who loved throwing slimy fish to the begging sea lions. But on the way home, Abby had asked why they were in there and not in the ocean where they belonged. Lauren told her they were a little sick and as soon as they were better, they would return to their homes. "It made Abby feel better," Lauren said. "But the lie made me feel worse. Places matter too, Conner. Places and names."

When we pulled out of the Sea & Sky parking lot, Lauren turned right on the Embarcadero, which meant we wouldn't be heading up Pacific, the quicker way to the freeway that would take us the long way around again. I panicked at first, wondering if she was going to take South Bay by accident, simply out of years of habit. Or maybe it was intentional. Like bringing me to Braden's favorite candy shop and to the anchor memorial and telling me the origins of his name and putting the sweatshirt on me. Maybe she was purging, facing things more head-on. Maybe it had something to do with Peter's comment about moving.

"Oh, silly me," she said a few blocks down the Embarcadero. "I should have turned up Pacific. It's okay, I can swing back on Morro."

But before I could begin to untie all the assumptions I had jumped to so quickly, we were approaching Yakety Kayaks. Travis would surely be there, but hopefully he'd be busy with customers down by the water, or tucked away in his little shack. I had visions of him running us down, jumping on the hood, and dragging me out of the car by my collar.

Still wearing the brown sweatshirt, I slumped down as much as I could without looking like I was slumping down. But I didn't see Travis or his car. In fact I didn't even see the bouncy sign of Yakety Kayaks. Instead there was a new sign, blue and yellow and glossy, that read *Horizons*, and a half dozen construction workers were tearing down the wood siding of the place Travis had built from scratch.

CHAPTER 15

MY PARENTS WERE COMING IN FOUR DAYS.

That was two weeks earlier than they had originally told me, but even that I had forgotten. Through a four-part series of messages my mother left on my answering machine, she explained how the troupe had grown so big they were rapidly adding dates and splitting resources. They were currently in Mesa, Arizona, and while one half would cover Holbrook and all of Southern California, my parents were flying to Northern California for a two-day fair outside Lake Shasta, then they had one in Hollister, and before I knew it they'd be in San Luis Obispo. My mother's enthusiasm was profoundly irritating. She rambled on about my father the knight, and how much fun the fair was going to be with me there, how maybe I could even help out at the booth.

As quickly as I erased the messages from the machine, so too was the thought of my parents coming to town gone from my mind. Like pushing a button. There hadn't been room enough for anything else after that trip to the Embarcadero. Peter wanted to move. But in the past couple of days, Lauren and I hadn't spoken about it. She had driven me to practice, and we talked about nearly everything else except that. She complained often about Abby's absence. Only catching glimpses of her daughter in passing. This new boyfriend was now consuming Abby's life, which, to Lauren, was both a big concern and a big relief.

What if Lauren agreed with Peter? Where would they go? How far? And what did that mean for me? Did I follow them? Was I sentenced to a life of following around this broken family, trying to make it right? But entertaining the thought of the Thomases moving also led me to the implications of them staying. A future of wearing brown sweatshirts, chasing ghosts, going the long way around. Was that my penance?

Comfort the living. Honor the dead.

These simple words by someone with no more than initials engraved on a statue in the shape of an anchor, they echoed throughout my bones, my bones that weakened. Like walking around on rusty plumbing pipes.

Was I comforting the living? And which of the living was I indebted to? I wasn't giving any comfort to Abby. To Peter. Was it my job to comfort? Of course it was. Was I comfort for Lauren? She was certainly that for me, but how could I be that for her? And how dare I count myself in the list of those that need comforting. What more could I do? What more could I offer? Was it my job to fix what I had done? Wasn't that why I had survived? I had to do more. There had to be more. But it couldn't be *fixed*—that wasn't the right word. Comfort. Comforting. To comfort. The word ran over and over in my mind and on my lips and through the breezeway of my limbs until it lost all meaning. I wasn't sure it was the right word either. Comfort was a warm embrace. At best, temporary contentment.

Honor the dead. I wasn't doing that. At least not properly. What was the point of honoring the dead if they were dead? People said funerals were for the living. Before, I never much thought of funerals. Aside from a co-worker in Havasu, I had never been to one that mattered to me. But I thought of the Thomas funeral often. If funerals were for the living, then so were statues. The anchor statue wasn't for the people that died at sea. It was for their families, so they could come and look at the names and the giant anchor and think that those they lost were important. That their deaths meant something, and now they lived on. But they didn't live on. So what did it mean to truly honor the dead? Not what the statue wanted it to mean, but what it *really* meant.

I grabbed the keys to my truck and went outside. I didn't know if this was going to give me any answers, but it felt like something I should do. Even if I only drove around the block. The inside of the cab was as it was last time. Clean. Cold. It smelled sterile, like someone else's new car. My heart palpitations were already audible in my inner ear. The windshield was pockmarked with the stains of old pine needles. Little brown and orange hash marks all over the glass like a game of pickup sticks.

But the windshield soon transformed into a screen. I saw South Bay Boulevard, the base of Black Mountain, the wild shrub, all seen at a cockeyed angle from where the truck had settled to a stop. Cracks began to spiderweb their way up and across the glass. I shut my eyes hard and forced myself to think of something else.

The first thought was Lauren's story about her uncles, Braeden and J. Pierce. I distracted myself with initials and names. Jonathan? Joshua? Jacob? And then I thought of the child whose name she couldn't even say. Were they a family destined for loss? I let my mind roam into the bigger implications of what that might mean. With my eyes still closed, I started dipping into God and religion. And if they were a family destined for loss, where did I fit into that? Was I an innocent bystander? No, how dare I look for an out, an excuse. *I* was the one driving that day. *I* was the one cranking Neil Young at too loud a volume, taking the turns with familiarity and carelessness, turns I had taken a thousand times before. Of course my train of thought led me right back to the cab of the truck.

Around the block. Easy. I opened my eyes, put the key in the ignition, and turned it clockwise. Instantly the engine gurgled to a start and along with it, the radio. A random station. Some kind of country-rock. But there it was. *Bass-snare-bass-bass-snare*. One-and-two-and-three-and—the guitar lick eased into the beat. My chest tightened. *Click*. Engine off.

It was still fairly early when Lauren and I walked into the Frog & Peach, an English-style pub in downtown SLO that prided itself on a large beer selection and live music seven nights a week. It was the first time Lauren and I had done anything resembling drinking, but after seeing my reaction to the barrage of confrontation and news that had come at me in rapid fire that particular Wednesday, she didn't hesitate to call Peter and let him know she would be home a bit later. When we exited the car, I peeked inauspiciously down Higuera, part of me restless to see the new name, but I couldn't quite see the restaurant from that angle, and the signage probably wasn't up quite yet anyway. But still, like being around an ex-girlfriend, I felt the unease of proximity.

Seeing as how it was midweek and the sun was still lingering, there were only a handful of people—mostly solos at the bar—when we arrived. The Dodgers were playing the Mets on the half dozen or so TVs, and a band was lazily setting up their instruments on the tiny stage in the front corner.

"You wanna grab one of those tables, Conner, and I'll get us some drinks?"

"Sure." I eyed the handful of tall round tables that lined the wall.

"What would you like?"

"Any pale ale on draft will be fine. Thanks."

"Go sit, Conner. I'll be right there."

And so I did as I was told, picking the table farthest from the band and farthest from the front door, while "American Woman" played through the bar's speakers. As I waited for Lauren, who was waiting for the bartender to finish talking to one of the band members, I watched the rest of the band as they undid knotty cable-wire and pieced together a drum set. There were four guys in total, including the one talking to the bartender, and each of them had dark pomaded hair slicked up, to the right, and then to the back, with long, manicured sideburns. And tattoos aplenty. Two of them wore bowling shirts, black and turquoise, while the other two wore fitted white T-shirts with cigarette packs rolled into one of their sleeves. Along with their cuffed jeans and black Doc Martens, they were textbook rockabilly. The one was now leaving the bartender, and I caught a clear glimpse of his mustache, the kind that curled at the ends. He also had a large neck tattoo of a pinup girl rocking a guitar. Cliché.

As the song on the jukebox switched to "Roxanne," Lauren showed up at the table with a pint of beer and a glass of white wine. She was wearing dark blue jeans and a green button-up, and her hair was up in a ponytail that bounced around the back of her neck. If you only looked at her ponytail and not her dry red eyes, you would have guessed she was half her age.

"Thank you."

"Of course."

I took a sip, letting the edge of the glass linger on my lips.

"He said this band is supposed to be pretty good," Lauren said, with so little enthusiasm it sounded as if she were saddened by the fact.

"They look like tools."

Lauren shifted in her seat to look at the band, and I leaned out to the right to get a better look myself. The drum kit was nearly set now. The head of the kick drum was a mint green. In the middle was a skeleton on a motorcycle with vinyl records for wheels. Around the rim of the drumhead read *Hank Mardukas and the Dukes*.

"Guess we'll see," she said.

She turned back around and reached her hand out to touch my fingers. Both my hands were clutched around the base of my pint glass.

"So what happened today, Conner?"

"Jesus. Where to start . . ." I knew exactly where to start, however. But I stalled. Opening up to Lauren still didn't feel right. Not because I wasn't comfortable with her. But I didn't feel right having problems of my own.

She waited patiently as I hid behind sips of beer. She hadn't yet touched her wine.

"Okay. Well. Travis came over a couple hours before you picked me up for practice."

As soon as my beer was back on the table, she reached out and held on to one of my index fingers. Her hands were noticeably warm. And with her touch, I launched into my visit from Travis. He wasn't mad. He was matter-of-fact: I was out. Things were moving too fast, and he couldn't wait around for me any longer. If I ever wanted a job, I had one waiting for me in the kitchen, but I was out as a business partner. He didn't show up as friend-Travis with a six-pack of Firestone. He was business-Travis, and this was a meeting. I was fired from the very idea I had come up with. As I recounted the conversation nearly word for word, Lauren listened with kind eyes, and her hands held my one finger as if it was going to save me. Travis was partnering with Manny. Aside from the money Travis got from selling to Horizons, Manny also put in a large sum and became fifty-fifty partners. It was also no longer going to be called Further. They were calling the place Café Lola, serving upscale Mexican. Manny said he could nearly replicate Señora Garces's mole sauce, and they were still constructing a menu and interviewing executive chefs. Manny apparently had given up sex and was going to put all of his efforts into the restaurant. And so just like that, I was out.

"Does that make you mad?" Lauren asked. Like a mother. Or a therapist. "Did you fight back for what should be yours?"

"I didn't. Not even a little. I felt like I did when I read Rian's breakup letter . . ." Not knowing how to finish that thought, I took a long swig of beer. I had only a third of the pint left, and Lauren still hadn't pecked at her wine.

"And what feeling was that, Conner?"

"Like . . . I dunno. I didn't care. It was fine. He was right."

"But that was your idea. You guys started it together."

"I don't care anymore." And as I said it, I really felt as though I meant it. Earlier today, when Travis was over, I thought I cared. But it was as if I thought I was *supposed* to, so I acted the part. "I don't care," I repeated.

"So you're not even going to take the job he offered? Even if you're not part owner, you could cook there."

"Probably not."

"Hmm . . ." Lauren rubbed my forefinger between two of her fingers. "How did it end?"

"It just did. He gave me a hug and told me to call him soon, and then he left."

Lauren was out of questions. And I could read her face. She was confused. When she came to pick me up from the gym, she knew I was upset, and yet here I was telling her I didn't care.

"There's more," I told her.

A few more people had entered the Frog & Peach, including a group of half a dozen college kids that were clearly there to see the band. A couple of them had on Hank Mardukas and the Dukes T-shirts. They were lingering around the stage, trying desperately to engage the band in conversation.

I went on to tell Lauren about practice. I didn't bore her with the details of how shitty it was. How they were all shitty. I glossed right over the part where only eight showed up this time, not even enough for a proper scrimmage. A good forty-five minutes before we were set to finish, Coach Rich showed up and ended practice abruptly. He told the team he had opened up the pool for a free-swim, or they could go home if they could arrange an earlier pickup.

Coach Rich then asked me into his *office*, which was really a desk, bulletin board, and two folding chairs stuffed in one corner of the equipment room. It reeked of rubber.

"What the hell's going on, son?" was how he began.

"Yes," Lauren said, "from what I've witnessed, he's not the gentlest of people."

"Yeah, he is what he is. But then he told me that the team, my team, had approached him. Said they wanted to complain about my coaching. They told him they didn't even care that they were winless all summer, they wanted a coach who tried. Who cared. Even if a coach didn't know *how* to win, they wanted someone who *wanted* to win." There wasn't more than a smattering of leftover suds at the bottom of my glass. But I threw my head back and waited for a couple of the bubbles to slide down to my throat. "The kids. It wasn't even the parents that went to him. You know? It was the kids."

"I'm sorry, Conner. What did he say?"

"He said I need to get my shit together or he'll find a new coach when school starts."

"I'm sure you're doing your best with those boys."

"I'm not." I was interrupted by the drummer banging away on each drum one, two, three, four times, before moving to the next one. Meanwhile, Hank and the rest of the Dukes tuned up their guitars. "Anyway, I'm not. And maybe it's totally ridiculous, but I felt worse about myself after the conversation with Coach Rich than I did after talking with Travis. Isn't that dumb?"

"Not at all."

"Check, check," Hank spat into one of the microphones. "Check one-two-three, check." This went on several times before he gave the thumbs-up.

"The thing is," I continued, "with the restaurant it only really affects me. Travis, I guess, but he'll be fine. But with the team . . ." A few strums of a static guitar swallowed the rest of my sentence.

It was then that Lauren picked up the wine. Her lips were tight as she sipped. It was the tiniest of sips. A thimbleful.

"I'm sorry those two conversations had to happen on the same day, Conner."

"It's fine. Whatever. It really is. I didn't mean to complain. I just thought it might be nice to go out tonight instead of back to our cold houses, you know?"

"I do."

Over Lauren's shoulder, I saw the Dukes get set to play as the one with the mustache stepped to the mic. "G'evening everyone." His voice was a mash-up of the croon of Elvis Presley and the grit of Johnny Cash. "And welcome to the faaaabulous Frog & Peach."

The effect was entertaining but altogether fake. Lauren turned her attention toward the stage as did the other dozen or so people in the dark pub.

"We are Hank Mardukas and the Dukes. My name is Hank, and theeeeeese"—he turned and grandly swept his arm across the stage—"are my Dukes." The handful of fraternity guys were already clapping and whooping. This seemed to please Hank. "Now this first little ditty we're gonna play for you all was actually written and performed by a beautiful woman." A few of the frat boys whistled. "But I'm gonna try and do it justice. It's by a feisty, beautiful woman they used to call 'the Sweet Girl with the Nasty Voice.' Anyone know who I'm talking about?" Hank waited for a response. The bar was quiet until one of the frat boys yelled, "Your mom!" at which his buddies were highly amused. They were all bad caricatures of themselves.

"No, no, I'm talking about the great Wanda Jackson. And this here little ditty, yeaaaah, she recorded way back in 1957. It's called 'Fujiyama Mama.'"

Then the band kicked into a rocking swing beat. And they were damn good. The contrived wardrobe and fake accent aside, it was instantly apparent these guys knew how to play. The song was '50s sock hop with a pinch of '60s surf rock. The instruments were tight, and Hank's voice was all gravel when it needed to be but then as smooth as a diner milkshake.

With the song bouncing off the walls, there wasn't much room for conversation. Snare drum and kick drum and fuzzy guitars . . . sounds I had been trying to avoid from my own head. Bile started to climb from my stomach, and my head was swimming. I decided not to tell Lauren about the third confrontation that came my way that day. I had already spent too much time talking about myself and my petty bullshit. But had I told her, I would have said that after Coach Rich warned me to get my shit together, Jimmy was waiting for me in the parking lot on a bike a few sizes too small for him. He pedaled in circles around me like a bully as he talked.

"You didn't call anyone, did you, Coach?"

I had mumbled something incoherent.

"You didn't call a single fuckin' school, did you? There ain't nobody coming to Bakersfield to see me."

Again, I had forgotten. Didn't even know where his list of schools was. Whenever I talked to Jimmy, I always had the full intention of helping him, but then each time, as soon as he left, so did the motivation. As if he took it with him like the smell of cigarettes that hovered over his head like a cloud. Jimmy continued to ride in slow, crooked circles around me as I sat on the parking lot curb and waited for Lauren.

"You fucked me like the rest of 'em, Coach."

I had tripped and stumbled over a half-hearted apology and told him that maybe it wasn't too late. But the tournament was in less than a week. We both knew no one was coming. "Shit, Coach, shit." He repeated this several times as he coasted around me. "Shit, Coach." Then he rode off on his too-small bike.

As Hank Mardukas and the Dukes sang about drinking sake and blowing up heads, I decided I would spare Lauren that part of my day. She didn't need to hear how I fucked something else up. I felt for a moment that I might actually faint, but shook off the floating white light of my vision and focused hard on the band.

"Thank you! Thank you very much. Yeaaah, the Queen of Rockabilly! How 'bout it! She wrote that song when she was just eighteen! Talk about a fly lil' kitten!"

"They're pretty good," Lauren said when she swung back around to face me.

"Yeah," I said, "and loud. You want to go out back? To the patio?"

"Sure," she said, and smiled.

Lauren grabbed her glass of wine, I left my empty pint glass, and as we made our way out the back door, the band jumped into "Folsom Prison Blues."

I opened the door for Lauren, leaning on it a bit for balance. As she passed by me, she held out a folded twenty-dollar bill.

"Here, Conner. I'm a little slow." She held up her wine glass. "But get yourself another beer."

I took the money with a muttered thank-you. I wasn't sure what it was, but it wasn't the alcohol that was making me feel off-kilter. Another drink might actually help.

Inside, the Frog & Peach was slowly but steadily filling up. The crowd was a fair mix of college students and baby boomers. I sat on a barstool and waited while the lone bartender filled a pint of Guinness at the other end of the bar. The Dukes were playing the Cash song a click or two too fast, but they were tight and made it work. A bit panicky and eager to get outside, I leaned farther over the counter to get the bartender's attention, and it was then that I noticed the guy waiting for the Guinness was looking at me the way you look at someone when you want to stare but don't want to get caught staring. He steadily made an effort to look at the band, then back to the bartender, but those were just end points. Each time he moved from one to the other, his eyes swept across me with purpose. I didn't recognize him, not even remotely, and he was clearly older than me by a good margin, so there was no chance he was an old high school classmate. He had a strip of brown-gray hair along the sides and back of an otherwise bald head and was a good fifty pounds overweight. When the Guinness was placed in front of him, he appeared to shake himself free of me as he grabbed the pint glass and rotated to face the band. Looking at the back of his shaggy beige sweater, I dismissed him as a bored loner and ordered a shot of Maker's Mark and another pale ale. I needed that extra shot of numbness if I was going to have the conversation with Lauren I thought was approaching.

Squeezing my way through the crowd to the back door, I heard Hank onstage announcing the next song. "This next one we're borrowing from a cool cat by the name of Johnny Burnette. He died much too young, and we want to pay tribute to him tonight with this little rock 'n' roll number. Hit it, boys!" *Comfort the living,* I thought as I felt the cool night air on my face. *Honor the dead.*

About half the tables were occupied, but overall, the vibe was calmer, quieter than in the bar. I found Lauren at the back of the patio, alone at a round wooden table.

"Hey, thanks for this," I said, tilting my glass and sitting across from her.

"You're welcome, Conner."

The drums and bass were still present, but otherwise you couldn't hear much from the band except when the back door swung open. For a little while we sat and sipped and talked around things. And my body seemed to settle back into itself. Lauren asked if I'd heard from Rian. I hadn't. I asked if she'd met Abby's boyfriend. She hadn't. She told me Justine had called her again and left a long message. Lauren was thinking of calling her back if only to tell her she'd like to be left alone. I told her that was a good idea, and emailing might be safer. I shared the news about my parents coming to town, and how I wasn't looking forward to it, but I would have to see them at least once. Lauren hinted at wanting to meet them, and I hinted at the fact that they didn't know anything about me. We didn't normally talk so cautiously, not since our first meeting at the lake. I was finished with the new beer when I finally brought up the subject we'd both been avoiding.

"Has Peter mentioned any more about . . . you know."

"Moving?"

She had a way of being blunt without being abrasive. As if she simply didn't have those filters built from fear and insecurities that plagued me and everyone I knew. I often wondered if she had always had that quality or if that was new. A side effect.

"Yes, about that."

"Peter hasn't said another word about it. Or about anything, really. But I know he's still thinking about it."

"And are you thinking about it?"

"Well, Conner, how could I not?"

We both sat there looking at our glasses. Mine was empty, and I was chastising myself for not at least saving a sip for moments like these.

"So, like, what . . ." She was going to make me ask it. "What do you think about his idea? Do *you* want to move too?"

She didn't answer right away. The back door opened, and music poured out onto the deck like a flood of water. The Dukes were jamming on something much heavier now. And for a flash, for a two-count, it wasn't Hank's song, but Neil's song from that Monday. Pounding, relentless kick drums. My stomach turned, and I fought against the beat until the door closed and snuffed it out.

"He'd probably want to move to Rockford," she said.

"Where's that?" It sounded far.

"Illinois. Like an hour northwest of Chicago. He has family there."

Catching my eye to the right was the man who had come out the door. The same balding man from the bar, with the beige sweater. He had his Guinness in one hand and a notebook in the other. As he weighed his seating options, he glanced in our direction more than once.

"What do you think of Rockford?" I asked, turning back to Lauren, who was rubbing an index finger round and round the rim of her wine glass.

"It's okay. The winters are awful."

"But do you *want* to go?" I felt the alcohol swimming through my body.

My insides warm and swollen.

"I can't go, Conner." She lifted her glass to her lips but then brought it straight down. "But I can't stay either."

I understood, but I also didn't. I understood because that's how I'd felt nearly my whole life. Jumping from one town to the next, from one career path to the next. Both feet firmly planted in sand, one strong wave away from being washed out to sea.

"Part of me really wants to go, Conner. I'm tired. I'm so tired. I'm tired of avoiding South Bay Boulevard. I'm tired of living with two people who barely speak to me and don't look me in the eye." As she said this, she made eye contact with me and held it, like a challenge. In the light of approaching night, her eyes were glassy, her pupils huge. "And I'm tired of the looks I get. The mailman, the grocery clerk, the neighbors, all those people who knew me in passing, enough to smile and say hello. But now . . . Now they look at me like I'm a ghost. Like I'm a ghost who roams around not knowing she's dead, and everyone's too sad and scared to be the one to tell her." She sat back in her chair with a sigh and looked off at nothing. "And you have no idea how much I cry, Conner."

The last line was a punch to the gut, and I sat back in my chair to show her that we didn't have to talk anymore. We could take a break, catch our breath. I thought about what she said. I understood the loneliness, that much was easy.

A waitress came up and asked if we wanted something more to drink. She was a pretty girl. A little too skinny, but she had long black hair that looked as though it had been ironed. I began to wave her off, but Lauren sat up and asked the girl to please get me another pale ale.

As I watched her leave and then bounce between the occupied tables, scribbling drink orders, I caught the man with the Guinness looking at me again. This time it was with his eyes only. His head was down as he furiously wrote in his notebook, but even in the dim lighting of the patio, I saw his eyes creep up and shoot us looks from under the canopy of his forehead.

"But I can't leave either, Conner."

I turned back to Lauren, who was now leaning into the table, toward me.

"If I leave . . . I'm leaving *him*. How could I live in a house, in a town, that doesn't carry a single memory of him? That's all we have now, memories, so how can I give that away? What kind of mother would I be . . ."

The music swelled into the patio again as the waitress finished making her round and went inside. Then just as quickly, it vanished, leaving only a muffled thumping bass.

"I'd go with you."

"What do you mean?" Her big pupils looked strained. Hopeful and confused.

Comfort the living.

"If you moved," I said. "I could go with you."

"Excuse me." His voice was higher than I expected. The man with the beige sweater stood at our table, Guinness-less, but with his notebook tucked under his arm. "I'm really sorry to interrupt. But you're Lauren Thomas, is that right?" He gestured toward Lauren with his free hand. She eyed him with caution. "And you are Conner Robbins, yes?"

"Okay," I said. "And you are?"

"It would mean a great deal to me if I could sit and have a few minutes of your time." He put his hand on the chair, ready to pull it out at the slightest hint of permission. "I promise to get straight to the point."

My hand shot out to the chair and held it in place. "Whoa, whoa, wait a second. First, who the hell are you?"

"Oh, yes, sorry, my name is Dale Ruthemeyer."

The name sounded vaguely familiar. I looked to Lauren, but she sat there indifferent to it all. I asked her with my eyes if she knew the man, and she simply offered a shrug.

"Can I sit, please? I'll buy you a round."

"We don't want your drinks, sir," Lauren piped up, her voice irritated. "What do you want?"

He cautiously took a seat and placed his notebook in his lap. I didn't know who would know both Lauren and me, but it couldn't be good.

"Like I said, I'm Dale Ruthemeyer. I've left you both several messages."

Lauren and I exchanged looks. Still nothing.

On guard, we turned to face him. Up close, his face looked much older, covered in millions of tiny zigzagging wrinkles that looked as though they were earned and not just a product of time.

"I'm, uh, I'm from the *Tribune*."

"Oh shit," I said. I should have known. "Man, no, get out of here."

"Yes, please leave, sir."

Dale immediately stood and with notebook in hand, put his hands out toward us, pleading. "Please, please, one minute of your time."

"Go!" I said more forcefully. People began to look.

He shuffled clumsily away from the chair. His hand still out. "Please, Mrs. Thomas."

"Please leave us alone," Lauren said without raising her voice.

When she spoke I stood straight up, as tall as I'd ever been. Fists clenched at my sides. Dale backed away more quickly, eyes darting back and forth between Lauren and me.

"But Mrs. Thomas, if you'll just hear me out. I promise. I've already talked with Peter, and—"

"You talked to Peter?"

"Yes, Mrs. Thomas, I did, and if you'll—"

"And Peter talked to you?" Her voice was more incredulous than accusatory.

I relaxed my fists and sat back down.

"May I? Please?"

"Wait, you and Peter talked? When? Where?"

Dale took this as an invitation to sit. This time he laid both his notebook and his hands on the table. "Yes we did, and if you two would please just let me—"

"Fine," I said. "Out with it. Speak."

He took a big breath, and he began in a calm, albeit tinny, voice.

"First off, I'm deeply sorry for your loss, Mrs. Thomas. I am." He waited for a response, but none came. "Okay, as you both may know, or maybe you don't, the two articles that came out following"—he didn't know where to look at this point—"the accident. They were both very matter-of-fact. The who, what, where, Journalism 101. And that was it. But there's so much more to the story, and I want to tell it. People should know Braden." *Honor the dead.* "People should know Peter and Abby. They should know you, Lauren. And you, Conner, they should know you. There are so many stories here. Human stories. And maybe it will help people. Maybe it will help you all as well." *Comfort the living.* "You don't understand how many letters and emails the paper has received. About you guys. People hurting. People wanting to know more. Look, I don't know exactly what will come from this, but I think it's a good thing. And I think it's the right thing."

Lauren calmly lifted her palm up to stop him. "Who exactly have you spoken to?" This time she did sound accusatory. She was thinking of Abby.

"Well, I've talked to the policemen who arrived to the . . . Well, they weren't very helpful. Gave me nothing I couldn't have gotten from the report. And I spoke with Justine Bardales. She was the—"

"We know who she is," I said.

"Yeah, she was interesting. She had a lot to say. It has really affected her, actually. And, well, like I said, I've talked with your husband, Peter."

And appearing as if out of nowhere, the waitress was at my side, placing down a new coaster and a fresh beer. I hadn't even noticed the back door open and close. Maybe the Dukes were on a break.

"That'll be seven bucks," she said, and shifted her weight from one bony hip to the other.

"Here," Dale said, reaching for his back pocket. "Please, let me—"

"We don't want your money," Lauren said. Her hand was already reaching a ten across the table to me. I handed it to the waitress, and she was gone without so much as a thank-you.

"Yes, so, you talked with Peter, go on."

"Yeah, so, he answered one of my calls one night and agreed to meet me for coffee, and yeah, we chatted for a bit."

"You met for . . . but when . . . Oh, it doesn't matter. What did he say? Who else have you talked to?"

"That's all at the moment. I would love to talk to Abby, but I promised Peter I wouldn't approach her without your permission."

Lauren looked visibly relieved.

"And obviously I'd love to talk to you both. And now that I see you two are . . . well, spending time together, I think that makes the story far more fascinating."

"We're not here to entertain you," I said. "Or help you win some small-town bullshit journalism award."

"No, no, it's just a real story. Loss and tragedy, grief, timing, and fate or destiny or God or whatever you believe in, and letting people know Braden, and healing, and—"

This time Lauren held her hand up to stop him.

"I'm sorry," he said. "I'm passionate about human stories. How we're all existing and surviving on this big ball of water together. It's incredible, isn't it? Conner, I'd even love to talk to your parents. I know they'll be in town soon."

"How the hell do you know my parents will be in town?" I was embarrassed at their mention. I took a long swig of beer. It was cold and numbed its way down my throat.

"I wasn't going to approach them without getting your permission first. You have my honest-to-God word."

"Please leave my parents alone."

"And Abby," Lauren said.

"I will."

"I have a question for you, Mr. . . ." Lauren looked at him hard.

"Ruthemeyer."

"How did you know Conner and I would be here tonight? Are you following us?"

It hadn't even dawned on me, but to hear Lauren's question I grew a fresh hatred for this small, inbred town.

"No, no, nothing like that. I'm here for the, for the band. The Dukes. Local music, interesting group of characters. It's a tiny puff piece, but someone's gotta write it. Anyway, I recognized you, Conner, at the bar. At least I was hoping it was you. Look, clearly this is not the right time and place, and I know I bombarded you and . . ."

He leaned his large belly forward and reached for the back of his pants. He brought out two business cards.

"Here. Please. Each of you take one and call me. Soon. We'll set up one-on-one meetings at the time and place of your convenience. Wherever, whenever you want. But please let your story be heard."

Lauren took the card but didn't look at it. Dale held one out to me and then placed it on the table in front of me.

"And this way, you are in control of your story. Don't let the people of this town write their own story about you. Don't be gossip, don't be . . ."

"That's enough," I said. "Please."

"Again, I'm sorry. I just—"

"Don't you dare contact my daughter, Mr. Ruthemeyer."

"No, no, I wouldn't. Not without your—"

"We've given you our time," Lauren continued. "We gave you what you asked for."

"Yes." I jumped in to take the lead. "I think it's time you go. And we won't be calling you, but thanks."

"I'll go," he said. "And I sincerely hope you don't mean that. This is your story, not mine. I'm just the pen. The microphone."

"Good luck with your piece on the Dukes," I said with my face in my pint glass.

Lauren was looking at the business card. Not reading it so much as turning it over and over in her hands.

"There is one more thing," Dale said. He held up his chubby index finger for effect. "Syndication." He looked back and forth between us for some kind of reaction. "I've already pitched the idea to editors at both the *LA Times* and the *San Francisco Chronicle*. They're interested. And now that I know you two are . . . well, friends? This could be a big story. It's not anything about the money, but people are going to want to hear it. I'm not talking Netflix or *Dateline* or anything. But papers around the country. Hell, *People* magazine. Who knows?"

"It's time to go," I said, standing up. "We're not sideshow freaks for everyone to stare at. And we're not some fucking get-rich-quick idea you've been creaming your pants about." I shoved his business card off the table. "And if you call either of our numbers again . . ."

"Think about it. That's all." He backed away from the table, ignoring me, but staring at Lauren the whole while. She kept her head down. "Think about it, Mrs. Thomas. Please."

Lauren didn't say anything until we were back in the car, parked along the curb on Higuera, only blocks from what would soon become Café Lola. On her lap were the brown sweatshirt, Dale's business card, and her car keys.

"It's the little things like that that make me think maybe Peter is right, Conner."

"That guy is an asshole."

"But you heard what he said. About the letters. The emails. None of those people cared about Braden before. Their sentiments aren't real. They may *think* they are, but they're not. The town will never see me the same again. And I don't care about what people think or say about me. Not those people. But I should be able to live, right? At some point, somewhere in time, is there normalcy again? Happiness even? How, though? I dunno. I dunno what I'm saying. I'm sorry."

"Don't be. I understand exactly."

"I know you do, Conner. You're the only one that does."

"That's why I'd come with you. If you moved."

"But that's crazy. You've never been to Rockford. Where would you live? What would you do?"

"What do I do now? What do I have here? I've lost my restaurant, I'm about to lose my second job in however many weeks. I have maybe one friend, but who even knows about him anymore. What do I have here? I'd move to Rockford. I'd find a place close by. We'd do what we do now. Go places and talk and understand each other. Maybe eventually Abby will warm up to me. And Peter too. Peter will be different in Rockford. It could work."

I said it all with conviction as if I had run it over and over in my head, playing out every scenario, weighing all the pros and cons. But none of that had happened. The three beers and shot of whiskey had made my tongue loose. The moment the words left my mouth was the same moment they entered my head. I didn't know if it would work. I didn't know much of anything. But the thought of losing Lauren terrified me.

"I don't know. Let's go, Conner," she said with a tired voice. She started the engine and pulled onto the empty road. "I don't know, maybe it would work. If I had you . . . maybe it could."

It was three intersections later, all red lights, when she spoke again, though it sounded as if she were speaking to herself more than me. "I don't know how I could leave Braden."

We eventually made a left onto Foothill and headed toward the Thomases' house, only to pass it in silence. It lay dark, hidden among a long row of sleeping houses. We couldn't see it; it didn't exist.

The fog hit us as we climbed up Los Osos Valley Road, still a couple miles before the cemetery, which would be equally harmless hidden in the night. As if a switch had been flipped, the headlights suddenly illuminated an ocean of wet mist, a perfect blanket of white-gray cotton that we cut through like a razor.

It wasn't until we reached 11th Street, however, and Lauren was making a slow right turn into the fog, that she spoke again. This time, it was a simple question that didn't require an answer.

"Conner, can I spend the night?"

CHAPTER 16

I WOKE UP TO LAUREN CRYING INTO THE BACK OF my neck. Quiet, wet tears. We were on our sides, curled up inside one another. She spooned me from behind and wrapped an arm around my chest, holding me to her. The tears ran one by one down my neck, tickling almost, before being absorbed by the cotton of my white T-shirt.

Before that, we slept. We slept and we slept and we slept. We arrived back to my apartment around ten and there was no more talking. Not about moving, not about Dale, or Abby or Peter. I gave Lauren a glass of water and a hand towel for the bathroom, and that was that. We got into bed, both fully dressed apart from our shoes, and when her thin arm wrapped around me, her body pressed against my back, it was like a button had been pushed, and I fell into the deepest sleep.

When I awoke to the droplets running down my neck, I couldn't see the time, but it was late. My body felt heavy, as though it had slept for days. I didn't want to startle her, so only my eyes moved, blinking themselves into consciousness. It was then that I realized she was holding my shirt tight in her fist. Knuckles white and pink, so much held in that fist that I would never know. Even as I tried to lie still as water, Lauren sensed I was awake. A natural mother.

"Good morning, Conner," she said in a half whisper. "I'm sorry for this." She wiped the back of my neck. "I've been up for a while, but I didn't want to wake you."

I didn't say anything or turn to face her. I knew she liked me better with my back to her.

"Did a lot of thinking too." She unclenched her fist and patted down the pulled and stretched fabric on my chest. "I still don't know about moving, but I think I decided something." This time she waited for a response.

"What did you decide?"

"I think I'm going to talk to that guy. Dale."

I didn't know what I was expecting her to say, but it wasn't that. Last night, she had seemed as put off by him as I was.

"He's not really a bad guy, I don't think," she said. "And he may write the story anyway. I am the best person to represent Braden the right way. And that's important." She retracted her hand. We were no longer touching. "So yeah, I think I'm going to do it, Conner. I'm so against these things—the gravesite, the memorial—they represent his death, not his life. And I'm not doing it for Dale or for me or for the people that will read it. I don't care about them. I'm going to do it for Braden."

Honor the dead.

"But I won't say anything about you, not if you don't want me to. Not a word. And I don't want you to feel you have to talk to him too. That's your decision."

She left shortly after getting out of bed, and she agreed to come get me and take me to basketball practice the next afternoon as was our usual routine. When she left, I found $300 on my bathroom counter.

The more I thought about Lauren talking to Dale, the more it made sense. I could see why she might want to tell her story. Really, she'd already been telling it to me these weeks. But my story was different. What did I have to offer? To what, to talk about how horrible it had been? But something in Lauren's voice made me think that despite her words, she *did* want me to talk to him. Maybe she wanted to tell *our* story as well, but she couldn't do that. She couldn't do that to Braden. I would have to be the one to tell that story.

I spent all of Wednesday and most of Thursday morning in front of ESPN Classic—sporting events that had already happened, outcomes already decided—and only partly thinking about what would happen if I spoke with Dale. But really, most of my thoughts were consumed with the idea of moving. I would have no trouble leaving this town that had betrayed me, but what would happen in Rockford? I had no idea if Lauren wanted me there as much as I thought, or hoped, she did.

Before falling asleep on the couch in front of the 1978 Masters, I received an email from Travis. The subject was "Update," which didn't sound like a lecture or a guilt trip, so I opened it. It was as the title indicated. He began with a line Rian had also used in her letter—"I'm not giving up on you"—and then went on to update me on Café Lola. The menu was set. They were almost fully staffed and shooting for an October first opening. This didn't make me feel much except to wonder what Travis would say when I moved to Rockford, Illinois.

His email made me realize there was real mail I hadn't checked in who knew how long. The mailbox was stuffed, mostly with junk. Flyers and letters and cards, asking me if I needed my trees trimmed or my teeth cleaned, sales on mattresses and life insurance. There was a gas bill and an envelope from the sheriff's office, clean and ultra-white with a blue insignia in the upper left corner.

I sat down on one of the chairs outside my apartment and opened it. Inside was a single sheet of paper. A form. Official. An accident report full of dates and times and names and locations. I glossed over most of it, catching familiar-enough letters and numbers to understand. But there were two items, numbers thirteen and fourteen. Item thirteen was as simple and binary as it came. *Investigation,* it read, with two choices beneath: *Pending* or *Closed*. And next to *Closed,* in a neat little box, was a large, bold *X* in a slightly different font, done with a typewriter. My heart rate sped up and my hands started shaking, the paper quivering like a California tremor. Item fourteen read *Cause of Accident*. I couldn't even process all the options, my eyes darting to the *X* sitting slightly outside the designated box like a missed bank shot. *Other than driver*. That's all it said. Three basic, generic, ambiguous words. *Other than driver*. What did that even mean?

I stuffed the gas bill and the form into the overflowing mail holder by the phone, similarly stuffing those three words somewhere in the back of my brain to fester. I couldn't deal with them now, but I knew they'd surface later.

By midday on Thursday, I was going stir-crazy, and there was no food in the house. An empty pantry had been a common occurrence the last few weeks, so I had grown accustomed to deli sandwiches from Keeley's Liquor a few blocks up. Pre-made sandwiches wrapped ten times over with sticky cellophane, sitting in the refrigerated section between packages of sliced American cheese and generic cartons of half-and-half. Dennis always worked the day shift. A nice enough guy who graduated high school with more energy and enthusiasm than brains and direction, and woke up one day to find himself forty-two and still working the counter at a liquor store. What I liked most about Dennis was that he knew exactly what had happened but never brought it up.

I was walking up 11th, pine needles crunching under my feet, when I decided to text Lauren, asking her if we could stop at the grocery store today on the way home from practice. I could just as easily ask her when I saw her, but I missed her and longed to see her name in my messages. She didn't reply right away, so I turned the phone to vibrate and stuffed it in my pocket. The sky was gray, and the breeze was strong and chilling. I hugged my arms tight to my body as the air pushed through the fabric of my sweatshirt.

After deciding on a ham and Swiss, I asked Dennis to please break a hundred-dollar bill.

"Nothing over a twenty," Dennis said, pointing to a sloppy handmade sign taped below dusty bottles of brandy.

"C'mon, Dennis."

"Just this once," he said, taking the bill from me reluctantly. "But the boss will have my ass."

It was then that my phone vibrated.

Dennis counted and recounted my change on the counter, laying out each bill as if he were a blackjack dealer in Vegas.

"Dennis, you ever been to Chicago?"

"Chicago?" He said it with disgust, as if I had asked if he put ketchup on his ice cream. "Why would I go to Chicago?"

"Just curious."

"I like it fine right here. No reason to leave. Here you go. $89.37. You saw me count it out."

"Yes, fine, thank you," I said, gathering the fanned-out bills off the glass countertop.

"You thinking of taking a trip?"

"Maybe."

"I dunno why people always trying to go someplace else. Never 'preciating where they are."

I couldn't decide if that was the dumbest thing Dennis had ever said or if it was somehow brilliant. So I took my change and left without another word.

Back out on breezy 11th Street, with my ham and Swiss and bottle of 7-Up in a black plastic bag, I opened my phone to check the message from Lauren.

Can't come today. Something's happened. Will explain later.

That was it. No follow-up text. It didn't even sound like Lauren. She usually texted in full sentences and always found a way to say my name. Reading the text a second and third time, I felt stranded out there on the side of the road. I needed to get back to my apartment. I quickened my pace, holding tightly to the phone so as not to miss its vibration.

But it didn't vibrate again, and when I arrived home, I was just as lost and confused, but now sitting in an empty living room. I knew I shouldn't call, so after several rewrites, I settled on a brief and to-the-point text: *Don't worry about the ride. Is everything ok? Concerned.*

I thought of my truck sitting in my parking spot. Ready. Full of gas. And taxis took forever to get out here if not pre-ordered. It didn't take long to decide to cancel practice. I sent an email blast to the players, leaving out Coach Rich. When I logged in, however, there was a second email from Travis. This one titled "Update #2." There was an attachment, but I didn't open the message.

I picked at the ham sandwich all evening, the bread turning soggy from too much mayo. And like a lovestruck teenage girl, I sat and stared at the phone, willing it to light up or vibrate or tell me something. But nothing. *Something happened.* That could mean so many things, I didn't even know where to begin. Something with Abby? Peter? Had she already talked to Dale? Did Justine show up at her doorstep? Something else altogether unexpected for this family destined for loss?

Somewhere between watching Tyson versus Douglas and the 1980 NBA Finals, my mom called and left a message. Wondering if I had room enough at my place or if they should stay with the troupe. She was south of Monterey and didn't have a number for a return call. She would try again tomorrow.

On Friday morning, I still hadn't heard from Lauren. I texted her again around eleven. *Is everything okay?* I picked up another sandwich from Dennis, turkey and cheddar, and called a taxi for a two p.m. pickup.

Still no response to my question when the yellow cab honked twice outside my apartment.

The driver was someone I'd never seen before, and he was ecstatic when he found out I wanted a ride to Morro Bay High School. "Yeah, man, I went there!" And because of this excitement, he was more than willing to indulge my request and drive that long way round through SLO. It offered him more time to go down memory lane. Turned out he was four years younger than me, so we had just missed each other. I checked my phone as often as he said "Yeah, man!" But still nothing from Lauren. "Yeah, man, I used to love Mr. Pederson's classes. That guy was a trip!" "Yeah, man! I smoked out behind the trees every day at lunch!" "Yeah, man, football games were the best—fuck those Atascadero pricks though, yeah man, am I right?"

I nodded along and figured as long as I could keep him reminiscing, I could keep him from asking too many questions. Halfway down Los Osos Valley Road, as we passed the cemetery, he started the *Did you know* game. "Yeah, man, did you ever know Jessica, uh, uh, damn, what's her last name? Yeah man, what a rack!" Clayton Elster; Lindsey Manning; the Lawrence twins; Melissa, uh, something that starts with an *R*; that one guy they called Boom-Boom; the names went on and on. And although I'd only vaguely heard of a couple of them, I learned that "Hmm, I think so" was an effective response.

He was running out of names by the time we turned onto Foothill. The Thomases' house was less than a mile away. There wasn't any traffic, and I considered asking him to slow down once we got to their block. Maybe do a slow drive-by. Maybe there'd be a clue.

"Excuse me." I could tell I interrupted his train of thought, the flipping through old yearbooks in his mind. "Do you mind stopping for a moment? Yeah, right here is fine. I'll only be a second, but I'll be right back. Keep the meter running."

He pulled over across the street, one or two houses down from the Thomases'. There were no cars in their driveway, but that didn't necessarily mean anything. My heart was racing. I was praying that Lauren would answer. I could handle Peter, but I was deathly afraid of Abby. I took a couple deep breaths and walked to the front porch. The rickety mosaic table was still there, but now a terra-cotta pot sat on top, and in it a sad, limp cactus, its fleshy, bloated body yellow where it should have been green. A gift from a neighbor, no doubt. Lose a son, gain a cactus. The house was dark inside, but I figured it always was. I checked the cab, still there. Checked my phone, nothing.

I knocked twice, firmly.

I had no plan if Abby answered. Maybe retreat to the taxi as fast as I could. But no one seemed to be stirring in the house.

I knocked again, a quick three times.

The MBHS alum turned cab driver stared at me through his rolled-down window. A single car drove by, but otherwise the block was still. I took a step back from the door and waited. I figured Abby would have answered the door the instant my knuckles hit wood, eager to face whoever was intruding. Lauren most likely would have answered by the second round, having composed herself enough to be presentable to a casseroled neighbor. Peter, however, might take a while, mustering the strength to drag himself out of bed, willing each foot to move in front of the other. Or maybe he wouldn't answer at all. I looked back to the taxi again, the driver still watching with anticipation.

I knocked once more, three hard *whaps* with unplanned aggression. *Something happened. I'll explain later.* What did that mean? Still nothing. I left the doorstep and became stuck. The house, the phone, neither held answers. I felt as though I were drowning, grasping for anything to hold on to.

All the windows of the house had blinds shut tight as fists, but there were three small diamond-shaped windows on the garage door. Desperate for answers, I leaned up on my toes to see in clearly, but of course it was dark. I could only make out vague shapes: boxes upon boxes upon boxes, neglected gardening tools, a deflated basketball, an empty fish tank. Everything so goddamned dormant! Then I spotted three bikes, their twisted, sagging handlebars, desperate to collapse if not for stubborn rusty kickstands, all six tires deflated, drooping like melted clocks. The bikes huddled together—vultures, mocking me. Three bikes. Not four. "Fuck you!" I yelled, and pounded three times on the aluminum door with my palm, "Fuck! Fuck! Fuck!" screamed through gritted teeth. I paused, clenching and unclenching my fists, before pounding the door twice more. It banged and rattled but would not give. My top teeth released their grip from my lower lip, my tongue searching deep indentations for the iron taste of blood.

I scanned the door for a dent, something to show for my anger, but there was nothing. I pivoted and walked with purpose down the driveway. *Something happened.* My hand now pulsed with my heartbeat. Three bikes, not four. *Other than driver.* And as I passed the porch, I grabbed the little table with my right hand and flung it backwards with all I had. The crash was louder than I had expected and stopped me cold. When I turned, I saw the driveway was now littered with shattered pieces of tile and terra-cotta. The top of the table had snapped off from its stem and wasn't recognizable as a table at all. A million tiny pieces of green and blue and yellow sparkled like a rainbow of shattered glass. The pot was scattered in half a dozen pieces, and a large swath of soil striped its way across the driveway like mole sauce on a plate.

Taking in the scene, I didn't feel any better; in fact, just the opposite. I couldn't hide this. It was such a spectacle, everything sharp and broken and dramatic against the flat, drab driveway of this flat, drab house. Abby would likely assume it was me. Peter might not even notice. But what would Lauren think happened here? Would I tell her? Then I spotted the cactus, the last piece of this mess. It lay up against the base of the garage door like a dead banana slug. Not knowing what else to do, I lowered my head and returned to the cab. Autopilot. Muscle memory.

"Sorry," I told the driver. "Let's go."

"Shit, man, are you okay?"

"Yeah, can we just get to the high school?"

"Yeah, man, sure. Hey, did you ever know Katy Paxton? Her younger sister was in my grade."

With adrenaline still surging through me, it took me nearly half the drive to the high school to notice my finger was bleeding. The index finger on my right hand had an inch-long gash. Cut from a piece of tile, no doubt. The blood had run down my finger and filled in the grooves of my palm. I wrapped my finger tightly with the hem of my shirt, wrapping it tighter and tighter until finally it went numb.

As I walked into the gym, Kyle was leading the team in stretches at center court. Including him, there were only seven players. Numbers dwindling by the day.

"Hey guys," I greeted them, "we expecting any others? Jeremy should be here, right? And Sebastian?"

No one seemed to know anything. But their eyes had no trouble finding the blood that now decorated the lower half of my shirt.

"Well, we could play three-on-three, I guess. Maybe half-court. Work on our half-court game."

"Or you could play, Coach," Cody said, his elbow pushing against his propped-up knee, back in a full twist.

"No, no, I'm not gonna play."

"C'mon," Cody pushed. The others voiced their approval in single syllables. "Coach Rich said you were good back in your day."

"Yeah, you're not *that* old," Kyle said. "My dad plays, and he's way older than you."

I was wearing decent-enough tennis shoes, and with my shorts and T-shirt, I couldn't get out of it on a clothing technicality. I dabbed my cut finger against my shirt and rubbed at the palm of my right hand, already feeling the beginnings of a deep bruise.

"Alright, fine," I said. "Kyle, Cody, you're captains. Pick teams. I'll be right back." I ran to the equipment room turned makeshift office, where I put a bandage on my finger and changed into an old MBHS Fun-Run T-shirt that wasn't even mine, but fit well enough. Embarrassing and very physical reminders of what I had done, what the Thomases' driveway now looked like—the shirt like a neon sign, the cut like a penance. As I was re-entering the gym, my phone buzzed. A text from Lauren, answering my question about whether everything was okay: *Yes and no. Mostly no. Will call soon.*

But I didn't have a second to dissect the sparse words or make conjectures. The teams were chosen quickly, and soon I was in the middle of a full-court game of four-on-four with seven young teenagers who all had an overdose of energy.

They were short and bird-thin, but they were fast and didn't seem to tire. And naturally, they were eager to score on me, double-team me, box me out. All elbows and knees. And only four possessions in, I was spent. I tried my best not to show it, but my lungs were drowning, gasping for air like an asthmatic, and my thighs and back were on fire. I couldn't recall the last time I had done something athletic, not counting a walk to Keeley's or paddling around the bay. Years. My instincts on the court were still there, and it was easy to overpower the kids. But my shot was way off, my reaction time slow, and I made cuts as if in sand. This was nothing like lazily shooting free throws in Travis's backyard. I didn't just miss; I missed badly. And any time I handled the ball, the cut on my finger sent pain shooting up my arm. Everything a reminder. Each brick I threw up drew laughs and heckles from the kids, but I was far too short of breath to protest. I was just trying to survive. Sometimes I would barely schlep my body to half-court, and already the ball was heading back the other way. Wisecracks about my age or what kind of shape I was in whizzed by me, along with the blur of adolescent legs.

But then there was a moment, maybe thirty minutes in, where my body reached a tipping point. Collapse or push through. Sink or swim. Running up the court on a fast break, my legs were overcooked linguini. My sloppy layup clanked off the rim, and then back down around mid-court I stopped, bent over, hands on my knees, sucking air like there was none left while the pulse in my finger showed me how fast my heart was pounding.

"C'mon, old man, you need a stretcher?" They continued to heckle me. "My grandma runs faster than you!" All the kids laughed as they jogged past, faces rosy and flushed and youthful. And it hit me that Braden could have been one of these kids. One of these kids could have been Braden. And then as if a switch were flipped, I no longer felt as though I would throw up or pass out. I sprinted down to play defense, and while my legs and lungs continued to burn, I fell into cruise control, my body finally surrendering to what it was doing. I let competition and sweat and instincts take over. My thoughts and worry and guilt and stress and fear and uncertainty, they all got pushed down somewhere, turned off. I functioned purely on action–reaction. Muscle memory. For the first time in what felt like a decade, I lived in my body and not my head. My passes were crisp, I called out screens on defense, and even some of my shots started to fall. And although still strained, my breathing fell into a regular rhythm. But the sweat. I wasn't just covered in sweat, I was covered in *dripping* sweat. From any slanted curve or edge of my body, it poured down in moving streams. I blinked it out of my eyes and sopped it up with the borrowed T-shirt. I moved without the ball, I read passing lanes, I orchestrated fast breaks. They said exercise was a good cure for a hangover because you sweated out the toxins. I may not have had alcohol to sweat out, but I could feel the toxins evacuating my body, tiny little pollutants of guilt and grief and blame and sadness and pity, everything that had been trapped inside me like a disease, rushing out the nearest open pore.

And then like a fist hitting metal, it all came to an abrupt stop.

"Coach Robbins!" It was Coach Rich. He was standing in the doorway. "I need to speak with you. Now."

The game stopped and all seven players looked to me. This was the second time this week Coach Rich interrupted and canceled one of our practices.

"Sure thing," I said, and rolled the ball to Kyle.

Coach Rich scanned the gym, no doubt counting how few players there were. "I'll leave the gym open. You guys can stay or go, but practice is over."

As I bent to grab my things, my leg muscles nearly seized. And seeing my phone brought it all back. Rockford. Dale. Lauren. The Thomases' disaster of a driveway . . . *Yes and no. Mostly no,* she had said. Mostly no?

"Walk with me." Coach Rich was already four paces ahead, passing the trophy case and the equipment room slash office. He turned back. "Is that my fucking shirt?"

"What's this about, Coach?"

"I dunno, but you're gonna tell me."

I had no idea what he was getting at and couldn't make the effort to catch up to him, my legs one flex away from cramping. And frankly, I didn't give a shit about what Coach Rich was angry about. I just wanted to get out of there. He burst out the back doors and headed for the football field.

"Where are we going? Can't we talk here?"

"Let's go sit and have a chat so you can explain to me what the hell is going on."

Clearly the conversation was going nowhere until we reached his destination. So I followed him over the asphalt, and as I kicked up grit and loose pebbles, I was again haunted by the vision of the Thomases' driveway. Clay and tile and dirt, like a bomb went off. My heart dropped as the most obvious and simple question occurred to me: Who would clean it up? But I didn't have time to dwell on the image of Lauren out there with a broom, as Coach Rich and I crunched our way across part of the track and soon were clinking up the tinny aluminum stairs of the bleachers. My sweat was already starting to dry, the salt crystallizing on my skin. It wasn't until the seventh or eighth row that he finally sat.

"You want to tell me what you know about Jimmy?" he asked.

"What do you mean?" I thought back to Jimmy circling around me on his bike, radiating disappointment. But Coach Rich couldn't be angry about my forgetting to contact college coaches. Wasn't the whole reason Jimmy came to me because Coach Rich didn't give a damn?

He pulled his cell phone out of his pocket and hit a few buttons before handing it to me. "Listen."

Putting the phone to my ear, I heard a robot woman telling me the message was from last night at eleven thirty-nine. And then there was Jimmy's voice:

"Hey, Coach, I know you don't wanna hear this shit right now, but I gotta quit the team. Some crazy shit has happened and I gotta take care of it. Gotta be a man or whatever. Anyway, Coach Robbins can tell you more. I gotta go." *Click.*

I handed the phone back. "What? He quit?"

"He's our best fucking player. What the hell happened?"

"I don't know, I mean . . . I don't know why he said that about me."

"He wouldn't mention you for no reason. Out with it. Speak, son."

"Well, I mean, he was asking me to help him get D1 coaches out to Bakersfield, and I . . ."

"You what?"

"I kind of dropped the ball. But he wouldn't quit over that. And what was that about being a man? I don't know what that means." Though I did think of his family, what he said about his father, and worry set in.

Coach Rich glared at me. He wasn't buying it.

"I swear, Coach, I don't know what he's talking about." My right quad was trembling on its own. Not out of fear, but pure exhaustion.

"We got to talk to him. Fuck, *you* got to talk to him. Clearly he trusts you. What's this shit going on behind my back about scouts at Bakersfield? He doesn't need scouts at Bakersfield. It's goddamned summer league. Of course I'll help him come fall, but damn these kids, only thinking about their own stats and who's watching."

Something didn't add up. Basketball was Jimmy's way out.

The cross-country team entered, running in packs of two or three across the field. They held a steady pace, mechanical even, as if they had been running continuously for weeks. White shirts, blue shorts, and legs like the egrets out at Fairbank Point, they ran out of our line of sight as quickly and quietly as they had entered. I grabbed my leg to stop its shaking.

"Why do I get the damn feeling you know something you're not telling me. Why would he tell me to ask you?"

"I don't know," I said, and I meant it. "Look, here are the things I know about Jimmy: He drives a piece-of-shit car. He rolls his own cigarettes. He hangs out with a couple losers. He's got a messed-up family. He wanted my help with colleges. And, and, I dunno, according to you, he's got the best jumper this school has ever seen."

Coach Rich didn't look any calmer.

"That's it. That's all I know."

"What the hell is up with his family?"

"I dunno, he's got some asshole dad, I guess. But God, isn't that half the people in this world?"

"He beat on him or something?"

"I don't know. Maybe? I don't think so. But who knows."

"I'm gonna call him. He can't quit like this. I want you to call him too. I can't win league without him, and we can forget CIF."

With a direct order to call Jimmy as soon as possible, I was released. Sitting on the curb, picking at the bloodied Band-Aid, waiting for my cab, I became less and less concerned about Jimmy or Coach Rich, or basketball in general. Sure, I was curious about Jimmy's rash decision, but I had the feeling he would spend his life making rash decisions. And once Coach Rich was out of sight, speeding away in his old Camaro, my thoughts immediately turned back to Lauren. *Yes and no. Mostly no. Will call soon.* But there was nothing more waiting for me on my phone, so I sat in my cold, wet clothes, muscles quivering, waiting for a cab and again, waiting for answers.

When the house phone rang at ten p.m., I jumped from the couch and ran to the kitchen, my legs almost collapsing beneath me. That was the phone Lauren had first called me on. Our brief, stilted conversation. Her thin, hollow voice asking me to Laguna Lake. But when I answered this time, I was greeted with elation.

"Conner, my boy! You're home!"

"Hi, Mom."

"I've been trying and trying you. And you know I don't have a number for you to call back on while we're on the road. Oh, but here you are."

"Yes, I'm here."

"We're going to see you so soon. Are you so excited? Your dad says hello and he can't wait to see you too."

"So when are you guys arriving?"

"Well, we should be out there by four, but you know how the Faire folk are."

"No, Mom, I don't. I have no idea how the Faire folk are."

"Always late. Always, always. Just last week, we were supposed to be all packed up, but the Shakespeare troupe—"

"So you'll be a little later than four?"

"Yes, dear. But we do hope you come see us in action. You'd be so proud. But if not, I will call you when we arrive. Darling, do you want us to stay with you, or should we stay at the hotel? You know how much we want to see you, but we understand if you want your privacy. Oh, and your father says hello."

"Yeah, it would be easier if you stay at the hotel. My place isn't that big, and—"

"Oh, you know we don't care about that. We're family. In fact, your father and I have taken to falling asleep under the stars. Sleeping with nature. It's much more peaceful and restful that way, watching all those galaxies and planets out there, so full of mystery!"

"Well, I don't have a yard, Mom. You're not going to sleep in the parking lot of my apartment building."

"No, no, dear, I suppose not. We'll be fine at the hotel. Please make sure you are home around four because I'm gonna call you when we arrive."

"Yes, Mom, I'll try to be home around four."

"Here, your father wants to talk to you . . . Oh, no? Wait, okay no, no he doesn't. He said he will see you soon and tell you everything then."

"Okay, see you soon. I gotta go."

I spent the night on the couch, not really asleep and not really awake, as ESPN Classic droned on in the background. In the morning, my head throbbed, my entire body felt like one giant bruise, and my right hand was a mess. Though the bleeding had stopped, the cut on my finger was puffy and red around the edges, while my palm was blue and tender to the touch. Getting off the couch, my joints creaked, my bones ached, and my muscles simply surrendered. But much like the feeling of hunger that day in Santa Barbara, it felt good to be sore. As if my body were unfolding itself after a long, cramped hibernation. I shuffled my way around the apartment, starting coffee, locating clean clothes.

When I stepped outside, the cold late-morning air hit the coffee, and steam poured off the top like an old train. I brushed the pine needles off one of the chairs and sat down gingerly.

Even though it was early enough that Jimmy was likely still passed out, facedown, starfishing across his messy bed, I had to call him first. I had no idea what my call with Lauren would hold, but it could change everything. Jimmy was the opening act.

When I clicked on my phone, there was a new text message from Travis. He reminded me to check my email. He said I might be excited by the latest update. But I was disappointed it wasn't from Lauren.

My frustration quickly turned to nerves as I located Jimmy's number. I didn't know if it was nerves for the call or because the last time I saw him, he was riding circles around me and telling me how bad I fucked up. And now he had name-dropped me to Coach Rich. I took a sip of coffee and clicked the number.

One ring. Whatever it was, I could handle it. After all, he was just a kid.

Two ri—

Partway through the second ring, the voicemail clicked on. An apathetic Jimmy told me to "leave a message and I'll probably call you back." I hadn't made a plan for voicemail. Certainly not after one and a half rings. I hung up quickly at the beep. I could at least tell Coach Rich I tried, and it would be the truth.

Although the call to Jimmy yielded no answers, it wasn't a complete loss. It showed me to ready myself for the call to Lauren and all its possibilities. *Be prepared.* Sipping the coffee that was turning cold fast, I gave myself a pep talk. I was allowed to call her, I told myself. I was her friend, and I was concerned and wanted to know everything was okay. *Mostly no,* she had said. If she didn't answer, I would leave a message. Nothing long, nothing dramatic, just requesting, or asking, or everything short of *begging* for a call back. I also told myself I would claim responsibility for her driveway. "I am allowed to call her," I said aloud.

I put the cup of coffee down on the pavement and found Lauren's name in my sparse contact list.

I clicked her name and waited.

One ring.

"Conner."

Just as I was surprised by the abruptness of Jimmy's voicemail, I was taken aback by how quick Lauren picked up. Her voice was a near whisper, but it was her.

"Hey."

"One moment, Conner." I heard movement. And her breath, as if coming through my phone and making fog bursts in the cold air around me.

"I'm sorry if this is a bad time," I said, "but I—"

"It's okay, I just need to . . ." Her voice returned to its normal volume. "Sorry, I needed to step out."

"I know you said you'd call, but you haven't, and I needed to know you were okay."

"Yes, I'm okay, but . . ."

"What is it?"

"I'm at the hospital, Conner."

"What? What happened? Are you—"

"It's Abby."

And for that split second between the ending of one word, an imperceptible breath, and the beginning of a new word, I remembered her family. Destined for loss. My stomach dropped.

"She's pregnant, Conner. Abby's pregnant." She said it stronger the second time, as if telling herself more than me.

I stumbled over consonants and vowels, not really forming any coherent words.

"A couple days ago she was having really bad cramps," Lauren said. "She has endometriosis. We already knew that. So we took her in. But she's pregnant, Conner. My little girl is pregnant."

"You said you're at the hospital. Is she okay?"

"She is. But the pain is so bad right now. The doctors are trying to minimize that while keeping . . . everything safe."

"I don't know what to say." The mess I had made of their driveway now seemed insignificant, yet also the worst way for this family to return home from the hospital. My shame thickened.

"You don't have to say anything. I'm sorry I didn't call you sooner. But I have to be a mother now, Conner."

"Yes. Of course."

"I don't know what to do, but all I know is I have to be there for Abby right now."

And then like so many times driving in her car or sitting on my couch or lying in my bed, we were together and we were silent. The air between our phones without a blip of static. Only our breathing, inaudible but present.

"Her boyfriend, Conner. She said you know him."

"I know him?" But as those words left my mouth, I realized: *Jimmy*.

"Yes, he plays basketball. Do you know who—"

"Jimmy. Yes, I know him." Of course.

"We've met him. He seems a bit of a mess. He went on and on about how he's going to get a job, get two jobs, take care of Abby and the baby, said he knows how to be a man. Oh, I dunno, Conner, she's just a baby herself."

Abby and Jimmy. Their stories were just beginning, but they were already written. There were a million Abbys and Jimmys all over the world. They would be okay, and they wouldn't be okay at the same time.

"But I'm not sure about him. Something gives me a bad feeling, and I have to be . . . I'm her mother."

"He's not a bad guy, really. He has his issues, but he's not a bad guy." As I was saying those words, I was surprised to find that I genuinely meant them.

"I don't care who he is, Conner. She's only sixteen. She's my baby. She's not his, she's mine. She's my daughter and I'm going to look after her."

"I know," I said, but my voice wasn't there.

The volume of the noise in the background rose, and there were voices. I couldn't tell if they were talking to Lauren or not, so I waited. She whispered something, and everything got quiet again.

"There's something else, Conner."

I pushed the phone closer to my ear and closed my eyes.

"We're moving to Rockford," she said.

"When?" I thought it would be more of a surprise, but once I heard it, it wasn't a surprise at all.

"I know I said all those things about how I couldn't move. But things are different now. Abby needs a fresh start. She's adamant about keeping the baby.

And I have to be her mother again."

"When?" I repeated.

Silence, and then: "Right away. As soon as possible." Her voice started to waver. "We're going to stay with Peter's sister at first, until we find a place of . . . of our own. But we're moving right away, Conner. Peter said there's no point in waiting. Waiting for what? So once Abby is without so much pain, we'll pack up what we can, and . . . and . . ." She was talking and talking to fill the silence. Taking the long way round. "And Peter says we can sell our house even from Rockford. And that we can stay with his sister as long as we need. And oh, I don't know, but Abby needs me and I have to be there for her and she needs a new school and a fresh start and, and, and I dunno, maybe we all do. Nothing is forgotten, that's not what I'm saying. That's not at all what I am saying. But maybe we have to move forward. Not move on. I hate that. Moving on is forgetting. No one is forgetting. But we are moving forward, and right now forward is to Rockford and to family, and we're gonna be okay, Conner."

I took an audible breath as if to interrupt her, but I had nothing to say. Nothing came out.

"Also . . ."

How was there more?

"Also . . . I went to his grave site. It was the first time, the only time since the funeral. I don't know why I'm telling you, but I thought I should."

"I'm glad you told me," I said, although I wasn't sure I was.

"I cried so hard, Conner. It was horrible, but in a way, it also wasn't. I cried so hard my insides are sore."

There were more muffled words in the background, and something beeped.

"I have to go. The doctors want to speak with me."

"Yes. Yes, okay."

"I'll talk to you soon, Conner."

When she used to say that, I heard in her voice that even though she said soon, she meant sooner. But now her voice told me she didn't know when the next time would be. Or if there would be a next time at all.

CHAPTER 17

THE GROUND WAS DUSTY, AND THE WHINING whistle of bagpipes swirled from all directions. The women were all cleavage and the men all tights. Puffy white sleeves and flower crowns. Metal beer steins and giant turkey legs. Beards and braids and braided beards. The fair looked exactly as I suspected it would. My parents' wet dream.

My mother had left a message early in the morning. Told me to find her at the booth called Lancelot's Leather Goods. She failed to mention the $40 entrance ticket, though luckily I still had the last $300 Lauren had left me.

I passed King Arthur's Armory and a clothing tent called Wench Wear, and was stopped once to have a love sonnet forced upon me like an exorcism. I hadn't heard from Lauren since the hospital phone call, and I didn't know if I would. If I should even be checking my phone anymore. But naturally I did. Meanwhile, I was worried about my cut getting infected. It was swollen and tender to the touch. So before leaving the house, I'd glopped on some Neosporin and bandaged it up.

The crowd was an odd mix of costumed characters prancing around in the spring of 1580 and socks-and-sandals-wearing tourists arriving from feeding the sea lions. A couple yards ahead, I spotted a row of booths I hadn't yet seen and figured it was time to get it over with. The bagpipes fell silent and a jaunty drumbeat began, accompanied by what I was guessing was a flute and a handful of shrunken string instruments. This wasn't an environment I wanted to linger in any longer than necessary.

"Love looks not with eyes"—a short wood nymph was suddenly in front of me—"but with the mind." He or she had small horns popping out of a pixie haircut. "Therefore is winged Cupid painted blind?"

"Excuse me." I continued walking, but the fairy creature kept up, circling around me as they spoke, reminding me of Jimmy on his undersized bike in the high school parking lot.

"Lord, what fools these mortals be," they said before plucking a flower out of the hair of a woman walking by, though the woman didn't notice.

"Fools indeed," I said, offering a forced smile.

The wood nymph then handed me a piece of parchment paper rolled up like a scroll. On it was an invitation: *A Midsummer Night's Dream, today at 3 p.m. on the gilded stage beyond the grassy hillock.*

"Oh great," I said with another fake smile. "I'll try to make it." These people were in their element. I was the foreigner, and standard social norms didn't apply here.

"Are you sure that we are awake?" They were in my ear now, whispering. "It seems to me . . . that yet we sleep . . . we dream." And then they were skipping off to their next victim.

I put my head down and walked with purpose to the line of booths on the other side of the dirt field. Booths called Dragon Pets, the Apothecary, and the Sawdust Factory. I finally spotted my mother. She was talking to another woman and hadn't seen me yet. She wore a brown corset that pushed her cleavage up to her neck. Gross. Her shoulders were exposed, but thin white sleeves covered her arms. A long skirt hung to the ground, but with different colors and patterns that made it look more like layers of three or four skirts. Her hair, which was normally straight, was set in small, tight curls and pinned up with a large pink flower. She stood at the edge of a booth that sold leather belts, leather satchels, leather sandals, and other leather goods I didn't understand.

"Hi, Mom."

"Conner! My baby! You made it!" She came to me with open arms and kissed me once on each cheek. "It's so good to see you!"

"You too, Mom."

"What do you think of your old mother?" She twirled in a circle, holding out her skirt. I desperately tried to ignore the fatty flesh squeezing and stretching out from the top edge of her corset.

"You look . . . different."

"Well, thank you! You look a little different yourself. Did you lose weight? Do you have a cold or something?"

"No, I'm fine."

"And are you enjoying the fair? It's wonderful, isn't it? I have to introduce you to Annie and Nathaniel and—oh, where is Willa? She was just here."

"Where's Dad?"

"Your father? I think he's getting into his armor. I'll show you where to go. He's so excited to see you. Did you bring Rhonda or Travis?"

"It's Rian, Mom, not Rhonda. And no, I didn't bring either of them."

"Okay, good, I get you all to myself!" She grabbed my shoulders and kissed my cheeks again.

"I'm not going to stay long. This place is a bit much for me."

"Oh c'mon, it's fun!" She smiled and curtsied to someone behind me. "But we are having dinner tonight, yes? And we want to see your place!"

"It's an apartment. Nothing to see."

"My dear. We have traveled more than three centuries to see you. You're not getting away from us that easily."

"Okay, sure, you can come over tonight."

"Would it be easier for you to pick us up here or at the hotel?"

I sighed. The lies were about to begin. "I can't pick you up, Mom."

"Why not, honey?"

"My truck's . . . not working right now." I saw it clearly in my mind's eye. Sitting unabashed in my driveway. Working perfectly. Daring me to drive it. Begging me.

"Oh my, is everything okay?"

"Yeah, it'll be fine."

"Hmm, okay, honey. Not good timing, I guess. But your father and I will figure something out."

"Where is he?"

"If you walk back around the other side of these shops and head toward the stables, you'll see the jousting stadium. Look for a knight with a big purple plume. He should be dressed by now and is spreading the word about today's joust. It should be a good one. You see, the knight of—"

"Big purple plume?"

"Yes, the feathers on the top of the helmet. Your father's crest is purple, so the plume is too. Are you sure everything's okay, honey?"

I gave my mother a hug and left to find my dad.

The area behind the booths on the way to the stadium was much emptier. No poetry or Shakespeare was read to me. And only once did I have to wait for the royal procession to pass. Trumpets, pageantry, and carriages, the whole nine yards. "All hail Queen Arabella of Camdenshire!"

Was Rockford out of the picture for me now? I felt it in Lauren's voice. She'd repeated the words "I have to be a mother now" as if she was making a choice. A mother, maybe as opposed to . . . to what? In any case, I didn't know if I was welcome any longer.

Once the Queen and her royal subjects passed, I spotted my dad right away. The purple mohawk atop his helmet was practically a yard high. Ridiculous. He stumbled around in a full suit of armor, clunky, like a robot from the 1950s. It must have been impossible for him to see out of the metal face grid, as I had to nearly bump into him for him to notice me.

"Dad? Hey, it's me, Conner."

He lifted his faceplate with one hand, revealing the big grin hiding inside.

"Conner, my boy, how are you?" We attempted a hug but he didn't bend well, and I could barely get my arms around him.

"I'm okay. Wow, look at you."

"Did you know the word *knight* came from the Anglo-Saxon word *cniht*, which meant *boy*? Though I hardly think I look like a boy, now do I?" My father laughed his hearty laugh, which I'd always thought sounded forced. He had to hold his faceplate up the entire time we talked, like a scene from *Monty Python and the Holy Grail*. "Have you seen your mother? She's dying to see you."

"Yes, I just saw her."

"Good, good. And will you be joining us?" He handed me a piece of parchment paper much like the one I received from the forest fairy.

I read it aloud: "*Hear ye, hear ye. Thou hast been summoned to join Queen Arabella and Lord Jasper the Second at 2 p.m. in Squire Stadium to see the knights from the four kingdoms joust for honor, glory, and the hand of Lady Cassandra.*"

As I was reading, I felt it in my pocket: my phone vibrating. It would buzz once for a text message but pulsed like a heartbeat when it was a call. As I read the invitation, it buzzed off and on several times.

"Shall we be anticipating your presence at said event, my good sir?"

"I dunno, Dad. That's a long time to be here, you know. And you and Mom are busy. We'll meet up later, though. I already talked to Mom about it."

"You don't want to see your dad on a horse?"

"Wait, you're not actually jousting, are you?"

"No, son, we leave that to the young squires. But I am part of the ceremony. It's quite the spectacle."

"That's great, Dad."

"Do you know why all the old castles had spiral staircases?" He waited, although clearly I wasn't going to venture a guess. "They did that to make it harder for invading knights to run up and down them. Fifty pounds of steel plus those long swords. Well, one can imagine."

"That's great, Dad. I should let you get back to work."

"Oh, son, this is hardly work."

"You know what I mean."

We parted, and I couldn't get my phone out fast enough. The missed call was from Lauren, and there was a voicemail. After shimmying past a gang of pirates, arm in arm and singing a drunken tale, there was Lauren's voice in my ear.

"Hi, Conner. It's Lauren." So formal. "I wanted to let you know we are home from the hospital." Fuck. The driveway. My stomach clenched like a fist. "Abby's pain is manageable enough." She took a deep breath. "So she and I are heading out to Rockford tomorrow evening. The sooner we can start to get settled, the better. Peter will stay behind to pack our stuff, and then he'll join us." And then there was silence. I didn't hear a *click*, but I couldn't hear her breathing either. I stood in place, phone pressed to my ear, waiting, floating. "I need you to do me a favor." Her voice had lost the formality it had in the beginning. It was the Lauren I knew. The one who cried into the back of my neck, the one who sang John Lennon and talked about miscarriages and religion and saltwater taffy and Boy Scouts and uncles lost at sea. It was the voice she used when she talked about Braden. Heavy but soft. Like honey. "Forgive yourself, Conner." She said it slowly, careful to enunciate each syllable as if the words alone, spoken correctly, could make the thing happen. "It was an acci . . . For me and for him and for you. Forgive yourself."

~

My mom called the house in the afternoon to let me know they were going to take off early from the fair, figure out transportation, and should get to my apartment around six. After a cursory check, my suspicions were confirmed: zero food in my kitchen. I began my familiar march up 11th. Ralphs was a few blocks farther than Keeley's Liquor, but my parents needed real food. They thought I was an executive chef in an about-to-open restaurant. Shrink-wrapped sandwiches wouldn't cut it. The sky was a smooth gray. It didn't so much look like rain as it did fog that hadn't yet made up its mind if it was dropping in. I spent the walk thinking about Lauren. I tried to imagine her in Rockford. Couldn't picture the new house. Couldn't decide if it would be bigger, brighter, modern. Or if it would be an older ranch style, something more Midwest. Three bedrooms or four? Four. They would soon be four again. She wouldn't know any of her neighbors, and that would make Lauren relieved but lonely. Maybe she didn't know her neighbors that well now, but new strangers were lonelier than familiar strangers. Maybe it would be good for her. For them. A fresh start, she said. Maybe she would get Peter back. I didn't know what he was before.

I didn't have much of a plan when I arrived at Ralphs, so I roamed the aisles aimlessly, shopping on autopilot. Had she talked with Dale? Had she contacted him before Abby came to her in such pain, asking for her mother? Had there even been time? Maybe Dale was going to show up to the Starbucks downtown next week only to be stood up. Or maybe she had wanted to meet at the picnic benches around Laguna Lake. Eager, balding Dale Ruthemeyer, pen at the ready, fresh cassette tape in the recorder. Meanwhile, Lauren would be a thousand miles away, unpacking her things in her sister-in-law's guest bedroom, fresh towels folded on the bathroom counter. I left Ralphs with a bag of vegetables, wild rice, and sixteen ounces of skirt steak.

I crunched my way back down 11th Street, pine needles forever blanketing the side of the road. The fog was descending bit by bit as if lowered with a parachute. In my imaginary Rockford, as I played out Lauren's new life there, I kept hearing her words. *They look at me like I'm a ghost. A ghost who roams around not knowing she's dead. And everyone's too sad and scared to be the one to tell her.* She wouldn't be a ghost in Rockford. No one would know her tragedy and her sadness. They would look at her as the loving wife, mother, and soon-to-be grandmother that she was. Their smiles and hellos would be genuine, without the veiled sympathy and pity or whatever else it was she saw in their eyes. But so arrogant of me to think I knew how she felt. People didn't look at me the way they did her. Travis and Manny, Donnie and the waitresses, my basketball players and Coach Rich, even Rian from afar. There was a sadness there, but a different one from Lauren's. A confused and frustrated sadness. The opposite of Lauren's. They looked at me as if I was walking around like a ghost but didn't realize I wasn't actually dead. I wasn't yet a ghost. And they wanted to tell me, to shake me and scream it at me. Maybe that's what Lauren was trying to tell me in her message.

~

The steak wouldn't take long, so I decided to wait on that until my parents arrived. But I had vegetables for days to chop and a mushroom–red wine sauce that would only benefit from a longer simmer. I sharpened my chopping knife and washed a large bowlful of mushrooms: cremini, portobello, and button. I inhaled the smell of the mushrooms, earthy and strong.

I already missed Lauren. She was already gone. I was beginning to realize that. I was chopping the portobellos, long, flat discs like UFOs, when I noticed something was missing. Hesitant, I went to the stereo and knelt by my towering stack of CDs. Nothing jumped out at first. Some reminded me of Rian, which felt odd, and most looked nearly unrecognizable, as if I were looking at someone else's music collection. But then I spotted it, not in the stacks but on the entryway table. Neil Young. *Mirror Ball.* When did it make it back into the apartment? How? The case was cardboard, and the picture on the front was simple. In strict black and white, without any gray tones, was a large mirror ball surrounded by a smattering of white dots. *For me and for him and for you . . .* Going against everything my body told me, like swimming against the current, I put the disc in the player, turned up the volume, and returned to the kitchen.

The grungy guitar of "Song X" began to play, and my heart rate quickened as I sliced cremini mushrooms. They were mini portobellos, really, and had a deeper, more complex flavor than the standard white button mushrooms they resembled. The sauce would be better with a variety. I made a conscious effort to think of mushrooms. I made a conscious effort to stop listening closely to Neil Young's high, creaky, soulful voice, and simply to let it fill the empty space of the living room and the kitchen. I made a conscious effort not to think of ghosts or flights to Illinois. Only of mushrooms.

As the faster, more rocking second song, "Act of Love," came on, my heart still raced, but now my foot tapped to the beat. Muscle memory. I moved on to the button mushrooms and thought of titles. Titles were important. "Act of Love"—I didn't know what love looked like for me anymore. Who or where to give it. If I was allowed to receive it. But cooking, cooking for people, that was *the* act of love for me. So maybe this was the first step, the one thing I could do for Lauren. She asked me to forgive myself, and even if I didn't know how to do that, maybe I could do *this* for her. I could listen to loud music and think about mushrooms and cook a meal for my parents. I chopped the button mushrooms, white as little rubber clouds, and added them to the bowl. I remembered Mr. Candelaria telling us how all button mushrooms used to be brown until the 1920s, when a Pennsylvania farmer found a group of white ones growing in his patch. An anomaly, a mistake, a mutation. But they were the same mushroom. The farmer began to clone the white mushrooms and passed them off as an entirely new species.

She didn't *ask* me to forgive myself. It wasn't a question or even a suggestion. *Forgive yourself, Conner*. She said it like a command. Like a mother to a child.

When the third song began, it caught me off guard. "I'm the Ocean," the song that had been haunting me all summer. Knife in hand, music thumping in the background, I had been lulled into some kind of old normalcy. But that fuzzy guitar riff pulled me back under. The riff was six seconds long, and it played twice before all five musicians jumped in and never let go. My stomach bottomed out. Neil's voice, full of sorrow, desperation, and relief. I set the knife down, my hands shaking. I listened to the driving drumbeat—*bap-bap-bap-bap*—so simple, so repetitive, so relentless it punched through my weak apartment. Every detail from the summer swelled in me all at once, like a giant undertow. *This* song, *that* Monday, Lauren, so much of Lauren, and Peter and Abby, and Justine and Dale and Donnie and Jimmy and Coach Rich and Cody and Kyle and their young teammates, Travis and Rian and my parents. Rock shrimp tacos with mango salsa and brown sweatshirts and shattered tile pieces. I marched over to the stereo. I knelt down and turned the volume up. The windows shook with Jack Irons's stomping kick drum. I turned it up one more click, hit the repeat button, and returned to the kitchen to force myself to continue cutting vegetables for grilling and to make a mushroom sauce. To fight against the undertow. And as "I'm the Ocean" pushed on, it became even more than this summer. It was everything. I was again on my back on the Costa Mesa balcony, feeling each of my vertebrae pressing against the concrete. It was my six cities in twelve years. It was Anna and the girlfriends who came before and after: Maya. Natalie. It was my sweaty uncle in the desert. It was dark glasses of Guinness at Vesuvio and the stink of unwashed bodies on the BART. But the music was so loud there wasn't room for any singular thought to progress further than a flash. Not about this summer, not about the past, not about cooking, not about anything else. *For me and for him and for you. Forgive yourself, Conner.* It all just existed, without conscious or linear thought. I was browning onions and garlic in olive oil when the song began its finale. In the final chorus, all five members joined Neil and sang out in desperation as if the world might end at any moment. There was an effect on their mics, subtle and swimmy, as if underwater. "I'm the Ocean." The title, it made sense now. They were drowning. Their voices were screaming out for help, begging to be saved.

I added mushrooms and cabernet to the pan and turned the heat down. Flavor loved a slow simmer. I moved on to slicing summer squash. As soon as the song ended, there was a stark moment of silence before the opening riff started up again. On loop, like it had felt on that Monday, like it had felt all summer. I tried not to listen to the endless lyrics of the song, but to let the incessant drive of the music wash over me. Everything in the apartment vibrated. I added beef broth to the sauce and began on the brussels sprouts, perfect miniature cabbages that smelled bitter when I split them in half. I couldn't ignore the line in the song about homeless heroes. The idea that one-time heroes didn't always stay that way. Good didn't always remain. Maybe, then, neither did bad. And maybe if Lauren could forgive me, maybe I could forgive myself as well.

The song might have been on the third or fourth or eleventh replay when the bottom layer of rice reached its crunch and the sauce thickened from the cornstarch and the carrots and pearl onions and squash and sprouts, oiled and seasoned, were sizzling and browning on the grill, Neil again stomping through "I'm the Ocean," and me trying to figure out how to forgive myself. As the chorus continued to repeat, the meaning started to change. "I'm the Ocean"—the words taking on a new significance. Maybe they weren't screaming out for help;

maybe they were screaming out in celebration, yelling in pure exhilaration, wanting to tell the whole world they were not just alive, they were the ocean, the biggest, most powerful force on the planet. "I'm the Ocean"—was it a last breath before drowning or the exultation of a first *real* breath?

It was here that I noticed my parents standing in the doorway. Not trying to get my attention, not covering their ears, not trying to stop the music. They just stood and watched.

I ran to the living room, leaping the couch and slapping at the power button of the stereo.

"Oh my god, I'm so sorry!"

They looked so different than when I saw them earlier. Dressed plainly. Jeans, T-shirts, tennis shoes.

"No, no, honey," my mother said. "We didn't want to interrupt you. You really looked like you were on to something there."

"Come in, come in," I said, frazzled, as if waking from a dream.

"That song wasn't half bad," my father said, taking stock of my dull apartment.

"Oh, and it smells magical in here, darling." My mother gave me a hug. And as the world came back into focus, with echoes of the song rattling off the back of my skull like a pinball, much as it had been all summer, I realized there was something I had to do. If you were caught in an undertow, you weren't supposed to do what seemed most natural—you weren't supposed to swim directly to shore. Rather, you should swim sideways, parallel to the shore, and free yourself of the current. I knew what I had to do, and I knew somehow my parents, strange as they might be, would understand.

"I know you just got here," I said, "and I'm sorry, but I've got to go for a bit."

"Did you forget something at the store, sweetheart? Want me to go with you?"

"No, Mom. I need to take care of something. The rice, the veggies, everything is ready to eat. The steak needs like three to four minutes on each side. You guys can handle it, right? Enjoy the food, and then I'll be back and we'll talk. We'll really talk."

"Sweetie, I don't understand. Where are you going? How long are you going to be?"

My father gave me a look of understanding, even though he didn't understand at all. "Don't worry about us."

"Well, yes, your father's right. We'll be here, darling, take your time. But I—"

"Great, thanks, I promise we'll talk when I get back."

And *poof*, I was out the door.

But for all the momentum I had from the song, from the cooking, from the certainty of what I needed to do, it all froze in place as soon as I closed the door to my truck. The light outside was dimmer than it should have been, the tall pines shielding what little was left of today's sun. I held the steering wheel loosely with both hands. Gripped it tight, then relaxed. Squeezed the wheel again, tighter, my knuckles turning bone white, my cut searing, my bruised palm aching. My heart not beating faster this time, but harder, like a kick drum against my sternum. I closed my eyes, took a deep breath. This time I didn't try to distract my brain or run from it all. I tried to be present, to be present in the cab of my silver truck in front of my small apartment on 11th Street. This was the only place I was or needed to be.

As I exhaled, I released my grip on the wheel and let my hands slide down the curvature of it. I clicked the radio knob off before putting the key in the ignition and turning the engine over. It started without protest, and I instinctively put on my seat belt and turned on the headlights. Muscle memory.

With the lights on, I could see how dirty the windshield was. Dead pine needles and tree pollen blanketed the smooth glass. I pulled the lever toward me to shoot streams of water up onto the windshield, and it took four rounds before the wipers successfully cleared my view. Two large arcs of glass like crystal. The borders of the windshield were still beyond filthy, but I had the exact amount of clarity needed to see and to drive safely. Not everything had to be perfect to be good.

I released the parking brake, put the truck in reverse, and gently backed out of the parking spot. Muscle memory.

It felt good to be moving. The street was empty, and everything was quiet except for the hum of tires on asphalt. I came to full and complete stops at all the stop signs along 11th. The last thing I was in was a rush. With the silence came the return of my thoughts. But instead of being panicked or full of flashbacks, they were scattered, one idea bouncing to the next, and the only connection, the only certainty that ran throughout, was how much I didn't know.

I didn't know if I would ever see Lauren again. I didn't know if the Thomases were going to make it. I didn't know if I would stay in Los Osos, if I would ask Travis for a job at Café Lola. I didn't know if I would return to San Francisco or if I would ever see Rian again. If I would ever talk to Dale. I didn't know if it was some kind of fate or predestination that put me on that turn at that moment on that day, or if it was a freak accident without any reason or meaning beyond that. *Other than driver.*

What makes God good . . . one thing at a time . . . sink or swim . . . be prepared . . . find your belief . . . comfort the living . . . honor the dead.

So much I didn't know.

What I did know was what I had to do at that moment. To swim sideways. To swim out of the current before trying to find the shore. And maybe that was enough. I turned right onto Santa Ysabel, the last street before running into the Elfin Forest, the little patch of magic in Los Osos most people didn't know about. And six short blocks later, I sat alone at a red light, facing South Bay Boulevard. A couple cars zoomed across the clear arcs of the windshield, but no one came up behind me.

To my right was the long way around. Los Osos Valley Road and San Luis Obispo, clear skies and Laguna Lake. Cal Poly students and new restaurants. It was Foothill Boulevard and the Thomases' house. It was Carlock's donut runs and rolling into third period late on rainy days. It was longer, but the roads were straight and clean and predictable.

I glanced across the street at the Nazarene church, gripped and regripped the steering wheel, a thin layer of sweat between my palms and the plastic. *For me and for him and for you. Forgive yourself.*

To my left was the winding road of South Bay Boulevard. It was estuaries at high tide and egrets and blue herons. It was snakelike twists and turns and blind curves. It was the flooded twin bridges and Morro Rock. It was roadside memorials, candles and flowers, crosses and stuffed bears. It was rubber tire marks lingering on the road and tiny pieces of shattered glass lodged deep into divots of the asphalt.

The light turned green, and I made a slow, smooth left turn onto South Bay Boulevard and drove toward all that had been haunting me. But I was also driving toward myself. Not the ghost version of me, but the one Travis and Rian saw, the one even my parents saw. And I realized now, even the one Lauren saw.

As I eased out of the first curve, the silhouette of the giant rock and three smokestacks loomed in the distance, and beyond them, the ocean. I didn't know if Travis would even be home or what I would say if he was. But I knew I had to see him, and this was the way I had to get there.

ACKNOWLEDGMENTS

First, a huge thank-you to my wonderful agent, Carleen Geisler—for believing in this story from the start, and then making it exponentially better, and then finding it the perfect home. I have relied on you each step of the way more than you know, and this book would simply not exist without you.

This book would also not exist without all the wonderful people at Central Avenue, including Beau, Molly, Becca, and Audrey. I appreciate every bit of work that went into making this project a reality. An especially heartfelt thank-you to my publisher, Michelle Halket. From the moment we met, your passion for books has been inspiring, and I am forever grateful for all your hard work, enthusiasm, and transparency throughout the process. You have created such a warm family at Central Avenue, and I am lucky to be a part of it.

It is difficult to put into words the gratitude I have for my editor, Jessica Peirce, my word guru. From seeing something in this novel early on to the surgical precision with which you made it leaner, tighter, better, I cannot adequately express how thankful I am. Your care and razor-sharp eye are simply next-level.

Thank you also to Garrett Calcaterra and Jeff Wallace, who both graciously dared to read an early draft of the manuscript. Your feedback was invaluable, and your friendship is even more so.

Writing is such a solitary, internal act, and many of us would not survive without our writing groups. So I am very grateful to each and every member of the Biscuits, the Shippers, and the Sloths. Having these small, tight-knit communities over the years has given me the drive, the inspiration, and the support that was vital to writing this story.

Thank you to Jordan Loy for your law enforcement expertise. While much of our conversations didn't make it into the book, it is important that the bits that did are accurate. I'm so appreciative of your time and knowledge, and I still don't know how you do what you do.

Thank you to Amy Chase, my favorite go-to artist, for the absolutely beautiful map. Your talents are so immense and varied, and I'm grateful to have your fingerprints on this book.

I also want to thank Jeremy Tolchin. I think of the Central Coast as an important character in this novel. These small towns are where I spent my formative years, but my experiences, memories, and perspectives of them are inextricably tied to our friendship. These places and this book would not look, feel, or sound the same without you.

And of course a big thank-you to everyone in my family. I do not take your unconditional love and support for granted. In fact, it is just these things that give me the freedom to take risks and be vulnerable—key ingredients to being a writer. Thank you all so much. But a special full-hearted thank-you to my mom, Linda. From my first memory to the call we most likely had yesterday, you have always been my #1 fan, not just in writing but in life, and to this I owe everything.

Lastly, to my two girls, for whom the words thank you are not nearly enough. Aleja, love of my life, this life we have built together is a beautiful thing that I am grateful for daily. And Silvana, my darling, my dar, thank you for pushing me in ways you don't even realize. I strive to make you proud of me every day.

Book Club Questions

1. Between his affinity for outdated technology, watching sporting events that have already happened, and even naming the restaurant after a phenomenon of the 1960s, Conner seems to have a preoccupation with the past. Does this contribute to his difficulty staying in one place in the present and his uncertainty of what to do with his future? What is the difference between nostalgia and being stuck in the past?

2. Conner has a couple of theories, but ultimately is unsure what Lauren wants to get out of that first meeting at Laguna Lake. What is it that makes Lauren reach out to him in the first place? What is she hoping to accomplish?

3. After those first couple of meetings, Lauren continues to pursue spending time with Conner. Why? As they continue to grow closer, what is it she's getting out of this relationship?

4. Both Rian and Travis try to support Conner as he spirals into guilt, but ultimately, they each decide to move on without him. Did they try hard enough to be there for Conner? Were they right to move on?

5. Conner and Lauren's relationship clearly evolves over the course of the novel: from talking to spending an entire day together on a mini road trip, to sharing a bed and spending the night together. Did they cross the line? If so, at what point? Is there even a defined line given the severity and uniqueness of their situation?

6. Between driving Conner around town and giving him money, Lauren is also clearly supporting Conner in very tangible ways. Is she giving him what he needs to get through this tragedy or is she enabling him, preventing him from healing properly?

7. The small towns of Morro Bay, Los Osos, and San Luis Obispo almost function as characters in the book. How does living in a small town affect the characters? How does it affect the plot of the novel?

8. If you consider how differently Lauren, Peter, and Abby all process their grief, is there one way that seems to be more healthy? More natural? One that is more destructive?

9. Lauren often tries to make connections between Braden and Conner. Whether consciously or subconsciously, is she trying to replace Braden with Conner?

10. Ultimately, in thinking of Lauren and Conner's relationship, which character helps the other more? In what ways? Which one hinders the other more?

11. Given the rather open-ended nature of the novel's conclusion, where do you see each character in a month? A year? In five years?

Eric Scot Tryon is a writer and editor from San Francisco, California, where he lives with his wife, daughter, cat, and several poison dart frogs. His short fiction has been published in over fifty literary magazines, including *Mid-American Review*, *Indiana Review*, *Glimmer Train*, *Ninth Letter*, and *The Los Angeles Review*. He is also the founding editor of the literary magazine *Flash Frog*.